LUMINOUS BODIES

LUMINOUS BODIES

A Novel of Marie Curie

DEVON JERSILD

PAUL DRY BOOKS
Philadelphia 2026

First Paul Dry Books Edition, 2026

Paul Dry Books, Inc.
Philadelphia, Pennsylvania
www.pauldrybooks.com

Printed in the United States of America

Library of Congress Control Number: 2025949659
ISBN: 978-1-58988-210-2

For Jay

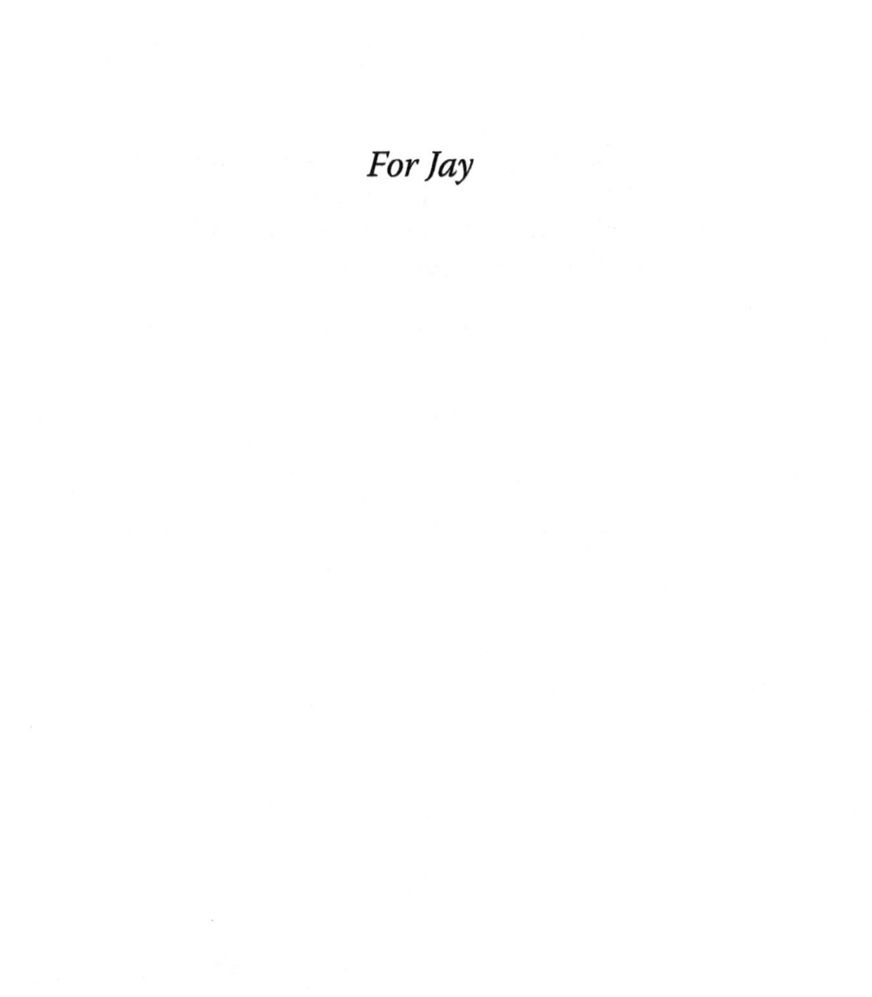

This is a work of fiction based on real people and events. The quoted documents are drawn from actual letters, journal entries, and newspaper stories—sometimes loosely and sometimes conflated.

Energy is Eternal Delight
—William Blake

Stockholm, 1 December 1911

Madame Curie,

In my letter of last week, I encouraged you to come to Stockholm to accept your Nobel prize, for which, as you know, I was an enthusiastic advocate, in spite of the delicate matter of the attacks on you by the family of Monsieur Langevin. I am writing again because things have changed. The lengthy letter attributed to you, written to Paul Langevin, which has been published in a French newspaper, has been circulating here. The situation has been aggravated by the ridiculous duel of M. Langevin, which gives the impression, I hope incorrect, that the published correspondence is authentic.

It is therefore preferable that you not come here on December 10. I beg you to stay in France. No one can be sure what might happen here if you were to come for the prize.

If the Academy had believed that the letter in question were authentic, it would not, in all probability, have awarded you this second prize. I therefore hope that you will telegraph me that it is impossible to come.

I also urge you to write a letter to the Nobel Prize committee of the Swedish Academy stating that you do not wish to accept the prize before the Langevin trial has demonstrated that the accusations against you are false.

Sincerely yours,
S. Arrhenius
Member of the Swedish Academy

Sceaux, 5 December 1911

Monsieur Arrhenius,

The action you advise would be a grave error on my part. The prize has been awarded for the discovery of Radium and Polonium. There is no connection between my scientific work and the facts of my private life. I cannot accept the idea that the appreciation of the value of scientific work should be influenced by libel and slander. I am saddened that you are not yourself of this opinion.

By the time you receive this letter I will have sent a telegram to the Academy announcing that I will be in Stockholm for the ceremonies. I am so sick that I don't know if I will be able to manage the journey. Nonetheless, I intend to be there.

M. Curie

Highcliffe-on-Sea, England, August 1912

When I wake up, I'm rubbing my nose in a scratchy sheet, and it takes a moment to know I have been dreaming. An image of Paul hovers in the upper right corner of my mind. He's sitting on the beach in his striped bathing costume, a scrim of sand on his slim, square shoulders, the sun glinting off his skin in tiny, jeweled bursts.

In my mind I go to him and say, "You're back."

"Of course I am," he says, sounding hurt that I could have doubted his devotion. He digs his toes in the dry sand and lets it sift between them. I kneel in front of him. I take his foot, brush it off, and cover it with kisses. Then he's in my bed. His heat spreads over me.

But Paul has never been here at all.

The throbbing in my kidney spreads to my groin and under my ribs. This kidney can't think for itself. It seems to believe it's of the same substance as my heart.

I lie still, trying to hear the sea. Sometimes, when the tide is out in Highcliffe, there's no sound at all, only a spreading emptiness.

A roaring sound begins in my skull. I breathe in to fend it off.

I want to talk to Hertha alone, and so, when I hear bustling downstairs, I get up and tread lightly past the room where my daughters are asleep, the door open in case of monsters, Eve with her doll clutched tight. I try to disguise the hitch in my gait. Despite appearances, I don't actually like to be dramatic.

I find Hertha in the drawing room with her strong back to me, humming a Hebrew melody. She arranges supplies on a bookshelf—permanganate of potash, India rubber, aluminum powder, gloves. She has extraordinary range, Hertha: mathematician, physicist, engineer, and inventor, all in one. She never wants to be away from her laboratory, so she has made one here in her rented summer house. What, I wonder, is the source of Hertha's energy? Was she born with it? One would think it was nothing to transport glass water tanks with sand and rollers and rearrange a drawing room. Or to host an ailing colleague and her daughters. Just this spring, she smashed windows during demonstrations with her sister suffragettes, and they're planning something for the fall.

She pours a bag of sand into a tank, a hiss of gold, and I think of the first time I saw her. She was on her scientist husband's arm, and I on mine. We stared at each other, recognizing like spirits. I knew her as an expert on electric arcs, and as the woman who, when *The Westminster Gazette* wrote that Pierre had discovered radium, had published a letter to the editor saying, "Errors are notoriously hard to kill, but an error that ascribes to a man what was actually the work of a woman has more lives than a cat." We stood there, in the lobby of the Royal Society, me in my navy wool suit, high neckline, tight waist (I'd had it made for my wedding in a style I could afterward wear to the lab), and she in a billowing, crimson cloak. "A royal color," I said, putting out my hand. She laughed and said, "Or the color of fresh blood." Later, I would wonder—did she mean that she felt like prey at this otherwise male conference, where we were the only women scientists? Or that, as women, we brought new life to these halls? The two of us were doubly outsiders, she a Jew and I a Pole. We had more in common, as it ended up: a parent who died when we were young, mothers who pushed for our education, daughters, supportive husbands. Both of us are widows now.

"Ah, Marie, you're up." She lays her gray-green eyes on me,

her eyebrows rising in the middle. I shrink a little. The light of her gaze is so honest, and she sees so much. Today she looks worried. I don't know how much is because of me.

I follow her into the kitchen, where the kettle already simmers on the stovetop. She hands me a cup of tea. The first cup of tea in the morning—it's still a comfort. I stir in half a teaspoon of jam, the way we sometimes drink it in Poland.

I rub my burned forefingers and my thumbs together—I can't break the habit. "Hertha, I hope you know, I never wanted to hurt anyone."

"Of course you didn't." She puts butter and toast on the table and sits down beside me.

"I worry that you hold it against me. What I've done. What I've been through."

She looks at me with surprise. "Have I been so dreadful?"

"No, no. You're an excellent nurse."

"I've done my fair share of nursing, it's true." In the last few years she's lost her nephew, her mother, and her husband, and she helped care for all of them.

"And here you are," I say. "Taking me in, and my daughters."

"If I don't get you back on track, how will I keep going with my research?"

I'm about to say I don't understand, but of course I do. I also need Hertha to be unstoppable, resolute, indomitable. It's strange to think that until six weeks ago, when I fled France and came to her in Dorset, our friendship consisted of three or four visits and a handful of letters. Yet for years we have given each other courage.

"I've been a fool," I say.

"You're human, thank God. Not the great and good 'Madame Curie.' I sometimes think that you believe in her."

"Hardly." There's an odd metallic taste on my tongue, the taste of a void. If I ever believed in that icon, I couldn't now.

"I sometimes think she's half your trouble," says Hertha, but she tempers her statement by putting her hand on my arm. "It's not your fault, Marie. You've been treated abominably. I hate to see you so disheartened."

Outside, the wind throws rain around. This rain has come up fast and hard. I have an impulse to walk out into it, head out to the sea, drift to another world where no one has heard of me. No one there to disappoint. Be disappointed by.

Hertha takes another piece of toast. Her father died young. Her mother went to work as a seamstress, leaving Hertha at home, age seven, to care for the baby. Her father had amassed secret debts; her mother paid the price. So did Hertha. Yet here she is.

Last night she made me walk up the cliffside with her, to a bench where we could look out over the ocean. Puffins ran on the surface of the water, a comedy of outstretched feet and wings. She couldn't stop laughing.

It's quiet upstairs in the damp house. Irène and Eve are sleeping in.

"I'm not ready to go back to Paris," I say.

A shadow of concern falls over her face. "Of course you're going back."

"Please understand."

"There's the Institute. Your teaching. The girls."

At this moment a neighbor sticks his head in the door, an old man wearing a Mackintosh and carrying a plucked chicken. "You said you wanted one, Mrs. Ayrton? Here it is." He squeaks the door open wide.

"Oh my goodness, Mr. Everett, you darling man."

He holds the carcass up proudly: fat as can be, with dimpled skin, and dripping from the rain. "You'll have a feast, you will. The wife, she cuts it up and fries it, but I like a roasted chicken. You'll never taste better than Dorset chickens. It's the little pebbles they eat."

Hertha takes coins out of her purse.

"I have potatoes too, and tomatoes," he says.

"I'll send the cook by later in the morning, shall I?"

He ambles off, and Hertha washes the chicken at the sink. It will take half the day in the oven, a chicken of that size. Strange, the way the world goes on. A person's life can change in an instant, yet the saws in the lumberyard keep buzzing, and the wagons deliver their milk.

"What will you tell the girls?" Hertha says. "They expect you to go home with them."

It's been months since I was there with them. "They have a very good nanny," I say.

"I had a cat once who lost her mother before she was weaned. She cried every time I left the room."

I wince.

Hertha shakes her head but doesn't turn around. "Really, Marie. If you cast yourself in the role of a spurned woman, that's how you'll be seen. You know how to hold your head up."

I can't say anything to this.

She puts the chicken on the stone slab and wipes her hands on a cloth. "You could come back with me to London for a while."

"To Norfolk Square?" I lift my face, and Hertha is looking at me, and the idea of being with her longer causes a river of hope to rise in my chest, a feeling that I'll pass through this place in my life, over rapids and rocks, and find something new on the other side.

I need Hertha now, her energy, her love. I don't know where to find my own.

PART ONE

I

Paris and Warsaw, 1894

THE SCENE IS FOYOT'S RESTAURANT, a reception after a lecture, on a spring afternoon of intermittent rain. I am chatting with one of my professors while observing Pierre, whom I've been seeing for a few months. We aren't exactly a couple—I have made up my mind never again to catch the idiotic fever that people call love—but I'm interested, alert, and can't stop looking at him. He stands alone amidst the poppy field of tablecloths, the soft clatter of conversation and cleaning up, compelled by a train of thought, his nose lifted slightly in expectation.

Suddenly he seems five inches taller. His ears twitch, and a smile breaks through his grave expression.

A young man has burst into the restaurant: trim, muscular, with dark, brush-cut hair and a tough, schoolboy face. An aura of volatility. I know right away this is Paul Langevin, the amazing student Pierre has been telling me about. "My thunder boy," he calls him. "He'll be the best of us. The best physicist in France. You watch." When he sees Pierre, his face opens up, shines. The two men go to each other.

My skin tingles. It's as though the atmosphere's particles have become electrically charged. I've felt this way in the brilliant, ionized air around a waterfall. What a wonder, what a thing to contemplate: two splendid men whose affection for each other makes the air around them shimmer.

If I had met Pierre when I first arrived in Paris, at twenty-four, I don't think I would have paid him any mind, in spite of his charm. I had made up my mind: no husband, no children. Only science. That choice had taken root in me long before I ever crossed the border out of Poland.

The path wasn't easy. Back home, under Russian rule, real opportunities were reserved for Russians or Poles willing to bend. After the failed uprising of 1863—just a few years before I was born—the empire tightened its grip. They tried to erase us. They took over the courts, the universities, the hospitals. Women couldn't earn degrees. Even our language was forbidden.

But in our family, learning was sacred. My father told us again and again that only knowledge could free us. Not violence, not grand speeches, just the slow stubborn work of the mind. The Russians could jail us for speaking Polish, banish our books, and rename our streets, but they couldn't change the laws of nature. They couldn't alter a chemical reaction or rewrite a mathematical proof, and this was our advantage. Evolution would unfold. It was our job to nudge it along.

My father lived that principle. Though he'd never been granted a degree, he studied science and poured himself into teaching, and into us. We listened. Helena, just a year older than me, struggled to find her footing as a singer, but Józef went to medical school in Warsaw. Bronia was already a doctor by the time I joined her in Paris, living in a neighborhood called "Little Poland"—we always planned to bring our knowledge back home. And who knows what my oldest sister Zosia, the brightest among us, might have done, if she had lived.

We weren't alone. All across Poland, people were waking up, beginning to think and to work. The movement we called *positivism* wasn't just for scholars—it was for everyone. Workers, peasants, women, children—we were all needed. As teenagers, Bronia and I snuck into secret classes held in private apartments—the "Flying University," organized by the fearless

Jadwiga Dawidowa—where we listened to lectures on physics, literature, history, philosophy. The windows stayed shut, even in summer. I'd sit on a blanket on the floor, knees pulled in tight, and hold my breath every time footsteps passed in the stairwell. We felt like part of a secret army, with books instead of guns.

When I shared my patriotic fervor—my passion for positivism—with my French friends, they actually laughed. To them it was romantic nonsense. They thought my maniacal work at my studies was nothing more than personal ambition. "That's because it's all *you* know," I snapped. Of course, they weren't all wrong. I did enjoy beating them out. But that wasn't the point.

In 1863, ten thousand Poles—farmers, students, dreamers—rose up against ninety thousand Russians soldiers. The bodies of our leaders soon hung from the ramparts of the Warsaw Citadel. My brother always claimed this was his first memory. It can't be—he was born that year—but I knew what he meant. It felt like we were there, as if we ourselves had seen a hundred thousand men being sent into exile, marching off in chains to Siberia—my Uncle Henryk among them. *He had no shoes,* my mother whispered once, as if she still couldn't believe it. *No shoes at all.* She kept his picture by her bedside, a young man with bushy blonde hair.

We knew, after 1863, that violence wouldn't save us. As my father would say, we had to gather up the stones of truth, one at a time, and build a new foundation for Poland. Each of us had to discover the path best suited to our nature, our own way of being useful.

I adored literature—novels, poetry, and essays—as well as science. For a while, I couldn't choose. Then, at nineteen, I stepped into a working laboratory and saw, for the first time, rows of workbenches all facing one way, with counters of polished slate, and a scientist working with a manganin resistor, and a wall of cabinets and drawers, their contents waiting to be discovered. The air vibrated—something, *something,* was about to be revealed. By then I'd practically memorized my physics and chemistry textbooks, but never had I seen an open, well-lit lab. My cousin Józef Boguski, its director, had studied under Mendeleev in St. Petersburg, which, perhaps, was why the Russians left him alone. After my first visit, Józio let me come in at odd hours to make experiments. I checked my results against the textbook, ecstatic when I succeeded, miserable when I failed. I spent weeks refining basic skills—measuring, filtration, precipitation—wanting to reach the point where I made no mistakes. I wasn't tempted to rush. I wanted solid ground. How surprised I was when, exploring chemical affinities, I mixed potassium chlorate and sulfur in a mortar. At first the white and yellow crystals seemed inert. I stirred harder with the pestle, stirred and pressed, and *crack, bang, fire!* A lovely explosion. Smelly smoke in my face.

Before I could start on my degrees, I needed to save money and send fifteen rubles a month to Bronia in Paris. When my turn came, she would help me. So I humbled myself and took a position as a governess with a family in the beet-farming countryside. That's where the trouble began—the trouble that nearly kept me from marrying Pierre.

The Zorawskis were almost rich: they managed two hundred acres of beet root and owned most of the local sugar factory. My primary charge was a ten-year-old girl, spoiled and unruly, but sweet. Her eldest brother, Kazimierz, a physics student, was away at university. He was the palpable joy of his parents, and when he came home for the Christmas holidays, I saw why: he was sunny and smart and his smile could charm the devil into the open. I lost my balance and toppled into love. When he went back to university we wrote each other once or twice a day. How could such a slim boy take up so much room in my mind? When, in the evenings, I couldn't study for thinking of him, I worked trigonometry problems—they allowed no lapses of attention.

His parents showered me with compliments. They loved my studiousness and moral grit; they wanted their daughters to be just like me. They dragged me along with them to dances and parties where the girls frittered their wits away. And I behaved myself. Indeed, I was exemplary—I hardly ever brought up higher education for women, or illiteracy, or the peasants' working conditions.

Then Kazimierz proposed. How could I have guessed how everything would turn? Kazimierz's parents, when he told them, were aghast. What was he thinking, to marry a poor girl? A lowly governess—really? Was he absolutely out of his mind?

Oh, how I would have known what to say, if I were in his shoes! But Kazimierz went mute. He swore to me that he would defy them, then returned to his university. I stayed on as governess under his mother's icy eye, hoping that he'd find courage. Two years passed. When Bronia wrote that it was time—high time—I came to Paris and made something of myself, I told her that I couldn't bear to leave our father. I said that she and Józef would have to be the ones to develop the amazing gifts of our family. Yes, I was still holding out hope for Kazimierz, but more than that, I'd lost faith that I would ever become somebody.

Poor Bronia, receiving my letter. She knew too well the depths to which I could sink.

It took me another year to break with Kazimierz completely and pull myself out of that hell.

On the journey to Paris, I thought hard. I had been plagued by outsized emotions all my life—and I had worsened them by devoting myself to a cause too small. Clearly, I had a taste for sacrifice; why else give up Paris for a boy? But sacrifice was only noble if the cause was worthy—if it was properly channeled.

I decided I had better stay single.

If only I had known in advance the freedom ahead of me! I had needed change, movement, life, and here was Paris, energy pulsing through the streets. Libraries open late at night, air and light in city squares. Paris had seen blood in the last decades—the Paris Commune and the Franco-Prussian war—but in her broad avenues, among fountains and aqueducts, people were free. My emotions no longer seemed too grand or big. I looked around myself, at the fruits of imagination, intelligence, and persistence, and I asked myself, what might I contribute?

I moved in with my sister and her husband, Kazimierz Dłuski (I cringed at his given name). Evenings, their household was open to Polish patriots. These gatherings were often sad—all of us far from home, and some, in trouble with the Russians, unable ever to return—but they were also fun. I was a hit when I dressed up one night in a flowing tunic and ribbons in our national colors and posed with one arm to my forehead, a tableau vivant: "Poland, Breaking Her Bonds." My father, when I wrote to him, bragging about my success, was not at all pleased. He reminded me that there were Russian spies about, and he implored me to do nothing that might get in the way of working in Poland and coming home to him.

I folded the letter back into its envelope. How could I have been so careless? My skin was hot; I hated to displease my father.

I decided to renounce my social life, not only the parties at my sister's house, but the group of Eastern European students who gathered in each other's rooms at the Sorbonne. ("Not even once a month?" my friends protested. "We need each other!") I knew I would miss them, but I was in Paris to earn a degree. My French, I realized, was not as good as I had thought, and my solitary scientific studies hadn't prepared me well enough. It was time to bear down. Unfortunately, my brother-in-law could not endure my doing anything but engaging in agreeable chatter with him when I was at home. How a man of thirty-six, with a child and a medical practice, had so much time for gossip, I couldn't fathom, but this being the case, I declared war with him.

"I'm moving out," I told him.

"I promised your father I'd watch over you. You're staying here."

"I'm twenty-four. I can manage on my own."

"I forbid it, Maria."

"Help me get my bag, will you? Where have you hidden it?"

I installed myself in a garret room near the Sorbonne. No heat, no water, no kitchen, very cheap. I carried coal up seven flights of stairs, but still the water froze in my basin. I found that if I piled all the clothes I had on top of me, I slept well enough. I scrambled eggs and heated up cocoa on the flame of my alcohol lamp. And there was no one to call me from my studies! No one to interrupt me for an extra lesson or to divert them with a game of chess! I was in Paris, my own master and my own servant. Within myself these two parts got along extraordinarily well. I washed glassware in labs to make ends meet.

At the Sorbonne my first professor was the mathematician Monsieur Paul Appell, later dean of the faculty. His entrance into the amphitheater brought us all to silence. How picturesque he was, in his white tie and evening coat, with his square beard and his Alsatian accent. "I take the sun, and I throw it," he proclaimed, in one of his demonstrations. Was there anything more marvelous than science? What novel could compare, what poetry?

My brother-in-law worried about the packs of young men who swarmed around women and escorted them down the boulevard Saint Michel, making rude gestures and loud-mouthed jests. He said I was naïve, I should be more careful—terrible things happen. He also said I was anemic. When I fainted at a lecture, and one of the students rushed to find him, he came running over. He made me come with him and eat a steak, and he was furious. It was true that my disinterest in food and sleep were making me light-headed. I had discovered new pleasures, better than food, drink, and kisses from foolish boys.

One afternoon, at an advanced calculus exam, in an amphitheater rich in portraits and statues, we students were given ten problems, not one of them familiar. I wondered: had the invigilator distributed the wrong papers? Surely this was intended for the students in year two? With faces of stone, René Descartes and Blaise Pascal glared down at us. I realized we were expected to use the calculus we had learned as a perch from which to develop solutions to much more complicated problems. I stared at each page of the exam, each problem like a solid ball, and, like an atom (or so we thought at this time), indivisible and indestructible. Was I going to fail? And then I recognized one small part of an equation that I understood: it was as if a tiny piece of the problem had broken off. My breath came faster. I could work with this and could show my work. Each time I reached a dead end, I moved on to another problem, and then another, and then I circled back, until again I recognized a segment of an equation: another tiny piece of a ball broke free, giving me a way in. My chest grew warm, and I carried on, nudging harder and a little harder, until all ten problems revealed themselves to me, all of them opened up.

At the end of three hours, when our time ran out, I had solved every problem. My lips were salty with sweat.

When exam results were posted, in our class of eighty, I had second place. I stood there in the hallway, and my eyes moistened when I saw my name.

It was in my third year in Paris that I met Pierre, through our shared fascination with magnetism. He was using a heat engine of his own design to bring substances to white-hot temperatures, studying changes in the force of their attraction—work that led him to Curie's Law of the magnetism of paramagnetic materials. I was finishing my last year at the Sorbonne and working for a magnet company, testing the strength of steel samples—a plum job I thought I'd earned on merit. Only later did I realize the eminent professor who recommended me had another motive: he wanted me in his laboratory so I could, in my "spare time," catalogue his collection of rock samples. He showed me his shelves of rocks with pride, waving a sheet of acquisition codes under my nose. "Women have patience for this sort of thing," he said. I could have cracked a piece of quartzite on his head.

When a visiting Polish scientist—one of my professors at the Flying University—came to see me, I confided my frustration. At once, he thought of Pierre, whose work he greatly admired, and invited us both to his boarding house for tea after dinner. Upstairs, in a narrow reception room, we drank smoky tea from a samovar fueled by pine cones. The sharp, sweet resin lifted in slow curls—the smell of Poland. We talked about my country and our work. Pierre stared at my acid-stained fingers. He couldn't offer me laboratory space—he himself had only a hallway outside his classroom—but from that evening, we began to see each other.

Pierre. Artless, brilliant Pierre. I liked his long, expressive hands, his grave smile, his auburn beard. He was careless about his appearance, yet elegant in his baggy, old-fashioned suit. I was twenty-six to his thirty-four, but there was something childlike about him. He was intense and serious, like me, and endlessly ambitious—you don't get where he did without a relentless drive to discover—but with a lighter spirit. On our first walk through the Jardin des Plantes, he plopped a frog in my hand and laughed when I shrieked. "Hyla arborea," he said.

We went to Physics Society meetings; we walked and talked. His father, a radical physician, had sent Pierre and his brother Jacques—then twelve and sixteen—out during the Paris Commune to drag injured men from the barricades back to their apartment, so he could treat them. He'd let Pierre roam the woods instead of going to school. Pierre's curiosity about plants and bugs and water and sun had grown into a passion for science.

Jacques, by the time I met Pierre, had long since moved with his family to Montpellier, but Pierre still talked as if he were missing a leg. The two brothers had done some fantastic experiments together when they were in their early twenties, discovering, with the aid of tinfoil, glue, magnets, and a jeweler's saw, that stretching or compressing a quartz crystal created an electric charge: the piezoelectric effect.

Pierre had that same brotherly devotion to Paul, who had come to study with him at seventeen. What I was to see that afternoon at Foyot's restaurant—that spark, that electric current—it was a gift Pierre had, or a need, for some one person to be at his side, two brilliant minds made brighter when they shared their fire.

I confessed to Pierre that I wrote poetry and in my notebooks drew elephants, oxen, monkeys, hawks. As it turned out, he wrote poetry, too. He urged me to read Zola, the "prose poet of a thousand nights." I recommended Eliza Oreszkowa, whose novels made me weep like a three-year-old child. If he read *On the Niemen*, I thought, he might understand my passion for my country, my blaze of longing to be useful, to move the world forward, at least a little. He might even understand, though I didn't tell him this, the hurt of being cast aside by a lover's family for being poor.

What was the risk, I asked myself, of becoming friends with Pierre? In a few short months I would leave Paris for Warsaw, to keep house for my father and seek a post at a girl's school, teaching mathematics and science. If I was lucky, I might find laboratory work. Perhaps I would risk Siberia and teach at the Flying University in my forbidden tongue, for Polish women were still barred from earning a degree.

So I told Pierre we could be friends, and only friends. What could he do but agree? But that afternoon at Foyot's Restaurant, when I saw the current running between him and Paul, unhidden and returned—I realized I wanted more. It was Paul, oddly enough, who made me see it. I wanted that same shimmer in the air between Pierre and me. But I didn't know how to say it, and our parting cheek-kisses remained chaste.

I found myself thinking about Kazimierz—how, when he came home from university, we would fly at each other. Whenever we could, we slipped away to a path by the river, kissing without stopping. Once he pushed me against a bullock cart piled high with beet roots; another time it was the red brick wall of the factory, its chimney spewing black smoke, his mouth closing over mine, his tongue thrusting deep. After a day with Pierre—his lanky body close enough to feel its warmth, but never more than the brush of a sleeve—I would lie in my garret bed, pull my nightgown up around my waist, put my hand between my legs, and remember.

Why didn't Pierre try anything? Had I scared him with my declarations of independence? In a sliver of my mind I worried that something was missing in me, as if a spark that maybe I'd once had with Kazimierz had been snuffed out, and maybe Pierre had sensed it. Or was it only friendship that he wanted? When he was twenty, he told me, he had been in love with a woman named Avril, who wanted every minute of his time. She had made it hard for him to work, hard to think, even, and he broke it off with her. She took it badly. A few months later, he heard that she had died from some mysterious cause. The whole thing haunted him.

Perhaps, like me, he planned never to marry.

One June afternoon as I read at my desk in my garret under the eaves, Pierre lay on my bed propped up on one arm (there was only the one chair), totting up numbers. My third-story neighbor had scowled when he and I walked up together. I said, "Madame Brune, you're looking unwell, shall I fetch you something from the pharmacy?" A few times before, I had been visited by a suitor, and I think she suspected that I was a prostitute. The French thought all of us foreign girls were loose, except for the Russian girls, whose Siberian blood apparently protected their virtue.

Pierre put his pencil down. "You'll graduate first in your class," he announced. He liked to calculate my ranking, which charmed me, though I wished he'd spend more time writing up his work on magnetism. ("I'm already on to the next thing," he protested. "Perhaps I'll get to it. I will if you want me to." But he wasn't really onto the next thing, he was back with his beloved crystals, exploring their symmetries.) I supposed he didn't really need his doctoral degree; he was a man, and French, and no one doubted his work.

"Wouldn't your mother have been proud?" he asked.

I tidied up my desk. In my family, we rarely talked about my mother, and when we did it was in reverent tones. "Oh yes, I think so. When she was in the Alps, taking her cure, she'd write us letters. 'Be kind to your friends, and helpful, that's your duty, but don't let them beat you in your studies!'"

Pierre put his palm to his forehead and laughed. "What a tremendous mother."

"She was the head of an elite girls' school when she was Miss Boguska, until I was born, baby number five. I've no right to complain if I end up following in her footsteps."

"Don't you want to stay here?"

"In some ways," I admitted. Soon it would be time to pack up my station at the lab, to put away the magnetizing coils, switches, wires and adaptors, and the metals and mineral samples: pyrrhotite, with its iridescent tarnish; sharp-edged lodestone, salty to the tongue. My employer would use my findings to build better products, with stronger steel. If I could only stay in Paris—of course I couldn't—the time I had put in for the magnet company's profit could lead to something better for me, to pure research, where I could ask my own questions, and follow them to their natural ends.

So many questions coiled inside; they almost frightened me. What if I didn't leave Paris? Wouldn't my father want a life in science for me, the life he had wanted for himself?

Traitor, I said to myself.

A breeze came from the window, cool and bracing. Pierre was studying me. "It would be possible to get a certificate and teach here."

"I don't want to be an exile." The very word sounded tragic. "Anyway, no Pole has a right to abandon her country."

"You're extreme, Marie."

"Extreme, to know my duty? Do you know how many educated Poles are in Siberia?"

"But how can you give up your research?"

"I guess I shouldn't expect a Frenchman to be sympathetic. Look what your country is doing in Algeria. Tunisia. You French and your 'velvet gloves.'"

I thought he might bite back, but he was quiet.

"Weren't you interested in taking another course?" he said. "Theoretical physics with Brillouin? You could teach and do that too."

I loved the way he spoke—slowly, thoughtfully, as if in every sentence he was searching for the truth. In fact I was unnerved by his lying there on my bed, so casually in his old-fashioned, large-cut suit, somehow both gawky and graceful. I said, "Guess who I saw kissing a woman in the Jardin du Luxembourg."

"Paul Langevin?"

"You know he has a girl?"

"I guessed. I doubt it's serious. He'll be leaving for Cambridge soon."

Paul had been awarded a grant to study at Trinity College, under the famous physicist J.J. Thomson—he had told us this with puppy-dog excitement, looking at Pierre with big open eyes, eager for approval. It's all happening in Cambridge, he had told us. Pierre should visit. It wasn't a world away.

Was I jealous of Paul? Probably. Yes, I was, because of his opportunities, but more so, because of the pleasure Pierre took in him. Paul had come to Pierre bustling and eager, but also awkward, bewildered, a working-class boy whose primary school teachers had recognized his potential. Pierre, at twenty-nine the youngest faculty member at the École de physique et chimie, had taken him on. He had been the one to initiate Paul into creative science. He had Paul explain to him new developments in science that excited them both, even asked him to collaborate on a study of damped motions, those back-and-forth movements that lose energy over time (the way a swing does, or a pendulum). Paul began to think like Pierre, even to walk like him, his head cocked to one side, his mind on higher matters and not on the sidewalk beneath his feet.

Pierre said to me, "J.J. Thomson wants to be the first to discover a theory of matter."

"I wonder if he'll pull it off."

"Cambridge is too theoretical. Even mystical. I keep telling Paul, science is not a religion."

"What does he say?"

"He agrees, of course. But he says it's your religion."

"Mine?"

"Yours."

"My family says I've replaced Catholicism with science." This was true. My brother teased that by driving myself hard, forgetting to eat, I was mortifying my flesh, a bride of science instead of Christ. He said that from a girl I had hoped to be canonized. Indeed I had been a religious little girl, in love with incense, chalice, and wafers, until I discovered flasks and beakers and chemical samples, instruments I could *use.*

Pierre smiled, shifting on the bed, lazily propping his head on his hand. "I like how extreme you are," he teased, getting back at me after all. "A passion for science is rare in a woman."

"*You* think it's rare."

"Yes, I do."

It occurred to me that Paul might find a woman in Cambridge and stay there for good, and that would be sad for Pierre. What kind of woman would Paul choose? A partner in Thomson's lab? A local girl selling potatoes at the Saturday market? A thought skittered through my mind: she would have big breasts. I squirmed. Why would I think such a thing?

"You'll miss Paul," I said.

"Yes, I will." Pierre swung his legs off the bed and stood up, towering over me. He stepped a little closer. "Do you want me to kiss you?"

I was startled. "Oh, I do."

"I thought so. I thought you did."

His beard was soft against my mouth. We held each other close, and delicious feelings spread throughout my body, a thrilling weakness and surges of strength. I took his warm breath into my lungs, and I breathed mine into his. I slipped my hands up under his shirt and felt the long muscles of his back.

When Pierre spoke, his voice was hoarse. "Come back to me," he said. "Go visit your father, but come back."

"You think because we kiss that you own me?"

"How can you say that?"

"Nothing has changed. My plans haven't changed."

We kissed again. From outside came the sounds of students shouting on the street. I said, "Don't you have a meeting at six o'clock?"

"Meet me after?"

"I'm studying."

"Meet me for an early dinner tomorrow?"

Pierre and Paul would follow each other anywhere, quite literally, as I learned the next day when I went to meet Pierre at his favorite cafeteria. Passing by the ancient building where he taught, with its crumbling stone, all locked up for the evening, I hardly noticed the dog shit on the sidewalk, or the people I passed. I was thinking about a paper Pierre had dedicated to me, on symmetry, which he loved to explore in crystals, and wondering about his finding that dissymmetries within phenomena can always be found in the medium within which they arise—if they appear in the effect, he discovered, they must be there in the cause. I had questions for Pierre, and I was thinking about his passion for crystals, and how lucky he was to live with few constraints, to have time and space to dream, and everything required to turn his dreams into realities.

There on the sidewalk outside Pierre's university, my eye was caught by a window opened on the second story of the building. A man's head popped out. I stopped and stared. The man looked out, surveyed the scene, and yelled, "Ahoy!" He disappeared a moment, and then a leg came out of the window, and then another leg, as he crawled out onto the narrow ledge that ran along the face of the building. I thought he looked like Paul, tall and lanky but powerfully built, and then I realized, it *was* Paul—loose red trousers and black boots, unmistakable and, at that time, just shy of flamboyant. Then another set of legs came out of the window, and another, and another—three young men carefully, gingerly, finding their footing and moving across the ledge along the wall, palms flat against it, a line of students in dull suits, led by the pied piper. Last of all, Pierre stuck his head out the window and called, "Langevin, you're an idiot!" Then he too crawled out and stood on the ledge. Instead of following the others, he wrestled with the window, trying to close it behind him. My heart thudded. I wanted to call up "Leave it!" but I was afraid to startle him.

By this time I wasn't the only passerby holding her breath; a small crowd had gathered, comrades in half-terrified and half-amused silence.

When Paul got to the drainpipe at the corner—bracketed to the building and covered in rust—he reached a hand out and grabbed it. Would the bracket hold? Would the rusty pipe crumble? He swung his leg around, gracefully, no trouble at all, and shinnied all the way down to the garden. One at a time, the three students shinnied down after him, Paul standing at the bottom, though there was little he could have done if someone stalled: the drainpipe would never hold two men.

When Pierre hesitated at the top, Paul called up, "Don't think about it."

"I never think," said Pierre. "I investigate." He reached out for the drainpipe and shinnied down, as deft and impressive as the others, though he was twelve years older than Paul. Then the drainpipe lurched, and Pierre froze. He was still a good three meters from the garden when the brackets broke from the building with a shower of crumbling stone. He tumbled backward and crashed on top of Paul.

When I ran to the garden, I found the two of them rolling in the grass, laughing, all sparks and boom and tingle, more of that famous thunder. Apparently, they had been working out a problem at the blackboard and lost track of time, and the janitor had locked them in.

Standing there, a little apart, I watched as the students brushed off their trousers, and Pierre and Paul got to their feet. Suddenly I was annoyed with both of them. I considered walking away, as if I had not been a witness to their antics. I wondered why I felt so bereft and annoyed and alone. It came to me then that what I wanted, I couldn't have: I wanted in on this—to be part of this game. Part of the rowdiness, the roughness, the camaraderie. I wanted to live large and free, to wrestle and love and try and fail, to argue all afternoon at a blackboard about formulas that no one had considered. Could it ever happen, even here, in Paris, that Pierre would come across me and a group of women scientists—or any women, really—shinnying down a drainpipe, and wrestling each other in the grass?

Pierre was almost right: I graduated second in physics. (This did grate a little. The year before, I had graduated first in math.)

I wrote to my father about when he should expect me in Warsaw. He replied that he would meet me at the train station with my brother Józef and his wife.

Pierre walked with me up the hill to the Gare du Nord to buy my ticket for three weeks out. As we got closer to the station, the train whistles grew louder. We passed street performers, acrobats and violin players, but we barely noticed.

"Don't look at me like that," I said.

"What? Like what?"

"I'm not being banished."

"No, of course not, I wasn't thinking that."

"This is my choice."

"Yes, of course it is."

"You look like a pouting dog."

"No one has ever called me a pouting dog. My brother Jacques says I pout like a donkey. I think it's my soft eyes and pointy ears."

I refrained from kissing him right then and there, outside the Gare du Nord, and from saying, you *do* have soft eyes, dreamy and soft and lovely. Instead I shrugged and said, "Your ears aren't as pointy as all that." He laughed. I loved to make him laugh. It was power of the sweetest sort.

I took the train from the Gare du Nord through vineyards and mountains, and through dense woods. I had to change trains half a dozen times, French then Belgian then German porters, until finally I reached Poland. It had been more than a year.

My father was smaller than I remembered. He stood on the platform next to a woman with pretty posture, a feather in her hat. I hesitated at the top of the train stairs. Jadwiga, Józef's wife? My father's eyes shifted, a twitch in his cheek.

I rushed to him. He stood stiffly as I hugged him. I straightened the handkerchief in the pocket of his green vest.

Jadwiga called him "Father." In the carriage, she put her sweet round arm on his. She was soon to have a baby.

"She's taken my place in your affections," I teased my father, when she had gone home to my brother and we were at last alone in his apartment.

He showed me my bedroom, the kitchen, and the parlor with our red velvet chair and green malachite clock. I lingered in front of our old glass cabinet that held his physics apparatus: test tubes, mineral specimens, and a gold-leaf electroscope, all locked up like forbidden fruit, glinting in the afternoon sun. I had stared at this cabinet since I could crawl.

He showed me his small, corner bedroom. He had nailed my mother's ivory cross above his bed, although he wasn't religious. When I was ten years old, I had kissed my mother goodbye underneath that cross, her scalp wet with sweat, and smelly, like stale beer. She was going to be with Zosia, she said. She longed to see her girl.

At that time I was going every day to the Old Town with my aunt, to the Chapel of Our Lady in Miasto Square, to beg God to heal my mother. When she grew worse, it occurred to me that God might need a sacrifice. I stayed up all of one dreadful night until finally I came to a decision: I would offer myself in my mother's place. The next morning, in the incense-filled shadows, among men crawling on their bellies to the crucifix, I asked God to take my life, and spare my mother.

She died soon after. I never prayed again.

Now, at twenty-six, back home with my old father, I had a vision of myself lying beneath my mother's ivory cross, frail and unable to get up, a silly thought that briefly frightened me. I wasn't about to die. I would be fine in Warsaw. I would make a life for myself.

After dinner, I went for a walk. It had rained all afternoon; mud trickled through the cobblestones. As if by chance, I found myself outside the laboratory where I had made my first experiments. My cousin Józio was still director, and I still had a key. I knew I shouldn't go in, but the streets were dark—I didn't think anyone would see.

A faint odor of acetone permeated the halls, exciting something in my belly. I lit a lamp, and there they were, the slate-topped workbenches, cool beneath my fingers, and the round furnace perching in its corner. Squatting on a shelf, amidst crucibles and ladles, was a creamy stoneware jug with decorative grape vines, the filter I had used to purify pressurized water. I picked up a copper blow pipe and puffed a bit of air through it. I had nearly dislocated my jaw on this pipe, pressing too hard on the silver mouthpiece, until I learned to use my chest muscles to make my cheeks a more efficient bellows.

It was here, while working in this lab, that I admitted to myself that Kazimierz was never going to marry me. The knowledge had come to me with a sudden chill, the feeling, even, of my approaching death. Yet I had gone on working with the blowpipe, blasting a thin stream of air over a gas burner—not harshly, nor gently either—bringing the flame to bear at a thirty-degree angle on a seed-sized substance, placed on a piece of charcoal, to discover what it was made of. I had questions to ask in a specific order. Did the substance melt? Did it vaporize or swell, crackle or explode? What color did it turn in oxidizing heat, and in a reducing flame?

I didn't have to think, really. It was more a matter of doing. Of being precise and refining one's attention. Science was more reliable than love.

Józio had liked to grab my arm and take me to the chart of elements—still on the wall, in blue and red and yellow, its columns arranged by atomic mass. Breathlessly, he'd tell me about how, in the 1860s, new elements were being discovered rapid-fire, but each one appeared to be an incidental fact of nature, and no one understood how the elements *related* to one another—not until Mendeleev. Józio pointed out the gaps in the chart for all the elements yet to be discovered. We wondered together: who would discover them, and how?

A thumping overhead. Footsteps? A night guard making his rounds?

I waited until it was quiet, and then I put out the lamp and double-checked that I had locked the doors.

My father was sweetly relieved when I took over the food shopping. There was a job coming up that might suit me, he said, teaching math at Gymnasium number three, where we children had gone to school.

Józio came to dinner. Over chops and potato soup, we talked about an article in the British magazine *Nature*, the physicist John Perry mathematically rebutting his teacher, Lord Kelvin, with calculations about convection in the earth's interior. If Perry was right, said Józio, slurping his soup, the earth was tremendously older than Kelvin claimed.

I went to bed with a hollowed out feeling in my chest. Was this who I was now, a spectator of science, a watcher on the side?

II

Warsaw and Paris, 1894–1896

Pierre Curie,
13 rue des Sablons, Sceaux
10 August 1894

Dear Marie,

I am glad you are taking in the fresh air and enjoying the summer with your father. I continue to hope you will return to Paris in October. We have promised each other—haven't we?—to be at least great friends. If only you won't change your mind! For such things can't be controlled by will. And yet it would be a fine thing, in which I hardly dare believe, to spend our lives near each other, hypnotized by our dreams: your patriotic dream, our humanitarian dream, and our scientific dream. Of these dreams, the last is, I believe, the only legitimate one. We are powerless to change the social order, and taking action, no matter in what direction, we can never be sure of not doing more harm than good. From the scientific point of view, on the contrary, we may hope to do something; the ground is solider. Any discovery that we make, however small, lives on.

See how it works out. But if you stay in Poland, it would be altogether too platonic a friendship. Wouldn't it be better for you to come and stay with me? I know that this question angers you, and that you don't want to speak of it again. And then, too, I feel unworthy of you from every point of view.

14 August 1894

. . . Marie, you say that you will not be influenced by me, that you are a free person, and will make decisions when and how you please. Is this not a little arrogant? We are all more or less slaves of our affections, slaves of the prejudices of those we love.

7 September 1894

. . . Marie, you have an amazing way of understanding selfishness!

When I say you must return, it is not the selfishness of a friend. I would grieve if you did not come back, but I dare to entreat you because I believe that here you will do more solid and useful work.

I put Pierre's letters in my desk drawer and closed it hard. All that afternoon, in a sweltering attic, over the clacking of hand cranks and foot petals, I'd read aloud to twenty women, seamstresses working for a pittance. Their little children, alone in stinking apartments, waited for them to bring back a bit of bread. Few of them, mothers or children, knew how to read. What did Pierre know of this? Was this not useful work?

I went to see my friend Klaudia, looking for commiseration. We sat in her mother's parlor just as we had as children, on either end of a wooden sofa, our legs curled under us and cushions tucked around. But before I could complain about Pierre, she blinked in an open-eyed way and told me she was marrying a German. She had waited to tell me in person. She knew I'd disapprove—one of Poland's three partitions was ruled by the German Empire; the Germans were our enemies. But fate, said Klaudia, had brought her and Dieter together. He loved her, and she loved him. I had no right to disapprove. Wasn't I a bit too rigid? Was *every* German an oppressor?

When news broke that Tsar Alexander II had been assassinated, Klaudia and I, as schoolgirls, had danced on the desktops in an empty classroom, until Madame Smirnov came in.

I agreed with the values I'd grown up with—and what was wrong with that? Could it be true that my fine principles were a form of rigidity, or arrogance, as Pierre said?

As I climbed down the stairs from her apartment, I thought to myself, at least Pierre hadn't proposed. At least in his letters he didn't mention love. He knew that what I needed was useful work, and that never again would I behave like a stupid lamb, trotting to the slaughter of my hopes for the sake of romance.

As I stepped out into the afternoon sun, a trolley came by, and a water-barrel wagon. Horses crossed the square in all directions. A man in a cap just like Pierre's stopped at a kiosk to buy bread. My heart thumped. But it was not Pierre.

I hadn't been honest with myself. Even when I wasn't thinking of Pierre, his image was awake in me. This whole time in Poland, he'd been a vibrant shadow in my mind. I hadn't wanted to admit that I had fallen in love again.

Paris beckoned because it offered me a chance to have a life in science. This was true. But just as important, maybe more important, was the fact that Pierre was there.

I went to my father and told him the situation. It was after a dinner of boiled potatoes and fried onions. I cleared the table and scrubbed the pans before sitting down with him. "Let me hear one of his letters," he said. I got one and read it out loud. I could see my father nodding, which gave me courage. "Nothing has ever given me more joy," he said, "than being married to your mother. But are you sure marriage is what you want?"

"You think I'm too independent," I said.

"You're stubborn, you want your own way. You won't even adapt your clothing to the weather." He accused me of this when I walked in the rain without an overcoat or wore my usual wool when the sun was hot. He was right that my lack of concern was a choice, and not absent-mindedness. I didn't want my attire to demand too much of my attention, whether for reasons of comfort or vanity.

He said, "Think about this carefully, Manya. Think about what you want."

"Go to Paris if you like," my brother said. "Your idea of duty is too punishing. Jadwiga will help Father."

We are all, more or less, slaves of our affections—these were Pierre's words.

I wrote to Pierre that I would come for a year, arriving four weeks hence. I would live in a flat in my sister's medical office, and he and I could see each other often.

My father and Józef drove me to the station. Once again I boarded the fourth-class ladies' carriage, and watched the forests and the wooden huts of Poland slip by.

Six months after leaving home, I was chagrined to write to Klaudia and tell her that her Manya was about to marry after all, to change her name and stay forever in Paris. But what was I to do? Pierre and I couldn't bear to be apart. I would bring him to Poland and ask him to love her, and to love our country.

I had to believe that, in marrying Pierre, I would gain in strength and not lose myself altogether.

• • •

Our honeymoon: July of 1895. We are twenty-seven and thirty-six. We ride our bicycles along the coast of Brittany, make love in the rocky coves. "Who explained menstruation to you?" Pierre asks me. "Who braided your hair?" "Bronia and Bronia," I tell him. He wants to know everything.

After, we travel to Chantilly, to the house Bronia has rented for her family, my father, and my sister Helena to go to after the wedding. When we arrive, she's digging up onions in the garden. She wipes her hands on her apron and scoops up baby Lou. "Hello hello!" she calls. The house is in a sunny glade near a wide golden cornfield, not far from the Oise River.

Pierre kisses her. "Thank you for being a good sister to my wife."

"Oh my," she laughs. "Father and Helena are out back."

But they aren't out back, they're circling around to greet us, Helena with her toothy grin, the look she has of being just about to break into tears or laughter, and Father without his tie, a little rounder. Bronia's husband follows, pushing his mother in a wheelchair.

We have four weeks in that country house, and I should be thrilled. Everything is better than I could hope—my father likes Pierre and his parents, too, who have rented a nearby place and join us every night for dinner. Everyone is cheerful. Dr. Curie starts political arguments, Mrs. Curie clucks her tongue, and Pierre groans and puts his face on the table. Bronia's husband fills our glasses with wine. But for me there's a fly in the ointment: I don't like it that Pierre and Helena go off for walks to the river, just the two of them. At first I see this a sign of Pierre's esteem, that he wants to know my family, but Helena looks at Pierre with too much awe. At night she dresses up and sings to the family, and I believe she is directing her songs to him. Pierre, I know, has a loyal nature, and yet I begin to doubt. Am I naïve, to imagine our love as smooth and secure? Can what I have with him be snatched away?

All this reminds me of when Helena and I were teenagers and had a crush on the same boy, one of my father's boarders. I thought, in my life, I was done with all of that. Will I never be rid of pettiness? But it isn't pettiness, it's the fear that good things don't last. Nothing lasts—every human being knows that. And I want a heart that accepts reality and transcends meanness. I don't want a wrinkled, jealous self. There's a longing in me that can't be appeased—this is what I say to myself.

My father sees me blinking—he knows the signs of my nervousness. One morning when the two of us are up before the others, he makes me sit beside him in the kitchen. "Are you all right?" he asks. "You're happy with Pierre?"

"Oh yes, Papa!"

He studies me. "You needed your mother," he says. "It's a shame."

I use a napkin to wipe my eyes.

"You don't need to worry about me," he says. "I'm all right."

One evening toward the end of September, my father and I sit on the terrace before dinner. There's a chill in the air and a bright slant of sun. Bronia's chicken and dumplings bubble on the stovetop, the aroma making me hungry. Father smokes his pipe and reads the French paper; I mend one of Lou's little sweaters and worry over Pierre and Helena, off on another walk from which, somehow, I am again excluded. I click my darning needles; if I concentrate, I can click away my doubts. A V of geese squawk overhead, and as I watch, I see two figures in the distance: Pierre and Helena coming through the stubbles of the cornfield.

Pierre carries a bouquet of wildflowers. He strides ahead of Helena.

"What is it?" I ask, when they get near. I can see he has something in mind.

He pulls a chair up and hands me the flowers.

"What is it?" I repeat.

"Najdroższa żono, daję ci bukiecik jaskrów wodnych," he says. *Dearest wife, I give you water buttercups.* He looks at Helena like a schoolboy seeking approval. She nods, and he continues, *"Kiedyś pojedziemy razem do Polski i pokażesz mi piękno swojej ojczyzny." I look forward to traveling with you to Poland so you can show me the beauties of your fatherland.*

The water buttercups have five white petals and a yellow center. I gaze at them to hide the wetness in my eyes. *"Dziękuję, najdroższy mężu,"* I say. *Thank you, dearest husband.*

My father and Helena beam. I go to my sister and embrace her.

That night I lie in bed as Pierre undresses. It's miraculous, that I get to watch him unbutton his shirt and trousers, the trousers that need a good wash, which he tosses to the chair heedless of the wrinkles he's making. The warmth of him is mine to smell. The covers he turns down are ones we share.

He reaches to turn off the lamp, but I stop him. I need to see his face.

"You won't like this," I say, "but I need to tell you."

"Yes?"

"I was jealous of Helena."

"You what?"

My face burns. "Are you angry?"

He sits beside me and takes my chin in his hand. "Look at me."

I lift my eyes.

A softness passes over his face. "Was it very painful?"

"Very."

He kisses me, turns off the light, and pulls me close to him.

• • •

I was sad when my father and Helena went home, and more so when Bronia and her husband and baby Lou moved to the south of Poland to start a sanitarium for people with tuberculosis—to do good, to help other Poles, as we'd all promised we would. But missing home, it seemed to me, was like a mother-grief we all carry. An intimation of wholeness that we crave.

Pierre and I knitted our lives together. He wouldn't touch the back of my neck or my hip as he passed by—this wasn't his way—but he wanted me, and I wanted him. Our lovemaking was fond, affectionate. At times I remembered Kazimierz, how he held me with such fervor that it hurt, and I could feel how hard it was for him not to push with the fury of his need. With Pierre it was lovely, but it wasn't like that. When we made love he often held my hand, as if to reassure me that we were friends. Only when he cried out—a haunted cry, as if he were in pain—did I experience an otherworldly quality. Just at the moment we were closest, I sensed his separateness. Then he would fold into my arms and we would cling to each other. We slept with our legs all tangled up, as if to keep anyone or anything from trying to separate us.

Nowolipki Street, Warsaw, 1871

Zosia puts cabbage leaves on a branch to make it soft for me, and she scooches me up. The tree has blossoms, yellow stars. I say they smell like lime. Zosia says they smell like honey.

Up climbs Józef, up to the top. Up comes Bronia, and Helena.

"Ouch!" I say. Bronia's leg kicks me, but she doesn't mean it.

Zosia knows about leprechauns. She's the oldest, the sister Mama, she comes up last. She bends over a branch, and her fuzzy gold hair lights up like the sun.

Our linden tree is old, old, old. Older than my Babcia, and older than her Babcia, but not as old as Poland. Mama says you take the bark and it cures anything.

One, two, three, four, my hare went out the door. That's about the rabbit that the hunter shot. *Two, three, four, five, he turned out to be alive.* Zosia tells me all the rhymes.

We are five Sklodowski children, and we all fit in our linden tree. Mama says, five is not too many, and it's just enough.

III

Paris, 1897–1898

When I consider my insanity with Paul, and I try to plot what came before—other times when I worried about my own mind—I would have to say that the craziest of all was early motherhood. Women aren't always honest about this, but it's plain to see that motherhood induces a kind of psychosis. There's something existential, terrifying, in the merging of mother and child. The vulnerability, the extreme feelings. The love and rage on both sides, and, worst of all, the times of no feeling at all.

When Irène was born, Pierre said, "She's an elf," because of her delicate features, but I said, "She's a queen." Though it wasn't the fashion, I nursed her. I wanted to do this, yet it made me anxious not to know how much milk she was getting. I wished I could measure it in a vial and analyze its nutrients. When she lost ten percent of her body mass in her first ten days, the doctor said it was normal, but I got frantic. Was my milk good? Could it keep her alive? I covered a notebook with linen, and I entered her weight before and after every feeding. I also noted her level of energy, ranking it from one to five. Ultimately, I had to accept the data and hire a wet nurse to supplement my milk. It felt like a defeat, but for nothing on earth would I endanger my baby's health.

At this time I was finishing up coursework for my teacher's certificate, and the magnet company had rehired me, so I was back in my old professor's lab, the one who made me catalogue his rocks, gritting my teeth as in days of old. "As society advances," he informed me, air faintly whistling through his teeth, "the division of labor between men and women grows more pronounced. And how is your dear little baby?" I went home every few hours to feed my dear little baby. She brought a big complication to my life.

I watched other mothers who smothered their babies with kisses. My parents had been formal—they had never treated us like that. Sometimes, when I kissed Irène, I felt like a pretend mother.

One chilly morning, I went early to the market with Irène, prepared a beef stew for dinner, and then, leaving Irène in the care of the nurse—with instructions for them to take a walk—I set out for an exam at the Teacher's Institute. The prompt for this exam? "Elaborate on the superiority of the French language." I rolled my eyes but was halfway through the essay when, in my mind's eye—but as if it were happening in front of me—I saw Irène's pram careening down a frosty path, rolling and rolling until it clattered down steps and pitched her into a pond. I stood upright. I bolted. I ran down the boulevard all the way to the Jardin du Luxembourg where, even from a distance, I could see the nurse in her umbrella skirt, idling by the fountain, one hand on the pram. I sat on a bench with my head in my hands until my heart stopped pounding. I walked back to the Institute and finished my exam.

Pierre said, "These X-rays. They're a high-frequency form of light, as Roentgen supposed." We sat drinking coffee and passing articles back and forth at the kitchen table, sharing our notes in the margins and asking each other questions. "Kelvin says they're impulses in the aether, not continuous waves."

I was marveling over Irène in her cradle, Irene-who-hadn't-drowned-in-a-pond, Irène with her slender fingers and pinched little nose. How had she taken root inside of me? Where did she get her glow? I felt a confused sense of something I couldn't work out. The life in my own spirit ebbed and flowed. At times it nearly guttered out. Could I keep this baby alive?

"I love my life," I said to Pierre, "and yet there's a feeling of wrongness. Something uncomfortable." I didn't want to admit to my panic, or that I'd spent two hours over Irène's cradle making sure that she was breathing. And doubts I thought I'd vanquished had come back around. *You aren't doing enough*, said a voice inside my head. *Will you ever do anything of any worth?*

Pierre put his article down.

"You have a big world here in France," I said. "Your crystals, your work. Your family."

He wrinkled his brow. "Your family, now."

"You see Paul every day." Paul was back from Cambridge and Thomson's lab—he hadn't married while at Cambridge, as I'd thought he might, but he was engaged to a woman in Paris (not quite the potato-selling maiden I'd imagined for him, but I'd been right about big breasts). He had picked up a course at the EPCI—the École de physique et chimie, where Pierre was on the faculty—and every day Pierre told me stories, things Paul had said, his vehement support of Alfred Dreyfus, the music he adored, and how he teased their colleagues, calling the director "Father Schütz," and another colleague "Bichro," because his beard was red like sodium bichromate. I was happy for Pierre to have such a friend, but I felt left out.

"Aren't you happy?" he asked.

He looked worried, so I tugged at his ear, which for no reason I could fathom, always made him smile.

"Of course I'm happy. But something niggles at me."

"Like when you straighten a painting on the wall?" He couldn't get over a visit we had made to the Louvre, when I'd shifted a Delacroix painting, *Liberty Leading the People*, a little higher on the right.

"I think so. A bit like that." It *was* a bit like that—something off-kilter inside of me. "Do you believe what Pasteur says, that the universe is a dissymmetric whole, and life is a consequence of dissymmetry?"

"In a physical system, if anything is to happen, the symmetry has to be disrupted."

"For something to happen rather than nothing." I didn't want to go too far with the dissymmetry analogy—it can be annoying when people apply science to emotional life—yet the notion comforted, gave meaning to my discomfort. Symmetry felt good; it brought a sense of harmony, of things being right and true, but it didn't create anything. To make something new: that took dissymmetry. First the discomfort, the disruption. Then the something new.

"You'll feel better when you have a dissertation topic," said Pierre.

"Yes, that's probably true. You are the best husband, do you know that?" I loved that he stayed with me in this conversation, right to the very end. He had a way of making me feel that some unnamable fear I carried was not, after all, a big problem. Once, after our wedding, when a photographer was making me his subject, I had felt myself stiffen into something wooden and ugly. Then Pierre stepped up to my side, and my body softened, grew supple and alive.

He was right about the dissertation. I needed to discover the work I could bear down on. I didn't need it to be grand, but I did need it to bewitch me. I wanted to focus all my energies in one direction, become a single mind. In my life this had been the only way to ease my restlessness. And I needed my efforts to have meaning.

"Roentgen's rays are astonishing," said Pierre.

They were astonishing. They could pass through wood and flesh, and from across a room, even when enclosed in a vacuum tube that itself was encased in black cardboard, they could light up a fluorescent screen. I shivered a little, picturing a skeletal outline of my pelvis and ribs, and ghostly space in between.

Roentgen called this high-frequency light "X-rays," because

they were so little understood, but in the year since he had shared his news, more than a thousand scientists had published on the subject.

In all this excitement, there was little room for new research by me.

Pierre's mother died around this time, and he was nearly struck dumb. He would stand in the middle of a room and tug his beard as if he didn't know where he was. I rubbed his shoulders and made him onion soup, and he politely thanked me, which made me feel like a stranger to him. I began to dream of my own dead mother. Always, in these dreams, she was floating on her bed, her hands folded over her belly. Twice, I woke up in just this posture, and shuddered.

One rainy evening, I had particular trouble coaxing Irène to sleep, and when I joined Pierre in bed, he complained, ridiculously, that I spent too much time with "that child," and I never paid attention to him. "Really, Pierre!" I said. I lay next to him in bed, but we didn't touch. I was listening to rain in the gutters when he began to sob in great, heaving gulps. I sat up and put my hand on his back. He smelled sour, of heat and sweat, or as if he had vomited. I had never seen him cry. I was conscious of the strangeness, of this being something new but somehow part of the mysterious, dark world we had recently entered—babies and spit-up and squalling and fatigue and death.

When finally Pierre could speak, he told me that Avril, the girl he'd been in love with when he was young—he had gotten her pregnant. She had been frightened of her father finding out. Pierre told her they could get married, but it took him two weeks to say it; she knew he didn't want to. All on her own, she went for an abortion. She had hemorrhaged and died.

"It's my fault," he said. "It's all my fault."

"Oh, my darling. No, no. Oh, how terrible, my love."

Moonlight lined the velvet drapes. I took Pierre's head in my hands, and he closed his eyelids so that I could kiss them. I pressed my lips to his salty lashes, and at the corner where his eye met his nose. He was here with me, with his tears and his breath; he had come back from the past, back to me.

• • •

20 January 1898: Irène changes her position by rolling on the bed.

30 January: She holds a rattle in her hand.

15 February: 6.2 kg before nursing.

• • •

That spring we moved from our tiny apartment to a bungalow with high windows, on boulevard Kellerman, at the southern edge of Paris. Pierre's grief eased. What he had confided in me became part of the world we shared; we held the knowledge tenderly between us. I felt stronger in myself as our connection grew, and I believe that he felt stronger, too.

My life became simpler when Dr. Curie, a widower now, came to live with us and help with the baby. His old face brightened when his granddaughter cooed, and he cooed back.

I began to believe I could trust the life in myself. The spring sunshine helped. One day I went out with Irène and, enjoying the magnolias and the daffodils, I mused on how plants need light to change water and carbon dioxide into glucose, allowing them to flower and grow, but Henri Becquerel's uranium rays—unlike these beautiful blossoms—emitted their power without ever seeing the light of day. How did this happen? Where did they get energy?

Becquerel's specialty was minerals that naturally phosphoresce: they glow when exposed to a strong light and slowly release the light they have absorbed. He wondered if there might be a link between X-rays and uranium rays that phosphoresce, so he wrapped a photographic plate in black paper that the sun couldn't penetrate, and over this he placed a copper cross, and over this, a plate of uranium salts. He expected, when he exposed the plate to sunlight, to find the outline of a cross on the photographic plate. But clouds covered the sun that afternoon, and he placed the whole contraption in a deep dark drawer. Days passed, and the sun in Paris refused to shine. Finally, he lost patience and developed the plate anyway. To his startlement, the photographic plate wasn't blank: a silhouette of the cross shined white against the black, as bright as if the uranium salts had been exposed to the sun.

How had they penetrated the black paper? Had anyone even tried to find out? I found myself walking faster, rattling Irène in her pram, over sidewalk bumps and crevices. Was there an opening here for me?

The men working in this field weren't especially interested. Uranium rays weren't dramatic; they couldn't be used to see inside of people's bodies. Becquerel thought that the emissions were a kind of "invisible phosphorescence," but what did that mean? He wasn't asking this question. Instead he had returned to his previous work.

Unlike X-rays, uranium's rays didn't need to be produced in a vacuum tube. They happened spontaneously. Pierre and I had read a series of lectures by Lord Kelvin, in which he confirmed through his own research the claims of Roentgen and Becquerel: both X-rays and uranium rays electrify the air. He didn't know why. He too had dropped the question.

By the time I parked the pram at the side of our house and picked up my sleeping baby, I had a dissertation topic. I would devise a way to measure the amount of energy uranium gives off. My findings by themselves might not mean a lot, but people could build on them. I could build on them. Pierre's genius with instruments would help.

If I approached a subject so unknown, no one could say that my work was derivative. Nor would I need to spend weeks in the library, slogging through other people's research. I could ask my own questions, invent my own methods. I could discern the inklings of my own mind, and follow them wherever they took me.

Pierre persuaded the EPCI to allow me the use of a cramped and musty storeroom, down the hall from his classroom. I moved old crates and lumber, swept cobwebs off brick walls, washed windows, tables, chairs, and a set of shelves: voilà, my laboratory. My next task was devising a measurement apparatus. Electrometers, as all scientists know, are designed by the devil—they're temperamental creatures, and unreliable—but my devil was the angel Pierre. He lugged into my quarters a quadrant electrometer that he and his brother had invented fifteen years before, using a piezolectric quartz as a benchmark measurement, because quartz, they discovered, generates an electric current when it is compressed or stretched. Pierre stayed at my side as we adapted it to my purposes, and no number of courses could have taught me what he did. I learned from watching his long deft hands, his intuitive way of moving and making adjustments.

After two weeks, we had an apparatus that spread across three tables: an ungainly assemblage of cylinders, poles, boxes, batteries, and wires. The measuring process was essentially a standoff between the power of a uranium compound and the power of the quartz. On one side of me, an ionization chamber converted uranium's rays to an electric current. On the other side, I manipulated a tray of weights to put traction on a suspended quartz, so that it would generate a current. In front of me stood the electrometer, with its needle suspended between two plates, and attached to it, a tiny mirror. When electric charges caused the needle to move, the mirror moved with it, and this caused a beam of light to travel across a ruler. I fixed my eyes on this beam of light, while registering, with a stopwatch in my left hand, the time it took for the uranium compound to overpower the quartz.

This process, though complicated and demanding, was brilliant and efficient—or so I could admit once I recovered from twenty days of practice and twenty nights with hot water bottles on my strained neck, and cucumbers on my exhausted eyes. When I felt I had the right, I bragged to Pierre about my great finesse. He kissed me twice and said I was as boastful as our butcher, who claimed he never had to sharpen his blade, unlike the hacker at the end of the street.

Through all of this, I was still tired, of course—I still had a baby—but I didn't mind my fatigue so much. When each morning I stepped into the dank, tight quarters of my little kingdom, the dust of chemicals in my skirts, I would stand for a moment at the threshold and gaze at the apparatus perched on my worktable like an overgrown prehistoric grasshopper, all mandibles, jutting legs, and eyeballs on stalks. I felt like a child in a field of freshly fallen snow.

I still sometimes think back on this time with wonder, those early days of starting out as a mother and a scientist. It would have been nice to know Hertha back then. Hertha and I have talked about this, especially about the extremes we felt—the violent bliss of nursing, the nameless dread. Hertha, like me, developed odd fears and illnesses after having her baby. My doctor, when I complained about trouble breathing, examined my lungs and, knowing of my mother's tuberculosis, urged me to go to a sanitorium (I refused). Hertha, enervated, was sent away to the seaside with little Barbara and couldn't work for two years. Whatever else caused her illnesses and mine—the responsibilities, the exhaustion—most of all we were fearful of losing our lives as scientists. We were not only women, but mothers, now, which, in the eyes of the world, meant doubly disqualified. The charge against women like us was that we were anti-natural. We had to fight against believing it. Hertha and I agree that the mind doesn't have a sex. And yet, we have come to wonder if this is the whole story. If some of what we have achieved is not in spite of, but because of, being mothers.

I like to linger over the details of my early discoveries in science in the same way that, in the weeks just after, I rehearsed every moment of Irène's birth. Each of these happenings was a small rift in the universe that let me into a chasm of possibility, mesmerizing, glorious. After Irène, when I woke up in the mornings, I would call back to mind the first tugs of contractions, like intense menstrual cramps, but a good and promising ache. Then amniotic fluid dripping down my legs, its faint, sweet smell. Then contractions in massive swells, and learning to surrender, the pain peaking, intensifying, and passing through me, and coming back around. It was the pushing that most surprised me—not my own, but the force that muscled the baby from my body, and I pushed with it, because the pain was splitting me apart, and I needed to get this child out of me. And then she was there: an astonishing blue-and-red creature, squalling—a whole new sound in the universe. The timeless had somehow pushed into time and found a place for itself.

It was like that with radioactivity. I had the wondrous sensation that I, an ordinary mortal, had been received into awareness of primordial forces. This feeling started early on, when, in that dank storeroom, I discovered something baffling: the more uranium any compound or mineral contained, the more active its rays. It didn't matter whether it was solid or pulverized, or whether its atoms were combined with another chemical; its potency didn't change if I heated it or cooled it or dissolved it in acid or water. Nothing I could do to it changed its potency; no interactions between or within the molecules had any effect on my measurements. The only thing that mattered was the quantity of uranium, in any shape or form.

If this energy didn't derive from interactions among molecules, then what? It was too early for a theory. I only knew what Becquerel had shown: the energy of uranium rays didn't come from the sun. Could there be another source? Were there imperceptible cosmic rays suffusing the world, which only certain atoms knew how to absorb and radiate?

One afternoon, I saw through these questions into something completely new. I had been standing at my worktable, and it was raining outside. My breasts were tight with milk, though it was still an hour before I would head back home to nurse my hungry Irène. At the thought of her, my ducts released. Milk soaked through my corset and dampened my dress. I felt alive, inside of my own skin. The wind knocked a branch against the storeroom window, and from down the hall came laughter—Pierre, conversing with his students. I could almost smell him in his woolen suit. My corset tightened around my breasts with every breath, and I had that mysterious full sense of being right here and now, in a musty storeroom with the rain falling softly outside, rain that fell also on the house on boulevard Kellerman where my daughter slept in her cradle, and, in my mind, over farms spreading eastward and all the way through thousands of acres to Poland, where, in a small apartment in Warsaw, my old father, at this hour, was preparing his noonday meal of sausage and tea.

When I turned from my reverie back to my work, I picked up, with some tongs, a gold-and-green flecked piece of autunite, a type of uranium ore, and I placed it on the disk in the ionization chamber. At that moment the question came to me: Why assume that the energy of uranium comes from an outside source? The answer was clear: it was taken as a given that the atom was the smallest unit of matter, solid, inert, and indivisible—this was the foundation of modern chemistry. But in science there are no givens! What if the consensus was wrong? What if uranium's energy arose spontaneously from within? What if it possessed within itself a supply of power, built into the structure of the atom?

It was possible. There were no data to contradict it.

A marvelous tension grew in me, as if the ground were trembling with a coming earthquake.

In the days that followed, I developed a headache, a throbbing in my skull, but I couldn't stop measuring. I borrowed samples, I begged for them. I expanded my ambition—I wanted to know if other substances gave off similar rays—metals, minerals, compounds, salts, common and rare, whatever I could find.

One day I tested thirteen elements, none of which gave off any rays. A subtle nausea made it hard to eat, but I was nursing, so I forced myself. I did know that an engine in me was in relentless gear. At night after putting Irène to bed, I often went back to the lab, threw open the windows and worked into the night, the only human in the cavernous building.

Among my samples was a black chunk of pitchblende. One day I placed this on the disk and measured it. It took so little time to ionize the air to saturation—its rays were so potent—that I thought the electrometer was broken. I examined it but found nothing wrong. Pitchblende is a mineral ore of uranium, but in the samples I had, the uranium had been extracted for industrial purposes, for use in ceramic glazes: I knew that uranium couldn't be the source of this energy. Indeed, this pitchblende was more potent than uranium, *much* more potent than any known element. I knew this for a fact, because I had measured all of them.

I went to fetch Pierre from his classroom. Together we examined the electrometer, but we found nothing wrong. I consulted with colleagues: my measurements must be mistaken, they said. I needed to be more careful.

The next day I repeated my measurements ad infinitum. My readings were always the same.

I found Pierre bent over his crystals at his hallway workbench, pushed against the wall. He stood up straight when he saw me. He knew without my saying: my measurements checked out. We stood there containing our excitement. Within the pitchblende, there had to be an undiscovered element, generating these rays, an element listed nowhere, on any chart. We didn't hug or kiss. We never did in front of other people, especially scientists. Pierre beamed at me and I at him, and I could have stood there for an hour, just enjoying the energy between us. Then he began to clear off his workbench, the crystals that he loved so much, and a new apparatus he had built. I stood there watching him, this man who had only recently regained his passion after the death of his mother; only recently returned to his crystals, to study their growth structure. This man who, before I even met his parents, had told me that if I wouldn't stay in Paris, he would move to Warsaw for me. Now he was setting his work aside once more, because the task of finding a new element, isolating it from all the other elements in pitchblende, was too much for one scientist. Of course he would join me. Of course we would do this together.

I had an urgent need to drive ahead, but if word of my findings got out before I published them, and another scientist got the same results, I would get no credit. I gave the potent rays a name: radioactivity. I wrote up my results to date, though every moment of delay was an agony.

"Does it matter who gets the credit?" Pierre asked.

Sometimes, his high standards irritated me. "Clearly, you've never had to worry about being passed by."

"Not true," he said, holding up a finger.

"Oh, oh—I'm sorry." The Academy of Science had recently turned him down in favor of a man from a family with a coat of arms. This was galling, of course. For one thing, it would have been nice for Pierre, as a member, to present my findings to the prestigious Academy—where important findings were most often first delivered—instead of my having to rely on the Sorbonne professor in whose laboratory I had worked. I had tried to console Pierre, telling him he could try again, and the next time he would win, but he hadn't wanted to hear this. Paul, when he heard about the vote, had a different approach. He came over in high spirits with a bottle of champagne and raised a glass to Pierre's independent mind. "It's better this way," he said, an arm around Pierre. "You'd be fed up with those fools in two minutes. You're incapable of being superficial." By the time he left, Pierre was laughing.

Now in my lab book, Pierre's notes mingled with mine, my meticulous script and his floaty, airy one. Neither Pierre nor I had specialized training as a chemist, so we brought in a colleague, Monsieur Bémont, to advise us on the task of separating out each component of the pitchblende ore and measuring its potency. For months we hardly lifted our hands from the tasks of grinding chunks of pitchblende into a tarry black powder, dissolving it in acid, separating, purifying, measuring; separating, purifying, measuring. Pierre might have liked a slower pace—his legs began to bother him. The doctors diagnosed rheumatism and put him on strychnine. This worried me, because of course strychnine is a poison. The doctors assured me that correctly dosed, it relieves swelling and pain.

We precipitated one element after another from pitchblende residues, and one element after another, when we weighed it, failed to match the power of uranium's rays. Then one morning, to a pulverized sample of what I took to be silvery-pink bismuth, I added hydrogen sulfide, causing a chemical reaction that produced a solid, which, when I placed it in the ionization chamber, generated a charge 150 times more active than uranium. This bismuth wasn't just bismuth! I made careful notes while my exhilaration grew. Meanwhile, Pierre, beside me, was heating some of the bismuth sulfide to seven hundred degrees in a Bohemian glass tube, and the test tube cracked. A deposit of fine black powder formed in the broken glass. When I went to measure it—"Your hands are trembling!" said Pierre, so I drank a cup of tea and tried again—we found it to be four hundred times more potent than uranium. Four hundred times. We had found a new metal, a new *element,* in this black powder—we were sure of this—but when we took the sample to Demarçay, our spectroscoper, he came up empty-handed: our new metal didn't appear to absorb light at specific wavelengths, unique to it. Demarçay could detect only the characteristic spectral lines of bismuth, in the blue and green and yellow regions.

We couldn't yet corroborate our finding. There was nothing for it. We would have to wait for confirmation.

• • •

20 July 1898: Irène walks very well now on all fours. Says "Gogli, gogli, go."

15 August: Bathing in river, she plays with her hands in the water.

16 August: She plays with a cat and chases him with war cries.

• • •

Toward the end of that year Pierre and I had evidence of a second radioactive element in pitchblende. Alone in the lab on a Monday morning, an icy drizzle outside my window and inside temperature barely above freezing, I precipitated a barium chloride sample that registered as nine hundred times more active than uranium. Nine hundred times. I was frightened that its power would disintegrate, so I sent a student to collect Pierre, and I ran up two flights of stairs, the sample in my hand, and thrust it into the hands of Demarçay, to examine its spectrum. I shook with cold until Pierre arrived and put his jacket around me. With both of us watching, Demarçay directed his beam of light through our distilled barium chloride sample, and dispersed it through a prism: there was the barium line, yes, but this time, there was more: another line, a line like none other, intense and red.

Pierre and I stared at each other. Outside we could hear the rain picking up, and tree branches cracking. "Oh," said Pierre—I don't think he knew that he had spoken. I took both of his hands.

Out in the hallway, Paul was pacing, waiting for us. The student who had fetched Pierre had told him. When he saw my face—I must have been lit up—he picked me up and swung me around. He swung Pierre around too, in a fit of joy and bravado.

Pierre and I went home and had supper with Dr. Curie, and I put Irène to bed. That night—the only time in our lives—we went to Montmartre to a music hall and danced.

At three a.m., beneath our bedroom window, something was chewing on a shrub. "Do you hear that?" I said. Along with the crunching, there were noises like a baby cooing. "Are there two of them?"

"Porcupines. They're demolishing my father's rosebush."

I shivered. The coos were sweet but also somehow disturbing. It happened this way for me. When a project was all finished, I might be excited, but I also got a ghostly feeling, a metallic taste in my mouth.

"That beautiful rosebush," I said. "After all his work."

The street lamp filtered through the shudders, landing on Pierre's armoire. My hair smelled of the music hall. Perfume, cigarettes, sweat.

"You danced. How are your legs?"

"Painful." He turned to lie on his back. "I'm fed up with this."

I lay my hand on his hip. It wouldn't help him if I gave in to fear. "I'm going to put you on a diet of no wine and no red meat."

"All right. If you think it will help." We listened to the rustling in the rosebush.

Pierre said, "Are you sure you want to go ahead with this?"

"Aren't you?" I knew he was talking about radium, how much more there was for us to do. We hadn't seen it as a solid. We still didn't have a pure sample; there was a high proportion of barium in the compound. We thought it would take weeks to separate the radium. We would need a vastly bigger laboratory, and at least two tons of pitchblende—how to get and pay for all that? I pictured it arriving by locomotive from the German-Czech border. We would send a wagon to pick it up, hire men to carry the heavy sacks into our working quarters. When I opened the sacks they would smell of the forest, of mushrooms and loam, and wet tree trunks. I wanted to dig my hands into the pine needles and brown dust, mixed with black tarry chunks of ore.

Pierre said, "We already have our evidence."

"You know it's not enough." Though we had found the spectral line of radium, there would still be skeptics. Physicists were accustomed to working with mysterious rays, but chemists were suspicious of anything they couldn't see or touch. And unless we isolated radium from barium, we couldn't weigh it with enough precision to assign a weight. We couldn't place it in the Mendeleev table.

When I was twenty and staring with my cousin at the chart of elements, I never imagined that I would have the joy of finding and naming two more: radium, and polonium, which I had named after my country. I pictured my comrades at the Flying University, reading about polonium. They would know I hadn't forgotten them.

"But we have our element," said Pierre. "No one will doubt us."

"But they do doubt us. And I want to know its weight."

"You are the world's most stubborn woman."

"I think so. Probably."

Pierre drifted off, but I lay awake, thinking of the chart of elements. At my cousin's laboratory in Warsaw, I had spent hours learning my way around the normal and transition metals. I had researched the history of every element, its properties, who discovered it, when and how. In our lab at the EPCI, I'd also hung up a chart, but the newest version, beige and blue and black and red, including helium, argon, and krypton. Each rectangle was crammed with numbers and letters, with gaps for elements that scientists had predicted, but were still unknown.

Every day I stared at the dashes in those empty spaces.

IV
Paris, 1902–1906

Pierre and I did the work, the brute labor and the delicate procedures, famous now, described in any textbook published after 1903, our story told as if it's grand and heroic—and maybe this is, after all, not so very far from the truth?

We had expected to spend four or five weeks isolating radium chloride, and it took four years. Four years, and not two but ten tons of pitchblende to pulverize and boil in vats, five hundred tons of rinsing waters, and thousands upon thousands of chemical treatments. The roof of our cavernous hangar on rue Lhomond leaked in many places; it was freezing in winter, a furnace in heat. After each step of our process we had more potent distillates, but we also, necessarily, lost some of our radium: chemical reactions are reversible reactions, and radium vaporizes: it's terribly unstable. Would there be any radium left of whatever we managed to procure? This was the question that kept us up at night. After a test tube shattered for no reason while he was heating it, Pierre took to staring intensely at any simmering liquid in his glass tubes or his porcelain dish, fearful of another explosion.

The scientific community was poised for our results, and Pierre and I shared our strong distillates with others now working in this field. People came to visit. The chemist Wilhelm Ostwald was scandalized by our quarters—it was a stable, wasn't it? Or a potato cellar? He thought it was a hoax until

I showed him our equipment. But by and large, outside of our teaching—Pierre still at the EPCI, and I at Sèvres, the Institute for Teachers in Training—Pierre and I created for ourselves a world apart. We had lunch together, and after, arm and arm, we'd tour our shabby hangar, observing our operations and imagining our future. It was like the vision Pierre had wooed me with, in his letters: we lived close to each other, hypnotized by our work and by our dreams. Sometimes I thought of my father's words about nudging evolution along. It was a relief to know that I was doing something useful.

And we succeeded: we isolated one-fiftieth of a teaspoon of white radium salts, enough to measure (and the equivalent in energy of 10 billion kilowatt hours). Exhilarated, I assigned it the atomic weight of 225 and placed it in the Mendeleev table: number 88, after barium, in the column of alkaline earth metals.

"All's right with world," said Pierre. "Columns are filled. Pictures are straight."

"You're a patient man," I said, kissing him and tugging at his ear. He had indeed been patient with my excessive zeal. When alarmed by my overwork, my fatigue and loss of weight, he objected very little; instead he found a creative way to fund a full-time assistant, André Debierne, a round-faced chemist of about Paul's age, shy—wary, even—but attentive and meticulous. Henceforward he worked at my side.

Paul was among the few friends we had seen in those four years. He came over sometimes in the evening after Irène was asleep, and the three of us would sit in our garden, talking until long after our lamp grew dim and we could no longer see each other's faces. When Pierre and I began to recognize the degree of radium's energy—not a thousand times more active than uranium, but a *million* times—we confided in him about our fears. What if it got into the hands of criminals, especially politicians who start wars? Pierre said that we have to trust that the good that comes from science outweighs the bad, and I agreed—I'd staked my life on this. Paul wasn't sure; he was at the same time more idealistic about science, and more fearful of human nature. We all felt the tremble of what we couldn't know. Maybe the bedrock laws of nature were just as we all thought, and matter couldn't be created or destroyed. Or maybe we'd discover that inside the atom there's a kind of furnace, creating life out of nothing. Maybe our theories of matter would have to change.

Often, I would leave the two of them and go up to bed. Through my open window I could hear their murmuring voices, soft tones that rippled over me, both soothing and exciting.

Once, a sharp tone in their conversation woke me up. Paul sounded annoyed, but Pierre was standing firm. The next morning Pierre told me that he had refused to give back the manuscript of Paul's doctoral thesis on the ionization of gases; he planned to turn it in himself to Paul's editor, who had agreed to publish it. Paul didn't want to let it go, he was obsessed with edits, afraid of making a mistake, but the work was brilliant, and he needed to move on. I had never seen Pierre behave like that, against another person's will. But apparently, he knew what he was doing. The publisher thanked him, and Paul, a week later, poked his head in our laboratory, sheepish, saying that in all his life he had never had a better friend.

By the time Pierre and I isolated radium, Irène was five years old. She planned to be a scientist. She also wanted a little sister. I was thirty-five, and now that I was done stirring twenty kilograms of boiling pitchblende until my shoulder froze, done with coal and iron dust and transferring vats of liquid, and attempting fractional crystallization while rain dripped through the roof onto my neck—finally, finally, we could have our second child.

I wrote up my research for a doctoral thesis and—pregnant, nauseous, frightened, and ready to run to the bathroom—I presented it to a panel of three examiners, three men in evening dress, and a room overflowing, more and more chairs brought in. "Madame Curie," they announced at the end, "the first woman in history to receive a doctorate from the Sorbonne." Cheers and jubilance, a merry din, my friends and colleagues clapping hard, Pierre and his father beaming. My students, my Sèvriennes, with roses in their arms.

Paul and his wife threw a party for me in the garden of their house near Parc Montsouris. Paul filled our glasses with Chateau Margaux from 1900, the very best vintage—scandalous, considering he spent half his time scaring up another course to teach to make ends meet. Chinese lanterns, laughter. Madame Langevin, pink and strong, a third child coming after four years of marriage. She congratulated me on my thesis. "I think it's wonderful," she said, stroking my cheek as if I were a soft-skinned child. I admired her tarts and cheeses, strawberries and flaming orange nasturtiums—"As if you don't have enough to do!" She replied, "A wife does what she must."

Toward the end of that evening, Pierre ushered us all to the dark side of the garden. "Not another toast," moaned Madame Langevin, but I knew what Pierre was up to—he wanted to show off our radium. Some of our friends had seen it—he kept a test tube in his vest and flaunted the sores it made on his chest. But there was an aspect of radium that could only be seen in the dark: it was luminous. Its energy excited nearby electrons, and this created light. You could almost read by it. To heighten the effect, Pierre had partially coated the test tube with zinc oxide, because it was phosphorescent.

I stood by a hazel tree while everyone gathered, listening to insects trilling in the shrubs. The smell of gardenias and cat pee stirred my nausea, a sensation that I cherished, because it held the promise of new life. Lately I'd been missing my father, who was growing old without me. He hadn't felt well enough to travel to Paris for my thesis defense. It was hard to live apart from my family. But there in the garden on this lovely evening, it seemed to me that my choices were worth it; they were good. What would the study of radium spawn? What couldn't come of my alliance with Pierre? I thought of the embryo inside me, its arm buds and leg buds, its unformed face. Who would this child be? How would its life unfold?

"Dear friends," said Pierre, his words ringing out. The moon was barely a sliver, and I couldn't see his face, but I was stirred by the sound of his voice. He waited, and then again, with warmth: "Dear friends. I present you with the offspring of our collaboration." He must have reached into his pocket for the test tube of radium, because there it was, in the dark above him, an astonishing blue light.

"Look, look," someone said in a hushed voice, and across the crowd, there was a gasp. Against the night, the glowing outline of the test tube quivered. Ghostly. Blue. Unattached to anything material.

Nobody spoke. Nobody whispered.

We stood with our faces raised, to the blue phosphorescence caused by radium.

For the next three months, it seemed we were still living in that blue glow, our lives backlit with expectation. And then one morning at the end of August, in the fifth month of my pregnancy, I woke up with an ache in my belly. I didn't think it was unusual. We were on holiday with Irène in Normandy, at the seaside near Arromanches, in a cottage that looked out at the cliffs and a quiet beach. We had planned a picnic and walk with friends at a neighboring house, but I didn't feel well enough. I told Pierre to go ahead and to take Irène so I could rest. I stood on the porch and watched them dawdle down the beach (neither one of them ever moved at a pace), Irène perkily swinging her arms, Pierre squatting to pick something up from the sand—a shark tooth, maybe, or a bit of sea glass—and Irène inspecting it. Then I went back to bed.

When I couldn't get comfortable after an hour, I thought a swim would do me good. I had swum throughout my first pregnancy, and I wanted to float on the water, to let the ocean bear me up. The winds were calm, and the tide was high—gone was the broad and sandy beach. I made my way carefully across the rocks. My lower belly ached.

Oh, to lie back and unweight myself.

Finally, the water was up to my knees, and I swam into the surf. I was floating with the sun on my face, breathing in the smells of salt and kelp, when a cramp twisted through my abdomen. The pain took me under, and the cramp screwed tighter. I set out for shore, pushing myself. A wave came in with an undertow, and I couldn't fight past it. Panic. It pulled me out to sea. The pain blinded me, but I knew I mustn't pass out. I gulped salt water, and I kicked to stay afloat, aiming at the shore, with all the force of my will swimming in one direction, ducking under waves as they washed over me. The cramping eased as I fought my way, and I could stretch my arms. But the rocks near the margin were not coming closer. I was not moving toward the beach. I changed my tack, swimming at a diagonal, trying to find more strength. At last, the rocks came closer. I was making progress. I had called on the last of my reserves when the cramps returned. The pain took me under. A big wave came and heaved me up onto the shore.

I lay on my side, panting, but I was still in reach of the waves. I dragged myself higher up the beach.

I sat up and saw that blood poured over my thighs.

I looked around. No one to help. I steadied myself. I took off my swim shorts and squatted. A sick tide moved through me. It expelled my child from my body.

I should have been dizzy with shock and pain, I should have lost consciousness. But then I saw the baby girl. I picked her up and cupped her in my hands. She was exquisite. Her skin was translucent, her every rib a wonder. She had pointed ears like her sister's and faint, gingery eyebrows. She moved her head as if she were seeking something, her tiny, sublime mouth opening. I touched my finger to her tongue.

And then her skin turned blue, and her breathing stopped.

The roar of the waves.

• • •

It's a roar I've been hearing my whole life. I learned about it from my Uncle Henryk, when he came back from Siberia, when I was a child of six. My father unlocked the door, and it swung inward with a gust of cold. There on the step was a man in a huge fur coat, with a suitcase wrapped around with cord. Ice glistened in his whiskers. He smelled of engine oil. He walked as if his feet were blocks of wood.

My mother hugged him until he tottered. We had thought that he was dead.

I was magnetized and a little afraid as he devoured ham and Hungarian wine, sitting in our big red velvet chair. I didn't know him, nor did my brother and sisters—he was the one who left Warsaw in a chain gang in 1865, when he was arrested with other patriots, after the uprising.

My mother went to the kitchen and came back with a soaking bucket filled with warm salt water. She knelt in front of her brother and went to unlace a boot.

"No, don't." His voice was rough. "My feet are not so pretty."

"Do you think we care?" She pulled off both of his boots, then tugged at a woolen sock—soiled and smelly and stuck with bits of hay—and then we saw it, his swollen white-and-purple foot, with two toes in the middle, no longer flanked by sibling toes, but sticking out amidst scab and protruding bone.

I gagged. My uncle shrank in his chair.

My mother placed one of his feet in the basin. She rinsed her rag in the salt water, and then she took his foot in her hands, and she washed the hairless top, and the bottom, and between the two toes. Only once, she turned her head. She didn't want him to see her tears.

The wind picked up and blew hail against our window, and I sensed that there was danger outside our doors, a danger my parents had tried to keep away. But inside, in front of me, was my uncle and the coal fire and this baffling scene. The grotesque foot in my mother's hand. Love funneling through her.

"You think this is bad?" asked Uncle Henryk gruffly. "Frostbite is easy. Losing toes is easy. I nearly puked my stomach out of my mouth, and I was retching blood, and that was easy. What's hard—now let me tell you. What's hard is being a thousand miles from home. It feels like knives in every part of your body. It's like someone is burning you from inside out, and you'll have no relief until you can get home."

I sat closer to my father. He put his hand on the back of my neck.

"Did you never forget?" asked Mother. "Not for a few hours?"

"Sometimes, yes, when I found a friend or had a bit of work. But then I'd see a bend in a river that looked familiar, or a loon would call, and I would throw myself down, and roll in the dirt like a dog, and howl. I thought I was mad, but I wasn't the only one. There are men howling all over Siberia. They call it roaring."

And then he said, "God save you, Bronislawa, from ever feeling anything like this."

I could hear the men in Siberia, the ones who were still there. The coal crackled, and ice pinged on the roof, and a frightening wind rose up, blowing through our house, knocking down our walls, and hurtling us—my father and my mother, and my siblings, and the red velvet chair—farther and farther away from each other, until I couldn't see anyone anymore, and I was alone in outer space.

• • •

What is the point, I ask myself, of looking back at my childhood and my life with Pierre? What do these memories have to do with the story of what happened between Paul and me? Perhaps it's true that all strands are interwoven, and none of my stories has a separate shape of its own. Life is a broad black net where a disturbance in one corner sends waves out over the whole, shifting all the threads.

• • •

After my miscarriage, a month went by, then two. Pierre thought I should go back to teaching, and he needed me in the laboratory, but I stayed home and mended socks. Paul took over my classes at Sèvres. My father-in-law, Dr. Curie, looked after Irène. I was glad to have them near.

Pierre didn't understand. We'll have another, he said, but I didn't want another. I wanted the baby who had died, the girl with faint eyebrows and pointed ears, who had looked so like her sister.

I would have had the miscarriage no matter what, said the doctor, but I wondered: had I brought it on by overwork? Four years boiling tons of pitchblende, stirring with an iron bar? A colleague had written us a letter reprimanding us for self-neglect. Pierre had thought he might be right, but I had refused to be held back.

If I had stayed in bed that morning, would the cramps have gone away? If I hadn't had to swim for my life?

Earlier that summer, before the miscarriage, I had heard from my brother that my father fell while getting out of a tram; while recovering, he had come down with bronchitis. I was on the train to Warsaw when he died. When I arrived, I made my brother open up the coffin, even though he said I was morbid. There he was, my once dapper papa, the hair I used to trim, his skin loose around his neck, wearing the soft green waistcoat he'd kept brushed and clean since I was a little girl.

My poor, brilliant papa, like me, troubled by regrets. His physics apparatus under lock and key. His Russian "superiors" living and breathing for their all-night vodka parties.

Once, at the dinner table, when I was little, my father had told us a story, how he insulted the Russian headmaster, Mr. Ivanov, who had been harsh with their students for their "Polishisms." My father had lost patience. "The boys don't mean to make grammatical mistakes," he'd said, "any more than you do. And you've been speaking Russian so much longer!" My mother put her ladle down, her face gone still. My father nervously laughed. Two weeks later: Goodbye to airy schoolmaster quarters. Goodbye to the garden and the linden tree. Hello to dark and dank quarters on Karmelicka Street, where my father had to take in boarders. First two, then five. Then twelve.

By what measure of justice had I become the scientist?

After our mother died, he had given his life to his children, shaping our character, putting bread on the table, reading to us in five languages, leading us in exercises. When I was a governess, he had sent me math problems to work out and send back to him.

What kind of selfishness had made me break my promise to live with him in Warsaw and take care of him?

It felt cruel to me that Pierre carried on as if nothing important had happened. He didn't understand my self-recriminations. "It's just life, Marie. I can't follow what you think you've done wrong." Yet I was also glad that he was puzzled by my misery. It gave me hope that I could come to see things in another way.

He had wanted the child, too. When I told him I was pregnant, he had been so happy. He had grabbed me and spun me around. I breathed in the joy of him, and it doubled my own joy.

I found myself wanting to write to my friend Hertha. I had met her only a few months before my pregnancy, when Pierre and I traveled to London—at the Royal Society, on that occasion when she wore a billowing red cloak, both of us on our husbands' arms. We had met for breakfast. She told me she was gutted by grief for her mother, whom she'd nursed for a year, and a nephew who had died of smallpox, only recently.

I felt shy about writing, but I sent her a letter at her home in Norfolk Square. I told her that my world had turned all gray. My daughter Irène was unhappy; she sensed my misery. I could never bear to have another child. It would be a betrayal of the one who died.

I heard back from her with no delay. She had wept when she heard my news.

But dear Marie, please don't let this grayness of which you speak take hold of you. Even if you have another baby, this lost child will live in your mind. Let your pain be your source.

I didn't understand what she meant, *Let your pain be your source.* But she must know. She must have found a way to live with grief.

One fall morning I made myself attend a committee meeting at the Physics Society. We were considering scientists to present at our annual conference, and I wanted to recommend Hertha, to give her an opportunity to share her work in France.

Paul was on this committee. I hadn't seen him since the party after my thesis defense. He had dark circles under his eyes. Two weeks before, Madame Langevin had given birth to a baby girl. I wondered if something other than fatigue were troubling him. I knew of only good things in his life—his now published thesis on the ionization of gases had already become a classic, and because of it, he'd been asked to step in for a year as chair in experimental physics at the Collège de France. This was an honor for a thirty-year-old man.

When I suggested Hertha Ayrton to the committee, for her work on the formation of sand ripples, the room went quiet. I felt conscious of my weak voice—perhaps this was why?

I shouldn't have come. It was too soon, and I wasn't ready.

One gentleman proposed that Hertha's experiments were "wayward," and another had heard that she offered "a feminine running commentary outside of and complementary to her lectures." Paul stood up, indignant—he was always sympathetic to the underdog. He'd heard Hertha lecture on electric arcs in 1900, he said, when she came to Paris for the International

Electrical Congress, and he had learned a good deal indeed. The other scientists backed down and agreed to inviting Hertha. I agreed to reach out to her to settle the date, and we moved on to other business.

The sun ascended in the tall windows of the meeting room. It fell across the table, and I shifted a little to let it warm my face. My mind drifted, and it seemed to me that I was lulled by a rhythmic motion, and the murmuring voices of the others were like the sound of waves.

A memory jolt went through me—roaring waves at Arromanches. I couldn't sit still—I gathered my things and ran out to the sidewalk.

The wind picked up. A cat mewed pitifully, circling a drain in the gutter.

Suddenly, Paul was walking beside me, breathing heavily. "I'm so sorry," he said. "She would have been born about now, like my Madeleine. It's too hard."

Her arm had been smaller than my little finger. Her skin so thin I could see her beating heart.

I refused Paul's handkerchief but found one in my pocket and blew my nose.

He held his hands behind his back and continued to walk with me. He didn't seem to mind my crying; he had melancholy of his own. After a while, he said—to himself or to me, I wasn't sure—"I do take some comfort in the laws of thermodynamics." I had no idea what he meant, but I could see that he was sincere. In another mood, I might have smiled.

When we reached the station, Paul suddenly grabbed my hands. His eyes sought mine, and they scared me a little—as if they held a question only I could answer. I perceived in that moment his piercing willingness to get past conversation and everything trivial and false. I didn't quite know what he wanted, but I shrank back. He looked disappointed. We carried on, and he stayed with me until I reached my train.

I have sometimes asked myself: was this where it all really started between Paul and me? But at that time, I had no use for his love, not with Pierre so close and so alive.

"He's complicated," I said to Pierre that night.

Pierre threw his trousers on the chair and crawled into bed next to me.

I asked, "Does he ever talk about what ails him?"

"No, but I suspect he married the wrong woman. She's irrational."

"Is she?"

"And baby after baby!"

I was quiet for a while. "Well, Pierre, you can hardly blame her for that."

I wondered about Paul's promise as a scientist. Would he be able fully to achieve it? There was more to success than genius; it took perseverance, and confidence. When Paul had taken my hands, I had seen in his eyes a fiery particle of life. Could he keep it going? Apply that fire to his work?

"There's gloom underneath," I said.

"He's a man of substance, and she's just simple. Do you know how lucky I am to have you? Really, Marie. I wouldn't have married."

"I guess we're both lucky." I nestled into him and pulled his arm around me.

"*Ukochana żona*," he said. "Beloved wife."

I'd lost a child, but I had Pierre and Irène.

Gradually, I returned to myself. The painful memories didn't fade, but I consigned them to a compartment in my mind, which I would visit and afterward close the door. I knew how to do this. I'd done it from an early age.

I didn't know this at the time—Pierre didn't tell me—but early that fall, he'd gotten wind that he was being considered for the Nobel Prize for the discovery of radium, with no mention of me. He had told the committee that he wouldn't accept an award for work that had been initiated by me and accomplished by both of us.

In November, a telegram came from Sweden: along with our colleague Henri Becquerel, the two of us, Pierre and I, had won the Nobel Prize. I was so surprised I couldn't speak. I sat down at our kitchen table and was perfectly dumb for half an hour.

"I hate prizes," said Pierre. "They're demoralizing."

"Science should be done for the love of it," I teased. Both of us were playing down our exhilaration.

"You're scientific snobs," exclaimed our friend, the physicist Jean Perrin. "This is splendid news!"

The prize set a big wheel turning. Our laboratory hummed. The prize came with money; we hired a lab assistant. We put a bathroom in our house and donated to Bronia's sanatorium, and we helped my sister Helena, and gave Pierre's brother Jacques money for his research. Pierre bought me a briefcase—a leather bag in buttery yellow—to replace my one in tatters.

"The happy laureates," the newspapers called us. My house was "invaded by glory," and I was "the Madonna of Science." They loved the way I "fanned the sacred fire in Pierre."

This confection created by the press annoyed and slightly frightened me. They quoted us endorsing outrageous claims for radium: "No more baldness! No more gray! No more cancer!" and we were forced to waste our time writing and publishing disclaimers. When we tried to escape to Normandy, the journalists followed, sneaking into our living room, photographing the neighborhood cat and publishing conversations with seven-year-old Irène.

Their highest praise of me? "She's as good as French." Oh backhanded compliment, impugning my Polishness. So many French were suspicious of foreigners. I shivered when I read about Dreyfus, whose detractors still printed lies and trash every day of the week, though they'd sent him to Devil's Island. Sometimes I remembered my grandmother's warnings: Russians or no, hide your glories, my darling. She worried about witchcraft and the evil eye. My mind went to her in the weeks after the prize, rotund and regal in her purple-gray silk—a mourning dress which she wore for Poland, because our country had been erased from the map—partitioned among Russia, Prussia, and Austria—in 1795. Her own mother had also worn a mourning dress. *Babcia,* I would say to her, *come into the nineteenth century.* What would she have thought of my prize?

Around this time, Pierre discovered that a single gram of radium could melt a gram of ice and bring it to boiling in an hour—a finding that defied scientific experience—and all he wanted was time to wrestle with the implications. Being a mother, I was accustomed to interruptions, but Pierre had little tolerance for the hoopla around the prize. Sometimes I scolded him for his complaints. *Things will get back to normal,* I told him, *this is not a catastrophe.* But for him it was. He had lost the leisure to follow his own mind. It didn't help that the requisite public lectures fell to him.

Also around this time, the scientists Soddy and Ramsay, in an astonishing bit of work, discovered that decaying radium produces helium, which supported the idea that even when radioactive elements seem to be stable, they are spontaneously transforming into other elements. Pierre and I were excited—the scientific movement we had started, with the discovery of radioactivity, was gaining speed—but this news brought home to us that in the year since the prize was announced, we had done very little work. I had been the first to suggest that radium's energy might come from within, but Pierre had been uncertain—wasn't it as likely that there were emanations in the ether that radium was able to absorb? I had agreed with him—and I still do—that one mustn't jump ahead of the evidence. But others brought evidence forward while our time was being frittered away.

If I could reach back from the present and change the past, among the many things that I would do, I'm fiercest about this:

I would give my husband a spacious lab and surround him with tranquility. A lab where no journalists could find him. Every day he would enjoy the peace he craved. I don't try, in my mind, to make him live to seventy, that's too grand. But with all the fervor of my heart, I grant him the freedom to follow his inclinations, invent his instruments, and trace the strands of his thought. When I visit him there, in this imaginary lab, he turns his head with pensive kindness, and he says, as he always did, "Marie, how was your day?"

His leg and back pain grew worse, and he began to walk with a limp. I stayed encouraging, but inside I felt like my *babcia*, seeing his pain as an omen.

Often, I went to the laboratory alone at night, the only time I could focus and get things done. I'd stay there until two in the morning, writing letters to chemical factories, trying to forge alliances and develop better, quicker ways to purify radium. If the science of radium were to thrive, we needed extracts for ourselves and other scientists.

I did conceive again and bore a daughter, just before Christmas in 1904. Pierre seemed to expect this baby to be an answer to all my ills, but I couldn't rejoice. Bronia's five-year-old boy had suddenly died of meningitis. Irène had developed another cough, and I was fearful about her health. World news was generally terrible. A hundred thousand Poles had lost their jobs, and the Russian police opened fire on a crowd of protesters in Warsaw. The Germans were slaughtering the Herero, the Ottoman army was fighting Greeks and Bulgarians, and the Japanese and Russians were at war. How could I raise another child in this world? How could she be so fat and happy?

But baby Eve, with her dark curls, wouldn't tolerate my distraction. She screamed when I put her down. As I was not a stoic, I carried her, and over time, we adapted to one another. Her soft, unformed being rested over my heart. I began to revive. Tea and toast in the morning tasted good. It was as if I had, for too long, starved the animal of my body, and my baby, my girl, sucked at my breast and brought me back to myself.

At night, Pierre and I still wrapped ourselves around each other. His heartbeat, and the rhythm of his breath—these nurtured my life as well. As I grew more contented, Pierre did, too, and I became more aware of what he had suffered for my sake, during my months of unhappiness. How lonely and worried he had been. My gratitude deepened, as did our love.

By springtime it felt as if we were entering another chapter, lighter and freer. The Sorbonne created a chair for Pierre and gave us a space to work in, on rue Cuvier—cramped, yes, but they promised to build more rooms around a courtyard. My assistant and collaborator, André Debierne, became our laboratory chief, and even he—a straight line of a mouth at the best of times—hummed a tune and threw open the window of his new office, just off the entryway where he could monitor all who came and went with the eye of the eagle we needed him to be, both for our research students and to keep visitors away.

We even enjoyed a few benefits of our celebrity. We visited Auguste Rodin in his studio and saw *Adam and Eve Sleeping*. The dancer Lois Fuller, from the Folies-Bergère, insisted on setting up for a private performance at our house, with a team of American electricians. Our dining room blazed with her illuminated veils, comic and wonderful, our house instead of our laboratory caught in a strange light. When the troupe was gone, Pierre and I made love right on the sofa, in the hiss, buzz, and glow of a new light bulb. Pierre also dragged me to seances with Eusapia Palladino, fascinated by chairs skittering across the floor, pushed by an invisible hand, and window curtains swelling out, when the air was still and conditions were perfectly controlled. Were there forces, he wondered, beyond what we could see, making these things happen? How might a scientist study them?

Our friends took to gathering at our place on Sunday afternoons, in the dining room, or the garden if the weather was fine. André would sit in the corner with Irène, playing chess.

Jean Perrin, the physicist, gnome-like with his red beard and curls, would put on the phonograph in our dining room and climb out of the window onto the patio, singing in his rousing tenor, "*Wunder webend er sich wiegt!*" He called me Madame Radium and said that I was rich as Croesus, minting radium instead of gold, trying to provoke me into a speech about the free flow of information in science, because my earnestness amused him. He knew, of course, that Pierre and I had chosen not to patent our techniques for extracting and purifying radium chloride—and he would have done the same—but in his jesting he completely confused Madame Langevin—Paul's wife—who happened to have joined him that day, dressed in a pretty new frock and incongruous amongst our crew. She congratulated me with enthusiasm—"I've been telling Paul, *other* scientists make money"—and I had to disillusion her, explaining that Pierre and I had published all our secrets.

On these occasions, Pierre's father and Paul would argue with each other as they always did—"It's the imperialism of revolutionary committees," and "How arrogant, to underestimate people who are oppressed!" Listening to them, one wouldn't have guessed that they were on the same side: anti-clerical and anti-monarchist, advocates for the people. ("Better you than me," Pierre would say to Paul—he hated an argument.) My students from Sèvres also sometimes joined us, especially Eugènie Feytis, who brought buckets of apricots and cherries.

I wrote to Hertha that I was slightly embarrassed about all the fun Pierre and I were having. Soon I received the pale blue envelope and paper with her now familiar script. *Darling Marie, A person of science who has any genius must take delicious joy in living, working, and discovering, and must never be ashamed of herself. Can there be any genius without a love of life and its pleasures?*

I answered her, *You have a way of fending off my furies. Perhaps your power won't stand up to scrutiny, but I shan't investigate.*

The spring of 1906 was rainy, with the Seine threatening to flood.

Pierre had some bad nights with his legs, his moaning so intense that I was afraid he would wake up the girls. He urged me to go to sleep, but I never would. I wanted to be with him, even though I couldn't take away his pain. When he got too warm, I would take off his shirt for him, releasing the tender smell of his body, which still made my own body soften. His skin gleamed white in the dark. The hours ticked on. Sometimes he would sleep, and I would lie close to him. I was conscious of the sound of his breath and mine.

A new doctor diagnosed neurasthenia—not rheumatism after all. What Pierre needed was more time off, the physician said, and more walks in the country. After that I made sure that we left our laboratory by six o'clock. Pierre and Irène began a new ritual of Sunday morning outings, hiking to a pond in the woods with buckets and magnifying glasses.

And on a day in April, when the air was fresh and the sun new and bright, Pierre and I took the girls—Irène now eight, and Eve sixteen months—on a train to the country, to St. Rémy. We walked along a washed-out road. Pierre laughed at how Eve walked in every rut and climbed up on the stones. He was proud of her balance, excellent for a toddler. We were surprised to see broom shrubs in flower. We cut branches of flowering mahonia and made a large bouquet of large water buttercups. Pierre and I sat next to a millstone while Irène, in her blue knit trousers, ran after butterflies with a pesky little net that kept getting tangled, and Eve squatted in the meadow, pulling out clumps of grass.

I took off my underskirt and gave it to Pierre to sit on, so he wouldn't get cold. His legs were bad that day. "Marie, don't," he scolded, but he allowed me to spread the skirt out, and to lie with my head on his lap. The air was cool on our faces, the sun warm on our necks. We marveled that, from millions of kilometers away, a blazing ball of fire could touch us with its warmth. Ernest Rutherford had recently discovered that the source of the sun's energy was radioactive decay. "It will warm us for vast millions of years," I said.

"We should collaborate on something new," said Pierre, tugging at the tiny hairs on my wrist.

"Ouch," I said, but I didn't really mind. Our minds were sparking together. Something would come of this.

"Goeÿ thinks I'm insane, but I'd like to develop an objective method to study the paranormal. Everything has a vibration—atoms, sound, thoughts. Vibration produces radiation, right? It's a source of energy. So why couldn't there be a genuine telepathy, an influence of thought on thought?"

"From a distance, you mean."

"Like when you and I have the same dream. What is that?"

"One of us absorbing vibrations from the other?"

"Or back and forth somehow?"

We murmured about how stunning it was that radium could cure tumors. When Irène shrieked—she had actually caught a butterfly—I led her off to set it free. Then I leaned against Pierre, and we fell back to dreaming: What about a radium institute? What if we built one together? Spacious laboratories, vast research teams. Pure science for us, a second branch for medicine, run by others. Pierre would raise the funds. I would find the site, work with architects. And I would plant a row of linden trees the moment we had the ground.

I looked out over the green valley, the spring air sharp in my lungs. "Irène will work at your side in our lab," I said. "She's just like you."

"And Eve?"

"She reminds me of my mother—musical, good."

Pierre smiled and lazily stroked my arm. "We make marvelous children. Should we have another?"

These dreams were not to be.

Instead, back in Paris, walking alone in the rain and following a carriage to thread his way through traffic, Pierre let his attention wander. At the convergence of Pont Neuf, the quais, and the rue Dauphine, he stepped around the carriage and failed to see a thirty-foot wagon piled high with military uniforms coming down over the bridge, pulled by two Percherons. He grabbed onto one of the horses in an effort to steady himself, but it reared, and he fell under the wagon.

They said it was slick.

They said the driver tried to swerve.

The rear wheel of the wagon crushed his skull.

Bronia came from Poland. After the funeral, before my family left, I got a pair of scissors and took her into the parlor where Pierre's body had lain, before they took him away. His garments and his watch had been returned to me. I made Bronia sit as I pulled his bloody clothes out of the bag and cut them up, and kissed the tatters. I kissed what remained of him, and then I threw it all into the fire.

I remember Irène waking in the bed beside me the next morning, searching for me with her arms, saying, in her plaintive voice, "Mé isn't dead?"

And I remember Paul Langevin, slumped over on my husband's desk at rue Cuvier, days after the accident. It frightened me to find him there. For a moment I thought that he too was dead. When he turned his face, I saw a red gash at his hairline.

"What happened?" I asked.

He looked at me as if I were deranged by grief—as if I were asking him about Pierre, I saw this in his eyes—but then he remembered and touched his fingers to his forehead. He said abruptly, "Bicycle accident. I'm fine." It didn't look as if he'd had a fall; he had no other scrapes.

"What the devil do I do now," he muttered.

"Can I help?"

He turned from me, his back unnaturally rigid, his shoulders raised in a contortion of grief. I had a need to comfort him; I couldn't bear his pain. I put my hands on his shoulders—how they trembled—and leaned over him and pressed my cheek against his head. Paul had loved Pierre. He had been formed by him in the ways I had; he had looked into the eyes of my husband and found his own mind in the depths of Pierre's attention. I rested there, my hands on Paul's shoulders.

And then he twisted suddenly, a sinewy turn, and he pulled me onto his lap. He gave off an acrid smell of stress. His hands were on my back; I feared my ribs would crack. I didn't know if he was holding me or holding his own pieces together. Finally, he loosened his grip. He put his head on my shoulder and cried without embarrassment.

Nowolipki Street, Warsaw, 1872

My mama's trunk says "Pani Bronislawa Sklodowska." My biggest sister kneels by another trunk, drawing flowers around her name, Z-o-s-i-a. She wears her jacket and her bonnet, but the droshky is late. She will be Mama's nurse. She's thirteen and old enough. Zosia and Mama are going to Austria, to the Alps, because the water is pure and the air doesn't scratch your lungs.

When she plays the piano, my mama rocks. I sit on a hassock by her, and nobody can make me leave. She plays Chopin, "Opus 27, No. 2." I hate this one because my chest hums, like bees are inside, and I don't want the tears to come.

Mama stops playing and coughs, a dry, staccato cough. Staccato is like in music. She tries to play again, but the coughing comes.

"Here it is, Mama," I say, retrieving her handkerchief.

"Maria. I told you not to touch it."

"I'm sorry." My voice is faint.

When she takes the handkerchief away from her mouth, she tries to hide the red, a bright sun with dots scattering away from it.

I say, "You're taking Zosia. Take me, too."

She runs her fingers through my curls. My curls are wild, I'm like a little beast, and you can tell when she says this, that she likes little beasts.

"Zosia's the eldest," she says. "You're the youngest."

"Who will brush my hair?"

"My darling. Auntie Lucia will come. A year isn't so long."

"Auntie says I have to pray for the Russians."

She strokes my forehead. "My Manyusya. Auntie will pray for the Russians. You pray whatever is in your heart."

V

Paris, 1906

A FEW WEEKS AFTER Pierre's death I went to rue Cuvier when I thought that no one would be there. I tried but failed to take a measurement for a curve on which both Pierre and I had made some points. When the door opened in the entryway—André Debierne had come in after all—I slipped into my office the back way. I took out my journal and wrote.

> *Yesterday, for the first time since the terrible day, Irène said something funny and made me laugh, but I felt bad about it. Do you remember, my Pierre, how you reproached yourself for laughing a few days after your mother died? My head bursts and my reason is troubled. I don't understand how I can live without seeing you, without smiling at the sweet companion of my life.*
>
> *Today, in a letter to her cousin Madeleine, Irène didn't speak of you. She will in time forget you completely, yet the loss of you will weigh on her whole life and we will never know the harm this loss has done.*

André rapped at my door. He tried to come in and found it was locked. When I opened it, the poor man stood there, shifting from foot to foot.

"I'm sorry," he said.

"What is it?"

"Langevin is here."

I stared at him.

"He knocked. He might not know you're here."

"Tell him I'm not seeing anyone."

> *Pierre, I can't, I don't want to endure this. Among all the carriages of Paris, these wagons and automobiles, is there not one that could make me share the fate of my beloved?*

Walking home from the train, I stepped through an iron gate into a small cemetery off the sidewalk and sat down in the sparse grass.

Waiting there, my head against a gravestone, I thought of a Bible story that scared me when I was a girl, and still scared me, Jonah in the belly of the whale. I felt swallowed up like that, in a moist dark fear, gone to a place where no human being could follow. Jonah had called out to God for help, but that had become impossible once I lost my religion as a child. I closed my eyes. In my skull, an empty roar.

I pulled myself up and carried on down the sidewalk.

One Saturday morning, I was sitting at the dining room table with my father-in-law, answering letters of condolence, when the post arrived. It was a letter from the French government, offering me a widow's pension. Enough to live on. Enough to pay the bills. A minute before I had wondered if I could soldier on, but now my hackles were up.

I tore the letter in half.

"What? What is it?" said Dr. Curie. Even-tempered except in politics, he was also unaccustomed to displays from me.

"They've awarded me a pension for life," I said. Of course a pension sounded good, but embedded in this offer was the assumption that without my husband I was powerless. Take what you can get, it seemed to say. Had I died instead of Pierre, they'd never have given him a pension.

My father-in-law had a dent in his jaw where it had been shattered by a bullet during the February Revolution of 1848, and when he was annoyed, it grew prominent. He said, "Two hundred thousand workers on strike, and this is how they want to spend their money." I loved this about Dr. Curie—he was always on my side.

"I'm thirty-eight years old, why wouldn't I work? It's a matter of conscience."

"Conscience?" he asked. "Or pride?" He peered at me with his sharp blue eyes. "You have a high degree of both."

"Fair enough." Though I was idealistic like Pierre, I was not as pure as he had been.

"Grandpère!" came Irène's voice from the back door. Eve was napping, and Irène had been playing with Aline, the Perrins' daughter; our gardens were connected by an iron gate, and they came and went as they pleased.

He rose with alacrity. "I'm coming, *ma chère*." Recently, both children often called first for him, this man with silver hair and dented jaw, whose dignity was the more pronounced when he was in the company of children. After Pierre died, he had approached me to say that he could go and live with his eldest son, Jacques. I told him I'd be hurt, but he should do as he wished, swallowing my fear that he might leave the girls and me. He'd said, "What I wish is to stay with you."

A week after the government's offer, I received a second letter, this time from the Sorbonne. Like the first, it was intended as an honor: Would I take over for Pierre in the Faculty of Science? They made no mention of the chair Pierre had held—they would leave it empty—and the fee they offered was a fraction of what Pierre had earned. They wanted me to do everything he had done—the lectures, administration, advising, and laboratory oversight—all for a pittance. They thought they could get away with this because no woman had ever taught in their hallowed halls. Not at the higher levels.

This time when I tore up the letter, Dr. Curie was skeptical. He hovered over me as, on the spot, I wrote back declining the offer. "You should think twice," he said. "You know your money at Sèvres isn't enough."

Pierre had earned more than double what I did. The cook had asked for a raise, and there was the charwoman to pay, and the taxes on our house.

"Did you think twice, when you lost your patronage?" When his progressive politics, especially his alliance with the Paris Communards, caused him trouble with his bourgeois clientele, he'd lost his standing as a physician, and he'd taken work as a country doctor, with lesser pay. "Did you regret it?"

"I had Sophie to take the edges off. She made our lives comfortable."

I used to feel jealous of my mother-in-law's gift for homemaking. My first year of marriage I'd spent hours each day trying to replicate her recipes and meet her standards for the son she still loved to indulge. Then one day, when Pierre failed to comment on the beefsteak I'd prepared, I asked him how he liked it, and he said, "Did I eat a beefsteak? It's quite possible." He swore afterward that he was teasing me, but I was not sure. He was preoccupied with higher things. Not long after, I hired a cook to make our meals.

"You take the edges off for me," I said. "I don't know how I'd manage without you."

"I've never known you to be foolish, Marie. Especially not about money."

"I couldn't hold my head up."

Besides, was there any other scientist in France besides me who could take Pierre's place, who had the knowledge and capacity? Secretly, I held to the belief that the Sorbonne would have to come around and make me a better offer.

The rest of that day I walked around energized, but that night I woke in a sweat. Could I afford this house? Was it hubris, to decline the Sorbonne's offer? Would the girls and I have to move out with their grandfather? Share a house, even, with others?

A horse clopped down the boulevard; I listened as the sound grew faint. Dr. Curie got up and padded to the toilet. During the day my father-in-law was just as before, but at night he became an old man; his pee hit the toilet bowl in a thin, stop-and-start stream.

Eve called out from her cot. When I checked on her, I found she had sweated through her sheets, but her hands were cool. Bronia's boy was dead of meningitis. *Pray God Eve doesn't get sick.*

When, finally, I lit my lamp and picked up *Le Temps* from the floor beside my bed, I had a shock. The paper was a few days old. There, on the first page—why had no one told me?—was a letter from Lord Kelvin about my work with radium, published first in *The London Times*. My pulse thumped in my temples. He claimed that I'd misunderstood my data, and that radium was not a new element, not an element at all, but more likely a compound of lead and five helium atoms. As if all the research that Pierre and I did had been a farce. As if we hadn't isolated radium chloride. As if we hadn't weighed it.

Lord Kelvin was the lion of British physics. People listened to him. Why would he want to discredit me and the work that Pierre and I did? Why would *Le Temps* reprint a letter that sowed misunderstanding?

I imagined *Le Temps* on the table in the common room at the Faculty of Science, and committee members reading it, the ones who already would have read my letter, in which I had declined their offer of a job.

That morning I went in to see André in his office before I'd taken off my coat. He had assisted me in the work of isolating radium; he had a stake in this.

He was taking a bit of snuff, his window open to the clatter of the street. I thrust the newspaper at him. "Have you seen this?"

"No one will take it seriously."

"That's not true."

"I'm sorry. You're right."

"Who challenges scientific theories in the *Times*?"

"A man in his dotage."

"It's just as . . . You can't trust people with titles." I had been going to say, *It's just as Pierre says.* "The aristocracy is loyal only to itself," he used to mutter. "The Victorias, the Wilhelms, the Ferdinands—by God, they'll bring us all to ruin."

"And the Nicholases," I would add. "Don't forget the Romanovs."

Kelvin was a formidable adversary in part because he and I appeared to be on the same side. Presumably he believed that knowledge lighted the path forward. Many would see no reason to mistrust him. Would he have challenged our work if Pierre were still alive? I had given my life to science—would I not be allowed to contribute, would everything I did in the end come undone? I shivered, though I was still wearing my sweater and my coat.

Marriage had protected me more than I knew. Hertha's husband, Will Ayrton, a physicist and electrical engineer, had refused to collaborate with her, because he knew that he would get the credit for anything she did. I had thought he was extreme in this choice, since their interests overlapped so much. Because of it, her path had been harder than mine, but that could all change, now that Pierre was dead.

Will was sick now, too. Hertha was nursing him.

"Kelvin must believe he's right," said André. "He wouldn't risk his reputation." His round face had a worried look. He went to his cupboard and took out a tin of biscuits. "I'm peckish. Care for one?"

I took a biscuit, like a horse accepting a palm full of sugar. It was dry in my mouth.

"Have another," he said, holding out the tin. I shook my head, and he ate two quickly. "What shall we do?"

We both knew that the only way to refute Lord Kelvin beyond all doubt was to produce pure radium metal—not the compound radium chloride, but the pure element itself. Virtually impossible to do, because radium has no stable form. It's easier to handle when chemically combined with salt, but even then it emits radiation. It's always in the process of decay.

My gamble with the Sorbonne paid off. They made me a fine offer. Pierre's chair in general physics, his full responsibilities, and a salary close to his, of ten thousand francs. Whatever negative effect of Lord Kelvin's letter, it hadn't stolen this position.

When I opened the letter I felt a huge relief, and yet, minutes later, standing in the doorway of my house, I lost my confidence. I had detractors, I knew this, who whispered that I was a fraud, that all my accomplishments were, in fact, Pierre's work repackaged for show. Colleagues who refused to see that I had already proven myself, but had humored me, because I was the wife of Pierre. Could I face up to them, in this new position?

My daughters watched me from the parlor sofa, Eve with her worried, uncomprehending eyes, Irène, eight years old, ready to comfort me. Wasn't it true, that their father had been a hundred, a thousand times better than me? Who wouldn't prefer to listen to him? *I* preferred to hear him speak. When I lectured, I was stilted. Whereas Pierre had been alive, surprising, precise.

The position meant I'd have to retire from Sèvres, and leave my students. Alice, Mireille, Katya. I thought of how they looked at me, tender and full of hope. They would miss me, but they would also want me to go, to lead the way. To show that for them as well, a future in science is possible. They hoped one day to work in my laboratory.

Jean Perrin was upset when I confessed my hesitation. "You can't hand all this over to a stranger," he said. "The precious supplies, the instruments! You've got to save what you can out of this ruin."

I wondered if Paul would understand. Pierre had been his teacher. He knew what it felt like to miss Pierre and to try to fill his large shoes.

Since the afternoon when I asked André to turn Paul away at rue Cuvier, he had kept a respectful distance, yet he was often in the Common Room at Sèvres, reading a newspaper, while I sat at a desk in the corner, organizing my lectures. The silence we shared was vibrant, tactile. I felt less alone, and anchored by his presence, I found it easier to focus on my work.

• • •

They have offered that I should take your place, my Pierre. I accepted. I don't know if it's good or bad.

Irène has learned to swim, but she doesn't dare jump in the water.

Who will give her what you would have given?

• • •

On November 5th, the day of my first lecture at the Sorbonne, they expected a crowd, not only students, but society women, photographers, journalists. To learn about the ionization of gases? Likely not. To be part of a carnival, more like it, wanting to see the prize monkey, the first woman ever to teach at the Sorbonne. Six months after my husband's death.

Late that morning, I took a train in the opposite direction, to Sceaux, the suburb southwest of Paris where Pierre was buried. The talk was at 1:30. I believed that I had time.

No one else was at the graveyard. I went to the old chestnut tree which, until recently, had shaded all my visits, until its hand-like leaves turned red, then orange, then waved their way to the ground. Pierre lay in a deep grave, on top of his mother, Sophie-Claire Depouilly Curie, 1832–1897. I knelt by the stone. One day, at last, I would take my place in a casket on top of him.

I only want to carry on the work you did, my Pierre. Is this what you would want?

I must have lost track of time. I became aware of a presence. At first, I thought it could be energy coming from Pierre. This had happened before, when his coffin was still in our parlor. I had been resting my head on the cool wood, when I felt something strong and consoling, as if an emanation from his spirit had infused my body. My Pierre, who had wanted to study emanations. It lasted for a day, a glowing peace.

But it was Paul. I turned to see him, his hands clasped behind his back.

"Perrin thought you might abscond. He said to look for you here."

Perrin knew me too well to believe this, but I could imagine his saying it.

"Pierre wanted me to teach at the Sorbonne one day," I said.

"Me too, but no one's expecting me there at the moment." He glanced at an automobile idling on the side of the road, across the manicured green. "It's Goeÿ. He brought me."

"I told him I'd stop working if I ever lost him."

Paul squatted next to me, his long thighs in their flecked wool. "I hope he told you how foolish that would be."

"He said that if I died, he'd continue working, but like a body without a soul."

Paul shut his eyes, and a wind blew up, shaking the top of the chestnut tree. A pepper spray of birds against the white. His chin was tilted up, his face to the weak sun, and it seemed to me that the sky was in his mind, and his mind in the sky, in the birds and the tree branches—the universe thinking through him.

"You and Pierre," he said, "you both knew how to love. Know how, I mean. You."

He offered me his arm, and we walked together over the graveyard grass.

"We've been turning people away since noon," said Dean Appell. "You're making history again." He'd been waiting for me in a patch of sun in the courtyard of the Sorbonne, with its neo-Renaissance facades, its colonnade and square. We walked toward the amphitheater, and I leaned on his dependable arm. I had never fully recovered from my awe of him, this giant with great robes and long white beard, from whose pen emerged a series of treatises, equations, textbooks, and expositions. After Pierre's accident, he had been the one to come and tell me. I had been out on an errand. When I stepped into my kitchen and saw him there, with horrible compassion in his eyes, I knew the worst had happened.

"I'm a celebrated widow, if I'm to believe the newspapers."

"Irène didn't want to see the first woman ever to teach at the Sorbonne?"

"I don't want her to associate science with spectacles." I was annoyed by the throng who had packed the amphitheater, the society people with no true interest in science.

Dean Appell shook his head. "You're altogether too pure, Madame Curie."

He took me into the amphitheater through the speaker's door. Sunlight flooded through the towering windows, spraying the walls with gold. Applause thundered from the tiers. A student brought me a glass of water. My hand on the glass appeared to belong to somebody else.

Why was everybody clapping?

Forgive me, Pierre.

Pierre's students were there. And people from the Polish colony where I had lived with Bronia. The pianist, Paderewski, with that deep crease between his eyebrows, bending forward with his hands raised, as if even now he were poised to play his instrument. I searched, and there was Paul—dark forehead, his eyes sending out light. Next to him was Perrin and his wife Henriette, her hand on her chest. She was telling me to breathe.

Where were my students from Sèvres? Had they managed to find seats?

I stared into the crowd, but in my mind what I saw were Pierre's bloody clothes in the bag the police had brought. His wallet. His keys. The stretcher bearers, carrying him into the house.

In front of me was a long table covered with instruments; I grasped it, and I looked ahead, over the tops of the ladies' hats. Finally, the clapping ceased. The silence in the room was craterous.

"It is surprising," I said, "how much our ideas about electricity and matter have been changed by the progress that has been made in physics in the last ten years." I had memorized this. It was the last sentence of Pierre's last lecture.

In front of me was a blur of faces, sadness brushed over them. A young man wiped his eyes. A movement in the front row caught my attention: my Sèvriennes. Katya, Fleur, some twenty of them. Katya bowed her head, a Polish sign of respect.

At last the marks on the pages of my lecture assembled into French, and I got through the lecture. More applause, and people rising to their feet. People swarming, telling me my lecture was a triumph.

Were they imbeciles? Didn't they know that Pierre was dead?

I felt Dean Appell at my side, his unobtrusive but persistent kindness.

Out on the sidewalk, Perrin wanted me to go for a drink. "There's a group of us," he said. "We'll celebrate."

Henriette looked at me and said to her husband, "I'll take her home." She looped her arm through mine. The night of Pierre's accident, it was she who had fetched Irène; she had coaxed her to stay with their family for a while. She was with me when I told Irène that her father was dead. "No, no," Irène had cried. Before I could get the words out, she clamped her hand over my mouth.

The gray in the sky had deepened. A bit of garbage blew

across the sidewalk. "Are you all right?" I asked Henriette. She too was unusually quiet.

"I'm all right," she said.

The children didn't hear me come in. I stood in the echoing entryway, listening to the voices coming from their grandfather's room. Irène's questions, Eve's soft babble. Dr. Curie's patient tones. All the life of the house was there in that one room.

The next day I would turn thirty-nine. How tired and lonely I was.

Jean Perrin told me he was worried about Paul. We were at a cafeteria at the corner of rue Monge and rue Censier, where Pierre had liked to order cutlets, spinach, brie, and bread, for forty sous. My beef stew had an oily smell. I stirred it around while Perrin flirted with Natalie, one of my Sèvriennes. He offered her a cigarette. She sensibly refused.

"She's half your age," I scolded him, when he joined me with his tray.

"What?" he protested. "What did I do?"

"Why is Paul depressed?" I asked.

"I don't know. His wife's overwhelmed with the four children. It's rough at home sometimes." He looked uncomfortable, as if he knew more than he was saying.

I thought of my fears after Irène was born, and after Eve, my discouragement. I thought also of times when Pierre and I had seen Paul's gloom, how the light went out of his face, the way it sometimes disappeared from mine. But I'd had Pierre to warm me with his life.

"We used to see each other," I said. "But not since I left Sèvres." I felt, confusingly, both that I was guilty of avoiding Paul, and that it would be wrong to reach out.

"When Chateau Latour and a night at the opera won't raise a man's spirits, I don't know what will. Really, I don't know what to do."

"You're a good friend to him, Jean Perrin." He'd been good to Pierre as well. However unruly his humor sometimes was, his kindness was unfailing.

"Do you remember when Paul made me walk up that endless staircase to the top of the Eiffel Tower? Oh my God. The middle of winter. The lift was broken."

I laughed. "Only the air at the top was pure enough for him." He had asked Pierre to come too—he had installed an apparatus on the tower, to study variations in electric charges in the atmosphere, and he wanted Pierre to see the experiments. Pierre couldn't, because of his legs. In the end, Paul discovered, to his surprise, two kinds of ions—larger, slower ones that efficiently condense water vapor, and smaller ones that only exist above five thousand meters. When he told us this, he'd been joyous as a child.

I watched young Natalie get up from her table and fasten her bag, dark curls on her ivory neck.

"And you," said Perrin. "Are you feeling better?"

"Much. Thank you for insisting." He had seen me on the street, looking pale, and had grabbed my elbow and taken me to lunch. Gone were those early days in Paris when I could subsist on bread and hot cocoa for a week, before it caught up with me.

"And now you must come and see our new ultramicroscope. The light is brilliant, you can't imagine. You can see the millionth part of a millimeter! I'll be able to count atoms."

"But this is astonishing. You'll put an end to the rebuttals of atomic theory."

"That, Madame, is precisely what I'll do."

I did go to his lab, and he showed me a transparent body containing ultramicroscopic particles. It wasn't that the optical parts of the microscope had been improved. Rather, it made use of a new a method of throwing intense light.

I thought I was looking at the starry heavens. Stunning. Beautiful.

This meeting with Perrin buoyed me up. Over the next few days, my mind circled around Lord Kelvin's challenge. With advances in technology, and help from factories producing radium, might there not be a way forward, a way to refute him?

At lunch with Perrin, I'd chosen not to tell him about an awkward encounter I'd had with Paul in the Common Room at Sèvres, in the last week I taught there. I'd been at my usual desk, when I felt eyes on my back: Paul at the entrance to the room, one hand on the bookshelf, with ruddy cheeks. The room buzzed, like an electric light. I flushed.

"You've been to hear the paper?" I asked him. There'd been a Physics Society meeting.

"You'd have been shocked by the way physicists carelessly used the word 'symmetry.' They didn't distinguish among scalar, polar vector, and tensor."

We both smiled. Pierre would have been scandalized, was what our smiles said.

He pulled a chair up next to me, and then pushed his chair back a couple of inches, as if, like a frightened cat, I needed extra space. He was right. I felt like that.

"Marie," he said. "I need to tell you something. I'm drawn to you. What I feel for you, it's strong."

I looked at him, his wistful mouth and deep black eyes. Could this actually be true? Did Paul think he was falling in love with me?

"I'm not stupid," he said. "I don't expect anything. I just need you to know."

"It's not me you want. It's Pierre, and you can't have him. He's dead."

"Don't be angry, Marie."

But I was angry. How could he talk to me like this? Can't he keep things straight, I muttered in my own mind. He seemed to want me to welcome what he offered, and yet any pull we felt toward each other could never be satisfied. I was in love with my dead husband. Paul was a married man. Adults should remember their positions.

"Don't ruin things," I said.

He pinched his eyebrows together.

"I would like you to go away."

"All right, yes, all right."

If he was upset, he didn't show it. He put the chair back in its place and left.

By the time of my lunch with Perrin, I knew that Paul had come to his senses. Probably, he was embarrassed that he had imagined feelings for me. But seeing myself through his disillusioned eyes was in no way comforting.

He had popped his head into my office at rue Cuvier to apologize, a few days after he'd overstepped. "The madness of grief," he said, rolling his eyes to make me laugh. His phrase had stung—"the madness of grief." It did seem mad, to imagine that I would find love again.

One day when I was getting off a train, I happened to see Paul buying a newspaper. Amidst the crowd in the gray mass of the station, its smells of brake dust and creosote and rotting fruit, he stood out in relief, crisp and handsome and well-pressed, with his air of intelligence. Refined as he was, he still looked like a street boxer wearing a suit, muscled and ready to fight, a bit of a storm on his face. The working-class boy who didn't take anything for granted.

"Marie," he said when I approached him.

"How are you?"

"The better for seeing you."

I blinked, yet I believed him. "There's something I've been wanting to ask you," I said.

"Anything at all."

"You read Lord Kelvin's letter, yes?"

He looked at me, curious. The time board said that the train to the suburb of Sèvres, where he still taught a few classes, would be leaving in three minutes.

"Am I being stupid? I need to know if the threat is real. I need you to be honest with me."

Though his eyes were on the people boarding his train, he didn't seem to see them. "I will always be honest with you."

"What do you think?"

"I think they've got their knives out for you."

"They?" I asked, but I knew who he meant: the upper-crust, the established. The members of the French Academy, who rarely worried about how to fund their research.

He said, "They don't like being bested by a woman."

"I didn't think it was a competition," I said primly.

He took his pipe out of his pocket and filled the bowl with a loose pinch of tobacco, tamping it down with a gentle finger, and then, as if he had all the time in the world, sprinkling in a little more. He lit a match and moved it in a circular motion over the bowl. Finally, he breathed wisps of smoke out of his nostrils and said, "It seems perhaps it is."

"You think I'm right to be on guard."

"Yes, I do."

Strangely, I felt better after this. Paul agreed with my course of action. And I knew my enemy.

One cold morning at rue Cuvier, I went again to see André, who was at his desk, worrying over figures. I stood a moment observing him, his bald head and creased brow, the suggestion of a scowl. Before I met him, his sister had taken her own life. I didn't know what this meant to him, because he never talked about it. I liked the cordial distance he kept between us.

He stood up. "Madame. You should have spoken."

"What do you say we isolate pure radium metal, you and I?"

He took a quick little breath, and his face woke up. I loved this about André: he was always ready to hatch a plan with me. He said, "You've done the impossible before."

"We'll need a team."

"Pfft," he said, pushing air through his lips. "A research team, in France."

"All it takes is money."

"That's all, is it?" But he looked happy.

I had thought a lot about what Paul had said—"they have their knives out for you." I didn't want to be cowed anymore. I would find the money. I didn't know how, but I would move forward, I would figure it out.

Karmelicka Street, Warsaw, 1878

I wake in the black of dawn, in Papa's bed.

In the room next to me, the sad floorboards creak. The boarders, Papa's students. They take turns peeing like horses. Papa will be getting up from the moleskin couch where I should be, in the dining room, where Józef and Helena sleep on pallets.

The servant girl scrapes around the kitchen, making groats. They smell like ash and mud. Through the cracked windowpane, I hear the Wistula River, pouring through the city. It's half a mile away, says Józef. He doesn't believe I can hear it.

Bronia sleeps where Mama did. How can she? Bronia doesn't cough anymore.

Tomasz, our boarder, brought home the typhus, that's what I think. He's flunking his exams because he can't speak Russian; not even Papa can teach him. Of Papa's twenty students, Tomasz is the worst.

Zosia, her white hands folded on her chest. Shorn white hair. I followed behind the casket in my mourning clothes. Mama watched from the window.

Mama didn't die of the fever; she died of tuberculosis. Beneath her ivory cross.

It's not Papa's fault. He walks with his shoulders tipped forward, making a cave for his heart.

The door handle rattles, and Bronia comes in, still in her night dress. Now she's the oldest girl. She says, "It's time to get up, Maria," but I won't get up. She gives up and leaves.

"She won't stop crying," I hear her say to Papa.

"She'll stop eventually," he says.

I stuff the sheets into my mouth, so they won't hear.

When I wake up again, the apartment is quiet. Papa is sitting on the bed. He smells of shoe polish and pine tar soap.

I ask, "Where are the boarders?"

"Everyone is out. Come, I have something to show you."

He leads me to the dining room. A stream of light: I cover my eyes. Papa pulls me onto his lap. We are at the long long table.

When I take my hands away, there is Papa's gold-leaf electroscope, not in its locked glass case, but on the table, shining in the sun. It has a circular base and a brass support rod with a little sphere on top, and two pendants, fine gold leaves, one of them half the length of the other, all enclosed in a delicate shimmering bottle.

"Here," says Papa, leaning over me. "Let me show you how it works."

VI

Paris, 1907

A YEAR AFTER PIERRE'S ACCIDENT, I sold our house on boulevard Kellerman and moved half an hour away to the suburb of Sceaux, where Pierre was buried, and where he had grown up. Dr. Curie had room to cultivate a garden, and the girls could play outside.

I never talked with my daughters about their father. I wanted them to move on. Each morning I rose early and settled the affairs of the household, instructing the maid and consulting with Dr. Curie, who, along with a nanny, took charge of the girls' activities. I took the 7:55 train to Paris, arriving at 8:34. In all my orderliness, I lost the habit of conversation without a set purpose. I don't suppose it was pleasant for other people.

One Saturday, alone with the girls, I sent them out to the garden. I had installed a cross-bar and trapeze for Irène, to practice her gymnastics. She had strong arms, and I trusted her. When, twenty minutes later, I checked on them, the girls were throwing clods of dirt. Irène picked up some kind of metal disk at the edge of the garden—a bit of trash from the previous owners that I hadn't cleaned up. I yelled, "Irène!" but she flung it in the direction of her sister, a spinning wheel of rust. Eve turned her pudgy face toward me. If I hadn't yelled, she would have seen it coming. She would have ducked. Her eyes said, what's the trouble, Mé?—and the disk skimmed the side of her head.

Her wound bled profusely, but it was shallow. I daubed it with cotton soaked in carbolic acid. She made a show of squinting her eye, happy with the attention. She would be all right.

"What were you thinking?" I asked Irène.

I examined a big bruise on her arm. "You really don't know how you got this?" She had come home from school with it. "Mé," she said, "can I put my monkey puzzle tree in your bedroom? Please? It isn't happy in mine."

That night I lay awake, worrying. I had tried to focus on my daughters. I oversaw Irène's studies, and I read to Eve and taught her Polish songs, but whatever else I was doing, I was always listening, my ear cocked to the southwest, the direction of the graveyard from our house, as if, through static, Pierre's voice might materialize, the frequency of some celestial transmitter suddenly just right. I feared that if I stopped listening, at that very moment Pierre would speak. The circuit would pick out his signals, and I wouldn't be there to hear.

What was wrong with me? This was what I asked myself. I had friends, work, and two healthy daughters, but nothing stirred life in me. Grief was one thing, but it felt as if, since I lost Pierre, I had gone numb, inert, the taste of metal on my tongue. In my mother's last days I had watched the light die in her eyes, a guttering candle that finally went out. I hoped to survive until the girls were grown.

Irène's monkey puzzle tree sat in my window, but I had drawn the line when she tried to bring in her hamsters, Filou and Tigrette, spinning on their squeaky wheels. "But they'll miss the monkey puzzle tree," she had argued.

She hadn't meant to hurt her sister, but she did bully her, and she wasn't doing well at school. Her copybook was smudged and careless. Academically, she was bright, but she wasn't a conventional learner. She was like her father, who always said he had a "slow mind." To the extent that this was true, his mind was slow like a glacier, changing the landscape as it passed. He couldn't shift the course of his reflections to suit the external environment, nor, I worried, would Irène submit herself to formal schooling. If, the next year, I enrolled her in a lycée, the teachers might brand her stupid. She could become discouraged.

Oh, careless Pierre! He should have been here to raise the girls with me. If he'd been paying attention that day on rue Dauphine when he stepped around the carriage, he might have seen the wagon and the Percherons coming. His poor old father, when he heard the news of the accident, had said, What was he dreaming about this time?

The bedroom was cold. I folded my thin blanket in two. Finally, I slept.

Toward morning I dreamed of Zosia, the most gifted child in our family, the one whose stories made us laugh and shudder, before her typhus-inflected moans kept us up at night. In the dream she was so real—her hair a voluminous white-gold, her eyes a dreamy gray. The goofy hands and feet of adolescence.

Then her hair and eyes went pale, and she floated through the wall. I clung to my mother's waist to stop her from leaving, too.

My father appeared in the parlor: "Stay back, Bronislawa, my love. You'll join your daughter soon enough."

A pain in my throat woke me up. I lay very still, and slowly, the past receded. Nothing horrible was happening now. It was morning. A breeze came through the window.

"I had a bad dream," I said to Pierre, slinging my arm over him.

My arm dropped into empty space on his side of the bed.

The next day I thought of how my father-in-law had kept Pierre home from school, letting him roam the valleys and the woods and do his studies on his own, because he would have failed at the lycée. On the spot, I came up with an idea for Irène: a cooperative school, for the children of faculty friends, taught by us, their parents.

"It's a splendid plan," said Perrin. "Better drown the children than subject them to a French lycée."

We were drinking sherry on the Perrins' terrace, and a mere sip had my head swimming. Henriette threaded a needle to do her mending. The Perrin children, Francis and Aline, were about Irène's age. Until I had moved my family, all our children had to do to visit each other was to pass through an iron gate. Now they were together again, playing hide and seek. Eve was always first to be found, because she was always singing.

"We'll teach by means of experiment," I said.

Perrin said, "Oxygen combustions."

"Measuring, electrolysis, building a thermometer."

"No recitation of dull, interminable rules. No fire down the children's necks."

"You'll teach physics, and I'll teach chemistry," I said. "Alice Chavannes will teach English and German and geography. Henriette, you'll teach history and French."

"I know the sculptor Magrou," said Henriette. "We'll get him to teach the children to draw."

"From models," said her husband. "I'll hire the models."

"In good weather we'll cancel classes," I said.

Perrin said, "There will be lots of good weather." He took a drag of his cigar, watching the children circle, kick, and scamper like a troop of foals. "It's love that motivates learning, isn't it," he said, and I thought of my mother, reciting poems that I still knew by heart, and my teacher, Monsieur Slosarski, risking his livelihood to instruct us in Polish history when the official school-day was over. Love indeed.

"Will you also teach math?" I asked Perrin.

"Heavens no, we'll get Langevin to do that."

"Oh, of course we will."

My arms tingled. A goldfinch darted over us, bringing a strip of bark to its nest in the Perrin's arbor. On the terrace, Henriette had put begonias and lamb's ear, and vines with purple leaves. The sun filtered through the branches of the trees, flickering on the stone.

"It's bliss here," I said. I took a second glass of sherry and let the goodness spread through my body.

Paul said yes to the cooperative school. I shouldn't have been surprised—he was often going on about French education—how deadly it was, the "ossifying dogma" our children were taught. "Children need to see that science is a living, breathing thing."

On a Thursday at lunchtime, I walked fifteen minutes from rue Cuvier to the EPCI, to meet with him and plan the curriculum. The day was lovely, fresh. That morning, as I got dressed, I had caught a glimpse of myself in the mirror and saw that I was blonde and relatively young—not brittle and gray, after all, though not so young as Paul's wife, seven or eight years my junior, vigorous and fresh even after her fourth child.

Paul didn't hear me when I stepped into his classroom, with its familiar scent of beeswax and old wood. He sat in front of a wall of windows where the midday sun glowed in milky glass. I watched him marking papers, tight-faced, his shoulders raised, face pinched in concentration. Pierre had taught in this room. On the chalkboard, dusted in white, were the memories of equations written in his hand, erased and written over. The very chalkboard where Paul and Pierre had stood arguing in front of their students and gotten locked in. The windows they'd crawled through that day when they shinnied down the drainpipe.

When Paul looked up, his tightness broke, and I felt my own face soften. He stood, and for a few quiet moments, we stayed looking at each other.

He said, "I'd almost forgotten."

I didn't think to ask him what he had forgotten.

He said, "I don't have much time, I—"

"—Oh, I thought—"

"—I'm sorry."

"No need to—"

His voice grew heartier. "My wife will have my head if I'm not home by one-thirty. She thinks I don't like her mother. Her mother's visiting."

"Do you? Dislike her?"

"She's a harridan. A fishwife. A coarse-mannered bitch." He said this with gusto, enjoying himself, and I felt flattered to be brought into his mood. Yet beneath his high spirits I sensed, as I often did, that something grated on him.

"Whereas to her, you're as charming as a courtier."

"Marie, you've found me out." He looked as if being found out gave him pleasure. "Listen, there's a steak-frîtes special around the corner. We'll have a glass of wine, and we can work out the curriculum."

"But you just—"

He gathered his exams and stuffed them in the desk drawer. "My wife can have my head if she wants it. She can just—have my head."

"What makes you change your mind?"

"Data: Every time I have spent time with Marie, I've come away the better for it. Hypothesis: If I go to lunch with Marie, I won't regret it."

I imagined us at the café, Paul with his brush cut hair and signature moustache, the two of us drawing attention. I said, "You're leaving out a fair bit of data. French widows don't appear in public with a man." I'd thought of this even with Perrin at the cafeteria.

Paul straightened out some chairs and dumped a glass of water in the classroom sink.

"What's going on?" I asked.

"Am I that transparent?"

"You're not ill, I hope."

He rubbed his palm over his standing-up hair. "My wife wants me to apply for jobs in industry. There's one coming up."

"Where? Not at Saint-Gobain." This company had courted

him before, manufacturers of glass and mirrors. Paul's recent work with Brownian motion had brought his genius more fully into view. He was probably, just as Pierre had predicted, France's leading physicist, and he'd been offered two lucrative jobs.

"Saint-Gobain, as a matter of fact."

"Why? Why would you reconsider?"

"I do have four children. My wife has a point."

I thought of Jeannette Langevin, her silly pride, her striving. "Oh, I know. Your wife likes parasols, caviar, and dinners at le Grand Colbert. You'd better get working on some patents. There's a new world coming, and it's going to be expensive."

"Saint-Gobain pays very well."

"Is money really so tight?"

"I don't have to tell you."

"But your research, Paul. It would kill you to leave it." If he took this job, his mind wouldn't be his own. He'd have to devote himself to working out methods for making—I wasn't sure—denser and more stable glass? Or whatever Saint-Gobain wanted. Gone, the drive to discover, the experimental joy, the hint of a mystery, a theoretical conundrum, and the pursuit of a means to explore it. The Paul I knew would disappear. He wouldn't lose his friends, but he would lose colleagues, the community of science that he treasured. I had an impulse to kick the chair in front of me. Here was a brilliant man who had the privilege of living in a free country, a man with every opportunity, on the brink of throwing this away. And why? Due to a misguided impulse to please his wife? And why was he telling me—for sympathy? Or in hopes I'd persuade him not to go to Saint-Gobain?

"Let's go for lunch," he said. "We'll talk."

"I can't go to lunch."

"You can't or you won't?"

"I won't."

"Well then, I'll keep my head after all."

I flushed. I hadn't wanted to make him unhappy.

He said, "You and I, we're scientists." As if, by regarding propriety, I was bowing to the irrational.

I rolled my eyes. "My point entirely."

He laughed, and we sat down together and applied ourselves to sketching out a crude curriculum for the children's math and chemistry classes.

Walking back alone to rue Cuvier, I observed men and women together in cafés, teasing, arguing. It would have been fun to go for a steak-frites special. Could I not have overcome my scruples? Instead, I'd acted like a middle-class Frenchwoman who wouldn't go out without a chaperone. I'd always scorned such women: no sense of purpose, brought up in drawing rooms, trained in intrigue and romance, adopting ideas as if they were new clothes, never taking anything to heart. They had rights to education that Polish women didn't, but they didn't value these rights.

Why did I let their notions of propriety influence me?

Left on rue des Patriarches, right for a few meters, left on rue Monge. Marching off my anger at myself, and my embarrassment. I had been too eager to see Paul, too pleased by the way he looked at me.

Were we drawn to each other because of Pierre—or was this something refreshing, aching, new?

I didn't want to give up on my yearnings, that was the truth of it.

I walked down rue Monge all the way to the market, but the vendors were closing up shop. All I could find was a jar of sauerkraut.

In September, on the first day of our cooperative school, I sat at a table in our upstairs sitting room with eight children and a pitcher of lemonade. Paul's sons were there, Jules fresh-faced and round, his pocket full of coins and bits of wire. He was going to build a radio. "Papa says I'm smart and can figure it out myself," he said.

Irène twirled a finger in her hair. "I could do it myself if I wanted to." She had just turned ten, without a father to know it.

The air was heavy, and even before the lesson, I was at the end of my reserves. Twice, Irène knocked over her glass of lemonade, and twice I helped her clean it up. But then it happened a third time: her elbow flying, her drink soaking the papers—and before I could think, I raised my hand sharply, I lurched at her and slapped her face. All eight children jerked back. In their faces, white and frightened, I saw myself as a monster.

Isabelle Chavannes, with her neat little bows, shrank in her chair. Irène, her neck and face stained red, said to her, "Mé doesn't hit me."

I caught a sob in my throat. My mother, if she had lived, never would have hit me.

Some of the children turned suddenly toward the door. It was Paul, with a puzzled look on his face.

"Irène spilled," said Jules.

"Let's clean it up," Paul said lightly. I didn't think that he had seen.

After everyone left, I was cold to Irène. This was how my father had punished us when we had misbehaved—once he didn't talk to me for three whole days. But Irène was miserable, chewing on her fist like a little girl. I took her damp hand into mine and told her I was sorry. We clung to each other that night.

A few weeks later, Paul came to see me at rue Cuvier to tell me that he'd made it to the third round of interviews with St. Gobain. He expected to receive an offer, and he planned to take it. I was more than annoyed. I couldn't congratulate him.

Then he told me a piece of news: Lord Kelvin had died. He'd caught a chill at his estate in Scotland, and it got worse.

"Really? You're serious?" He might as well have said that Mars had dropped out of its orbit.

"Before you had a chance to rub his nose in his mistake."

"We haven't even managed to buy pitchblende yet." André and I were practicing with barium because it was chemically similar to radium, and we couldn't risk the radium we had on hand.

Paul and I were sitting in my office, which stank of our smelly children, on the verge of adolescence. Earlier that day, filling in for Perrin, I'd had them dipping bicycle bearings in ink and rolling them down an inclined plane, to learn the law of falling bodies. I'd found my rhythm with them.

"But we detest competition, don't we?" said Paul. "We believe in cooperation, sharing information. It doesn't matter who gets the results, as long as one of us does?"

I spun his swivel seat around. "You're goading me with Pierre's words."

"Since he's not here to goad you."

It pleased me to see Paul's black eyes and bright face. "Pierre loved you," I suddenly said.

He said, "That excellent man," and instantly I teared up—it didn't take much for me to tap into the water underneath.

Paul surprised me with a glare. "You should stop this."

"Stop what?"

"You've mourned enough, don't you think?"

"What are you trying to say?"

"You talk about Pierre as if he were a saint. You've made him into a religion."

I stared at him. A blush burned over me,

"And you drift through rooms like a ghost."

"This, coming from you? A man who broadcasts his unhappiness? You make it other peoples' job to cheer you up!" I felt foolish saying this, but I didn't know how else to defend myself.

"What must your daughters feel? What about Irène?"

For a stabbing moment I thought he knew something I didn't—that she had typhus, or had been in an accident. "What about her?"

"You terrorize the girl."

When I could speak, I said, "I hit her once in my life."

He looked at me as if he hadn't known. I hadn't had to say it.

"It's the iciness," he said. "Better to hit her and be done with it."

When I got up and moved toward the door, my body floated alongside me.

"Surely you can rally for Irène if no one else," he said, a touch of pleading in his voice. And then, "Someone has to say this to your face."

A crowd of people appeared in my mind, people I had thought were friends—Jean Perrin and Henriette, André, the Borels—all of them shaking their heads. *She drifts through rooms like a ghost. She should hit her and be done with it.*

When I opened the door to the hallway, André was close by, flushing, embarrassed. "Do you need anything?"

"I'm fine." I left without looking back.

The girls were in the garden with their grandfather. I watched from the gate as the old man showed Irène how to harvest beets, pulling gently, brushing off the dirt. Nearby, Eve squatted in the grass, pulling up an earthworm.

What did Pierre matter to Eve and her earthworm?

Dr. Curie had lost his son, yet he dug up vegetables and planned for a spring garden.

I entered the house without their seeing. Mutton stew on the stove. I took my journal out to write to Pierre, but sitting at my desk, I only put my forehead to the page.

You've made him into a religion, Paul had said. But what else could I do, in the pointlessness of Paris and the whole dreary world? If I acted as Pierre would have done, at least I had a path. His death had drained me of my confidence, and with it, my imagination. Without Pierre, I wasn't able to open my spirit and trust.

What was it about Pierre that had eased me so? What was it about his loving gaze, and our synchronized breath, and the smell of his sweat, that made me stronger than I knew how to be on my own? When Pierre and I made love, the more I lost myself in him, the more I was delivered back into myself. My own awareness grew quiet, deep. We would lie together after, sometimes softly chatting, and I would feel how strange and wonderful it was to be alive.

How did being known by another person create such a charge? As a phenomenon it was unverifiable, untouchable, and yet it had the power to raise a person from the dead. It was as potent as radium, and as miraculous. But where did it go, this being-known-by-Pierre, when Pierre himself was extinguished?

The garden door screeched. Time for dinner. I put away my journal.

When the stew was eaten, schoolwork done, and bedtime rituals accomplished, I wiped down the table and sat there with a letter from Pierre's brother, Jacques. I had sent him a photograph. "The two little girls are a pleasure to see," he wrote, "but you! How sad you look! My wife cried when she saw how thin you are. Marie, your children need you to last a long time still." Rally, rally, this seemed to be the cry.

Dr. Curie came into the kitchen and poured himself a glass of wine, pulpy and dark, homemade by one of our neighbors. What a tall man he was. Age had hardly bent him. "Would you like some?" he asked.

"Yes, please."

He poured me a glass. "My beets are thriving. We'll have a nice salad tomorrow."

"What a treat." With him, I could feel that a day would come when I would be all right.

"You're tired, Marie."

"Yes."

"Shall we both go early to bed?"

"I have exams to correct."

"Ah."

"I'll do them in my bedroom."

He shrugged. "As you wish."

I ran a finger around the rim of my glass. "Today a colleague told me I've been grieving too long. He told me to stop."

He shook his head. "Sometimes people speak when they haven't been invited."

This was comforting. "What do you think? Have I grieved too long?"

"You're a grown woman, Marie. I can't tell you how to grieve."

When Irène got up the next morning, she looked peaked. Her mouth turned down at the sides, but this was her habitual expression. Her hair was a fuzzy mess.

"Do you think she's a little gray, Grandpère?"

"She's healthy," he said.

"I'm very healthy, Mé. And I have some beautiful new scrapes on my legs from playing outside, see?" She pulled up her nightgown to show me some dotted red scratches on her knees.

I poured her a glass of buttermilk. It reminded me of the sour koumiss my mother used to take—fermented mare's milk, to cure tuberculosis.

"Drink up," I said, and she tilted her head back, her gullet bobbing.

Who did Paul think he was? And what did he know about my daughter and me?

That morning I delivered a lecture to my Sorbonne students as my scientific self, and afterward, I sat in my office at rue Cuvier, listening to rain in the trees. Was Paul being worked over, wined and dined, perhaps even now, by Saint-Gobain? His criticism still stung, but I was angrier about Saint-Gobain, his willingness to betray himself and the colleagues who had nurtured him. Was it all his wife's doing, or was he also drawn to a fashionable life?

The postman scuffed down the hall—a note for me from Paul. I knew the meticulous script. Might he importune me to come to the EPCI between 15:00 and 17:00?

I sat for a while. No, you may not importune me, I thought to write, or something stilted, with anger bleeding through. Instead, I put on my raincoat and walked to the EPCI.

He was in his gray-flecked flannel, at the blackboard, writing rapidly. The chalk clicked.

"You can see what I'm doing?" he asked.

The first equation was familiar—Pierre had come up with it. "You're working with a two-state particle."

"It can align its magnetic properties with a magnetic field, or against it."

"Paul, what about Saint-Gobain?"

His chalk got louder. "I'll burn in hell before I work for them."

"Oh. Thank God. Your wife agrees?"

He turned his compact chest toward me, his face open and pleading. "Every day, there's something I want to ask Pierre. It would be easier if he were here."

I stood very still. "You criticize my emotions, and then you try to make me cry?"

"I miss him every day of my life."

"You have a funny way of showing it."

He came and seized my wrists, the way he had that day when I fled the Physics Society meeting and he followed me out. I wanted to pull away, and I wanted to stay. He was near enough for me to feel his body's heat.

"The worst of it," he said, "is I've lost you as well."

"You haven't lost me."

"Those evenings at your house in the garden, with the Perrins and Debierne and the Borels. What a grand time we had."

"We're still colleagues. We still talk."

He let go of my wrists, and I felt the sudden loss of heat, and a quick disappointment.

"Nothing's the same," he said.

"I'm sorry." I saw myself as thin and shallow.

"You see, I've done it again. I'm the one who's sorry. I am sorry, Marie. I have no right."

The room darkened; wind and rain thumped against the window.

"I'm a good mother, but I've been hoarding my grief. Storing it inside." This was the true reason I didn't talk about Pierre with the girls, I suddenly realized. I wanted to wallow in my grief. To hold it close, for fear that otherwise it would slip away.

Light played over Paul's expression. "You're the most loyal person I know."

"Thank you," I said softly. "I should go."

He stood in the doorway and watched me leave.

When I think back on this time when Paul and I were moving toward each other, it's easy to see that I wasn't being honest with myself. But as Hertha reminds me, it's easy to look back and judge our ignoble choices. Perhaps, in some other world than the one I lived in, with some other history than the one I had, I would have recognized other options.

After that day in the classroom, he and I relaxed with each other. I was less afraid of his temper, which I knew was born of deep feeling, and he owned up to it when he spoke sharply. Little by little we confided more in each other. He was unhappy at home, and at times I perceived a far-off look in his complicated eyes, but he said little about his marriage. Implicitly, the subject of his wife was off limits, and in this and other ways we tried to protect the innocence of our friendship. We never met for lunch, and Paul never again pushed me on this point.

As for the offer from Saint-Gobain, within a week they had withdrawn it, having discovered that Paul had supported their workers on strike, even joining them on the streets. Paul found this amusing, and the episode disarmed his wife, who, for the time being, withdrew and recalculated.

I found myself looking forward to Paul's company, storing up in my mind the parts of my days that would make him laugh, sharing my successes and failures in the laboratory. We continued to meet about the cooperative school. On fine days we canceled classes and with Henriette Perrin took the children on bicycle rides. We saw each other at the Society of Physics, and when Paul and his family moved to Fontenay-aux-Roses, a suburb close to Sceaux, we often took the same morning train. I had a friend whose life was tied to mine, who cared when I came and went, whose eyes brightened when he saw me.

I told the girls stories about their father. The time in the Jardin des Plantes, when we were courting, and he plopped a frog into my hand. Our honeymoon, when we went bicycling and got lost by the river Oise, and had to sleep amongst the cows. The girls were shy—they were accustomed to my reticence—but I could see they liked it.

Paul, too, was happier. Perrin said he'd become a less expensive friend, requiring only ordinary wine to lift his spirits. Also, he said, he was relieved to be able to listen to the opera without having to filter out Paul's lugubrious sighs.

Imperial Gymnasium Number Three, Krakovsky Boulevard, Warsaw, 1880

Monsieur Slosarski stares at our pale faces and bloodless lips. "Jakub Kunicki thought he was joining the Resistance," he says to us in Polish. We are a dozen thirteen-year-old girls, stationed at our wooden desks.

Jakub Kunicki is dead, hanged that morning in Saxony Square. Three of us stayed up all night with his sister Léonie, bathing her swollen eyes. When the bell tower rang the hour of the execution, Léonie called out, fell to her knees. I grabbed the wash basin and vomited.

Monsieur Slosarski paces, his chin up, his brown curls falling back. "But we," he says, "we *are* the Resistance. We don't carry rifles. We have empirical knowledge, patience, discipline." He rubs his hands over his hair. "Take out your books."

Two girls lift the floorboards, uncovering our Polish history texts. But already we hear a whistle from the landing: three short notes and a long one. Back go the books. Down go the boards. Up come the lids of our desks. Out come Russian texts.

The inspector wears a blue tunic and gold pantaloons. He walks among our desks, leaving puddles of melting snow.

"Please, join our biology lesson, Inspector," says Monsieur Slosarski. He is casual, cool, but his jaw tightens.

"Biology, Professor? After school?"

"We are making up lost time," says Monsieur Slosarski.

The inspector opens Hanna's desk: pencils, a bit of embroidery. He opens mine: the same. I know what is coming. I am nauseous. Hot, then cold.

"Call on one of the girls," the inspector says.

"Mademoiselle Sklodowska," says Monsieur Slosarski, and I rise.

"Tell us about our Tsar's accomplishments," the inspector says.

"His Majesty Alexander II, Tsar of all the Russias," I begin.

"Also known as . . . ?"

"Alexander the Liberator." Every syllable tastes of ash.

"Go on."

"He brought in an era of modern reforms. In 1861, he freed the Russian serfs."

"And in Poland? What are his accomplishments in Poland?"

I hesitate. Monsieur Slosarski's brow tenses. I remember his wife. His children.

"In 1863 he put down the Polish insurrection," I say. "He made Poland a Russian province. He russified the schools." The room begins to tilt and sway.

"And the courts," the inspector says. "He russified the courts."

When he leaves, I can hear every girl's breath.

"Maria," says Monsieur Slosarski. "Come here."

I walk to the front of the class. He looks at me, his gray eyes serious.

"Thank you," he says, and he shakes my hand. Like a comrade. Like a patriot.

VII

Paris, February–March 1908

WHEN ANDREW CARNEGIE came to Paris, Dean Appell called me on the laboratory phone to say that the great man had requested a meeting with me.

When famous people came through town, they thought they had a right to my time. They expected me to spend the afternoon with them, as if a laboratory could run by itself. Pierre had been driven mad by this. I believe he would have returned our Nobel Prize to get back the peace that we once knew.

"Give him my regrets," I said.

Silence from the dean. Yet he didn't try to change my mind.

I woke the next morning to the sound of the milk truck rattling down the boulevard, and the dean's silence came back with a start. I had turned down a meeting with Andrew Carnegie, a man who, for the last decade, had made a point of funding charitable causes. And why? Because that's what Pierre would have done.

It wasn't easy to see Dean Appell. He oversaw all the sciences and their faculty, taught classes, and, when seized by mathematical inspiration, locked himself in his office. To get to him, I had first to pass a secretary whose desk was in an alcove by his door.

"Please, Madame Colbert. May I see the dean right now?"

She looked at me over her pince-nez. "You may knock."

The dean's white sideburns had grown shaggier, his Alsatian accent stronger. He leaned back. "You really thought it was wise to refuse a visit from Andrew Carnegie."

"It was reflexive. I was wrong." I felt like a child, though I'd worked hard at overcoming my awe of him, now that we were colleagues.

"You have an odd relationship to people who offer you good things. A history of tearing up letters with"—he waved his hand in the air—"job offers, money, etcetera."

"I deserve your mockery, and I bow before you. Look, I know it's awkward, and I'm terribly sorry, but could you phone him back? Apologize, and let him know I'd like to see him?"

"I already have," he said. "I knew you'd come to your senses."

"The famous shed," said the philanthropist. We were in the old laboratory on rue Lhomond, with its cracked windows and packed dirt floor. He ran his fingers across crumbly plaster, and a cold wind poofed dust in his eyes. The place was leaky as ever. He added, "Where the magic happened."

I pulled my neck higher. "Happened? I assure you, Mr. Carnegie, my discoveries aren't dead and buried with my husband."

He chuckled. "Yes, I know."

He was a portly man, with the broad flat face and the scarf I'd seen in photos. His voice was higher than I'd have guessed. No trace of a Scottish accent. The years in Pittsburgh must have wiped that away.

He said, "I thought the papers had exaggerated your shed's decrepitude."

"Before we took it over, medical students learned to do autopsies here."

"The cold is good for autopsies."

The thermostat I had nailed to a post read nine degrees Celsius inside the shed. It had at times been colder.

"We immigrants," he said, "have the stamina to endure the worst conditions."

"You were twelve, weren't you, when you stoked boilers, twelve hours a day? That took stamina." I knew the points of his vanity. I had done my homework.

"A dollar twenty a day. I had a plan. I didn't know what it was, but I knew I had a plan."

I laughed. "Would you like to see my current lab?"

André later asked me why I hadn't hired a carriage, but it never crossed my mind. We walked through chilly streets to rue Cuvier. After the windy spaces of the shed, the walls in my lab seemed even closer, Mr. Carnegie taller and broader. I introduced him to the office manager and showed him our cramped offices, one for André and one for me, and the lab where a student, shoulders lit with dust-specked light, practiced with an electrometer.

Mr. Carnegie observed it all with his chin up high, the air of a man who makes splendid plans and needn't bother with details. "Your radium," he said. "They're saying it cures cancer and blindness and baldness. One day it will heat our houses."

"They say a lot of things."

"You don't have confidence in your product?"

Radium, a product? I hoped he wouldn't provoke me too far. "In science we're interested in what's real. We don't invest in a particular outcome."

"And the practical applications?"

"My area is pure research."

"You disdain the practical."

I felt, of a sudden, on a team with Paul, and on the other team, Mr. Carnegie and Madame Langevin, shaking fingers at me. "Pasteur said that progress in applying science comes from scientific disinterest. I believe that, Mr. Carnegie."

"You scientists. The more certain you are that your work is good for nothing, the more superior you feel."

"Let's just say we take the long view." He seemed to be wanting a fight, and I had a mind to throw him out. I said, "Mr. Carnegie, they call you a Plutocrat, don't they?"

"A Plutocrat? That's Vanderbilt. They do call me that, though. And worse. William Jennings Bryan calls me a commercial highwayman." He said this with pleasure and scorn.

"I've read your comments in the press. You've been unkind about France."

"Everything's dead. The soil is miserably farmed. Paris is decadent. Nobody has ambition."

"I don't think you mind what people say about you, as long as you get what you want."

"I do get what I want."

"I want something, too, Mr. Carnegie. I have a vision and a plan. A radium institute. One building for pure research, which I'll direct, and another devoted to investigating medical applications—your sort of thing. I'm determined to make this happen."

He nodded as if there were no friction between us. "That was my strategy, in business. See something all the way through. Not just the steel, the mining, the production, but the railroad itself. All the way through."

"And now you're turning to philanthropy. A thousand libraries, I understand."

"I was turned away when I was a lad. Couldn't borrow books."

"That's the thing, to make available to others what we've lacked ourselves." Perhaps I sounded superior, but the moment required it. "My husband never had a bona fide laboratory, all these years. Just this tiny one, and only at the end of his life."

You see? I said to Pierre in my mind. *This is for our dream.*

I made a cup of tea for Mr. Carnegie, wondering if it should have been brandy or scotch. "I'm afraid I can't let you smoke," I said. "It interferes with our equipment."

"I don't smoke. Least of all in front of ladies." He drank his tea in a few gulps. "What do you need?"

"First, a research team and money for supplies, to put radium on an undeniable footing. Ultimately, funding to build a radium institute."

"Interesting." He stood up. Apparently our meeting was over.

Dean Appell called me into his office not long after. Mr. Carnegie, he told me, had said that I dressed absurdly and made no attempt to charm, which in itself was charming. We were to have a research team. He had written a check for fifty thousand dollars.

I nearly laughed out loud.

André, out of character, disappeared from the lab, and when he came back, popped open a bottle of champagne. Jean Danysz and a couple of other students gathered round, and we all clinked glasses. "To new pursuits," said André. "New collaborations."

The cool bubbles spread over my tongue. I itched to get started. If I could I would forget about meals and nannies, lessons and chores. I wouldn't mind living in the freezing garret of my student days, if only I could coil my energy around my work. That wasn't possible now, with my teaching, my daughters, my house. But I could work in the time I had.

"Publicly he supports the trade unions," Paul said, when I told him about Carnegie, "but when it came to his steel mills, he got his way. Pretty bloody awful, really."

We were sitting opposite each other on a train, heading home after work, passing houses dusted with snow. I was a bit peeved, wanting heartier congratulations, but I only said, "Maybe he thinks he can wipe out his dirty deeds if he gives to charitable causes."

"Tell that to the poor bastards he fired."

"Are you saying I shouldn't have accepted the grant?"

"Now that you mention it, Marie, a penance is in order. You should join a strike."

"The sandpits in Dravail?" There had been arrests and violence there.

Paul took out his pipe, then put it back. "You don't fancy a little time in jail?"

"I don't fancy a hangman's rope. It's the Polish girl in me."

"You could help organize for suffrage. It looks like French women might stir up some trouble, like their English sisters."

Paul was teasing, but sitting there, night falling, the train clacking and swaying, I became aware of how I had contracted to protect myself, shutting out anything that wasn't science. Paul had signed Zola's letter, charging the government with anti-Semitism and illegal acts in the Dreyfus case. Zola had been charged with libel and fled to England to escape imprisonment—Paul had stuck his neck way out. Hertha, even with work and family illnesses, devoted herself to women's rights. I had sacrificed as much, but for science only.

I could feel Paul studying me, and when I raised my eyes, he closed his, as if daring me to gaze at him. And so I did. I gazed at his clear forehead with the crooked scar from the bicycle accident, after Pierre's death. The fleshy, exposed bit of his upper lip, his Cupid's bow, the rest hidden beneath his mustache. My nostrils filled with the smell of hot metal, smoke, and old fabric. Paul's shoe polish and pine tar soap.

We were in between stations, but the train engine shuddered to a stop, and the lights went out. This happened sometimes. There was no way of knowing how long we would be stalled.

Paul was a shadow opposite me. "You there?" he joked. His voice reached me as physically as touch. He reached forward as if blind and grasping. I laughed and gave him my hands. He squeezed my fingers. "Don't be angry with me. I'm not being critical."

"Aren't you?"

"I get worked up about injustice. I'm like your father-in-law. But I'm tremendously glad about your grant."

"I'm annoyed with myself."

"Ah, I know that path. I don't advise you to go down it."

"Sometimes I'm tired of my own company." I heard how tedious my melancholy was.

He took one of my hands, palm up, and with his index finger, explored the rough tips of my fingers. "That's where we're different," he said. "There's no one else I'd rather be with."

His words released the tears that must have been waiting there. How long had it been since anyone had comforted me like this?

The train rumbled forward, still in the dark, all the way to Fontenay-aux-Roses.

When Hertha came to Paris in early March, I was excited, almost unaccountably. She had delayed her presentation to the Physics Society because of her husband's death, but she was back full force. I had been mildly angry with her, in an irrational, beneath-the-surface way, as if she'd neglected me after Pierre died, when she was caught up in her husband's illness and her work. Of course, she could have said the same about me.

There was a tug in me, a feeling of wanting to see her. It was as if she had some knowledge that I needed, and I couldn't find my way to it except through her. I planned to introduce her to Paul; I wanted to show my two friends off to each other, but I was also nervous. Paul admired Hertha, but what if they didn't actually like each other? What if Hertha disapproved of Paul? And why did I care so much?

The afternoon of the presentation was clear, with a bright ball of sun in the sky. I walked Hertha from her hotel to the Sorbonne's science library, she in a black duster and a purple dress, with glorious, full hair. She pointed to the electricians who were installing new metal filament lamps along the boulevard: "My invention is already surpassed." She had figured out how to stop the hissing of arc lamps in London, when she discovered it was caused by contact with the air. "Never mind," she said. "There are always more ideas."

"Are there?" I laughed. No matter Hertha's losses, she was charged by some mysterious source. She seemed to live in the eye of a creative storm, endlessly renewed. I took her arm. "You're marvelous. And you're not even nervous. I vomit before public talks."

"No wonder, with your reputation. It's like being a figurehead on a ship, driving into the winds."

"I don't think about that. I'm just inherently skittish."

"Really, Marie. You leave out how hard it is to be a woman."

"Why shouldn't I leave it out, if I can?"

"Because we need a foot in reality."

"I find that a foot in the impossible helps me get to the impossible."

"You have a point," said Hertha. "But our uncomfortable knowledge is fuel for the fight."

"I'm not interested in fighting, really. Nose to the grindstone is more my style."

It was splendid to walk into the library, arm linked with Hertha's, the Sorbonne with its grand sense of itself, its rich wood paneling, medallions, and portrait of Lavoisier above our heads, all of it fresh and clean and expecting to last through eternity. A young man in a stiff white coat was setting out pastis and savory biscuits. Hertha had come in earlier to set up her tank on wheels, a meter long and thirty centimeters wide, filled with water and a layer of sand. The seats were filling up. Paul came in with Perrin as the clock chimed four.

For the first time since Pierre died, I felt ready to step out into public. My stomach fluttered as I introduced Hertha, and a brick of grief still lodged in my chest, but I could breathe around it. When I looked out at the sea of mustaches and beards, bellies and pocket watches, I thought I saw amusement on several faces. Two women speaking to the Physics Society—ha ha! Had they laughed before, without my noticing? Was Hertha right, that I had my head in the sand? Or was it harder for these men to overlook my femaleness when I was with Hertha? A droll smile never left the mouth of Monsieur Laurent, and Monsieur Martin scowled.

Hertha's presentation wasn't showy but vital, bold. When she asked for questions, Monsieur Durant, who hadn't bothered to disguise his yawns, leaned forward and spat out his words. "You're describing back pressure on a vortex, and that's impossible."

She looked at him steadily. "Back pressure on a vortex is impossible, yes, of course. What I'm describing is a difference of pressure between a stream flowing in one direction, and another stream flowing over it the opposite way. The vortex is produced by the difference." When her questioner looked at her over his glasses—skeptical, superior—she said in a strong voice, "Monsieur, if you hadn't been sleeping through my presentation, you'd actually have seen a ripple vortex."

Paul laughed out loud, and Perrin shouted "Hear, hear!" Hertha carried on with more questions. She made me think of a time I went swimming in a river as a girl, and my older cousin came flying down the bank on his bicycle, and rode it right off the dock, flying across the water and landing with a splash. How wonderful, and could I ever dare such a thing? I was self-conscious when I spoke in public—Hertha was right. I worked to find the best frequency, like someone plucking on a cello and looking for just the right point between the bass bar and the sound post. Always I tried not to be too large for a woman, without letting the men think that I was smaller than them. In my mind I'd compared myself unfavorably to certain scientists, like Ernest Rutherford, whose hale and hearty manner brought his audience to submission. Or Paul, whose explosive intelligence kept students at the perilous edges of their seats, or Pierre, whose dreaminess had cast a spell. How would an audience respond if I were dreamy or explosive? No wonder I was nervous. My audiences doubted me a priori.

After the questions, a young man circled the room, offering glasses of pastis. I stood talking with Miss Sharp, Hertha's friend from London, a petite, pretty woman in a ruffled blouse who said to me, "Mrs. Ayrton is the soul of tolerance, unless you're a man condescending to a woman."

"Some were so scornful!" I had my eye on Hertha, who was talking to Paul and Perrin. I was dying to know what they were saying.

"That man Durant was goading her before the talk. 'Women have their own unique responsibilities, don't you think?'" She did a perfect likeness of his pompous voice. "'Don't you find that only ugly women go to marches?' The usual blather." When she saw my dismay, she said, "I'm sure your colleagues normally pass well enough for human beings."

"Hertha must get a lot of such nonsense," I said. "Yet she seems unscathed."

Miss Sharp looked dubious. "After the Mud March for women, she was blocked from publishing her work. Turned down by the Society of Fellows. I wouldn't say unscathed."

A man of about fifty strode toward us, in a tweed jacket and brogues. He had a strong bearing but a humorous mouth.

Miss Sharp said, "Oh, here's Henry."

"Evelyn, I'm late," he said, "and I've no excuse whatsoever." His posh voice seemed to make fun of itself.

"Madame Curie, meet Mr. Henry Nevinson." Her expression said, *For all his quirks, he's simply wonderful.*

He touched my hand to his lips, exactly as in Poland.

I said, "Miss Sharp has been educating me about the consequences of being a suffragette."

"Miss Sharp is a terrifying wit, but too nice to run away from."

"Why do I think there's no danger of your doing that?"

"Madame Curie, you understand me in a moment."

I was wary of Mr. Nevinson's charm, but I liked his sweetness with Miss Sharp. "We're going to Le Dôme for dinner. Will the two of you join us?"

"We're headed to a meeting with the French Socialist Women," she said. "We're organizing for a convention."

I said to Mr. Nevinson, "You're going, too?"

"I'm not good for much, but I ride my white horse out in front of the suffragettes."

"He founded the Men's League for Women's Suffrage," said Miss Sharp. "He's an advocate, but he can't give up his chivalry."

"It's such a *nice* horse," he said.

At dinner, at Le Dôme, we were eight at the table, amidst the café talk, light gleaming on the wood, bottles clinking at the bar. Hertha sat next to Paul at the end of the table, and I next to her, so that I could anxiously eavesdrop.

When Hertha ordered a gin martini, Perrin said, "How American of you!" He ordered martinis and oysters for the table.

Paul said, "Our waiter has no mustache, did you see? Lucky for us, he didn't walk out like the others, though the poor bastard's probably paying for that choice, too." Paul had lectured me about the waiters' strike, and their right to a mustache. He had even taken Jules and André-Phillipe with him to join the picket line.

"We all pay for our choices," I said. I was thinking of Hertha's activism, but he looked at me curiously.

"I want to hear about your diamagnetism theory," Hertha said to Paul.

I turned to the student on my left and half-listened to his troubles with his landlord, allowing Hertha and Paul to talk. The dinner was going well. My martini was sharp and frosty. The taste of excitement, jazz.

The waiter brought plates of pear-shaped oysters, smelling of salty mud flats. I watched Paul detach the meat with a tiny fork and tip the oyster and its liquid from the wide end of the shell into his mouth.

He looked at me. "Delicious," he said.

"Mr. Nevinson's a force of nature," I said to Hertha, who was enjoying her oysters, too. "Are he and Miss Sharp engaged?

"He's a war correspondent. He exposed British atrocities in the Boer War, those ghastly concentration camps."

I must have looked startled, because she said, "You wouldn't have guessed this of Henry?"

"He seems rather glib."

"He nearly died on a trek in Angola, exposing the slave trade, for *Harper's*. Quite heroic, really." She took another oyster and said, "But no, they're not engaged. Mr. Nevinson is married."

I felt shocked. "But they seem so close."

"They're lovers." She said this not as gossip, but as simple truth.

A picture of Paul and me together flew across my mind, bicycling through the countryside, the two of us. Stopping at a café, with tables in a garden. "I would have thought she had more respect for herself."

"You're harsh," said Hertha.

"In France, a woman can have lovers, but she's ruined if anybody mentions it. Look at Madame Claretie." Madame Claretie was all over the newspapers for divorcing her husband—the gossipmongers said that she and the Minister of Finance, Joseph Caillaux, a married man, were having an affair. "The vitriol is cruel. They might as well shear the woman's hair and brand her with an A."

"The English also love their hypocrisy," said Hertha, "almost as much as they love their Royals." She turned to me confidentially. "Monsieur Langevin's theory. It explains your husband's results, doesn't it? Curie's Law?"

I paused for a moment. Why had Hertha shifted to speaking about Paul, at just this moment, when we were talking about affairs? What had she perceived? I said, "Where the teacher's mind goes, the student's mind follows."

"Remarkable man." She wiped her fingers on her napkin. "Is his wife a person of substance?"

"I don't know if I'd say that. A person of substance, no."

She looked disappointed. "Men like that, they're for equality in principle, but they marry women they can lord it over."

I said stiffly, "Madame Langevin can hold her own."

"That's good, then."

"Yes, I suppose it is."

When Hertha and I embraced and said goodbye, I was left feeling pleased but a bit unnerved.

Not long after, I received an invitation from Madame Langevin to come and have coffee and help her set up a room for Paul's lessons at the cooperative school. He'd been teaching the children at the EPCI, and she wanted him sometimes to hold the classes at their house. I didn't have time for this, but I wanted to stay on good terms with her, and, though I did find her annoying, I also somewhat enjoyed Paul's wife. I liked the pulse of her femininity, which was a calling for her, and the spell she cast with her flattering attention. She sometimes went too far in speaking her mind, but even this could be refreshing. She reminded me of my Aunt Karolina, whom we used to call "the silly one," because she gossiped about Polish society and was dedicated to fashion, and yet, somehow, if you weren't the object of her prejudice, had a salt-of-the-earth appeal. I was nervous about Madame Langevin's invitation, but I attributed it to the shiver of envy I sometimes felt when I stepped into an intact home—Father, Mother, children, everyone alive and well. I had nothing to hide except what had a right to be hidden in the privacy of my heart.

The Langevin's stone house perched at the intersection of two streets in the lovely old village of Fontenay-aux-Roses, now a suburb of Paris with plane-lined streets. Their house itself had genuine charm, with a second-story balcony and arched entryway, reminiscent of the house where I was born, but inside there were gilded mirrors and newly installed ornate ornamental molding, which I confess made me smile. Madame Langevin was the daughter of an imitation sculptor—that is, he imitated famous sculptures—and this house also aspired to something it couldn't reach. What did Paul make of it, I wondered, in his heart of hearts? He dressed elegantly, and he and Perrin talked nonsense about fine wines, but then again, he was scornful of pretense and spoke proudly of his locksmith father. There was much I couldn't make sense of when it came to Paul.

When Madame Langevin saw me, she took my hands. "Madame Curie, how good it is to see you." She smelled faintly of roses.

"What do you think of this room?" she asked. "Will it do for Paul's classes?"

"It's perfect, but this table"—a white side table with cabriole legs—"It's too small to be of use."

"Of use!" Apparently that had not been a consideration. Nevertheless, she had the maid carry it out. Meanwhile the baby, child number four, squalled in the next room, and somewhere a dog barked. Madame Langevin disappeared—there was a torrent of language, and then laughter, and then she came to fetch me. "Do you know how long it's been since I've had adult conversation? Come." She led me to a bay window where a table had been set with bread, butter, and a lovely apricot jam.

For reasons I couldn't fathom, Madame Langevin, ten years my junior, was treating me tenderly. At first I was wary, but I found myself starting to relax. The coffee was good. Out in the garden, a baby rabbit skittered about, one way and then the next. Madame buttered my bread for me and scooped jam on it. "You see, I can't stop being a mother, and you need some mothering."

I thought of Paul, offering me comfort on the train.

"How are you doing, ma chère? It's two years, isn't it? People go on about their lives, but you mustn't think we've forgotten. Not a day goes by when we don't pity you."

I swallowed my bread. I hadn't been thinking of Pierre, but the loss of him surged back. I said, "Much worse things have happened."

"That's of little comfort, don't you find? When your heart is broken? I don't know what I'd do if I lost Paul. Goodness,

I wouldn't have your courage. Here—" She buttered another piece of bread for me.

"I've done a lot of hard things, but moving on without Pierre is the hardest."

"Life is terrible," she said indignantly. "Tell me, do you wish you'd never met him? So you didn't have to suffer this?"

I looked at her. In the midst of her drama, her expressiveness, there was also genuine feeling. "Oh no," I said. "I've never wished that."

"It's so romantic. Terrible, but romantic. My love for Paul—we started off with trouble. We fought a lot, not like you and your husband, but I wouldn't give him up for anything. He's so good to me."

"Pierre thought highly of him," I managed.

"Ah, but it's a burden sometimes to be married to a man of genius. Maybe it's easier if you're a genius, too, but I'm just ordinary. Really, I can't imagine why he chose me."

I felt a sting of sympathy and guilt—I had thought these things myself. I had believed that Paul was unfortunate in his marriage. Pierre had thought this, too. It seemed I was seeing another side of Jeannette—as womanly, appealing. This house, for all its affectation, had the bustle of a real home, the chaotic, joyous energy of family life. The smells of hot irons and linen and wet socks.

"What's wrong with ordinary?"

"I can tell you, I feel stupid sometimes."

"But you shouldn't—"

"—I know. Paul tells me I should respect myself."

Did I hear in her voice a stagey note? Was she managing me, keeping me in my place? When, at that moment, four-year-old Madeleine came running to her mother, who tore a piece of bread and jam for her, kissed her on the forehead and sent her off again, another voice in me countered, *See how loving she is, how warm, whereas you are cold and condescending.* Irène's pale face floated into my mind, the day I had slapped her, her misery. No wonder Paul had confronted me.

I had a strange sensation of being unsure why I was there.

"There's no accounting for love," said Madame, pouring herself more coffee. "My husband treats me as if I'm something special. He's as courtly now as he was when we first met. And when we go to bed, what does it matter that he's a genius and I'm not?"

I felt as if she were pushing my head underwater, but I said, "It doesn't matter at all."

Later, when she saw me to the door, she put her arms around me and pressed her full round breasts against my chest. For a moment it was as if I were in Paul's skin, with her pressed into him in just this way. I was stirred, fluttery. She was making me feel her power.

"I hope you'll come and see me more often," she said, yet I had the sense that she was turning me out.

It was a foggy afternoon, the air somewhere between mist and rain. I lingered in the garden, admiring Paul's daffodils—he'd put in bulbs in the fall, he'd told me, and now there were clumps of yellow by the sidewalk, freckled with water. A cherry tree bristled with bright green buds. Soon, here and in all of Paris—along the rue Monge, the Jardin des Plantes, the Parc Monceau—would come the soft explosion of pink and white, followed by blossoms falling like snow, and the faintest of fragrances. A few weeks later, it would all be a memory.

PART TWO

VIII

Paris and l'Arcouëst, Summer 1909

AT FIRST, I REFUSED the invitation to summer at l'Arcouëst. I was flattered to be invited, but I didn't want to leave rue Cuvier.

"Why flattered?" Paul asked me. "You're top of the heap." He and his family had also been invited. His remark struck me as crude, as if I were social climbing, but it did feel good to be asked to join this elite group of professors, mostly scientists and mathematicians, who spent every August on the English Channel sea, in Brittany. Journalists called it "Port Science." Activities centered around the thatched-roof cottage of the historian who had invited me, Monsieur Seignobos, an aristocratic man perennially in a white flannel suit, who had a sprawling property with six rowing boats and two sailboats.

Things were going well for both Paul and me, and I liked to think that our friendship was partly responsible. With my encouragement, he had published his "Langevin's equation," his elegant approach to Brownian motion, the work that Hertha had asked him about, and already, it had become the standard treatment. My own work was also moving forward, with a new supply of radium and our laboratory humming with a team of researchers, courtesy of Mr. Carnegie.

In the three years since Kelvin's challenge, André and I had solved many problems in our effort to isolate radium metal, but each time we attempted to reduce the barium amalgam using electrolysis—we still practiced our technique with barium—the hydrogen attacked the amalgam, and the barium reacted to infinitesimal amounts of carryover moisture or oxygen. Our usual procedure for purifying hydrogen simply wasn't working, and I couldn't imagine taking a holiday until we found a solution.

Then one day as I sat on the laboratory steps drinking tea with a group of research students, my Polish student, Jean, said, "What if we heated the tubing?" André and I looked at each other: this was a good idea. In our next experiment, we placed the platinum tubing in the electric furnace, and then, carefully, we hooked it back up to the apparatus and released the hydrogen through it. Lo and behold, the barium amalgam did not react! With this problem solved, we were just months away from attempting the experiment with radium.

And so, with André himself headed to l'Arcouëst, I dismissed my qualms. Paul and Jeannette (we now used our given names) invited the girls and me to share a house and a nanny with their family. They found a place right on the sea, in a hamlet inhabited mostly by sailors and peasants. I was excited by the prospect of getting out of blazing Paris and into the ocean breeze, and spending time with Paul.

Did I think of how Jeannette had pressed her breasts against me at the door, that afternoon at her house in Fontenay-aux-Roses? Did it cross my mind, the competition between us? If so, it was like the flutter of a bird as it passed by. We were three adults, two of us scientists—this was my attitude. Surely we could figure things out. Irène, nearly twelve, would enjoy time with the Langevin boys, and Eve, at four, adored their six-year-old sister Madeleine.

The holiday began brilliantly. Each morning when the sun came out, a gang of us would converge on the beach in front of the Seignobos cottage: Monsieur Seignobos and his sister, Madame Parat, a sharp-nosed, older lady who apparently had outgrown social niceties; Paul with Jules and André-Philippe; Irène and me; the Perrins and their children; André Debierne; Marguerite and Émile Borel; Monsieur and Madame Charles Maurain, whom I had recently met; and others whom I barely knew. Jeannette didn't come, because she was squeamish and wouldn't set foot in the ocean.

"I hope you're not wearing your ridiculous swimming costume," she said to Paul as we set off the first morning, her face tilted up at him, like an adoring leading lady. "Those stripes!"

He flushed. "It's the only one I have."

I expected him to brush off the silliness, but he seemed upset.

She gave him a kiss. "It's fine. Go. Don't worry about it."

There were rituals to learn. On the beach, people greeted one another with a chorus of "bonjour!" Many of the men, women, and children wore pea coats of twill flannel, woven by a seamstress from the village. Established members of the tribe could be discerned by the wearing of this garment. It made me laugh, the pretentious lack of pretension, but still I coveted a twill pea coat. I played along with the delicious notion that among us there were no hierarchies—no prejudice of age or nationality or sex, and no family distinctions. Most of us had important work to go back to, and this was the unspoken thing. We belonged to the bigger world, and we were working to make it better. The fact that it was taboo to talk about our work (sport and amusements were the proper topics) only made us feel more grand. Young Marguerite Borel, however—wife of the mathematician Émile Borel, and daughter of Dean Appell—had just published her first novel, a romance, under the pen name Camille Marbo, and she was taking notes. "Scribble, scribble," Paul teased. "My work," she replied, "is more amusing than yours."

Each morning the children detached a few rowing boats from their buoys and made their way around the treacherous rocks. The rest of us would climb in, four sets of oars per boat, with the master of each at the rudder. What a glory, to feel my muscles as we pulled in rhythm across the bay, the sun flashing and the water spraying, as Monsieur Seignobos, ironic and gay, shouted commands, and Madame Maurain sang, in her rich tones,

> My father built a house of bricks
> (Pull, pull on your oars!)
> The youngest mason gave me a kiss
> (Pull, pull on your oars!)

Often, when we reached the channel, Jean Perrin lost control and spun our boat around, making Irène grin. "You're an elephant," his daughter Aline would shout into the wind, because there was, after all, a hierarchy at Port Science: philistines, who must be ejected; elephants, who were visitors without nautical know-how; sailors, with know-how enough; and crocodiles, who were experts on tides and currents and the code of the sea. Like Perrin, I was an elephant, and the butt of jokes. One day, perhaps, I could become a sailor.

"My dear, if you don't pull when I say, we shall all be drowned rats," said Perrin, on the morning I'm remembering. He was literally at sea, where no amount of bonhomie could save him.

"Maybe I should take over," yelled Aline, and Irène looked at me to see if I was shocked. French children were not as subservient as Polish children, but generally they knew their place. *What are the rules?* Irène seemed to ask. What *were* the rules? The oars splashed water in my face, and I licked the salt from my lips.

In ten more minutes we reached Roch Vras, a giant rock of an island. By then the sun was boastful and lavish; we rushed to escape it, changing into our suits behind a jagged rock and diving into the cool, transparent water. I went in first—for this they called me eager, but really I was shy of showing my arms and legs, especially to Paul, who was up to his ankles in smelly mud, smiling and unembarrassed. Each time my arms rose high into the air I could feel on my skin the eyes of my companions: I was an excellent swimmer.

I was out treading water when Monsieur Seignobos was

astonished by a long-armed swing of mud from Marguerite Borel. Irène swam out to me, bewildered. I put my arms around her middle, and we treaded together, with wriggly cold limbs. We watched Perrin stepped out from behind a rock, saying, "I warn you, Langevin, my wife is possessed of a fury." On cue, Henriette, mud-drenched and looking like a golem, rushed Paul with an armful of seaweed.

Irène said, "They're having fun?"

"Why don't you go lob some at Aline?"

She swam back to shore and awkwardly threw seaweed at her friend, then looked back at me, her forehead crinkled. I nodded, and she bent with skinny eager arms to try again. Before long my growing-up daughter was shrieking and running across the rock, flinging seaweed, making it whip and sting. In the zest of her release, I felt both pleasure and a pang. I had held her back, and myself as well. I saw how constrained and tight I'd been, and I saw my daughter perched on the verge of womanhood, tentative and uncertain. In my limbs I felt a surge of anger. I didn't want to hold back anymore.

By seven o'clock the next morning Irène had eaten breakfast and was ready to go back to Roch Vras. "It was fun yesterday," she said.

"Wasn't it?" We were at the table with Eve and Paul and Jeannette.

"I hope we weren't gauche," said Paul. "Monsieur Seignobos won't want us back."

"There were some crocodiles in the mix," I said. "They'd let us know if mud-slinging was out of bounds."

"Slippery, rubbery, horrible seaweed," said Jeannette. "I don't know how you stand it. It looks like snakes."

Paul said to me, "She's afraid of the fish." Little Hélà was on his lap, pulling at his mustache. "Ouch!" he said, and she giggled. Eve ate bread and jam and observed them as if they were foreigners. Outside the other children shouted and played.

"But you can swim, can't you?" I asked Jeannette.

"I do the doggie paddle."

"Her lovely rear-end pops up out of the water," said Paul.

"For you and you alone," she said. "I'm not an exhibitionist."

Paul gave me a conspiratorial look. Was he implying something about his wife—she surely liked to show herself—or maybe something about my swimming at Roch Vras? There was something forced in his good cheer. Often around Jeannette, he covered his irritation with kind and patient chatter. Other times he seemed to enjoy her. She said what came to mind, and she flirted, in her way, with men and women alike.

I got the coffee and poured it around. I loved l'Arcouëst, but sharing a house was a mistake. It was hard to be amidst Paul's family, the children running into his arms, the bickering and cooing between him and his wife. I didn't need my nose rubbed in the fact of my widowhood. It made me see what I didn't share with Paul and how alone I really was.

I said to Jeannette, "Shall we go for a bicycle ride, you and I? There are some paths up the cliff." I hated missing Roch Vras, but I didn't want her to feel left out. Also, I thought that spending time with her could right a balance and protect me from my feelings about Paul.

"Bicycles make me sweat," she said.

"Princesses hate to sweat," said Paul.

"I know you think my parents spoiled me," said Jeannette, "but that's only because you were raised by—"

Paul looked at her. She stopped mid-sentence. I didn't know what this meant, and I pretended I hadn't seen.

That afternoon as I folded the girls' clothing in our bedroom, I watched them through the window, splashing and throwing themselves at the waves. Paul, out on the beach, sat with his back to me. He wore his striped bathing costume. Something about the sand on those slim, square shoulders, the way the sun glinted off them in tiny, jeweled bursts, beckoned me. I set the basket of laundry on my bed and went outside and sat down next to him. "Hello," I said.

"Hello! That daughter of yours just beat my son in a swimming race."

"Good for her." The children were bobbing up and down, all but Eve, who crawled on her belly through the shallows, the nanny watching her.

"She's your girl, all right," said Paul.

This was the first time that we had been alone together since we had been at l'Arcouëst. I played with little pebbles on the beach.

"How's your interstellar travel?" I was breaking the unspoken rule at l'Arcouëst about not mentioning work, but I knew that Paul's mind would be on his current obsession, Einstein's "clock problem," a consequence of special relativity, to do with time travel.

"Twins instead of clocks, don't you think? Gaston stays home and minds the cattle while Gustav hurtles through space in a rocket at the speed of light. When Gustav comes home, he's two years older and expecting a feast, a fatted calf, only to find that poor Gaston has been dead two hundred years."

"I still don't understand this."

"Ah, but you will when you hear my paper."

"I know. You're the best at explaining this." Paul had in fact been very near formulating a theory of special relativity—Einstein acknowledged that if he hadn't gotten there first, Paul would have gotten there shortly.

He dug his toes into the sand and let it sift between them. I had an impulse to grab his foot, to take his feet in my hands and cover them with kisses. And his face. The forehead sloping down in a nearly straight line to the slim straight nose. I wanted to draw my finger down that path.

I stood up. What was happening?

"Stay." He tugged at the bottom of my dress.

"I shouldn't."

"I think that means you won't."

"I won't, then." I imagined Jeannette peering out the window behind me.

"Haven't we had this conversation before?" He looked up at me over his shoulder and smiled, but when he saw my face the smile disappeared. "Are you all right?"

"I have some folding to do." I walked stiffly back across the sand and rocks.

"Mé!" called Eve and she came running on chubby legs, in her big wet suit. I scooped her up, the dripping heft of her, and carried her into the house. It was a relief to be needed as a mother, to disappear into my relationship with my little girl.

That night I lay in bed with my daughters sleeping nearby, in cots under the window. How strange, to feel my nightdress brush my nipples, the tender insides of my legs, bright with electricity, when my spirit, for so long, had been like the dead, shell-less, hermit crab Eve had shown me on the beach the day before, desiccated, stiff, curled up on itself. Could it be that even this was changing? After Pierre died, I'd written in my journal that no one else would take the place in my heart that belonged only to him. Had I done wrong, to allow these feelings for Paul? Or could it be—and this came with guilt—that I'd been using Paul all this time to find my way back to the kind of love I had with Pierre? My feelings for him were not truly all-of-a-sudden, though I had tried to hide them from myself.

The wind, which had been knocking the shutters of the house, suddenly went still, and from the beach came the sound of bubbling and spilling, like a thousand lapping tongues. These were the moments of highest tide, before the ocean yielded to the pull of the moon and was sucked back into itself. Something scratched inside the wall—a mouse? I lay there on the cotton-stuffed mattress, aware of my weight and the cottage smells. Lamp oil, musty towels, cedar. In the room behind me were Paul and Jeannette in their own bed. I couldn't have what

I wanted. In spite of this, in spite of everything, a restfulness came over me. I imagined all the sleepers who had lain in this bed, and those who had made love in it in other seasons, other times, amidst these same sounds and smells. My struggles were not surprising. It comforted me, to acknowledge the truth of my feelings.

Irène and Eve breathed evenly. Earlier, the three of us had peered out at the night sky, at Scorpius, with its stinger and claws, Antarus at its heart, and a little further east, Sagittarius. And then—it was haunting—a lone swimmer, a stranger, had come up out of the ocean, up through the shallow waves. When he stood up, the water dripping from him had shone with a blue light. His body glistened blue. Eve had pointed, "Look, look!" and I whispered, "Sea sparkle." Their father had seen this same phenomenon, I told the girls, on this very coast—tiny plankton beneath the surface, creating phosphorescence. The young man, still in a blue halo, picked up a towel from the rocks and walked down the beach, disappearing into the night. I had the feeling then that Pierre had sent this swimmer, to me and to the girls. A tingling sensation spread across my arms. Eve squeezed my hand, as if she sensed this too.

Down the hall, baby Hélà fussed for a moment. There was an answering murmur in the bedroom behind me, then waves washing along the shore. Everything I felt had been felt before. It would all pass, and it would also circle back around. I pulled the blanket higher. The air was chilly on my face and hands. I had a sense of being in my body but outside of it too, amongst a household of creatures breathing with me, all of us mostly carbon and water, each of us assembled for a while into a person with a name.

It was one thing to get some perspective on my feelings for Paul, quite another to live with wedded love so near—pecks on the cheek, collar-straightening, and, at night, muffled whimpers through the walls. And worse, their squabbles. Jeannette's mother was coming for an extended visit. *She doesn't feel welcome,* Jeannette complained—the walls were very thin—and Paul laughed caustically. They had the luxury of argument.

I counted the days until I could return to my laboratory and my house in Sceaux. I missed Pierre's father, his undemanding talk, his way of brushing crumbs off the table after breakfast. I even missed my fatigue. At home, at least, I got through my days with purpose.

"Is something wrong?" Jeannette asked me one morning. We were peeling carrots and potatoes over a newspaper. I planned to take the children to feed these scraps to a goat.

"Why do you ask?" I hoped I wasn't putting a damper on their holiday, clammed up and remote.

Jeannette looked out the window at baby Hélà, who was playing with the nanny. "Paul told me not to interfere, but he sees it, too."

We talk about everything, including you, she might as well have said. Had she been alert to my feelings for Paul, even before I was? I dropped my knife in the sink and rummaged in the drawer for another, sharper one. "I'm perfectly fine. I wish you'd leave me alone."

Her eyes grew big, offended and triumphant. She puffed up her chest and pulled her shoulders back. "I've done nothing to deserve this. I take you in, I cook for you—"

I wanted to scream, but I had nothing to gain by speaking my mind. "I'm sorry, Jeannette. I've had headaches all week, but it's no excuse."

"You're lucky to have a friend like me. Most married women wouldn't even want you around. Most of them would try to get rid of you. Any way they could."

I stood frozen, but Jeannette, for all her disquiet, looked somehow proud and happy.

The front door of the cottage opened, and I heard Paul say, "Here we go, let's wash our feet." There was a bucket to rinse off sand.

I've always found that the timbre of a voice conveys a person's character. When someone speaks, I know instantly whether or not I'm attracted to that person. I feel a certain revulsion when I hear too-polished, self-satisfied tones, or the unctuous drawl of certain merchants. But some people in their voices sound true, and when I hear this, my heart drops in gratitude, and I feel a hopefulness beyond reason, as if I were thrashing at sea and someone approached me in a lifeboat. Paul had a voice like that.

"That's better," he said. "Now it's your turn, that's a good girl."

"Oh my Lord, she stinks," came Jules's voice.

"Hush, Jules."

"She stinks worse than Hélà! Oh, my Lord."

Paul appeared in the kitchen holding Eve's hand, his bag over his shoulder like a boy on a lark. The stench of feces filled the room.

"When's lunch?" said Jules. "What are we having?"

"I didn't mean it," said Eve. She was trying not to cry.

Jeannette said, "Paul, I need you upstairs."

"She hasn't had an accident in years," I said.

"Children never want to come inside when they're having fun," said Paul.

"Right now," said Jeannette.

Paul glanced between the two of us.

"I didn't feel the poop coming," said Eve.

Paul followed Jeannette upstairs, his shoulders drooping. What power did she have over him?

"Is Eve in trouble?" said Jules. "What's for lunch?"

"You could help by peeling the rest of the potatoes."

He was startled. Boys didn't peel potatoes.

"There's a knife in the sink." I grabbed some rags and took Eve outside to a patch of grass behind the house. She lay passively as I peeled off her suit and wiped down her bottom and legs.

"That hurts," she said. "You're scrubbing too hard."

"You're too big for this. You know better, don't you?"

"Are you mad at me?"

"A little. It doesn't matter."

"Is Madame Langevin mad at me?"

I looked at the length of her, the curls sticking to her forehead, the chubby legs already longer than the month before. "Do you care so much what she thinks?"

"I don't like it when someone's mad at me." She turned her cheek to the side.

"Never mind, my darling. We'll be going home soon."

When Eve and I came down for breakfast the next morning, Jeannette was at the table with baby Hélà, playing patty-cake.

"Here you are, and are you hungry?" She said this with tender solicitude, which confused me. I had had a bad night. Was our disagreement over, for her? How had that happened? "I've made coffee," she continued. "Do you think Monsieur Seignobos is a homosexual? That white flannel suit. Homosexuals can be charming. I have a mind to figure him out. Did you see how he eats potatoes? Men don't eat like that."

"You remind me of my Aunt Karolina," I said, pouring myself coffee. This was because my aunt, like Jeannette, had absorbed all the usual forms of disgusting prejudice, but when Jeannette looked at me, doubtful, I said, "She was pretty. Our favorite aunt." I couldn't believe I was stooping to this, but I was relieved that for whatever reason, Jeannette and I could carry on. I wouldn't have wanted to make a scene by leaving early.

The girls and I rode bicycles into Paimpol that morning, the next town over, with a harbor and a post office, a vegetable stand, and a row of shops. Eve was attracted by a mannequin with pert breasts in a plate glass window, and bolts of velvet and twill. Peering in, we saw two girls in peasant caps bending over sewing machines, and a sturdy woman with her hair in a braid who appeared to be giving orders. This, I realized, must be the seamstress who made the twill pea coats.

I found myself thinking of my mother, who had big gray eyes like this woman, and a purposeful manner; my mother who had set up a corner of our drawing room to be her cobbler's bench, to save a bit of money, and for the pleasure of turning out fine pairs of shoes for her family. On a shelf she had nails for her hammer and awl, and a stash of leather and glue. My father was proud that his wife, a well-bred woman who had run a top school, didn't find it beneath her to work with her hands and master the cobbler's trade. "Look at her," he would say to us. "The daughter of Polish gentry, who speaks five languages, making shoes with her own hands. Your mother isn't boastful, though she has reason to be."

A hollow opened under my breastbone. It had found me again, that hunger for my mother.

In the seamstress's window I caught my own reflection: Irène at my shoulder with her wild mass of hair, Eve beside her with her white ribbons. Were my girls as proud of me as I was of their grandmother? Another thought intruded: What would it have meant to my parents, had they known that their daughter would one day covet her husband's married protégé?

On the last night of August, Paul and I stood on the beach watching an orange sun plummet toward the sea. He wore a broad-brimmed floppy linen hat, stained with his sweat. In the last week I'd been cool to him, as cool as I could be without creating suspicion. But this was the end of our holiday, and I'd had a glass of wine, and I wanted to snatch the hat from his head and put it onto mine and run my fingers through his hair.

Nearly all the vacationers had come down to the beach to catch the last of the summer glory. The children played leapfrog, and the dying light turned the girls' white dresses pink and orange. When the ocean had fully swallowed up the sun, we all drifted toward the Seignobos cottage.

Paul and I lingered by the vines and passion flowers that climbed the low wall of the cottage. The children were all crazed, running across the sloping lawn with arms spread wide. Fireflies flickered over the shrubs. Irène and Aline Perrin were digging out firefly lighters and sticking them on their fingernails. They waved their hands, bright jewels in the dark. Paul's pipe smoke curled its way into the night and disappeared, and then came another curl.

"I think you'll be glad to get home," he said. "Living with us has been hard."

"And you'll be glad when it's you and your family again."

He sighed. "Let's be honest with each other."

I hesitated. "You make that sound easy."

"I've wanted to believe I can go on as I am."

I wasn't sure what he meant. Yes, he was to some degree unhappy with Jeannette, yet what I had seen at l'Arcouëst was something more alive and complicated. I didn't like it, but it wasn't mine.

"I'm sorry you're unhappy."

"Don't do that, Marie."

"I don't know what you want from me."

"I want you to give me a reason to hope."

"Don't say any more, Paul."

"You don't mean it. I know you don't."

"It would change everything. We wouldn't be able to be friends."

"I don't want to be friends."

"Oh Paul, please stop."

"I don't want to stop."

André walked toward us, but when he saw our expressions, he stopped and gave us a salute. Eve ran to him, crying, and he picked her up. She was upset about the lightning bugs, how the older girls dug out their lights. André said, "There's a live one, shall we examine it? It's a beetle, really. It lights up from within."

Inside, ragtime music—Jean Perrin at the piano.

"Are you traveling this fall?" I said to Paul. I could feel his disappointment, that I would turn to niceties.

"To Milan. To give my special relativity paper."

"André and I have a conference in Brussels."

"Ah, Debierne." He added quietly, "He's devoted to you."

"He always has been, to Pierre and me. And to the girls."

"I hope you're kind to him."

"Have I done something unkind?"

"No, it's just . . . don't you see it?"

"Perhaps you could speak plainly."

"All right. He fancies you."

I was startled.

"You're blind sometimes. It's charming but a little cruel."

"You're mad at me."

"Never." He moved his hand across the stone where we were sitting until he touched my leg. The girls were coming across the grass toward us, Irène and Aline. I felt the heat of his fingers through my skirt.

"Stop."

"I don't want to stop."

"The children are coming."

"Hush."

He took his hand away, and I felt it like a panic, the need to have it back. Then his hand ran across my leg, finding the inside of my thigh.

The girls twirled in front of us, being ballerinas.

"Papa!" called Jules. He appeared on the porch of the cottage carrying a tall drink. "Mama wants you."

"Tell her I'm coming."

Jules stood waiting. Paul climbed the steps and disappeared inside.

By the time I joined the others, I was bitten up by sand fleas. The children were taking turns at the piano. I felt the flush of my face. The panic and guilt, and the hunger for more. Paul's hand back on my thigh.

Jean Perrin brought me a glass of wine, and the two of us watched as Henriette danced with Eve. André and Paul spoke seriously in the corner, making me a little nervous. Jeannette chatted away to Monsieur Seignobos, who bent his head with the expression one gets when one is bored and cornered.

"My great-aunt married a respected barrister," she was saying. "He had a sister who almost married a baron of the Laval family. They lived in an ordinary neighborhood, and he wanted to move to the Avenue de l'Opéra, and they certainly could have, but she simply put her foot down. Her mother lived nearby, that was the reason."

"I see," said Monsieur Seignobos.

Madame Parat had apparently assessed the company. I could see it in her eyes. She looked at people and decided whether or not they interested her.

"My grandfather sold some of his art to the nobility," Jeannette went on. "And my great-grandfather—"

"—Oh for God's sake," said Madame Parat, her nostrils flared. "Do shut up."

In an instant, Paul was at Jeannette's side.

"Take her away, will you?" said Madame Parat.

Jeannette reddened and grew larger. "Well, I don't think you can be from so refined a family as all that. No one in my great aunt's family ever talked that way."

I was mortified for Jeannette—as frustrated as I was with her, I didn't want her exposed—but Perrin whispered in my ear, "Her great-great granny was a lady."

"Your wife is full of stories," said Monsieur Seignobos.

Paul wore a faintly ironical expression, but he was seething, I wasn't sure at whom. "Let's go home," he said to Jeannette. Her nose was literally in the air. To Monsieur Seignobos, Paul said, "She's not accustomed to brandy."

When they got her to the door, she turned and announced, "I'm not the one with bad manners, am I. And I haven't had any brandy."

I waited for an hour before returning with the girls to the cottage. When, a few hours later, low bitter tones began in the bedroom next door, I couldn't, thank God, understand what they were saying. At one point, Jeannette laughed strangely, more unsettling than the bitterness.

The next morning André came to our cottage to say that he had room in his automobile for the girls and me. I accepted. I said goodbye to Jeannette and Paul. There would be no more breakfasts together. No more evenings in the garden or sunsets on the sea.

Jeannette said, "We once shared a cottage with Madame Bisset. She's a widow, too, but she has some life in her." This landed in my gut with a thud. Some part of me knew to dismiss what she said—Jeannette wouldn't recognize life in a woman, if it wasn't dressed up in a frilly frock—and yet my face stung hot.

Paul was upset. I could have set him at ease, but I wanted him to suffer. I couldn't help feeling that if I suffered, he should, too.

Driving through the countryside, André kindly left me to my thoughts. He stared ahead and grasped the steering wheel, and a bright smell of cologne wafted over to me from him. Oh dear, I thought. I'd never known André to wear cologne. Could Paul be right about his feelings? I was annoyed with Paul for making me embarrassed around André. Couldn't some relationships be what they seemed? Wasn't cordiality enough? Yet I recognized now that even if Paul were wrong, and I hoped he was, there was a lack of equality in our relationship. André anticipated my needs before I knew them myself, and he often brought presents to the girls, while I had little curiosity about him. I respected him, I was fond of him, and I appreciated him, but I hadn't extended my imagination in his direction.

I sighed and shut my eyes. I would have to do better.

After forty minutes, as we turned onto the road for Saint-Brieuc, André asked, "Are you well, Marie?"

"Oh yes. I'm just resting, if you don't mind."

I did try to rest, but my thoughts were like water running downhill to Paul.

Szczuki, Poland, 1886

Kazimierz puts a stick in the snow and ties a cord to it to draw a perfect circle, two meters in diameter. We are making a marvelous igloo. With Andzia and Bronka, his two sisters, we pile snow bricks of diminishing size on top of each other, sloping to the middle.

For the past two months in the Zorawski household, where I am governess, every sentence has begun, "When Kazimierz comes home from university for Christmas . . ." In spite of the gushing, I am not prepared for the arrival of their eldest son. He has apple red cheeks and blue eyes—the clichés do fit. We are in love with each other.

Although I am poor, Madame Zorawski invites me to go with Bronka to the fancy balls in Karyacz, the gossip center of the region. She'll have a dress made for me, she says. I decline. The girls in Karyacz are like so many geese, with nothing to say, or else they are provocative. I refuse to fritter away my wits. Kazimierz says there are some intelligent ones I haven't met.

A rosy glow falls over the plains. Our noses are frozen. Kazimierz rubs his mittens together. "Go in to Mother," he says to his sisters. "Tell her Maria and I will be in soon for tea."

Andzia glances between her brother and me: I swear, that girl has a sixth sense. She takes her sister's hand and follows our footprints back to the Zorawski manor.

Kazimierz leads me inside the igloo, where a pink light filters through the seams of the snow bricks. "Your eyes are shining," he says. "You're the cleverest and most beautiful girl in the world."

We kiss, and it's as if there are ferns in my chest, unfurling.

"Will you marry me?" he asks. I say yes, and we kiss again.

He wants to know: when will we tell our parents? I'm modern, I tell him; he doesn't have to ask my father.

"I can see you'll be the one to get the glass of vodka," he jokes. At the wedding ceremony, there's one glass of water, and one of vodka, in indistinguishable glasses. Whoever chooses the vodka is in charge.

Kazimierz holds my hand as we walk back to the house, and my heart sings. I will write to Bronia right away. Our plan is for me to follow her to Paris to get my degree. We didn't count on Kazimierz!

We stomp snow off in the entryway. Kazimierz pulls off my boots, and we can't stop laughing.

IX

Paris, 1909–1910

BACK AT HOME after l'Arcouëst, I found myself reactive to any slights, as when, after a meeting at the Sorbonne, my male colleagues went off for drinks and a smoke, assuming I wouldn't join in. How could I join, when they went to a men's club? When they disagreed with me, they were overly deferential. They didn't bite in, the way they did with each other. I had imagined that I'd been accepted into the inner sanctum, but this existed only in my mind. Hertha had said, when she visited Paris, that it's better to have one foot in reality, but it didn't feel good to look at the world from her perspective.

When André bent my ear about a researcher who wasn't fulfilling his obligations, I said, "We'll have to let him go."

"Really?" André could be harsh, and he monitored the lab like a raptor, but I was the one who made difficult decisions. I called the young man into my office and told him we had a right to more than he was giving; it was time for him to move on. I wasn't wrong. We'd already given him a second chance, and in a laboratory, people absolutely need to play their parts. André spent the afternoon taking snuff.

I bore down on a treatise on radioactivity, compiling the research to date. I wanted to set the record straight, outline my own achievements in the context of the research gathering steam around the world.

At l'Arcouëst something had happened to me. It wasn't only that I fully admitted to my feelings for Paul, and his for me. I'd made contact with something deeper, at once softer and more violent. For too long I'd been binding up my energy, focusing on duties instead of joy, as a scientist, a mother, the widow of Pierre. But in Brittany, I had swum and thrown mud; I had pulled oars through waves with salt on my tongue. At night, in that musty bedroom, I had opened myself to sounds and smells and vibrations. I had sat in hot sand next to Paul's gleaming body, and in the dark of night, the girls twirling in front of us, he had put his hand on my thigh.

A current of life ran through me, and I didn't want to be afraid.

Paul had asked me for a reason to hope. What did he mean? Was there anything real to hope for? I determined to avoid him. How else could I let him go?

I didn't know what to do with my desire. Everything inside of me had changed, but nothing outside of me had.

Our last day at l'Arcouëst, we had gotten the news that Henri Becquerel, who had shared the Nobel Prize with Pierre and me, had died of a heart attack while vacationing with his wife. I had mixed feelings about Becquerel—he had favored his chums over Pierre when it came to grants—but the time for pettiness, his and mine, was past. Two of the three of us who had won that prize were gone. The funeral had been delayed, something about bringing the body back from Brittany, but finally it was to be in Châtillon-Coligny, and Paul would be there.

That morning, Dr. Curie set off with the girls to the Grand Palais to see an aeronautic exhibition—balloons, dirigibles, and airplanes. "Don't let go of Eve's hand," I said to my father-in-law. "She'll enchant a pilot and wander off with him."

"She enchants her grandpère, and I shan't leave her side."

Irène said, "Dirigibles use hydrogen. They're lighter than air."

Eve said, "Can we have a strawberry ice at Tortoni's?"

"What do you know about Tortoni's?"

"Madame Borel told us, at l'Arcouëst."

"So that's what she was teaching you." Marguerite Borel had told me that my daughters needed supplemental education but had only laughed when I asked her what she meant.

I had a foreboding as I said goodbye to the girls and their grandpère, dread rising up from my feet. I wanted to run after them and make them stay home, but I refused to burden them with my unfounded fear.

On the train to Châtillon-Coligny, we were practically Port Science redux: Paul and Jeannette, Dean Appell, the Borels, the Perrins, and André were there, all of us in a single compartment. Marguerite Borel looked touchingly young in her long pearls (I scolded her about Tortoni's). She had wrapped a piece of fabric about her head and wore that excited look she often had at the beginning of a social event: material for her next novel. Jean Perrin and Henriette settled into seats while Paul tucked the women's handbags overhead. When I passed behind him, my knees felt watery. *Easy,* I told myself, like a jockey talking to a mare.

Jeannette insisted that I sit by the window, next to her. "You look good in black," I told her, and indeed she was queenly, her gown cut in the new style, with a raised waistline and slim, empire silhouette, and a hat with brilliant blue feathers. Her shiny black silk certainly out-glossed my workable wool. I wanted to feel smug about the difference in our values, but instead I felt a pang of unloveliness.

Don't set your mind on what you lack, but think of what you have already. Marcus Aurelius. I'd read it that morning, browsing through my philosophy collection. Whatever arises in one's life can bring about growth, Aurelius said; everything has a hidden purpose. If I lived virtuously and accepted what happened, not judging events as good or bad, perhaps I would find my "inner citadel."

"It took two washes to get the sand out of my hair," said Jeannette. "I'm never going back to that place. I wanted Paul getting on with a better class of people, but what good were they? I've seen better-looking women in the fish market. Now the Becquerel family, I understand they're a fine class of people. Their own chapel, Paul says."

"They're a grand family in science," I said.

"What do you mean?"

"Monsieur Becquerel, and his father, and his grandfather, all three of them were members of the French Academy of Science and held the chair in physics at the Museum of Natural History. Henri Becquerel was born at the museum. Right in the laboratory."

"That's not even decent," she said.

The train rattled through a tunnel, and when the light came back it revealed Paul standing in the aisle talking to Madame Borel, her hands moving animatedly, him in that posture of his, head bent thoughtfully, hands behind his back.

If you are distressed by anything external, the pain is not due to the thing itself but to your estimate of it, and this you have the power to revoke at any moment. It was rather like science, really, working with one's emotions. A person had to learn not to trust assumptions and strong feelings, but to step back, observe, and question.

"Honestly," I said to Jeannette, "I would rather have spent the day with my girls, but I knew your husband would tell me I had to come." "You would miss the funeral of your fellow Nobel-winner?" he had said at l'Arcouëst.

"That's funny, he told me I'd be better off taking a miss. Paul!" She gestured at him—he was talking still to Madame Borel, and when he came to her, she scooted over to make room. "Didn't you tell me I should stay home?"

"I worried you were getting a cold, but you're looking very well indeed in your new dress."

Jeannette was pleased in spite of herself. "This from a man

who had a fit of temper last night over a badly made fruit compote."

Paul blushed. "The cook is getting lazy."

Jeannette raised her eyebrows as if to say, *There's more to this story, but I'm too polite to tell it.* "Marie said she wanted to stay home, but you made her come."

"One does need the support of fellow scientists," he said. "It's in Marie's best interest to attend. To see and be seen."

I bent forward to see him, past Jeannette's cobalt blue feathers, sticking every which way. He wore a perfect, public face. I wondered what was underneath.

"Pierre never exploited his connections," I said. "You supported him in this."

"Pierre could be overly sincere."

Jeannette straightened the fingers on her gloves. "Don't speak ill of the dead. I wouldn't miss this funeral for anything. I'd come to see the hats alone."

I leaned back and looked out the window, cheered unaccountably. I congratulated myself on doing a fair job of living in my inner citadel.

The service was set for two p.m., and at ten past the hour, the widow had not yet arrived. In the front pew of the chapel, a majestic lady with a helmet of white hair whispered to the man beside her. A fresh-faced boy serving as usher shifted from foot to foot. I sat next to Jeannette.

A wave of relief passed over the congregation when, on the arm of her son (another physicist), Becquerel's petite widow entered the cool stone church in the largest hat I'd ever seen, its broad brim drooping like an enormous mushroom. She smiled radiantly, as if she were walking down the aisle to get married to the man in the coffin. The woman was in shock.

It had been three years since Pierre's coffin was lowered into his grave. If I could show a little strength, maybe it would help the widow; she would see that it could be all right.

Jeannette handed me a handkerchief. "Too soon," she whispered. "I don't care what my husband says, I'm sorry we brought you." She put her arm around me and squeezed, and I felt again for her that salt-of-the-earth connection.

Two rows down from me was the scientist-statesman Raymond Poincaré, whom some believed would be President of the Republic. Pierre would have abhorred being among so many people so conscious of their lineage, these holders of purses and grants, and military men, weighed down by Royal Medals. They would die too, with their bushy side whiskers and soup strainer mustaches. *All that you see will soon have vanished, and those who see it vanish will vanish themselves.*

At this very moment Hertha was at the House of Commons in London with a suffrage petition, trying to wrestle away some of this male power. She had also been in a procession to Albert Hall to promote the Conciliation Bill. Streams of women had filled the streets. Miss Sharp had told her of a bus driver who called out his window, "Oh, for God's sake give 'em the vote, but don't let 'em hold up the traffic!"

In the receiving line after the service, Madame Becquerel swayed, a little drunk with grief. She had a fine, thoughtful forehead, and under her mushroom hat, even in shock, she had an air of dignity and, it seemed, a sense of her own worth.

"Madame, I'm so sorry." I put my hand out, but she didn't take it.

Henriette Perrin, just behind me, waited.

Jean Becquerel stood beside his mother. I could see in his profile the lineaments of his father, and his father's cheeks, which, even at eighty, were smooth and childlike.

"Your father was lucky to have you at his side," I said to the younger Becquerel, and to his mother, "And you to have a fine son still at yours."

"I know I'm blunt," she said, "but I'm tired of scientists who pride themselves on being objective, when they can't see in front of their noses."

Henriette put her hand out. "My condolences, Madame Becquerel."

I said, "What am I not seeing?"

"Henri had burns like yours on his fingers, and on his chest. They wouldn't heal." She seized my wrist and held my hand in view. "Just look at your fingers. Look!"

Henriette whispered, "Move ahead."

Madame Becquerel said, "You're exhausted, anyone can see it. Just like Henri."

"But it wasn't—"

"I might not be a scientist, but I'm not an idiot either."

I tried to move down the line, but she had hold of my wrist.

"Why do you think your husband fell?"

I said coldly, "It was an accident."

"He'd been limping for months. He couldn't sleep because of leg pain. Neither could Henri, but he was blind like the rest of you."

I pulled my wrist away and went to join the mourners gathering on the sidewalk, but I heard her saying loudly, "He had burns on his chest, and on his fingertips, just like hers."

That night I dreamed of laboratory rats, dead in their boxes from breathing in radium. I tossed around in my bed until I realized that this wasn't a dream. It was a memory. Pierre had done an experiment. He had written it up and concluded that radium was toxic to the respiratory system.

He had sometimes been in agony in his last months, but he hadn't blamed radium, not about his legs. After the rat study, he'd written a paper about radium's health-giving properties. Thermal waters were healing because of radioactive content, he said.

I'm not an idiot either.

Of course radium had potential for harm and had to be handled with care, and we might have underestimated its toxicity. Both Pierre and I knew this. We had chosen not to dwell on it. How does science go on otherwise?

That night I continued to toss around in bed, anxious about an ache in my hip and a jittery feeling along my spine. More so, Madame Becquerel's words knifed into me—*you're exhausted, anyone can see it.* Others had heard. I felt ugly and exposed, not about effects of radium, but shamed about some lifeless part of me. I had sensed this part of myself for as long as I could remember, something numb and unfeeling at the core of me. *Madame Bissette's a widow, but she has some life in her,* Jeannette had said at l'Arcouëst. Had she seen into me and discovered something dead, at the very moment when I thought that I was stirring into life?

The next morning I went straight to André's office. As always, he wore his lab coat and a key around his neck, the key to the radium cupboard. He was on the new office telephone, but he put it down and waved me in.

I said, "Madame Becquerel believes that Pierre was poisoned by radium."

He shrugged. "The woman is in shock."

"Did Pierre ever say anything to you, suspecting radium?"

"Certainly not."

"Can we go over our safety precautions? I'd like to hear your recommendations."

He raised his eyebrows. "What a good idea."

He had been asking me to do this for months, and I had accused him of being fussy. I wasn't one to worry overmuch about laboratory dangers. I'd sacrificed so much for radium, it was by now a habit, and I suppose I'd taken on the braggadocio of my male colleagues. Pierre showing off the sores on his chest. Becquerel joking that he owed radium a grudge because of his sore fingers, but seeming delighted by this.

"It's always a better idea when it comes from you," André said.

"You're forbearing, André. You're a saint, and I should listen to you."

"Indeed, you should."

We agreed that wearing our long lab coats was de rigueur, to protect from spills and radioactive dust; I would stop setting a bad example by neglecting to don my own. We had coached the students to keep their small lead castles, containing radium, as far as possible across the table while still in reach, and we all used tongs to handle radioactive sources. Only André and I had the key to the cupboard shielded with lead bricks, on the far wall of the laboratory, opposite the big row of windows. André now urged me to move the cabinet to the cellar, but on this point I disagreed; it would be too inconvenient. But I did agree that all of the lab workers must get outside at midday for at least two hours, to get fresh air. No more lunches in the building.

I grew increasingly annoyed as I remembered the funeral, the way Madame Becquerel had called out after me. Would she have done that to a man? She was neither a scientist nor a doctor, and her husband had died of heart failure. Yet I began to imagine an alternate history, one that might have spared Pierre, in which I chose a different topic for my dissertation, not uranium rays. Pierre would have gone on with his crystals. Radium, this decade later, would still be undiscovered, because who else would have worked with such precision and against such odds, through years of debilitating labor?

In fact, I couldn't un-wish radium, nor everything Pierre and I had been through with each other, everything we'd felt and thought and accomplished, as dearly as I wanted him back.

One evening, sitting on a park bench while the girls played hopscotch, I recited to myself the ways that radium was doing good. It could go where X-rays couldn't, near the eye and in the throat. It could cure lupus, as it did for a little boy whose mother had written to thank me. Radioactive tampons had cured cervical cancer. And this was not to mention the advances in science—the transformation of our understanding of the structure of matter, still ongoing.

"Mé," called Eve from the playground. "I can do it better than Irène!"

It was time to put my worry away. We were taking precautions with radium, doing what we could.

That night I startled awake from another nightmare—another memory. My dead baby on the rocks of Arromanches.

The cooperative school was by this time a well-oiled machine. We met less often as a faculty, which made it easier to go many days without seeing Paul. When we met by chance on the train, he seemed nervous and rather flat, and I found myself concerned about him. Our friendship had kept him going as well as me. How was he really doing now?

One evening, I went over to the Perrins after dinner. The afternoon had been clear, and Henriette, pouring out cognac, said, "At least Paul had a good day for traveling."

"What traveling?" I said.

"Didn't you know? He's giving a talk in Lausanne. He's so charismatic, he's much in demand, of course. He took Madame Langevin with him. He promised to buy her Swiss lace." Henriette seemed amused by this. "Her mother has the children," she added.

I couldn't decide whether this news was tragic or hilarious, it cast such a light on my folly. Paul had his young and vigorous wife—his fancy for me was probably passing away already. Wasn't I four years his senior? And gangly in black wool, the widow of his friend, a woman to whom he was kind, and over whom he had briefly lost his head?

That night getting ready for bed, I brushed my hair a hundred times, the way my sister Helena taught me to do. I was unbuttoning my blouse when a yearning twisted through me. It was as if I were under water, deep in a river, and had used up all my breath, and I had to get to the surface. When I looked in the mirror, a woman looked back at me with wild eyes. For a frightening moment the mirror seemed to reflect itself, a thousand mirrors descending in a hall behind me, and in my head, the sound of thunder, the sucking sound of a roar.

I breathed. I got ready for bed.

Later, trying to sleep, I thought of my Uncle Henryk, how he had appeared at our door when I was six years old, in his big fur coat in a gust of snow, smelling of engine oil, when we'd all thought that he was dead. He told us that evening that he'd carried a torch for a woman from Warsaw, a woman named Magda, the entire time he was in Siberia. When manacles dug into his open sores, and the winter cold reached into his marrow, and bedbugs ate at him as surely as crows on a carcass, then his mind had called up an image of Magda Bluesky, with her hair loose, in a cream dress that dipped in front. His hunger for home, and his hunger for her, had kept him alive for nine years.

• • •

How much of life is chance? Are there patterns which, if we can see them early on, might warn us of what is to come? Are we humans made like crystals after all, with internal, ordered patterns of atoms, and particular ways of snapping new atoms into the same arrangement, again and again and again?

• • •

In early December, on her fifth birthday, Eve came down with a cold, a fever and a stuffy nose. I taught her to use her handkerchief, but she often missed the mark; she would sneeze, spray everyone around her, look around, then remember her handkerchief and hold it to her mouth, looking like a guilty little thing. Irène, twelve now, came down with it next, and then our housekeeper, then me. Our heads filled with mud; our limbs throbbed. I didn't mind the sickness. It was real, it mattered, and it fit with my grayness inside.

After exhausting himself being our physician, Dr. Curie himself took ill. As the rest of us began to mend, his cough settled into his chest. Each morning and evening he chewed three cloves of garlic for their medicinal properties. You could smell it from the entryway.

By January he was seriously ill. I went into Paris to keep up with my teaching, but otherwise, all I did was take care of my father-in-law. I brought him pastilles, illustrated newspapers, reviews. This was a month of driving rains, alternating with snow; the Seine filled with debris, murky and yellow and moving with massive force. I distracted my patient by telling him about the workers I had seen piling stone and sand along the quays to defend against the coming flood, and the boxes and barrels, tree trunks and trash cans crashing against the bridge posts. I sat and read to him as long as he would allow it. Our usual cook prepared meals for us, but I made the chicken broth for Dr. Curie the way my grandmother had, with a beef bone added. Sometimes he was unable to pick up the spoon. Then I would help, pretending almost not to notice.

How did you do it? I wrote to Hertha. I found myself thinking about all the people she had nursed, most recently her husband. No wonder she had little time for her research. Also she was hurting from two cracked ribs after being assaulted by a policeman in a suffrage demonstration. The officer had worn plain clothes—he was dressed like a ruffian—and had yanked back her hair until she thought her neck would break, and she lost consciousness. She must have fallen and been trampled in the crowd, because after, her breasts were black and blue. *I'm in an inward white rage*, she wrote. *We fight, waste our energies, and yet nothing has changed.*

Eve became obsessed with the Paris Zoo. Parts of Paris were three feet underwater, and we'd read in the newspapers about animals, hungry and confused, throwing themselves around in their cages. Photographs showed bears stranded on the highest part of their pit, and zookeepers in sea boots trying to capture crocodiles before they escaped into the river. "Why are you crying?" I asked Eve, when she was unable to put on her shoes. "For the bears," she said.

Pierre's father thrashed around in bed. "Did you wash these sheets in sand?" he would bark at me. I moved him to the drawing room so I could be on hand.

"Is it scratchy, Grandpére?" Irène pulled back his sheets and brushed off imaginary grit.

"Well that's better," he muttered. He allowed only her to console him.

"It's true what they say about physicians," I told him. "You're a terrible patient. An impossible invalid."

"You're poisoning me with that soup."

Irène said, "Grandpère, did you see the postal employees are striking again? They've thrown down the gauntlet. They say they have the same right to strike as workmen do against private employers."

"It's open revolt. Good for them."

"People are saying there will be another revolution."

"Don't you worry, my girl. The Republic is not in danger."

She had the knack of bringing her grandfather back to reality. When he moaned, she wiped his forehead with a cloth. Dark circles appeared under her eyes.

As he grew weaker, a sentence circled in my head: *We're dying in the wrong order.* If he died now, I wouldn't be next in the family plot; I wouldn't lie on top of Pierre. I could go on nursing my father-in-law, and happily. I could wash and fold his clothes, mash up garlic, and spoon him his soup forever. What I couldn't do was bury him on top of Pierre.

Jacques and his family came from Montpellier to spend a few days. I got people to fill in for my classes and spent most of my time at the sickbed. Eve sat in a corner with her doll, looking at picture books. She didn't remember her father. In the years to come, she would forget her grandfather, too.

I wondered if I should contact Paul. He and Dr. Curie had argued and laughed together. Both of them had loved Pierre.

One night, I heard my father-in-law getting up out of bed, and I went to see if he needed help getting to the toilet. I found him standing at the window, the drapes pulled aside, looking out at the moon. I stayed in the doorway as he drank it in, his face raised to the sky. What was he thinking of, or remembering? His back was straight, as if he had recovered his strength. Rumpled pajamas. Bright white hair.

He must have sensed me behind him. "It's perfect," he said.

I came to see. It was less than half a moon, a glowing crescent, but its shadow side was lit by earthshine, so that the whole of it was visible, the old moon in the new moon's arms.

He turned to me with gentle eyes. "I'm not afraid. It's really very easy, Marie."

I helped him back to bed and pulled the sheet up over his shoulders. He raised his hand to cup my cheek. "My daughter," he said.

He fell asleep, and his breath was smooth and even.

I wrote to Paul to tell him that Dr. Curie would die within a day or two. He appeared at my door within hours, a silhouette against a sheet of snow. When he stepped inside, the fragrance of cold fell out of his overcoat.

I led him to the drawing room, where I had lit a lamp. It shone on Dr. Curie's face. His breaths were shallow and far between. I saw Paul taking in the room, the sofa where I had been sleeping, my robe folded onto a pillow. The brass bucket beside the fireplace, and burning coal.

"Is it very hard?" he asked.

That morning I had changed my patient's soiled bedclothes, and when I made up his bed, disturbing him as little as I could, I had used my finest linen. I had plumped his pillow and combed his hair and oiled his dry skin.

"It's beautiful."

Dr. Curie's forehead seemed to glow, and around his mouth was an air of expectation.

Paul put his hand on the back of my neck. Even before he touched me, our closeness had been tangible. Our hesitation during these last weeks was the stuff of silliness now. The coal in the fireplace warmed my arm and the right side of my face. We had been close, the two of us, on other such occasions—after my miscarriage, and at Rue Cuvier, when we had held each other after Pierre's death. Now death approached again, but gently.

"What is it?" Paul's eyes rested on my face.

"I'm grateful for the chance to nurse him."

"Yes, thank God." He knew I meant that I could nurse him as I hadn't Pierre.

Outside a horse whinnied and clopped down the street. Through the window, a gust of snow in the branches of the elm. We had stood just there, Dr. Curie and I, the night he showed me the moon.

His eyelids fluttered. His breath rattled faintly and smoothed again. The old clock ticked on the sideboard. The room smelled of smoke and nutmeg oil.

Something would change, I could feel it. Something was about to change.

He died on 25 February 1910, Eugene Curie, a physician like his father before him. It happened in the early morning. I was asleep on the sofa, and I woke to the surprising whoosh of a deep inbreath, and then a long, loud sigh. This was his last breath. I sat beside him as light came softly into the drawing room. At seven o'clock, I woke the girls, and I brought them to him. Together we raised the sheet over his head, and then I called the morgue.

His obituary spoke of his commitment to radical equality and how he'd lived by his principles, treating people ill with typhoid when other doctors had deserted the infested neighborhoods. I loved him for all that he was, his sharpness and simplicity, and how he raised his sons to think for themselves. He had gone on gardening when the worst had happened. He had gotten up each morning to care for his grandchildren, and he had freely loved me as a daughter and a human being. He had never questioned my choices, never asked me to be anything other than myself.

After his body was taken away, I went to see the people at the cemetery. In a way I was at peace, but underneath, another kind of current flowed: one of determination to have things go my way.

The funeral director was a sallow-skinned man who lived at the desk in the back of his shop. "The soil's near froze, like I've never seen it," he said. His walls were covered with death notices, and a display of coffin hardware.

"Because of the flood?"

"Even gravediggers got to sleep a few hours."

What was I trying to prove? For nearly four years I'd imagined my resting place above my husband. It was as if, in death, I expected to be made whole, the way I'd felt sometimes in life, when I had lain next to Pierre. The rational me could have made an argument against it, but it didn't change the fact that I wanted my bones to lie above my husband's bones.

"Monsieur Basset, haven't you someone extra, someone you can call in?"

He eyed me warily.

"I'm sure you can find a way."

And so, Pierre's coffin was lifted out of the spot where it had settled for four long years and placed in amongst some evergreens, at a discreet distance from the grave, under a new cloth.

At Grandpère's burial, we gathered around as his casket was lowered into its rightful spot, above his wife, Sophie, under the chestnut tree that was now like a member of our family. After the service, and after everyone had left, eight men in blue overalls would carry Pierre over and shimmy his coffin back down. For Dr. Curie I had brought a basket of chrysanthemum blossoms, but for Pierre, mimosa branches, covered in bright blossoms, yellow as the sun.

I was glad my brother Józef wasn't there; he would have chastised me. "It's too much, Maria," he would have said, as he did when I made him open up my father's casket.

"Help me scatter the blossoms," I said to the girls, after the burial words were spoken. Eve tossed hers from a distance, and they fell short. Her older cousin Maurice, the son of Jacques, picked them up for her to try again.

I held the basket as the others filed by: Uncle Jacques, his wife and Maurice, the Perrins, the Langevins, André, some older friends of Dr. Curie, including Henri Brisson, former president of France, who had been his classmate—they had, in recent years, played chess together—and patients from days of old, and local socialists whom Dr. Curie had supported. Big hands and small, rough and delicate, reaching for a fistful of red.

When it was done, and most everyone had left, Jacques offered me his arm. He'd planned a luncheon for us.

I told him I wanted to stay and asked him to take the girls.

Jacques was physically very like Pierre, only with a cannier look. "You should come with us," he said. When I refused, he walked away with his wife and the children.

Perrin and Paul came toward me, and I braced myself. Their wives were watching. The men in blue overalls were going for Pierre's coffin.

Paul said, "You should come with us, Marie."

"I'm going to bury my husband." And then again, "I need to bury Pierre."

Through his ears, and in the mirror of his eyes, I recognized what I hadn't yet seen: I truly was burying Pierre. I was saying goodbye to our life together, and at the same time I was proving to myself that no matter what came next—whatever adventure, whatever future love—Pierre was first and last, and nothing could change that fact.

I was doing what I had to do to free myself.

c/o the Zorawski family
Szczuki
10 December 1887

Klaudia, my dear friend,

Don't believe the report of my approaching marriage; it isn't true. This story has been spread about the countryside and even in Warsaw. Though it's not my fault, I'm afraid it may bring me trouble. My plans for the future are modest indeed: I would like a corner of my own where I can live with my father. The poor man misses me a lot. He would like to have me at home, he longs for me! To get my independence again, and a place to live, I would give half my life. On the other hand my heart breaks when I think of wasting my abilities, which must be worth something, anyhow.

With all my duties as governess, I am busy from eight until half-past seven without a moment's rest. At nine in the evening I take my books and get to work. At the moment I am reading:

Daniel's *Physics* (I have finished the first volume)
Spencer's *Sociology*, in French
Paul Berts' *Lessons on Anatomy and Physiology*, in Russian

Dear Klaudia, don't judge too harshly the backward spirit of the town where you now live. Social and political conservatism usually comes from religious conservatism, and the latter is a happiness, even though, for you and me, it has become incomprehensible. So far as I'm concerned, I should never voluntarily contribute to anybody's loss of faith. Let everybody keep their own faith, so long as it's sincere. Only hypocrisy irritates me, and it is as widespread as true faith is rare.

Your loving friend,

Manya

X

Paris, Spring 1910

A week after Dr. Curie's burial, Jeannette wrote asking me to come and see her in Fontenay-aux-Roses. What did she want? To pry into what had happened at Dr. Curie's funeral? To ask outright about my relationship with Paul?

Her note was delivered to my house when my mind was on other matters. At rue Cuvier, after three years of preparation, we were ready to produce radium metal. We had arrived at all the parameters in the process of electrolysis: the right voltage, the amperage, a mercury cathode, and an anode of platinum iridium. Our skills were honed. We were expert at producing an amalgam which, when put through the distillation process, yielded a few granules of pure barium metal. Within the week, we would risk it with radium, the real thing.

Since my father-in-law's funeral, I had been riding on a new wave of energy. I didn't know where it would take me, nor did I need to know. I had come out of the sickroom and was done as well with all my second-guessing of my own intentions. It was the same in my attitude toward Paul. I knew what I felt toward him, and I thought I knew what he felt toward me. I had to live day by day, and I found that I could do it.

I would have rather put my arm out to be stung by bees than visit Jeannette Langevin. There was a note of urgency in her letter which made me especially wary, though it was like her to be impatient even about trivial things. In the end, to keep on good terms, I wrote back that I would come that afternoon. First, I had breakfast with the children and took the train to Paris.

I got off as usual at the Gare de Luxembourg. It hadn't been long since I had emerged from the months of Dr. Curie's illness, and my legs were charged with the energy of being free. The Latin Quarter was recovering from the flood. People covered their noses with handkerchiefs as they walked by mounds of rubbish where workers were cleaning up. Few shops had electricity, yet they were open. A gallery owner had set up on the sidewalk, selling ruined paintings for charity. I felt a surge of pride. Though my French Pierre was gone, I was feeling more French.

At rue Cuvier, the radiators smelled of disinfectant, and there were faint water marks along the lower walls, but we were back in operation.

"When shall we do the electrolysis?" André asked. "A week from Thursday?" We sat at his desk making a list of preparations.

"A week from Thursday," I agreed. If we succeeded in procuring a radium amalgam, we would plan the distillation for the following day.

At lunchtime, the rooms emptied out as per our safety instructions. André and I took a tour around the laboratory, surveying the stations. One of the new students had forgotten to seal flammable materials, and his bucket of sand for extinguishing a fire was near an aisle, where it could be kicked over. André agreed to put him through the training again.

Early afternoon, I rang the bell at the Langevin house. Within another hour, I assured myself, I'd be outside again.

The door opened instantly: the maid, Babette, with Jeannette behind her. Jeannette's brow was tight. Her eyes were precarious, unsteady.

"Hélà is well?" I asked.

"She's a screamer, that one." She led me into the drawing room and tapped her foot while Babette poured coffee. "I can be frank with you, can't I?"

I was wary, but I said, "Of course."

"It's Paul. He won't listen to me. He says I don't respect him. And he's too harsh."

I didn't want to hear anything but good about Paul, especially from his wife. "He's harsh with you?"

"And the children."

I knew that Jeannette could be harsh, but Paul? At l'Arcouëst, the worst I had seen was a sardonic edge toward Jeannette. "I know he can be moody," I said, "but also generous."

"Oh, generous! To everyone but his family. You know when that school of his flooded, at Sèvres, he wanted to bring home two of the girls. Here! To live with us! 'Don't you feel bad for them?' he asks. As if it's my job to take in every stray. 'They lost their mattresses,' he says. Their mattresses! Two nubile girls under my roof. I wasn't born yesterday."

Why was I there? I didn't know, but the conversation went on this way, with Jeannette abruptly shifting topics, jumping from the rooster to the donkey. She herself was impossible, she said: she was a bottomless abyss. She made Paul tell her that he loved her a dozen times a day. It was no wonder he grew frustrated. "I'm not saying anything against him," she added.

"Of course not, Jeannette."

She let out an ugly laugh, and I wondered briefly if she'd been drinking. "I'm a person who's honest. I'm not like fancy people who hide everything. With me, you know where you stand."

I flushed. I, of course, was holding back. Of course she didn't know where I stood.

She shook her head woefully. "No wonder he loses his temper."

I knew I was taking her bait, but after a while I said, "He loses his temper?"

"I'm not saying anything against him."

I wanted to snap off her head. She claimed to be transparent, but here she was making vague hints and swinging between blaming herself and blaming Paul. I took in her pinched brow and the shadows around her eyes. She wasn't making this up—she was weary and miserable. For whatever reason, she had reached out to me. My shell of protection softened. I began to feel for her.

"If he understood you and was gentle, maybe you wouldn't doubt yourself so much."

"Do you think so?" She looked at me with yearning.

"You don't deserve to be treated harshly, even if you sometimes . . ."

She stood up and paced. "You know I told you about the fruit compote?"

"A compote?"

"On the train, I told you. He slapped me."

"He slapped you?"

"Babette made a mess of the fruit compote, and he blamed me."

As if unconsciously, she pushed up one sleeve of her blouse revealing, on the inside of her wrist, a spreading bruise in the shape of a hand.

For me, everything changed in that moment. Before my friendship with Paul, it was as if I had been stranded on an island; all around me, nothing but the roar of the sea. Then one day I looked out at the horizon and saw a ship—it was heading my way! Now, suddenly, the ship changed course. It wasn't coming for me.

But there was only this bruise. In fact I had no evidence.

Jeannette took my dry hands in her moist ones. "Could you speak to him? For the children's sake. He would listen to you. Ask him not to be so harsh."

I wanted to push her away, her smell, her touch, but she looked at me beseechingly. How could I not help? "I'll try," I said, "but I don't know if he'll listen."

There was a spring in her step as she saw me to the door. Was it relief on her face, or triumph?

Gauthiers-Villars wanted the page proofs of my *Treatise* by the end of the week. I put up a sign on my office door at rue Cuvier so no one would interrupt, so I could make corrections, but my mind buzzed. Had I ignored in Paul what I didn't want to see?

Only once had I seen him in a rage, and that was when the courts, in their scheming, leached the dignity out of Alfred Dreyfus, forcing him to choose between a guilty verdict with a pardon, or returning to the penal colony. Paul had appeared at our door in a fury so fine that the air around him sizzled.

Wasn't this the Paul I knew?

He'd told me he was impetuous. That day in the classroom at the EPCI, when we planned the children's curriculum, he had seized me hard by the wrists. Too hard? He'd once quoted Bertrand Russell, "Life is passion and rage, and only intellect keeps us sane."

I flipped through the proofs, barely concentrating. When I confronted Paul, would he be angry with me for interfering, or, worse, would he lie? The prospect sickened me. Surely, he would never strike me, or bruise my arm.

Many men did hit their wives.

All my life I had believed that if I made the right choices, I would never have to be frightened of a man.

A flicker of a thought: *I could be free of him.*

I had finally immersed myself in the *Treatise* when I heard something in the hallway. Someone rapped at my door, in spite of the sign to deter them.

It was Paul. My stomach lurched.

He poked his head through the door in that way that was becoming familiar. "Have you threatened them all with lashes? It's quiet as a nunnery." He saw me, and his face changed. "What's wrong?"

"What are you doing in this neighborhood?"

"You're just about there, aren't you? I've come to share the excitement."

"We'll do the distillation next Friday if we get the amalgam."

"Show me?"

We both reached for lab coats, and our hands brushed—a thrill went through me. I felt like a traitor. To Jeannette. To my sex.

I led him through the stations. Agata, my new student, had wired her electrometer and was practicing her technique. She gave him a huge smile. She was a pretty girl, Agata. Paper-white skin and lips like a child's, red, as if stained by berries. I saw Paul appreciating her.

"Are you getting reproducible results?" he asked.

"I try to keep everything still," she said, "but when I place a charge on the electrometer, it jiggles, or the reading is off scale, or the light moves off the screen."

"It may be in your breath," Paul said.

"That's what Madame tells me."

In spite of myself I was eager to show Paul the decomposition cell, which we had made from a test tube by softening its bottom with a blowtorch. Then I had pushed a platinum wire through it, projecting 0.5 cm into the tube; I'd flattened the bottom on an asbestos plate and allowed it to cool very slowly, to toughen the glass. I watched Paul as he leaned closer, the calm surrounding him, the calm of a scientist who knows that even the smallest inner agitation can disturb an experiment.

This, I thought, was what Agata was trying to learn.

This man, a brute to his wife?

"Do you have trouble with the amalgam adhering to the sides of the cell?"

"At first we did. Now we wash the mercury twice with alcohol, and twice with diethyl ether, and when we can't smell the ether anymore, we put it in the desiccator until we weigh it. Then it doesn't adhere."

"Will you distill the radium amalgam like the barium?"

"The temperatures are too hot. We'll use a quartz tube and put the iron boat inside it, and heat it in an atmosphere of hydrogen."

"That could be a fine explosion! May I come?"

"If you bring your goggles!"

I had promised Jeannette to talk to him, that was all.

I unlocked the lead case in the back of the lab and retrieved the tiny iron boat where we stored the barium metal, the metal we practiced with, to show Paul the silvery white granules, a bit like table salt. Then he wanted to see my *Treatise on Radioactivity*. I was touched as he sat at the edge of my desk, skimming the introduction, flipping through sections as the noon hour chimed—two volumes of synthesis of current research. Outside my office, the laboratory emptied out.

"It's irrefutable," said Paul. "Are you pleased?"

"Satisfied, not pleased."

"You've spent a lot of time defending your kingdom. You must be ready to move on."

He felt he had a right to say these words. Yes, I had been fending off my enemies. Yes, oh yes, I was ready to move on.

I had the impulse to go to the sink and spit in it, and wash my face, pretend I'd never seen Jeannette, but I girded myself and said, "I have a difficult topic to broach. In friendship. I had coffee with your wife. She asked me to speak with you."

He raised his eyebrows. "What's she playing at?"

"Do you think you might be too harsh with her, and the children?"

He grasped his head in both hands. "Will the evil of that woman see no end?"

"She's suffering, Paul. I think she's being sincere."

"Christ. You fell for that."

My hands trembled. "I won't answer your sarcasm."

"You reproach me when you know nothing. If you had to spend one day in my shoes, one night, you'd be lobbying for me to get the goddamn Nobel Peace Prize. And she knows I can say nothing."

"But why can't you say anything? She asked me to talk to you."

"I know it's quaint, but I do have some chivalry."

"You leave me to imagine some horrible crime on the part of your wife. I don't call that chivalry."

"Jeannette plays the subservient wife, but she undermines me at every turn. I will spare you the details."

I thought of the bruise on her wrist. Ugly, purple. "She feels . . . powerless."

"She's insolent."

I had been feeling foolish—why had I believed Jeannette, when all along I felt she had been managing me?—but now I was angry. I took my green wool coat from its hook, put it on and buttoned it up. "A child is insolent. A subordinate is insolent. Jeannette is not a child."

He said, "Don't go, please. I'll tell you what you want to know."

I stopped. Did I? Did I want to know?

"It's worse than you think. The children, they—they see their father degraded." He held his head as if his brains might burst from his skull.

I leaned against the wall with an old, helpless feeling, and a countering frustration. "Why do you put up with it, Paul?"

"I have no recourse."

"How can you say that?"

"I don't trust her, Marie. I don't know what she'd do."

I said, uncertainly, "There was a bruise on her wrist."

Paul was quiet a moment, and then he said, "You think I would hurt her on purpose?"

"I . . . I don't know. Perhaps in the heat of an argument. In self-defense."

"She was coming at me like a maniac. I gripped her arm."

"Awfully hard."

"I won't try to convince you."

"Paul, I—She said you slapped her about the compote."

"I slapped her once. It wasn't about the damn compote. Marie, I'm not proud of the kind of husband I've been, but I'm not what she says."

I went to the window and stared out. I thought I believed him. I wanted to. It was all so murky and difficult. I hated it, that he had slapped Jeannette, and I had slapped my daughter. Many parents hit their children and believed it was right, but I did blame myself. I couldn't find clear ground. An image of Jeannette rumbled around in me. *I'm a person who's honest. . . . He would listen to you.* I saw her as if in a pit, clawing her way to safety. Had she been driven mad by suspicion about Paul and me? If she lost him, what options did she have?

"I don't understand why she brought me into this."

"We fight, and she feels wronged. She wants an ally. It's not all her fault."

"But it's terrible, Paul. Terrible for everyone. For you."

I heard Paul sigh, and I sensed his relief. One bit of sympathy was all it took. He had been so alone.

The muscles softened in his face as he looked up at me. "I have nowhere to turn. Only the children, and they're too small."

"I'm sorry I haven't known. I haven't been a good friend."

His eyes moistened. "Your sadness, your grief. You've been a sanctuary. Because what you feel is honest."

I wanted to go to him. Overwhelmingly, I wanted to go to him.

"I'm ashamed, Marie."

"Of what?"

"Of needing love. Of needing it from you."

He sat on the edge of my desk in a band of sun, coming through the window. It seemed as if I could see his human heart. Tender, stupid. Beyond stupidity.

"I've tried to stop wanting you," he said.

I had the sensation of falling through the sky, but Paul was there, sitting on my desk in that stream of sun, particles of dust scattering the light. I went and stood before him, inches from his face. Pale scar across his forehead, light on his neck. His smell of shoe polish and pine tar soap.

He took the lapel of my coat between his fingers, examining its texture, studying the green wool, rubbing in a circular motion. Slowly, he undid the button at my collarbone, holding the fabric with his left hand, and with his right thumb and index finger, pressing the side of the button and passing it through the buttonhole. Next he unfastened the button below it, over my chest, and then the button after that. Slowly, with precision, he proceeded all the way down, pinching each button and passing it through its buttonhole. When I was all the way unbuttoned, he stood up. He slipped the coat from my shoulders, and let it fall.

After Paul left, I took a walk through the Jardin des Plantes. Two men raked the edges of the path, preparing the soil for planting. At the Fontaine aux Lions, a little boy lingered with a toy sailboat, ready to launch it as soon as his mother turned her head.

My breath was freer, filling up the backs of my lungs. It was as if I had been on a journey outside of my life, and now I had returned to my body. At the same time, an unexpected world, the world to come, pulsed red on the borders of my vision.

Paul and I didn't see each other for a week, but we sent notes when we were in the city, sometimes by messenger, sometimes by pneumatic post. We said nothing explicit about our new relationship—just little nothings of exchange: where we were, what we ate, funny things that people said. This brought me joy. Underneath was a pitching deck on a tumultuous sea. I tried to walk on it.

I wrote to Jeannette that I'd done my best. Paul reported that he had been both miffed and conciliatory with her, while she had been haughty. He took her out to dinner at a nice restaurant, and this seemed to calm the waters.

One afternoon, on my way from the train to the Sorbonne, overcome by a yearning for newness, for the crisp, scratchy feel of new cloth against my skin, I found myself stepping into a dressmaker's shop that I had passed many times without ever imagining walking through its doors. I had two serviceable dresses, one black, and one with fine gray stripes, both suitable in the laboratory and, with a necklace, on any other occasion. My sisters had made sure they were well cut (they didn't trust me in this), and I mended them myself.

"A special occasion?" the dressmaker asked.

"No. I mean, yes. Something for evenings in spring and summer."

Naturally I went to the blacks.

The dressmaker, Madame Mercier, clucked her tongue. "Black is for funerals. You're still young, Madame. You need something to bring out the color in your cheeks." She led me to racks of tender green and peach. Surely I was not in my right mind, shopping in the middle of the day, and without my sisters.

Madame Mercier saw that I was at risk of flight. She took my arm and walked me to the back corner, saying, "You need something fresh but strong." She pulled out a bolt of lovely white fabric. "Beautiful." She unrolled the bolt enough to drape it over my shoulders and led me to a mirror. "Do you see? You have some pink in your cheeks after all. Madame shouldn't hide it. You're from Poland?"

"How did you know?" I hadn't thought she would be one to pay attention to the Nobel hoopla.

"My son's wife. She talks like you, soft r's. The Polish girls, they're pretty but shy with their looks. My son took a mistress and I told Lena—that's his wife—you have to try a little harder. What do you expect, you go around like a poor little mouse? A man likes a woman with a little oomph. This dress will become you, Madame. And then you need new shoes, little white ones. And a visit to the coiffure."

Pencil in mouth, she wrapped a tape measure around my bosom, then my waist and my hips, and marked down the numbers. "It's a fine thing," she said, "to be in love."

On Thursday morning, the day of the electrolysis, I left my wedding ring on my bureau. If the mercury spilled, if it touched gold, the metals would amalgamate. The damage to the ring couldn't be reversed.

Of course, if the mercury spilled, I'd have more urgent things to worry about. For one, losing our precious radium sample.

That morning André and I procured, at last, an amalgam of radium and mercury large enough to distill—a few drops of radium bromide solution in ten grams of mercury—but to our astonishment, it didn't produce crystals like the barium amalgam. It was liquid, entirely liquid. We transferred it quickly to its iron boat, big as the littlest segment of my thumb, which we'd kept in an atmosphere of pure hydrogen. We placed this boat in a quartz tube, and I sucked the oxygen out of it. We didn't dare store it. It was too reactive. We had to separate out the mercury. We had to distill it right away.

I sent a note to Paul, inviting him to join us. André and I canceled our afternoon plans.

After the midday break, we got to work. We had placed the tubing in the furnace when Paul arrived, bringing in the wind and a scattering of blossoms on his jacket.

"Hello!" I said.

"Am I in time for the explosion?"

André looked back and forth between the two of us. He said, "Let's get you a rubberized apron."

Paul said, "Shouldn't you have a container around that tube?" He was worried about the mercury vapor.

"The tube won't fail," I said.

André had asked the same thing, but the quartz was safe at tremendous temperatures, and I needed to see the tube from both sides. Would Pierre have sacrificed an unobstructed view for added safety? Would Rutherford?

"No cigarettes," Paul declared to the little group of onlookers, as if they would be so stupid. Jean Danysz was there—he had prepared the hydrogen for us—and Agata, and a couple of other scholars, one of them Paul's student. They chatted in the background, but when André took the tubing out of the oven, everyone hushed. He passed the tubing through the sintered joints of our apparatus and connected it to the hydrogen tank.

"You ready?" he asked.

"Ready."

He opened the white clip to release the hydrogen, and I monitored the pressure, which needed to exceed the pressure of the vapor of mercury at the temperature of the iron boat. I watched a thermo-electric couple, one of its junctions inserted in the iron wall of the cup.

We fired up the gas burners. The hottest part of the flame, clear blue, allowed us to observe the contents of the boat. As the temperature rose—to 200° C, 300° C—the amalgam remained in its liquid form. Finally, at 400°, it became solid! But as the temperature continued to climb, it melted and gave off mercury vapor. André and I looked at each other nervously. When we reached 700°—the fusing point—there was still no distillation of mercury, and no condensation on the tube.

But look again! The vapor was attacking the quartz tube. Without a word I turned off the burners and André the hydrogen.

Inside the iron boat: a brilliant white metal, the size of a pea.

After the radium metal—black now, having been exposed to air—was sealed in a vacuum tube and locked into our lead cabinet, after the apparatus was washed and put away and all the aprons were hung up, Paul produced a bottle of champagne on ice which he had brought with him and stashed.

I put my arm around André. "I'm so proud."

He gave me a squeeze and said, "Bring in the people from the street!"

Paul poured the bubbles into glasses and flasks he'd collected from around the lab, and we were a jolly group. André for once was completely relaxed, no twitch of the mouth, no hawk eye over the place. Agata, odd but beautiful, her eyes so glad—she had succeeded in replicating her research results, so we would not have to send her home. Paul poured out more champagne, but I was already giddy. The nonsensical challenge to radium was behind me, the facts established. More research questions, brighter ones, lay ahead. Already, in my mind, I was planning a trip to Leiden to collaborate with a colleague.

Paul's eyes rested on my face. "Congratulations, Marie."

Later he would tell me that as I had been watching the tube that afternoon, he had been watching me. That the joy that came over my face was a state change as extraordinary as any going on in our experiment and as marvelous to watch. That when he saw it happening, he wanted to bring it about himself, with his own hands, to watch my face transform, because of what he was doing.

Warsaw
31 January 1892

Manya, my daughter,

Bronia tells me that you are looking well and the laborious life you lead in Paris doesn't tire you. I am glad the pressing iron for Bronia is all right. I didn't know who to get to make the purchase. Even though it was in the feminine domain, I had to take care of it myself.

Your last letter saddened me. I deplore your taking such an active part in the organization of these theatrics, these tableaux vivants. Even though this is done in innocence, it attracts attention. There are people in Paris who inspect your behavior, who record names. Those who wish to earn their bread in Warsaw will find it in their interest to keep quiet and remain unknown. Events such as concerts and balls are described in newspapers here, by correspondents who list names. It would be a great grief to me if your name were mentioned one day, or an indiscretion made it difficult for you to come back home to me.

Your concerned father

XI

Paris, Spring–Summer 1910

IF THERE IS AN allotment of joy in a person's life, mine, since Pierre's death, had been stored in another place like grain in a silo, locked up and out of my reach. Now, suddenly, the hinged door opened and the golden wheat came blowing through—it was boundless, it deranged me, I was jubilant and rich. The wheat distilled, and Paul and I were drunk with love. It would have felt like blasphemy to reason it out; it was truer than right and wrong. Our love was a blissful calamity, and we ran into it.

Paul found an apartment on the fifth story of a building on rue du Banquier in the Latin quarter, and there, for two hours at each midday, we made love to each other. The sweetness was intensely painful, like warming up flesh after frostbite. I held Paul's head in my hands; I searched his eyes; with my finger I stroked the curves of his ears, the runnels between the tendons of his neck. I kissed his hairline where the smell of him was stronger. I started at the cleft of his collarbone and kissed straight down his middle until he couldn't stand it anymore and took my head between his hands and pushed me down down down, and the force of his need sent through me a delirious blade of desire.

The world, of course, wanted to reclaim us, but in these sweet weeks, or however long it was, the requirements of life were a backdrop to our love. We performed our research duties twice as well with a fraction of the care. I felt calm before my lectures;

why would I be frightened of that meadow of faces opening like flowers? The students' eagerness surprised me. I no longer tried to earn their respect, yet they were rapt; they blushed when I stood near them. One young man came daily to my office to talk about his research and tell me about his life. He hovered behind me as I wrote a note for him. I could swear he was flirting with me.

In the laboratory, work hummed along. We'd had our success with radium and now, we all felt it, we were launching a new era, rich in ideas, experiments, and energy. We were becoming a place that future scientists would look back on and say, *rue Cuvier, that's where we made some leaps*. André worked out how to obtain a source of pure beta particles, not contaminated by other forms of radiation. With Agata, I was studying their absorption. With the physicist Heiki Kamerlingh Onnes in Leiden, I was setting out to show that radioactivity doesn't conform to known controllable forces. That spring I was awarded five honorary titles from European universities and a medal from the Royal Society of Arts in London.

I felt that something was amiss with André, and I could guess what it was. One morning, after pushing open the heavy wood and glass door, I went to his office to see if I could make things right. My passion with Paul had changed me; the honest expression of emotion seemed essential. I regretted having pretended that I didn't know how André cared for me. I found him locking his notebooks into a file drawer. Years ago, someone had stolen information from his notebooks and published it, and he wasn't going to let that happen again. It was a Thursday and so, as always in a Parisian gentleman's world, his shirt was newly pressed.

"Good morning, Marie," he said with his usual kindness, and as usual, he didn't quite meet my eyes. I wondered, was he embarrassed? Did he ever cringe about that afternoon when he'd overheard my argument with Paul, when I'd opened the door to find him loitering in the hallway, red-faced? I had never thought to ease his mind, to tell him that I knew that he was only protecting me. He never made me feel that I owed him anything, although, in fact, I did.

I closed the door behind me. "Don't think I don't notice all you do for me, André. I wouldn't have made it through these years without you."

"Are you going somewhere?"

"I'm thanking you."

"I'm always glad to help. I consider it part of my job."

"Ouch."

He blushed.

I began to laugh, but with an open heart, and I thought that André felt it, because his face relaxed, and he smiled.

"You're the best there is," I said. "And your company—even when you're across the way, talking on the phone or working with a student, I always know we're on the same team, and that you'd do anything for me and the girls."

"It's true, I would." Our gazes actually met. All this time, I realized, over these last years, he might have looked me in the eyes, if I had been more willing.

"I'm sorry it hasn't worked out as you—" I had been going to say, "as you might have wished."

"In a perfect world," he said, "I would have married you."

I bowed my head. I had been seeing this man in caricature, as less than he was. I hadn't given him my full attention. When he had joined forces with Pierre and me, he had set aside his own trajectory. What had he wanted for himself? Did he mind being alone? I'd seen a photo of him as a younger man, with a headful of hair, a curl over his temple, playful, looking at someone—who? A woman? What would he look like if he were loved, truly loved?

"I'm glad we can be close," I said, "even though it isn't the way you wanted."

"Oh, that's me. My brother always said, *André will be busy dotting his i's and crossing his t's and miss—*" His voice trailed off. "I don't mind, really."

Another gift from a gracious man.

"On the other hand," he said, "I can't not be a lion on your behalf, so don't let anyone take advantage of you."

"Understood." I opened the door of his office, and we walked out together.

He said, "What are we up to next?"

The strain of my life simply eased. I might have imagined that love given and received in secret, in a seedy apartment on rue du Banquier, would be a thing unto itself, sealed off from real life. I should have known, because I'd experienced it before, that the flow of love is never a closed circuit. It always radiates out.

My daughters warmed to me, and this broke my heart a little. They had needed more tenderness. Irène, normally so demanding, relented some, and was less apt to torment her sister. She had her usual classes with Paul, but he and I avoided being together with the children, who were apt to notice the invisible threads between us.

At home, I sat next to Eve at the piano while she played "La Marseillaise" and "il pleut, il pleut bergère," with lovely plump arms, her tongue on her upper lip, her shy fingers somersaulting over each other. This reminded me of sitting on a hassock as a child as my mother played, watching the feeling move over her face. In my own small body a hum of longing would grow so intense that my frame couldn't bear it, and I would run from the room and cry. "What is it, Manyusa?" my mother would say. I didn't know how to answer.

I began to believe that Eve's musical gift was something special. A child of five would not normally be able to play like that. I wrote to Jan Paderewski and asked him to assess her talent, reminding him of those days at Bronia's when we Poles gathered together. On a morning in May, Eve and I took the train to rue d'Allemagne in Little Poland, where he still lived. At his door we heard a flourish of notes and color. Was it Liszt?

"Mé, wait," said Eve, tugging my hand before I could ring the bell. Was she frightened? Or did she know already the joy of playing uninterrupted, in one's own musical world, and did not want to intrude? We stood together listening. Paderewski played as if the beauty and meaning of each note made it unbearable to leave it and move on.

He still wore his fiery hair pushed back. The crease between his eyebrows, which formerly came and went, now was permanently etched. The Bechstein in his drawing room was inlaid with mahogany, ash, and walnut. Eve approached it courageously and played "La Marseillaise" and a Clementi sonatina. Paderewski listened gravely. When she was done, he turned to me. "She has exceptional ability."

I suspected this, but I was moved to hear these words from the mouth of a great musician.

"Your mother was a fine pianist," he said.

"You heard her play?"

"My sister was her student at the Freta Street School."

"My grandmother?" said Eve. She came and stood by my side.

"She favored Chopin," I said. "She was a patriot."

"If times had been different," said Paderewski, "she might have been a great musician."

In the bus on our way home, Eve wanted to know about her grandmother. Had she really played so well? What had she played besides Chopin? Had I taken lessons myself?

"My mother taught me to play, but I had only a small gift," I told her. "Not like yours."

"Did you practice?"

"When your grandmother went away to the Alps, when she was sick, I practiced twice a day, to make a present for her when she returned."

"How old were you then?"

"Just a little older than you."

"Was she happy when she got back?"

"I think so." She had been weak—no kisses, but she gave me a faint smile. There was something in her nature that caused her to hold back from physical affection, though this wasn't uncommon in Poland, between children and their parents. Zosia, anyway, covered me with kisses.

"Where is her piano?" asked Eve.

"When she died, we had to sell it."

"Were you very sad?"

"I had stopped playing it by then."

"I mean, when your mama died."

"Oh. Our family didn't talk about it." I gazed out the window, remembering, and when I looked back at Eve, there was anxiety behind her eyes, as if I'd gone away from her again. I had held back so much, for so long.

I took her hand. "Yes, darling, I was very sad. Even now I can hardly bear to listen to Chopin."

I brought fresh flowers every Monday to the place that Paul and I shared, first daffodils and tulips and branches of lilacs, and then all kinds of lilies. We made varieties of love—vigorous, languid, adventurous, funny. We drank cognac and ate lunch, shared stories about our children and our work. Paul got it into his head to encourage me to put my hat in for the Academy of Science the next time a seat came up, which I found preposterous but flattering, since women were forbidden even to step into its halls.

We still never talked about Jeannette. This was our way of paying her some respect, to keep her privacy, and never to speak ill. What I enjoyed with Paul should by rights be hers, and I bore the guilt of this. As for her treatment of Paul and the lies she told, I might have been righteous, if we were not betraying her. Instead, I felt how complicated of all of our positions were.

Late that spring we held the last classes of the cooperative school. It had been a success, but Irène would be fourteen in the fall, and Aline Perrin thirteen; for many reasons, it was time for our children to attend a lycée. The Perrins hosted a gathering for the faculty on a Sunday evening, to enjoy a celebratory meal. I didn't expect Jeannette to be there or to find her wearing a new pendant brooch of silver and pearls.

Paul stayed close to her side. He caught my eye and made a face: so sorry, I couldn't help this. It was the first time I'd seen her since our tête-à-tête at her house. She was dressed in pink gossamer, a pink ribbon in her hair. One rosy color from head to toe.

Dinner was the usual Perrin chaos, with Henriette producing platters of food, and her husband bursting into arias. He was particularly merry that evening. He'd had success with his ultramicroscope—had estimated the size of water molecules—and so he poured wine and incited arguments. Alice Chavannes was there in an elegant scarf, and her husband Edouard, and the sculptor Magrou in his dusty jacket. "You've turned my daughter into an artist," I said to the latter. At Christmas, Irène had given me a clay sculpture of a girl petting a lion. "I've copied her sculpture in bronze," he said. "It will make me famous."

"Drink up," said Perrin. "All the flooding has destroyed the grapes. Enjoy this while you can." He filled Paul's glass. "There will be champagne riots, but you'll keep us well stocked, won't you, Langevin?"

"Watch it," said Paul, "or my wife will make me find a company that will actually have me." He liked remembering being turned down by Saint-Gobain, the irony.

"If you weren't so foolish," Jeannette said blandly, "you would already have a good job."

I drank my wine rather fast. I thought that Paul was behaving as he must, yet I felt that in his mind he had blocked me out. Henriette kept glancing at me.

Perrin said, "Do you see that the suffragists are presenting candidates?"

"My husband is against the women's vote," said Jeannette.

"You are?" Henriette and Perrin said in a chorus, and I said, "Have I gone to the wrong dinner party? Is the real Paul Langevin somewhere else?"

"It's my wife that's against it," said Paul.

"Mirabeau says it's our nature to tend the home fires," Jeannette said. "Woman is not a brain, she's a sex. We make love. We create harmony and grace." She had an impish look on her face, as if she were playacting, yet she also seemed to mean what she said.

"And make your husbands buy jewelry," said Paul.

"He thinks my brooch is gaudy," said Jeannette.

"And the exceptional women, the artists and inventors?" said Perrin. "You're with Mirabeau?"

"I don't know what he says about them."

"He prefers prostitutes because they're in harmony with the universe."

"Then he's very naughty."

Paul and Perrin smiled indulgently. My hands were hot. I could hardly sit.

Alice Chavannes said, "Did you see that Caillaux is divorcing his wife? To marry Madame Claretie."

"Caillaux's a good egg," said Perrin. "He'll be Prime Minister if he doesn't ruin himself with this bitch."

"Why is she a bitch?" I said. Everyone looked at me.

Henri Magrou said, "You're defending a society woman? You?"

"She's studying to be an art historian," I said. "At least that's what I read."

Magrou said, "*Le Figaro* has proof of their affair."

Perrin groaned. "She'll bring the man down."

"And you believe *le Figaro*," I said.

As soon as the attention was off of me, I stepped out into the garden, where I could have some peace. The shrubs in the garden had been severely pruned, the moonlight cold on the grass. I was miserable pretending about Paul. In the last couple weeks he had stopped holding back about Jeannette, describing her erratic behavior, her eye-rolling contempt. His stories made me want to go home and scrub the dirt from my skin. It sickened me now to see him controlled by her.

The door opened behind me, and Jeannette stepped out. She stood a moment, her eyes adjusting to the dark. She found me and looped her arm through mine. It was all I could do not to jerk away.

Inside, Perrin had everyone laughing. Earlier that week, I'd seen him coming out of a florist. When he saw me, I thought he was embarrassed.

"You look peaked," said Jeannette.

"I'm fine."

"I want you to know, whatever you said to my husband, it actually worked. Since then, he's been so kind. And happier, can you see?" She shivered and pulled closer, as if to warm her bare arms. "A kind word from him is all I needed. He says he didn't know it would be so easy, or he'd have tried it earlier. We're man and wife again. Who cares if I'm a nobody? I've got what I want."

It was an upward stab under my breastbone.

When we went inside, Paul was wiping lint off his elegant jacket. I said, "I'm glad to hear that you and your wife are doing well."

He made the tiniest eye movement, as if to say, people might hear. Alice and Henriette were nearby, talking about the explosion in Siberia, an asteroid or comet.

"Have a chocolate," Paul said. "From Angelina's."

I escaped as quickly as I could. At home, Eve and the nanny were asleep. I'd had someone living in, a girl from Poland, since Dr. Curie's death. Irène was waiting up.

"Cuddle, Mé?" she said.

I had a brief impulse to slap her. "You can put yourself to bed. You're a big girl now."

I avoided Paul for a couple of days. Yes, I was hurt and jealous. I also hurt for him, and I was angry, ashamed on his behalf, to see him so reduced, playing at being half the man he was. I knew I had no right to feel let down, but I was, in fact, disappointed. I had allowed myself to believe that he would sever his tie with his wife if he could. Now, I wasn't sure. He'd never said that he would leave her.

One morning after lecturing at the Sorbonne I returned to rue Cuvier to discover Paul in my office, tapping his fingers on my desk. "Cowardly, don't you think?" he said. "To cancel our meetings with no explanation?"

"What are we doing, Paul? Because I can't be your mistress."

"Mistress." His mouth twisted.

"Well, you've had mistresses." I said this as if I knew, though I did not. Until this moment I hadn't consciously realized my fear that, even now, he was seeing another woman, someone who wondered why he didn't come around so often anymore. I couldn't abide that. I could shrug my shoulders if he'd had women in the past, women below his station, like so many French and Polish men. I didn't need him to be a saint. What I needed was for him to be honest and clear with me. Not like he was with Jeannette.

"There's been no one since I fell in love with you. I need you, Marie."

"I can't come second to anyone."

"You're the one who matters to me." His voice was pleading. "I don't know what I'd do without you."

"You can't live without me, but you're married to your wife."

He looked at me with his miserable, intelligent expression. "That's just the thing. I don't want to be married to her. I want to leave her. Don't you want me to?"

I pulled my sweater around me.

"Don't doubt me, Marie. I'm not your beet-farming boy, who couldn't stand up to his parents."

"Aren't you?" I went to the window, so he couldn't see how his words affected me. Here I was again, these many years later, with the same impossible need.

"Are you saying you'll get a divorce?"

His eyes moved slightly. "Yes. I am."

"I have no interest in forcing you."

"It's just, let's be honest. If I look at this logically, you should leave me."

Now I was confused. I didn't know if he was asking for reassurance.

He rubbed his forehead, standing with his long thin feet apart. "Oh God, I'm an ass. With someone else you could have an uncomplicated life."

"But I'm not in love with someone else."

"Logically speaking, you should walk away. The risk to you is especially high."

"And you shouldn't? Walk away?"

"The thing is, I ought to for your sake, but I don't think I can."

"For God's sake, Paul, what are you saying? That you will or you won't go through with a divorce?"

"If I leave now, she'll punish me. She could punish the children."

"What do you mean?"

"She's unpredictable. If you want me, my love, you have to give me time. I have to prepare the ground."

I took a long breath. "I know."

From the laboratory, there was a commotion of rumbling chairs. Jean Danysz said, loudly enough for us to hear, "I did it! I finally did it!" and Agata laughed.

Paul had laid his cards on the table, and now the decision was mine. In the beginning, after months, even years, of resisting him, I had flown into his arms. For this I could hardly blame myself. But now I had to decide whether to go forward or to end it between us. I had to make a choice. Never to see him anymore—the thought made my throat close up. Yet the risks of waiting for him to take action were also high. So far, no one knew about us, but how long could that last?

Paul put his arms around me and whispered into my neck, "I don't want to ruin this. I always make a fatal mistake. In my work, too."

I pulled him close. "Hush, Paul. Stop it." I knew this side of him, the working-class boy who had risen to the top of his field but could never quite believe that he had already proven himself.

I drew Paul even closer, as if I could wrap my confidence around him. As if, with the heat of my body, I could give him the strength he needed.

He and I were different in this way. I had the blood of proud people in my veins, my mother's family, who, though they had no money, were rich in education. And yet my father had been like Paul. When he had lost his money by investing in an uncle's crazy scheme—money he had saved for his girls' education—he had blamed himself, and oh, how he despaired. I used to say to him, *Papa, your daughters will find their way, you've done everything a father possibly could.* But I could never convince him.

I had a choice about whether or not to stay with Paul, but that's not how it felt. There were only two paths ahead of me. One way was life, and the other, death. To me, it was just that plain and stark.

A month after Paul and I made up, Madame Mercier sent a note that my dress was ready. I put it on for a gathering at the home of Émile and Marguerite Borel. Jeannette would not be at the party. The air was fresh. The sidewalks of Paris were happy.

My daughters were surprised to see me in white. Together we went out to the rose garden their grandfather had planted, and Eve chose a pink one whose petals were open, with no brown edges, and we pinned it to my belt.

I was late setting off and missed the train, and so, when I saw a cabbie tightening a wheel of his carriage, I approached him. He had a mustache like Paul's.

"Good evening, Mademoiselle, would you like a ride in my carriage?"

Mademoiselle? "You flatterer," I said, and I climbed in.

A purplish light stretched across the sky. I thought of the people I might see that night. The Borels often hosted other scientists—Émile was a mathematician and the dean of the École Normale Supérieure—but also politicians, writers, and artists, men and a few women who gathered at the salon that Marguerite held in her yellow drawing room, where she produced her overwrought novels. I'd met the historian Ernest Denis at their house, and the artist Suzanne Valadon, much lovelier in person than in Renoir's paintings.

When the carriage pulled up to the apartment in the rue d'Ulm—Émile Borel's position came with lodging on campus—there were party noises out back. Instead of ringing at the door, I took the path to one side of the building, past honeysuckle and dwarf roses.

Marguerite's laugh rose above the murmur. Cedar scented the air—Paul's cigars, *la aroma de cuba*. He had probably passed them around, though they cost more than he could afford. I lingered by the bushes, partly feeling shy, but more to savor my appreciation—for Paul in his dove gray suit, Émile and Marguerite Borel, the light on the building. The cigars, the roses and the honeysuckle. From where I stood, I could see a table with champagne and Dean Appell, Marguerite's father, with his bushy white sideburns. Marguerite came into view, wearing a gold kimono, and I wondered how this intimidating man had produced this free-wheeling woman, though her outré appearance and her drama were cover for a piercing mind.

"My husband says that an infinite number of monkeys typing random letters, over an infinite amount of time, will reproduce the books at the National Library," Marguerite was saying about Émile. "Surely he's in jest?"

Émile said, "Randomness shocks our feeling of psychological freedom, but that doesn't mean it isn't real."

"Freedom," said Paul, "is not increased by ignoring statistical laws."

I loved to hear him talk to others, this man whose hair I had recently grasped, whose mustache had covered my mouth. I wondered if we could leave the party early and go to our place. How delicious that would be.

"The thing is," said Borel, "an education in probability could actually help people."

"You show what happens when the rich get richer and the poor get poorer, how it hurts everyone over time," said Paul. "You work it out statistically. It's social mathematics."

"Exactly!" Borel was pleased: he had been understood. That was Paul, so tuned in to others' minds that he could help them advance their thinking while straining nary a muscle in his brain.

There was a footstep in my direction: I risked being accused of spying.

Jean Perrin said, in his booming voice, "Your hearts are so pure, you think that men who see the light of reason will renounce their selfishness."

As I stepped into the garden, Paul was saying, "I don't know why not," and Marguerite was saying to Perrin, "Everyone but you, my darling, their idealism doesn't go that far."

Perrin didn't hear the insult: he was looking at me. Marguerite turned with her glass.

The whole party stared, and a few long seconds passed. Heat spread over my face. I didn't know where to look or what to do.

Marguerite strode toward me and took my arm. "I'm glad you're here. Have some champagne. I don't know why my husband goes on about probability. He's always been disgusted by low-level mathematics."

A year later, in Genoa, when I went with the Borels to a conference and, worried about Paul, I invited Marguerite into my confidence, she listened at my bedside, all ears, all frankness, and I asked her, What happened that evening at your house? Was it the dress? Should I not have taken advice from Madame Mercier? She told me it was not so much the dress—it was lovely, just right—but I was, to put it bluntly, glowing with sex. She said that it radiated out from my body about a foot and could be seen even by those not normally sensitive to such emanations. My hair, she said, was voluptuous, my skin moist and bright, my eyes had a yielding quality, and my posture had relaxed.

I interrupted her. "You're not putting me in a novel, are you, Marguerite?"

"I was saying," she continued, "that you couldn't have hid it, if you had walked in wearing a burlap sack."

Piwna and Podwale Streets, Warsaw, July 1894

The air is like steam from an oven. I raise my voice to be heard over the hand cranks and foot pedals. The seamstresses pause to wipe their brows. If sweat stains the linen, their pennies will be docked.

On the first stroke of five o'clock, a woman rises—faded blonde hair, a certain way of cocking her head. Justyna? I hurry after her, but she disappears into the crowd.

She stops to buy bread, and I catch up.

"My boy is waiting," she says. She reeks of attic heat. I remember her from school—soft skin, pink dresses, hair ribbons the color of cherry blossoms. Her papa's darling. At fifteen she left the Gymnasium; at sixteen she married a man whose pockets jingled with coins. I remember disliking her.

"Can we visit?" I ask.

She glances at the bread. Not enough.

I buy more—bread, cheese, milk—and I follow her up the stairway of a tilting house that smells of urine and tobacco. Her boy, four years old, sits on the bare floor in his underpants. There are two broken chairs, a pallet, and a clock that doesn't tick. Rags are stuffed in the windows.

"There's milk and cheese," she tells him.

He doesn't speak. He eats.

Her husband died—suddenly, nothing saved. Her father had made bad investments, and he lost everything, too.

I ask her if she might work as a governess. She tried, but her students spoke better French. *But you draw, you play the piano.* Not well enough. *You'd be an elegant saleswoman.* The customers want men. *Could you work as a servant?* No one will take her son.

"I don't excel at anything. I'm not a genius like you." She looks at me flatly. "Whatever happened to your young man from Szczuki?"

I flinch.

"Turned you down, did he? His family too good for you—the beet factory people?"

"I wasn't who they wanted."

"I heard you stayed. Worked at their house, after they'd already rejected you."

I had. For five hundred rubles a year, I had lived with people who scorned me.

"I wouldn't wish such torment on my enemies." Her eyes grow heavy. She leans back and begins to drowse.

I have coins in my purse, but charity can feel like a blow.

She murmurs, "The first time I accepted charity, I vomited. The second time, too. And the third. Then I got used to it. Then I began to expect it. I would plan in advance what I'd do with the money, a bit for rent, bread, maybe an apple for the boy. Now, I'm angry if it's not enough. As if it's mine already. As if I'd be right to take it, even if it isn't offered."

She opens her eyes and looks at me—not bitter, not pleading. Hollow. "What have I become?"

I leave six rubles on the arm of my chair.

XII

London, Paris, and l'Arcouëst, Fall 1910

OVER THE SUMMER I received an invitation to lecture at the University of London, arranged by Hertha. She asked me to stay at her house in Norfolk Square, and, playing off of a description of her in an American newspaper, she wrote, "Though my life is a puzzle, and you might set me down as odd, I feel certain that upon knowing me better you will declare me a most charming woman in my home life, a delightful companion, and in every way a woman."

I was eager to see Hertha. This was months before I was to confide in Marguerite, and the strain of my secret life was wearing on me. Hertha might be the one person I could tell. And so I traveled to London in September, leaving the girls with their nanny, and I lectured on the current state of radium research. The publicity beforehand was respectful—no sensationalism or even comments about my sex. William Ramsay was in the audience—the Scottish chemist who won the Nobel Prize for his discovery of noble gases—and John Perry, the one who had proven Kelvin wrong about the age of the earth, as I had proven him wrong about radium. Everyone clapped enthusiastically. I was very much cheered.

It was my first time in London without Pierre. If he'd been alive, he would have been the one asked to speak. The occasion was bittersweet.

Norfolk Square was a respite within the city, a garden with pretty ironwork and rowan trees around it, framed by terraced houses with balconies and grand windows. Hertha and I took a walk after the reception. "Don't you think it was rather fun," she said, "to be only three ladies among so many well-known men?" Miss Sharp had joined us at my lecture, accompanied by Mr. Nevinson.

"This from the great suffragette!"

"One needn't be overly consistent. Life is too grand. And by the way, I saw you glaring at Mr. Nevinson. If looks could slay!"

Hertha had earlier told me, almost accidentally, that Mr. Nevinson had a second mistress, a woman named Nannie, an Irish anarchist. At the reception, after one glass of sherry, I'd been merciless with him, congratulating him for his sophisticated taste in trophies, and telling him that he should leave Miss Sharp in peace if he didn't plan to marry her. He'd braved the battlefields of the Boer war—didn't he have the courage to follow through with what he had started? Half-amused, he'd tapped the cone of ash from his cigar and said that for a judge, I was ill-informed, but he was listening to me.

"It's not all Mr. Nevinson, you know," Hertha said. "Miss Sharp does have a choice."

"I don't know what it is about that man. I like him, but he gets under my skin."

My desire to confide in Hertha seemed to grow as she gave me a tour of her house. In Paris, I'd convinced myself that all was mostly well, but here, I was less certain. Finally we sat down for a cup of tea in her drawing room, where she'd also set up her laboratory. Troughs and sand rollers, engines and coveralls made happy company with tasseled drapery, family photographs, quirky vases and wall hangings, and books crammed into shelves and stacked on the floor. A portrait of Hertha's husband presided, along with a gilded silver medal he had been awarded by the Royal Society. This was a household built up by a married couple, very different from my sparsely furnished household.

"I have my choice of so many rooms, but it's more sociable to work in here," Hertha said. "After Will died, especially."

"Do you still miss him?" He had died the year after Pierre.

"Every single day."

I ventured, "Do you ever think about finding someone else?"

She laughed. "What I think about is turning Catholic and finding a nunnery. A flexible kind of nunnery, where I can work on my inventions. I do so want to finish my difference of pressure gauge. I want to show those bastards." These were the ones who, with uninformed objections, had turned down her article at the Royal Society. She looked at me earnestly. "You'll help me get back to it, won't you?"

"You want me to lock you in your lab?"

"I wouldn't mind."

We sat in silence for a while, and I got up my courage. "It was good to see Miss Sharp," I began.

Hertha poured us both more tea. A shadow crossed her face. "Did she tell you?"

"What?"

"She's part of a large demonstration next week. She's been working around the clock."

I hesitated. At the reception I did notice that she seemed weary. "Are they planning violence?"

"Of course this is all secret. Evelyn's been assigned to break windows in government buildings. She grew up with brothers. She's got a good aim."

"Ha!" I tried to keep neutral, but my body tightened.

Hertha observed me coolly. "You disapprove."

"Yes, I do." I set my teacup down. "This kind of thing always has unintended consequences. It requires patience to—"

"Patience?" She also set her tea down. "We've petitioned Parliament for decades, you've no idea. We thought we had a bill three years ago, and then the bastards tossed it out. We're denied the right to put questions at political meetings, and they've even rescinded the power of petition. It's *impatience* we need."

"People never want to believe this, but things can actually get worse. If you'd grown up in Poland, you'd—"

"Things *are* getting worse." She went to the window and gazed outside. "After the demonstration, when we're brought to court, the newspapers will say how irrational the suffragettes are, and loathsome and misguided. They'll blame us. You blame us. Evelyn says, it's like in the Oresteia, when Clytemnestra comes out of the house and says why she's murdered her husband. The old men in the chorus chant about how sordid and evil she is. No one points out that her husband had killed their daughter! It's always a woman to blame."

"I thought Miss Sharp promised her mother not to risk going to prison."

"Her mother saw the light." Hertha looked at me as if she were pleading. "I feel guilty not going myself, you know? My daughter won't allow me—I still have bruises on my chest. But Marie, to stay home, when the others—you should see them, they're so brave."

"And your daughter?"

"Barbie will be there."

"Oh, Hertha." I put my hand on hers. She had written to me about the women in Halloway, how brutally they were treated.

"I'm terrified," she said, "but proud."

She told me then about hunger strikes, how prison guards would tie the women down, drive feeding tubes through their noses. After weeks, their noses would "bite" the tube, and it would no longer pass into the throat, so the guards would cut their gums and cheeks, and shove in gags to keep them from biting or screaming, and then tubes. When the force-feeding stopped, and the tubes were taken out, the women still felt gagged. The sensation stayed in their throats.

This was not the time to bring up my own troubles.

That night I tossed in my bed in Hertha's guest room. Her stories had set off an alarm. I had been privileged, I had honor and prestige, but the regard I was granted as a woman was optional, that was the truth of it. It was not backed up by law.

If people found out about my relationship with Paul, there would be a scandal. The ground of my respect could shift. Since Pierre's death I had been able to sustain myself by keeping good relations, and my confidence conveyed itself to colleagues, which seemed to help. But I, too, could be treated as less than human.

I sat up and turned on a lamp. I needed to make a plan.

By morning I had worked it out. Paul needed to separate from his wife, sooner rather than later, and once he did, the two of us must rarely meet until a year had passed. Meanwhile I would bear down on my research, publish more, go to more Physics Society meetings, and as far possible, make myself unassailable.

I was packing my bag the next morning when Hertha appeared at my door in a yellow dress. "Cook has made an English breakfast for you. She says to come while it's hot. Eggs and mixed grill and tomato."

"Will you sit down? There's something I need to tell you."

She looked surprised. She sat in a chair in front of the window. She said, "Are you well?"

"You remember Monsieur Langevin. You met him in Paris, at the reception after your talk."

"The young man who was Pierre's assistant?"

I blushed a little. "Yes, Pierre's prize student."

"Brownian motion. A wife and children. Charming man."

I busied myself with my suitcase. When I faced Hertha, she was looking at me with concern. "What is it, Marie?"

I told her about my friendship with Paul, and my efforts to stay away, and Jeannette's treatment of him, and that we were lovers now. I told her about his wish for a divorce and his fear of leaving, his unhappiness, and my longing to make him happy. He was, as she knew, a brilliant scientist, perhaps the most intelligent man that I had ever known. We loved and needed each other. I didn't know any other way except with him to get what I wanted out of life, or to give what I could give. It sounded selfish, I knew it did. My nature was to feel too keenly, and I could hide that, but I couldn't change it. With Pierre, I had learned what it meant for love and work to be twined together. I could hardly do without this now. Paul needed me, too. It was imperative that he be free to do his research, and he needed my support. He would of course do everything to care for his wife and children, financially and otherwise. For years my life had not made sense, not even my daughters could reach me. Since Paul, everything was different.

Hertha sat with her hands on her knees, allowing me to speak until at last I had nothing more to say. She looked heavy and sad. "I do understand," she said. "The two of you. What a relief it must be, to have each other's intelligent company."

"You can't imagine, Hertha." I sat down on the bed.

"She has four children, Madame Langevin?"

"That's right. I taught the older boys. They're very dear. Paul wants to direct their education."

"Is she mentally stable?"

I didn't like this line of questioning, and I felt my stubbornness. "She's volatile."

Hertha sighed as she stood up. "Another woman with no education and few opportunities. I don't have much to say, except. . . ."

"Except . . ."

"Be careful, darling. I don't have to tell you. Women need to be careful in this world, more so than men."

"Oh, I know, I—"

She shook her head. "No matter what I know, I'm always surprised by how vile people can be. The press especially."

As we walked down the stairs, toward the smells of sausage and coffee, Hertha stopped and said again, "I'm serious, Marie. Be careful."

Back in Paris, I went to meet Paul at our place, but he never came. I had set out bread and breast of duck prepared by the butcher, and a carafe of red wine. Paul had been complaining of stomach trouble, but I noticed that he ate better when the wine was good and we had time to spare. It wasn't like him not to let me know about a change in plans. I left a note saying I would stop by again at eight o'clock. When I did, the duck had congealed on the plate and nothing had been touched.

I took the train back to Sceaux. The girls were staying at l'Arcouëst with an older Polish cousin. I was to join them after a trip to Holland, to continue my research at the lab of my colleague Onnes. I fed Irène's goldfish and watered her monkey puzzle tree. I spent an uneasy night.

The next morning at rue Cuvier, I got a note from Paul: I should come to our place right away.

He was at the table with his hand on his neck, his hair ungroomed. "Jeannette has the servant spying on me," he said.

I didn't embrace him. I was too alarmed. "Why did you come here?"

"I haven't been followed. She found a note I wrote to you in our letter box, ready to go out. It doesn't prove anything."

"Did you admit anything?"

"No, but she's suspicious. Marie, you should leave Paris right away."

"Why? What are you saying?"

"Jeannette said that she was going to get rid of this obstacle. That's exactly what she said."

"What does she mean?"

"It means she'll try to kill you."

Though my heart was beating fast, I laughed. "That's ridiculous. You can't believe her. She's scared. She's extreme."

He shook his head. "You've no idea. She's evil. She can be. Marie, she threw a knife at me."

"*At* you? Really?"

"Let's just say I wasn't surprised."

I pictured Jeannette in a fit, throwing the knife past Paul, to upset him, to provoke. It was bad, but I refused to overreact.

I said, "But why would you post a letter to me from home?" He was sentimental about our letters, this I knew—he kept mine to him locked in the desk, bound up with a string, in this very room. If ever I needed to assure myself of his devotion, I had only to think of this bundle. "Why didn't you use a public mailbox?" I persisted.

"I know, I know. We're in trouble, my love."

I had a flash of anger at Paul. I wanted him to straighten his spine. I wanted him to feel what I did: rage toward this woman who bested him at every turn. I thought of the putrid water that had surged up during the flood, through manholes and drains. The smell of sewers, rot, and excrement, that all had to be cleaned up.

Paul couldn't see what he had to do. I would have to reach out my hand and help him out of these filthy waters.

I went to see Jean Perrin at his home that night, and I told him everything. Henriette was at l'Arcouëst, with her children and mine, but he took me in and gave me brandy. He wasn't surprised, he said, that Paul would "seek refuge" with me. He offered to visit the Langevins in Fontenay-aux-Roses and try to calm things down. I should come see him again the following night.

When I did, the news wasn't reassuring. In front of the children, Jeannette had greeted him by saying, "Well now, Monsieur Perrin, this is not a pretty picture, you're going to see quite a scandal in the newspapers." She had grabbed Jules by the elbow and said, "Are you going to be like your father? Are you going to take a mistress?" He believed she was capable of blackmail and worse.

Several days in a row, Perrin returned to the Langevin house, trying to restore sanity. On the fourth day he sent me a note that Jeannette had spoken more calmly and had "promised to try to be nice."

One night, after staying late in the city, I got off the train to Sceaux and saw two figures looming by the station. Were they private investigators, people Jeannette had hired? Was my imagination getting away from me? It was nearly eleven p.m., and dark and drizzly. Though I felt foolish, I walked in the opposite direction of my house, turned into an alley, and leaned against a toolshed at the back of a cottage. A heap of rubbish smelled of rotting fruit, and something moved—the wet brown gleam of a rat. In a while, I walked back toward my road. When I turned from the alley onto the street, two pale faces stared out of the darkness: Jeannette and an older woman who looked like her, with a bitter mouth and pushed-up sleeves. Her sister. There was no one on the street but us.

The sister turned her neck and spat. "You cunt. You ugly cunt."

I stepped into the light of a lamppost—surely someone would look out and see—and she stepped closer. My lips and mouth were dry.

"Is he insane? He wants a cunt like you when my sister is in his bed?"

"Jeannette," I said. I had known her all these years.

Jeannette's eyes bulged strangely. "Just wait and see what we're going to do to you."

The sister said, "Get out of France, do you hear me? Do you understand? We're doing you a favor. Do you hear me?"

I saw her coming toward me, and I stepped back. She stomped her foot on top of mine and grabbed a handful of my hair, and pulled. My neck yanked back. Searing pain across my scalp. The next thing I was aware of was two women's backs as they walked away. Jeannette lifting her skirts. Her sister's dress hem dragging through puddles. They walked in the direction of the station. I seemed then to rise above my body, well above the lamppost, the figures below me small and unreal. It seemed as if another woman—Hertha, maybe—was hovering with me. We looked down on three women with tangled hair, one of them under the lamppost, the others walking away. Three women who might have escaped from prison, they looked that desperate.

In a while, when I could think, I walked through the dark streets to my house. My foot hurt, but I could walk on it. I pushed through the gate and stood for a while between a blackthorn bush and the chicken coop. Rain had turned the grass to mud. What if someone was lurking in my entryway? Jeannette's sister had a husband, Paul said, who would do anything for money.

The air smelled of worms and chickenfeed, though we'd given away our chickens after Dr. Curie died. I wished he were inside. I wanted him to open the door and lean his white head out and say, "Marie, come in from the cold."

I was afraid to enter the house. There was one more train into Paris, if it hadn't left. André would let me stay with him, but I'd have to face his disapproval—he'd never chided me about my relationship with Paul, but he didn't like it. Better to go back to boulevard Kellerman, back to the Perrins' house.

In the train car, I fell in and out of sleep. My neck and scalp hurt. I felt with my fingers. A small bald spot.

Would Jeannette and her sister tell Paul what they had done? Would Jeannette throw another knife? Might she provoke Paul into behaving like the brute she said he was?

I had a confused sense of being a character in someone else's play, and I was angry with Paul without quite knowing why. More than that, I was frightened for him. No wonder his stomach pained him and he couldn't work. There was no more room for fine considerations. He had to get away from her.

Perrin advised me to leave Paris. "Be sensible, Marie. Go now." We were in his office at the Sorbonne, which was much like mine, with a tilting floor and musty books.

"And give in to the devil?" My rage had twisted my insides. My defiance was growing, too. I had learned as a girl what to do with an enemy: you let them fuel you, drive you on. When they try to pull you into the sewer, you grab onto something undeniably worthy, show that you are better than them.

"I won't see Paul," I conceded. "Otherwise, I'll go about my business as before. Would you leave your research because of her? I don't think so."

"Marie, you are playing with fire."

I needed to understand, he told me, that the assault on me was not an aberration. Once, she had thrown a metal chair at Paul. In the first months of their marriage, she and her mother had hired an investigator to find incriminating evidence, in case of a court case in the future. Paul's own mother had witnessed enough to suggest that he divorce her before they had a child. And the scar on Paul's forehead? It was not from a bicycle accident. Jeannette had broken a bottle on his head.

I felt stunned. Why hadn't Paul told me? How could he hold this back? Yet slowly I realized that he had in fact told me similar stories, but always with a faintly comic edge. I had thought, could it really be as bad as all that? I hadn't been able to take it in, because he half made a joke of it. And I had never seen Jeannette like this.

The next morning I left for Leiden, to collaborate with my colleague. He must have wondered why I jumped when he so much as dropped a pencil. From Leiden I traveled to l'Arcouëst to join Irène and Eve and their cousin.

The four of us bicycled for miles on my first day there, and that night we went to a party at the home of Monsieur Seignobos. When he politely asked me about the Langevins, remembering that my family had lived with them the year before, I politely answered. Monsieur Langevin was preparing a paper, I said, and the seaside wasn't Madame Langevin's cup of tea.

Why, I asked myself, didn't Paul hold Jeannette accountable? He was the one who called her evil, but what did he do about it?

In the end he saw her through a sentimental lens, as if he were an old-fashioned gentleman: no surprise if the wife is hysterical and controlling, and violent, even—after all, she can't help her moods. If anything, he blamed himself. Isn't the man in charge of moral guidance? This angered me—the condescension to all women, not only to Jeannette. But even as I raged, I sensed I was engaging only half the story. Paul seemed unable to resist Jeannette, especially when she cried. Perhaps he didn't believe himself worthy of anything better. He had held back the worst of Jeannette's behavior from me—because of shame, or out of loyalty? Perhaps he couldn't explain, even to himself. The cords that tied him to his children were also strong.

I carried on in a simulation of acting like myself, but that simple notion, of being myself, confused me. Was Marie Curie the one who rejoiced when she scooped up a netful of shrimp, who rowed with the children across the bracing green water to Roch Vras? Or was it she who spent her nights in a fever, imagining Paul's mouth on his wife's breast?

After the assault by Jeannette and her sister, I had found no one home at the Perrins' house on boulevard Kellerman. I'd been reduced to wandering the streets. Finally, Perrin approached—a jaunty black shadow in the lamplight. I will never forget his expression when he saw me. The pity, the dismay. I knew from his face that I looked like a beast at bay. Cornered. Frantic.

I still felt like that.

l'Arcouëst,
25 September 1910

Darling Paul,

Last night I spent the evening dreaming of you, of the hours we've spent together and my delicious memories.

How I wish we were able to see each other freely, to work together, and walk and talk, and lie together every night. The instinct which led us to each other was powerful. So much could come of this feeling, instinctive, spontaneous, and so compatible with our intellectual needs. I believe we could derive everything good from it: work in common, a solid friendship, and courage for life.

I have discussed this with the Perrins, and we all agree that you shouldn't argue for joint custody of the children. That would only lead to battles with their mother, which would be horrible for them. Even leaving the children with their mother would be better than a continual state of war in your family. If you were separated from your wife, she would quickly stop paying attention to the children, because she's bored by them and incapable of guiding them. Little by little you would be able to take over their guidance.

It's obvious that your wife, no matter her promises or her best interest, won't be able to control her violence. Nor will she easily accept a separation—she lives by exploiting you. You must decide to do all you can, methodically, to make her life with you unbearable. She will vacillate in what she says. The first time she proposes that she would like a separation, you must accept without hesitation before she has a chance to use blackmail.

For the children, the change wouldn't be as big as you think and it would certainly be better for everyone. It's enough for now that Jules continues to board at the lycée; you could take a faculty apartment near him and see your other children at the Perrins' house. For them it will be less bad than living in a family in a state of war.

And there are not only your children, my Paul—there is you. Think of your future as a scientist, your moral and intellectual life. All this has been at risk for several years. Your friends know this, and you must realize it, too.

We can't go on living in the current state.

The first thing to do is to sleep in a separate bedroom. I'm worried about unforeseen events. I fear crises of tears which you can't resist. Paul, she will ambush you, she will take advantage of your need, in order to become pregnant. Please, be on guard against all that. Don't make me wait too long for you to sleep in separate beds. When I know that you are with her, my nights are atrocious. I can't sleep, I am lucky if I manage two or three hours. I wake up with a fever and I can't work. Do what you can to be done with it.

Don't ever come downstairs from your bedroom unless she comes to look for you. Work late. As for the pretext you've been looking for: tell her that because you work late and rise early, you absolutely need to rest, and if she insists, you will sleep in Paris with Jules.

Do this, my Paul, I beg of you, and don't let yourself be moved by her crying. Think of the saying about the crocodile who cries because he has not eaten his prey; the tears of your wife are like that. She must understand that she can expect nothing from you. Once she has seen that you absolutely intend to separate, she will no longer be unhappy, since you will give her the means to live as grandly as she pleases. She will be able then to look for pleasure, and even love, elsewhere!

There is the danger of a scandal. If you limit social occasions with your wife, she'll have less opportunity to gossip. Too many people already know about us. . . . If your wife got pregnant, they would judge me even more harshly. It would mean a definite break between us, because I can risk my life and my position for you, but I could not accept this dishonor. If your wife understands this, she will use this method right away.

Please read this letter carefully and discuss any of it with the Perrins. I will try to return to work, though my nerves are so stirred up.

I await the joy of seeing you with impatience, and I hope to have news of you tomorrow by way of Henriette.

Your loving Marie

Paris, 26 September 1910

My dear Marie,

I have read and reread your letter but I don't have time to respond in detail today. To the extent that I am able to judge our situation, I also believe that a separation is best and I will do everything I can to make it happen without violence. My existence at home is extremely difficult for me and everyone. I only try to imagine what the change will be like for the children.

One thing is clear, my entire moral life will be profoundly changed thanks to you.

I embrace you,
Paul

• • •

When I got Paul's letter, I had the impulse to take the next train back to Paris and make him talk to me. His cautious tone was chilling, as was his stance of wait and see. *My entire moral life will be profoundly changed thanks to you.* Was he placating me? Was he seeing me as a woman he had to manage, like his wife? Had I become that woman?

13 rue des Sablons, Sceaux
10 September 1894

. . . If you return to Paris, would you like to rent an apartment with me on rue Mouffetard with windows overlooking a garden? It is divided into two independent parts.

Your devoted friend,
Pierre Curie

13 rue des Sablons, Sceaux
17 September 1894

You are returning to Paris! This makes me very happy.

Your picture pleases me enormously. How kind of you to send it! Thank you with all my heart.

If you were French, you could easily be a professor in a secondary school or a girls' normal school. Would this profession please you?

Your very devoted friend,
Pierre Curie

P.S. I showed your picture to my brother Jacques. I hope that is all right. He admired it. He also said, "She has a very decided look, maybe even stubborn."

XIII

Paris, October 1910–March 1911

IT TOOK PAUL FOUR DAYS to send me a note when I got home from l'Arcouëst. He'd been waiting, he said, until Jeannette went to see her mother with the children. He stood by the window of our place in his rumpled white shirt. I hesitated by the door. He said, "What, not even a hug?" As we embraced, I felt his tenderness rising to meet mine, and my need for an explanation disappeared.

"I'm sorry for that terrible letter," I said.

"No, not terrible—"

"I'm afraid, Paul, but I won't try to manage you."

We swayed in each other's arms.

He said, "André-Philippe is taking the brunt of Jeannette, now that Jules is boarding at school. If I leave, I'll feel so guilty."

"My darling. Your happiness does count for something."

I thought of my own father, how, when he was fired from his teaching job, the changes were hard for our family—the move to dreary quarters, and boarders crowding in with us—but hardest of all was my father's unhappiness. He looked ashamed, bent over on himself, like a tree on a windswept cliff. I would have done anything to bring him joy. I had tried to tell Paul this.

We talked. We made love. When St. Anne's bell rang twice, I smoothed the wrinkles out of Paul's shirt and straightened his mustache. It could be a while before the bristles on his chin scratched my face again. When we kissed goodbye, I had the physical sensation of his wife's body wedging between us.

At rue Cuvier, André was at his desk with his snuff box, curiously still. "Hullo," I said. "Are you all right?"

He blinked. "Just resting a moment after lunch."

"Resting on your laurels?"

He smiled. "It is astonishing, you know. Radium in its metallic state. Impossible, and yet, we've done it."

"André, are you having a tipple?"

"Why do you ask?"

"You're not quite yourself."

He lifted a small glass with golden liquid in it.

"In the afternoon! I thought you had only the one vice."

"Twice a year, I have two vices."

"How do you decide which days?"

"The spirit comes upon me."

"Do I need to worry about you?"

"Twice a year doesn't justify worry, in my humble opinion."

Was there something he wasn't saying? Did his tippling have anything to do with me? I didn't think so. He looked relaxed and rather pleased with himself, as if he were indeed rewarding himself for work well done, a bit of happy indulgence. Once again I saw that there was much I didn't know about this man.

"All right, well, I'm going to lock myself into my office."

He pretended to tip a hat. "It won't be the first time I've guarded your door, Madame."

I went to my desk and took out a piece of paper and my fountain pen, and I made a list.

1. Radium Institute, fully funded, under my control.
   Like Cavendish Laboratory, Kaiser Wilhelm Institute.
   One branch research, one branch biological/medical
   applications

2. Involve more factories. Radium for researchers internationally
3. Create international standard for radium
4. Collaboration with Onnes
5. Decay sequence of polonium
6. Copper research?

I had a start on each of these items.

I had learned a lesson from my letter to Paul from l'Arcouëst, and his response to it: I must allow him to make his own choice. I was resigned now to waiting for him to leave Jeannette, but I didn't plan to let that drama take over my life, like those mistresses drifting through apartments all across the city, keeping themselves fresh, on the chance that their lovers might stop by.

In November, Dean Appell, still head of the Faculty of Science, sent a note asking me to meet him and our colleague Gaston Darboux, for drinks at a restaurant. Immediately I worried that this could this be about Paul, but the Dean, I thought, if he wanted to take me to task, would call me to his office, not the Flicoteaux on rue Champollion.

The heavy restaurant door, when I pushed it, seemed to push back, as if forcing any lady to ask for help. I made my way through anise-scented rooms, past men with loose curls and women in off-the-shoulder blouses, twirling green absinthe in glass mugs. I avoided eye contact; even poetic types were likely to recognize me. In the back, at an ill-lit table, two gentlemen with pince-nez and mutton chops were finishing a bottle of wine, Gaston Darboux and Dean Appell, each with a shock of bright white hair. "I hope," Marguerite sometimes said, "that my hair is like my father's when I grow old."

"We're sight-seeing," said Darboux, pulling out my chair.

"The prices are not what they were in Balzac's time," said Dean Appell. "That couple"—he nodded toward a man and woman with similarly long brown hair and identical black glasses—"they're reciting poetry to each other. About insomnia."

"At their age, insomnia?" said Darboux.

"And death."

It was flattering to join their good-humored, wine-soaked mood. Whatever they had to say to me, it couldn't be terrible.

The waiter brought another bottle of wine and a glass for me: Haut Sauternes Bordeaux, Goenaga & Co.—Paul would want to know. At first, out of anxiety and an instinct to catch up to the two men, I drank too fast. Then I pushed my glass away.

"Drink," said Darboux.

I poured wine into all three glasses. "I can tell when two gentlemen are about to ask something of me."

"Listen before you say no, that's all we ask," said the Dean, and to Darboux, "She always says no first."

"You know Gernez has died," said Darboux.

Gernez had replaced Pierre at the Academy of Science—in spite of his ambivalence, Pierre had allowed himself to be a candidate a second time, after the Nobel Prize, and this time he had been voted in.

"And?"

Darboux said, "We want to nominate you to take the place of Gernez."

"What a lovely surprise. But I'm disqualified, aren't I, as a member of the inferior sex? Not allowed to cross the temple threshold?" The Academy of Science was one of five branches of the Institute of France, and governed by rules of the larger body.

"A three-hundred-year-old policy," said Darboux. "We also have three hundred years of glorious pomp. You might enjoy that part. I do, I must say."

"The time is right to challenge the rule," said the dean, and he cited arguments for my candidacy: my achievements, which made it an embarrassment to the Academy that I didn't already belong; my honorary membership in the Dutch, Czech, Swedish, and Polish Academies, and the Imperial Academy in St.

Petersburg; my strength as a candidate compared to Edouard Branley, who would be my competition; and their feeling that the time was ripe. Everything he said echoed the points that Paul had been making to me.

"You'd be a lot in the public eye," said the dean, "until after the election. But you're an upright woman and the only woman whose merits might embarrass the Academy into making a policy change. Plus, we need you on the committee. We need someone to evaluate funding applications to do with radium. Will you think it over?"

I promised that I would, but as I walked out of the restaurant, past the lovers kissing, through the wood and iron door (which released me to the sidewalk more easily than it had let me in), I knew I would say yes. A place in the Academy would give me influence over the direction of research in France. I could argue my research assistants' merits, help them get grant money. Even a Radium Institute would be easier to fund if the people I lobbied were fellow Academy members. Every item on my list would be easier to accomplish.

And Paul? He would adore that I was doing this.

As I walked to the station, there was a revving in my veins, as if the wreckage on the track ahead of me had just been cleared, and I was set to go.

Within days after our meeting, Appell and Darboux put my name forward, and the newspapers blared with excitement. At rue Cuvier, the mood was just shy of ecstatic.

"You're the Reverend Mother of Science," said Jean Danysz, "didn't I tell you?" We were all having tea on the steps. Agata, breaking apart bread and chocolate with her fingers, said, "With you in the Academy, at last I have a chance in science," and my nephew Maurice, Jacques's son, said, "Think of the research we can do when you're immortal!" He was only half ironic—people called the members of the Institute "Immortals." I loved having

Maurice around, though it unnerved me to look at him and see Pierre, his eyes and the curve of his neck.

I said, "One step at a time," but I was giddy, too. I had allies. I had friends.

"What a carnival that will be," said Maurice, and he made a pantomime of descending from a carriage in a cloak and entering the Palace, as a hundred members of the French Institute would soon be doing: all five academies convening in a sudden meeting. The question they would vote on was, Should women continue to be excluded from membership, and from the halls of each of its branches—science, the humanities, fine arts, the French language, and the moral and political sciences? Dean Appell believed that the members of the Institute would vote yes to allowing women. If they didn't, I couldn't be a candidate for the Academy of Science.

"You look more like a peacock than an immortal," I said to Maurice.

"The immortals *are* peacocks, aren't they? Oh Aunt, I can't wait until you have a long black coat with green embroidery."

André joined us. "I don't believe in jinxes," he said. "But don't put a jinx on this."

"Your tea, Sir Skeptical." Maurice handed him a cup. He was the only student I had ever known to tease André.

"I'm right to doubt this," said André, and I said, "Yes, you are."

Jean Danysz said, "We all know you're the best candidate, Madame."

"The best candidates have lost before," I said, but secretly, I believed my luck had turned.

"Along with her fame she has nobility and beauty," Paul read out loud. We were looking at the paper in our chairs by the window at our place on rue du Banquier. "Nothing is missing, not even the poignant poetry of grief, from her pure and perfect image." He showed me the full-page renderings of my face, facsimiles of my handwriting, and an analysis of my character based on it. "They say you're obstinate," he said. "They're onto you."

Two months after Jeannette and her sister's attack, we'd gone back to our midday routine, taking special care that we weren't being followed. Without admitting to our relationship, Paul had pacified Jeannette with a ruby ring and a promise not to see me, even as a colleague. I hated that he bought her off, and it galled me to think of the hours of teaching he would need to do to pay for it. Hours he could have used for his research.

"And you're private and conservative," he said. "They can tell by the spacing and the hooks at the end of your words."

"Private, yes."

"Undemonstrative. That's not true."

I kicked his leg. "And tender-hearted, don't leave that out."

My playfulness masked how unnerved I was. The French press, we all knew, was a furnace in which reputations were destroyed as quickly as they were forged.

"Unswerving, dogged." Paul's head was still in the paper.

"Do you mind?"

"That you're dogged?" He put the paper down. "No genius without will power. You are superior, you know. You're a scandal. A woman who thinks well of herself?"

I took his paper away and sat on his lap. "And of you. I think very well of you."

He kissed my lower lip. "You taste of honey."

I nuzzled into him. We hadn't made love that day. "You smell of sex," I said. "Of wanting it."

He laughed, but it was true. Tobacco smoke perfumed his clothes and neck, and pine tar soap, but when he wanted sex, there was another smell, too, like a riverbed heated by the sun.

"Where did I get you?" He arched his back a little, the way he did.

"I don't want to leave. I want to stay here all day."

He pulled me closer. "All week."

He'd been in a bad mood when he arrived, because of an article he hadn't been able to finish. He kept making little changes; he couldn't stop himself. His publisher threatened to steal the paper from his desk to put an end to it, as Pierre had done before. Our talk of my candidacy for some reason cheered him up.

In the last few months, Paul had come into view for me in a different way. Whereas I had put him on a pedestal, and still did, scientifically—his mathematical mind was beyond anyone I knew—I was more aware of his weaknesses. He was passionate about equality among people, and I didn't doubt that he would sacrifice himself in a time of war. Yet with his wife, with women, he lost courage; he resorted to masculine pride and control. He could also be irritable and fussy. At restaurants, he'd send the food back if it didn't meet expectations and report this to me with indignation. I remembered Jeannette's comment on the train about Paul's fit over a fruit compote, and her account began to sound more realistic. He was also prone to complaining about his reception as a scientist, although he was held in very high esteem indeed.

None of this overly worried me. He treated me with respect, and who wouldn't feel injured, with a wife pouring salt in every wound?

With my head on his chest, listening to the pumping of his blood, I felt how fragile his life was. His heart would stop one day. Mine would, too.

"You're something wonderful," I said, pulling back to look at him.

He smoothed my hair from my face. "Compared to you, I'm wobbly."

"I wish you could see yourself the way I do." Not the wounded one, but the truest Paul, the future Paul, free from guilt and the absurd demands he placed on himself, free from Jeannette. I loved to picture him, this Paul-to-come: a lightness in his being, following his own sweet inclinations. His mind lit up with his research. All the pressure of his intelligence finding its proper channel.

This was the Paul I wanted to love into being.

If the first news stories about my candidacy were hymns of praise, the ones to follow were Juvenalian satires.

"It is abhorrent when women want to be like men," Irène read aloud at the breakfast table. "They will by doing so certainly lose their virtue." She put down the magazine. "What does that mean?"

"Throw that garbage away," I said.

"Men have hair on their backs," said Eve. "I saw at the beach."

Irène read, "Madame Curie has done nothing either before or since her husband's death, and yet she is greedy for prizes."

"The people who matter know better," I said, but my skin felt thin as paper. "You needn't worry, darlings."

With the Institute vote approaching, the mood was volatile. The press had turned to fear-mongering, invective, mockery. One would think a stray comet had struck Paris and civilization was coming undone: streams were becoming rivers, rivers becoming torrents and carrying dikes away, and all of this because of over-reaching women. I began to receive hateful letters. In one, I was accused of perverting good French men. In another, written with words cut and pasted from a newspaper, I was told that I was an instrument of Satan, and my death was coming soon.

"It's a case of hysteria," Hertha wrote. "It will subside. Remember your friends in science."

It didn't help that strangers on the street thought they had the right to scold me. Even at the boulangerie, where I had bought my baguettes for years, the baker, Monsieur Robert, had to give me his kindly opinion. "The thing is, you're not a natural sort of woman, that's what it is." He was trying to make sense of it. A judge who lived on my street stopped me to say, "Never mind, it's not a crime to be an over-reacher."

I recalled Hertha's words about my being like the figure on a ship's prow, called on to cut through roiling seas so women coming after me could follow in my wake. I had never asked to be their ambassador! Would women feel betrayed if my candidacy was wrecked because of my relationship with Paul? At night, I dreamed of walking naked through the streets of Paris. Under the best of circumstances, I would have felt exposed by all this press.

My lab was my refuge. Jean Danysz saw my hand tremor one morning and brought me a cup of tea he had brewed with blackberry preserves. A little cup of Poland.

"*Dziękuję*, Jean."

"*Moja przyjemność*, Madame."

Thank you. My pleasure.

This young man had a way of bringing me to my center.

But at night, brushing my hair in the mirror, I imagined Jeannette Langevin reading the invective in the newspapers and feeling vindicated. It seemed to me that the world was on her side, pious and violent.

In late January, when the Institute met for the plenary session, I had a premonition that the vote would go against women. Admitting women in general, Dean Appell had told me, was the biggest obstacle, and the newspapers agreed. I went to the bakery and bought an apricot tart for dessert with the girls. No matter the vote, we would have a treat that night.

When I met Paul at midday—we had half an hour—he told me that he and Maurice had walked down the street in front of the Palace to see the show that Maurice had pantomimed: men descending from their carriages and automobiles in the famous *habit vert*, rich green embroidery on long black cloaks. Paul laughed—he thought it was delightful.

I said, "Don't you feel the danger?" I had a vague suspicion that he came alive in chaos, whereas all I wanted was for this vote to be behind me, even if it went against women.

Paul said, "You'll be on the board of the *Comptes rendus*. Think of the good you'll do. Imagine, research funding based on the merits of a proposal. Think of that!"

And not on the scientist's social class. And not on the scientist's sex.

When I stopped back at rue Cuvier, Maurice threw his arms around me. My apricot tart went flying. Yellow custard smeared across the floor.

"Maurice, what in the world?"

"Never mind the tart, Aunt."

My heart rose. "Did they vote for women?"

"No, they did not."

"Then what?"

"They won't admit women to the Institute as a general rule, but each academy can decide for itself. The Academy of Science has nominated you! You're their first candidate."

"And Edouard Branley?"

"He's the second candidate. You're set to win, Aunt Marie."

During the next four weeks I climbed majestic staircases and sat in drawing rooms covered in expensive paper, making the customary visits to court the votes of members of the Academy of Science. We drank coffee in china cups. Wives in their silks came and sat with us, and the men asked flattering questions, prompting me to show off what I knew. I rather enjoyed myself, steering as best I could between Scylla and Charybdis, conveying feminine modesty without pretending to know less than I did, and confidence without encroaching on male terrain. These ritual visits risked my being seen as lacking proper reserve, yet not to make them would have been considered arrogant. Dean Appell and Darboux made many of the visits on my behalf, which seemed a good compromise.

Finally, in March, the day of the vote arrived. André and most of our staff waited with me at rue Cuvier to hear the results. Dean Appell called me that morning. “Prepare yourself,” he said, in his crisp voice. “You’ll be asked to make a speech.”

Before lunch, Maurice arrived breathlessly with news: the Institute had doubled the number of guards; the media and hundreds of men and women were pressing for entrance. Finally, spectators were allowed inside—all except the ladies. A group of infuriated women said to Maurice, “Tell your aunt we’re counting on her.”

The vote was to be at four. Maurice and Jean and Agata, and all the research students, waited in suspense with André. I wanted to kiss their shiny faces. If I had been a Reverend Mother, as Jean Danysz said, I would have blessed them for their devotion.

At three o’clock, I shut myself in my office and leaned against the wall, thinking of Pierre, his wiry beard, his capacious, wrinkled jacket. I wanted him now. I wanted to fold myself inside his memory.

At nearly five o’clock the telephone rang. I picked it up. It was Dean Appell.

“Madame Curie.” I could tell from his voice that something had gone wrong.

“What happened?”

“Branley’s supporters used methods that would embarrass monkeys. It was a fiasco.”

“Oh. I see.”

“Marie, I’m so sorry.”

I choked a little. “After all your work.” I couldn’t take it in. “You’ve done so much for me, Dean Appell. I’m as grateful as a daughter.”

“I’m going to lose a lot of sleep over this, but I hope you won’t.“

“I already belong to the best academy. My circle of devoted friends.”

He blew his nose at the end of the line. "Thank God, you're too noble a character to be affected by this nonsense."

I whispered, "Thank you."

I went back to my office and rested my head on my desk.

What a waste these weeks had been. My name had become a rallying cry for ridiculous debates about women, my research dismissed by people who knew nothing. Edouard Branley's supporters, supposedly men of science, had committed themselves to preserving the France of their fathers. Darboux and Dean Appell had been unfailingly kind and gracious—but the others, the ones I had visited in their drawing rooms, who had engaged me so charmingly? I had been treated like a trick pony they could send back to the circus in the end: a feminine voice but a muscular mind, a delightful novelty. I was not to imagine I was one of them.

I had looked forward to Paul's face when he congratulated me.

Never again would I submit my research to *Comptes rendus*; never again would I choose to present my work to the Academy. My research would therefore receive less attention—this could hurt me and my students. Yet I could not, I would not, ever again, subject myself to these male arbiters.

A noble character, the dean had called me.

Pierre had always said that prizes and positions were degrading.

I heard a scurry in the laboratory. I got up and washed my face in my office sink. When I stepped into the lab, I saw Maurice quickly tucking something under the table—a bouquet of flowers. André stared at the floor, while Agata and Jean stood mute.

"You mustn't mind so much," I said.

Maurice said, "The place is a cesspool of intrigue and gossip, that's what Uncle Pierre always said."

I tried to smile. "Your uncle did say that."

"Madame." Jean pulled up a stool for me.

"I'm not suddenly old," I said. The poor fellow blushed, and I put my arm around him.

As I walked toward the Gare de Luxembourg, I wrapped my shawl around my head to avoid attention, though the news wasn't yet widely known. The streets were noisy with engine groans, clacking bicycle horns and snorting Percherons. People mingled in doorways. Swarms of young men crossed the street just behind a passing tram.

By now, I thought, Paul must be on the train to Fontenay-aux-Roses. He hadn't contacted me. We had decided it would be too obvious to Jeannette, if he stayed out late the evening of the vote, yet he could have taken precautions and used a telephone, or at least sent a note. In an instinct of fear, without checking who might be watching, I changed direction, heading instead to our apartment. I nearly collided with a barrel-chested man who wouldn't step out of my way. A dirty fog hung in the air.

At rue du Banquier, there was a scattering of feathers on the stairs. I hurried up. The landing at the top was white with feathers, the door to our place ajar. The old woman from the next-door apartment stepped into the hall. She had the smell of sickness. "He's come and gone," she said.

Who had come and gone?

I looked around wildly. Our mattress was on the floor, half unstuffed. The bureau drawer had been pried open. My letters to Paul were gone.

That night I woke with a start a dozen times, remembering what was in those letters. I held my own arms and squeezed. My poor girls. It was good my parents hadn't lived to see, or Pierre's father.

Pierre would never, in any conceivable life, have dragged me into such a situation.

I didn't go into the city the next morning. I took Paul's letters from my bottom drawer and burned them. Nothing from him arrived in the morning post, but I received a dozen personal letters, sympathetic and gloating, about the Academy vote.

When I stepped outside, I found on my doorstep a copy of *l'Intransigeant*, a paper I never read. Who had left it there?

On the front page: "Branley defeats Madame Curie!"

> Madame Curie has pushed her taste for recompense and honors too far. She has offended scientists who once admired her. The general public has become hostile to her and applauds the lesson in modesty that the Institute has meted out.

I ripped it up and threw it away before Irène could see.

Paris, May 1895

This morning Pierre and I are to make the expedition to Sceaux, so I can meet his parents. When he comes to pick me up, I tell him I have a headache.

He says, "Walk with me to the train station, and if your headache isn't better, I'll walk you home and make it right with my parents." I agree, and we set off. His step is buoyant. In the end, we take the train to Sceaux.

"You've nothing to be afraid of," he says. "My parents are exquisite—you'll see." But who can give an impartial account of the people they love? There are beings who, among their families and their social class, are lavish in affection and praise, but whose eye turns critical when it is cast outside their circle.

At the Curie house, on rue des Sablons, vines climb over a cracked wall, and along the path, a pair of apple trees tangle their limbs. A rake rests against a shed. The moment I see the father in a work shirt like Pierre's, and the mother, round and pale in a polka-dot dress, weak from an illness but eager, I know that my misgivings are unfounded. They show me around their little house; they give me the best chair, and the delicacies they pass around, they offer first to me. *Tell us about your research,* they say, and *What is the state of education in Poland?* When my sister and her husband arrive, Pierre's mother takes Bronia into the kitchen, and I hear her say, "Don't let your sister hesitate. There's not another like my Pierre." They are modest but not ingratiating, self-assured but not arrogant. When a humble neighbor stops by for a game of chess, they greet him with respect.

"Could you come to love them?" asks Pierre. We are walking back to the station.

I flood him with tears. I hiccup like a child.

"My darling! What is it?"

"I was afraid they'd hate me and turn you against me."

"Oh, my darling." He covers my face with kisses, right there on the street. "As if that could ever happen."

XIV

Paris, Liguria, Brussels, April–November 1911

PERRIN AND I CONCLUDED that the burglar was Henri Bourgeois, Jeannette's brother-in-law, married to the sister who had assaulted me, and a journalist for *Le Petit Journal*, a sensationalist paper that catered to the masses with scandal and spectacle. Perrin went to see Jeannette. She claimed to have the letters, and she threatened to publish them.

"You have to leave Paris now," Perrin said. We were in his Sorbonne office, as we had been after the assault, the summer before, and once more he was advising me to go, to buy time and appease Jeannette.

"And no contact with Paul, all right?" he said. "No notes, no visits?"

I heard the rebuke that Paul and I deserved—what had we been thinking, meeting when we knew that Jeannette was alert to us, and keeping letters in a drawer?

"Yes, of course. I'm going to Zakopane in July. The girls will go ahead of me and stay with their cousins."

"For God's sake, Marie, how can I make this plain? Not July, not June. Now."

"It's plain, it's clear, I'll go."

Even as I said this, I hesitated. André and I had isolated enough polonium to begin a more precise study of its decay—

counting alpha particles, measuring the helium they produced. I wanted results before an important conference in Brussels that November. Only twenty-four physicists had been invited: Planck, Rutherford, Einstein, and six of us from France, including Paul, Perrin, and me. The subject was radiation and the quanta, and even as tired and unsettled as I was, the prospect was thrilling to me. Most people had no idea how serious the crisis in physics had become. We'd seen it building since Planck showed that black-body radiation didn't follow Newton's laws, or even Maxwell's electromagnetic theory. If the new findings were right, we needed all new theories. The Solvay Conference might be the most important scientific meeting ever held. I wanted to walk in with something to show.

Perrin rubbed his curly head, grim and alert. I had troubled him too much.

"I hope one day to make this up to you," I said.

"For a brilliant woman, you have a way of not connecting dots."

This, I suddenly realized, was true. When it came to danger, I could sometimes behave as if nothing were happening. If I connected the dots, the room began to spin.

"What about going to Genoa with the Borels?" he said. "Émile is attending a conference. His wife's going, too."

"Marguerite will be there?" Paul had moved in with the Perrins the week before, the night our apartment was plundered, and I knew that he confided in Marguerite. If I went to Italy, I could speak freely to her—she knew everything already. It was a school holiday. I could bring Irène and Eve.

"Are you sure you want to negotiate with this Henri Bourgeois, after what he did?" I pictured the knifed mattress, gutted, and my hand went to the sore spot on my scalp. "You're the best friend in the world, but you don't need my drama."

"I'm going to get those letters back. I'm going to scare the shit out of him, Marie."

"Why does this not relieve me?"

"There's something else I should tell you. Another turn in this saga."

"What?"

"Little Hélà has a high fever. Paul moved back home yesterday."

I flushed, my heart like a fish flipping in my chest.

"Jeannette told him that if Hélà died, it would be only the beginning of his punishment."

This news tipped some kind of scale for me. I had to get out of Paris.

It was strange and unreal to arrive in Santa Margherita, a bright little town on the Ligurian sea with a promenade and palm trees, and colorful houses, and sunshine, and voluble Italians.

Each day, while Émile was in Genoa, Marguerite and the girls and I hiked up narrow alleyways, past dwellings cut into the cliffside, smelling of cat pee and the powdery scent of sheets drying overhead. Now and then we heard women's voices from within the cavernous houses. Irène and Eve, now thirteen and six, would squat and watch beetles rolling balls of dung. Late afternoons we sat in cafés while Eve ran through the arcades with local children and Irène pestered Émile, back from the conference, with questions about math. A craggy old woman held court every day, pinching the cheeks of little ones who came to greet her.

The general public has become hostile to her. The newspaper's words rumbled in my mind, but these people here, in Santa Margherita, seemed to be saying, "Nothing is as bad as all that." Could it be true? That my troubles would pass, and my life was not a tragedy? My chest swelled with nostalgia—not a longing for Paul, exactly, though he was part of it. I had lost track of the self that had existed before Paul, and before Pierre. In this foreign land I sensed myself as one person among many, no better and no worse, and this was comforting. I had needed to separate from my life in Paris to feel this deeper life, a river

I needed to be on, and waters I needed to drink. If there were a scandal, if Jeannette made good on her threats, I would need to remember these waters.

We ate on the rooftop of the pensione. The girls ordered pesto alla Genovese every time, and twirled the green-specked noodles on their forks. When they fell asleep, Marguerite would come to my room, her hair brushed back, to talk with me about Paul. This young friend who normally held forth so charmingly didn't move a muscle in her face, for fear of stopping my stories. I probably sounded like one of the women in her novels, praising Paul's force of mind, pouring out my fears, but my sentiments were real.

What, after all, would happen to Paul? His face, when he lost hope, went dark and flat; his lids grew heavy. He lost all faith in himself.

"You'd walk through fire for him," said Marguerite.

The last time I saw him, on a rare stolen evening before the intruder, before the vote, we lay under a blanket on our bed as the light sank down to dusk. I propped myself on an elbow and traced his eyebrows, nose, and lips. He said, "I'd shrivel up without you."

I wanted to heal him, but our love seemed only to make things worse.

• • •

> *Yesterday, I scolded Irène for I don't know what, and Eve burst into tears. "You love her even though she pushes you around?" I say.*
>
> *"Yes," says Eve. "Anyway I like that better than if it was me who pushed her."*
>
> *"My little girl, are you sometimes unhappy?"*
>
> *"Yes, when others are in pain."*
>
> *"Then you worry more about others than yourself?"*
>
> *"I like it better when others are happier than me."*
>
> *Surely, no one taught her to talk like this.*

• • •

July, 1911, Zakopane, Poland

Darling Mé,

When you get here I hope you will stop Aunt Helena from trying to make me eat, eat, eat, because I can't eat so much.

I love Poland, the Poles, and the Polish language because it is your country, your people, and your language, but as for me, I love France more.

When I see the sun burning in the sky and making beautiful reflections on the brook, I think that it would all be more beautiful if a sweet Mé were near me to look at it. When it rains, I think that these moments in my room waiting for a lightning flash would be sweeter if you were in a chair near me.

I kiss you with all my heart on your beautiful tired forehead.

Irène

• • •

On a late July morning, I got up before dawn and took the 6:02 train, arriving in Paris at 6:40. The girls were in Zakopane while André and I spent a few more intensive weeks trying to clarify the decay sequence of polonium.

The greengrocers on rue Paillet piled up beans and cabbages, and merchants swept their walks, life going on regardless of my inner weather. Paul and I hadn't even been able to say goodbye after the intruder. We'd had no chance to make promises, say words for the other to hold dear, and so I drew on memories. Making love to each other as if nothing in the world mattered more. Agreeing that we belonged together. But Paul was living with Jeannette. In separate beds? I didn't know.

Whatever Perrin had said to Henri Bourgeois, there were no more threats. The next I would see Paul was November, in Brussels at the Solvay Conference. Not even Perrin thought that one of us should withdraw. What scientist would?

The sun on rue Cuvier turned the old stones a golden peach. From a distance I waved at our charwoman, Madame Brun, as she walked away from the laboratory. She always came in early and was gone by 7:30. She waved back and seemed to gesture toward our building. This puzzled me.

The door to my office was cracked open, and I smelled him before I saw him, lavender cologne seeping through the crack, suppressing the smell of someone who hadn't bathed. Monsieur Bourgeois. I somehow knew this right away. No one else was in the building. I had an impulse to flee, but I thought of our wrecked flat on rue du Banquier, and was frightened of what he might do if I left him alone in our lab.

He was at my desk, in my chair—a stout man with acne scars, wearing a checkered waistcoat and a gold fob chain. His hat was on my desk. The lavender was so overpowering, I stopped myself from covering my nose with my handkerchief.

He stood with a slight embarrassment. "Excuse me, Madame, my impertinence, shall we say, of coming here off your reasonable hours. I am Monsieur Bourgeois and I am here with some shall we say some fiduciary business at the behest of our mutual friend and relative, Madame Langevin."

I stayed at the doorway. "I don't have any business with you."

"I do appreciate your condescension. I'm here as a friend even though we have not been acquainted as of yet. Now I stand here before you, and I do appreciate this opportunity. It's fairly unique for me, as one unused to this sort of acquaintance, to come into a scientific establishment, and I've been looking over the appurtenances." He nodded at the glass case containing an analytical balance.

"What do you want?"

"I will go straight to my point and not be circumnavigating the subject." He lowered himself back into my chair. "There is the matter of some letters."

I stepped in and closed the door.

"Madame Langevin has in her unfortunate way come upon some correspondence. If I may be blunt, letters of affection which have been written in your hand. There's a question of morality here, but as a man of business I choose to go around this impertinence. Which is to say, for a certain sum of money, we, me and she, would be willing to turn a blind eye, which is always best in these circumstances, because the opposite for a woman of your fine reputation would be unpleasant."

My legs were shaking, but I found my voice. "You stole these letters, and you're blackmailing me."

"As you perhaps know, I am employed by a newspaper of some reputation. I am a reasonable man."

"Blackmail isn't reasonable."

"I am coming here more from family duty than from a need to pressure or to be insolent. My wife and Madame Langevin, I probably needn't tell you are of the closest acquaintance, being sisters."

"As a newspaper man, don't you need to guard your reputation?"

"I've come here with good intentions and to make sure that nothing of this gets wind. As you have understood, I have access to an editor who, not being a man of high morality himself, would be only too glad to publish your amorous elocution."

"I appeal to your conscience, Monsieur Bourgeois. You're not a blackmailer, really. You . . . You're a respectable man, Monsieur Bourgeois." I didn't recognize myself in these words. To dissemble like this sickened me.

"And I appeal to your conscience, Madame." He pressed his hat on his head. "Madame Langevin is a woman of many moods and much passion. You being a woman of illustrious circles, there is everything to be gained by pouring oil on these waters."

I double-locked the doors behind him. I threw open my windows and closed myself in André's office.

Jean Perrin consulted with lawyers and asked me to boulevard Kellerman to discuss the issue of the blackmail. It was nine p.m. Henriette looked pinched. She lit a lamp and took me to the garden. The children were upstairs in bed.

"What's wrong?" I asked. "Is Paul all right?"

"Oh my dear, there's trouble." She waited until we were seated at the wrought iron table. "Paul took the boys with him to Leipzig. Jeannette's accusing him of kidnapping them."

"He didn't tell her?"

"He waited twenty-four hours to tell her."

"Oh no. That was rash."

"He consulted an attorney before he left."

To me this was hopeful—he had consulted an attorney, he was serious about divorce—but Henriette's face told me not to rejoice.

Perrin came in. "Have you eaten? Would you like a plate?"

"I ate early," I lied.

"How are the girls?"

"My family is stuffing them with sausages, according to Irène."

He poured us each a brandy. Henriette, who rarely took alcohol, drank half of hers right down.

"You'd better tell me now," I said.

"I met with the lawyer of Monsieur Bourgeois," said Perrin. "Jeannette has sued for divorce. Marie, there's going to be a trial."

I held my hand steady as I drank my brandy. We had wanted Paul to file first, for reasons of emotional incompatibility. "Did she charge him with abandonment?"

Perrin and Henriette exchanged a look.

"Please don't hold back."

Perrin said, "She charged him with abandonment, but she also charged him with consorting with a concubine in the marital dwelling."

The garden shrubbery, the house, the Perrins—all seemed far away.

Henriette said, "Jeannette has got herself an illustrious hostage."

"But we never—" I said, and Henriette waved my words away. I had been going to say, we had never been together at his house. Consorting. "Will I have to appear in court?"

"It's possible," said Perrin.

My glass slipped from my hand and the brandy spilled. Perrin poured me another. The burn traveled down my throat.

"What does she want? Is it money?"

"She wants 1000 francs a month, and she wants Paul to agree to no custody of the children whatsoever."

I shook my head. Paul would not agree to that.

"That's why she's brought you into this," said Henriette. "She thinks Paul will give in to her demands, to keep you out of it."

Her face came close to me, then pulled out far away.

I drank another brandy.

Bourgeois had written asking for 5000 francs to slow things down, they said. Perrin and Émile Borel had gone to the police with this letter, to see about a blackmail charge, but they got nowhere. Paul wanted to pay off Bourgeois, but he didn't have the money.

"But I have 5000 francs," I said.

"He won't accept it from you."

"He can pay me back." I stood up and moved unsteadily toward the house. Henriette followed me.

"Where are you going?" she asked. She sounded alarmed.

"I'm a little sick."

I went into the bathroom and sat on the toilet with my head in my hands. When I came back into the hallway, the Perrins were speaking in low voices, in the drawing room. He asked her something I couldn't make out, and she answered, "I don't know. That she'll jump off a bridge. I would."

"It's terrible, terrible," he said.

Oh yes, I thought. I could go to the bridge. The one by the quai where Pierre was killed.

Henriette wouldn't allow me to leave. She brought me a nightgown and helped me dress. She brushed my hair, and I said to her, "You must hate me." It was shock and the brandy talking, but it was also what I was feeling.

She pushed hair out of my eyes. "Why would you say that?"

"You're the wife of a scientist. Your husband, well, he isn't a saint, is he."

"Hush, Marie."

"And I'm not a saint. But I would never make love to your husband, I never would. You know that, don't you? You believe me?"

"I believe you, hush."

"Do you hate me? Henriette?"

"Listen, Marie. Look at me. My eyes."

I wavered, but I looked at her face. A good face. Good wrinkles around her eyes.

"My husband has done much worse than you," she said. "I know that, Marie. He also has a chair at the Sorbonne. He's sitting downstairs drinking brandy, and no one is bothering him. Don't question yourself, do you hear me? You can't be questioning yourself. You won't survive. Do you hear me? Later on you can ask yourself what part you played. Right now, do not question yourself."

On a blistering afternoon, I climbed the steps of the stately institution where I did my banking, to make the transaction that would drain me of my savings. In exchange for 5000 francs, Bourgeois and Jeannette agreed to keep my name out of the lawsuit, but they refused to hand over the letters. And there was nothing to bind them to their promise.

For the whole month of August, visiting my family in Poland with the girls, I managed to act as if nothing were happening, and almost to believe it. In September, back in Paris, I kept expecting a legal summons, or an urgent message from Jean Perrin, or lavender perfume under my door. October came, and none of this had happened. Apparently, by giving in to blackmail, I had given them what they wanted.

Henriette told me that since Jeannette had pressed charges against Paul, he had made a point of traveling as he pleased, traveling around Europe to conferences without informing her.

"Good," I said. "He's standing up to her. Maybe he's getting stronger."

"Stronger or more reckless," she said.

My girls fussed and complained and fought with each other. Irène tried to convince me not to go to the Solvay Conference, or to let her come along. She had added up the days that I was away from her that year. "One day I'll go to Brussels," she said, "to a great scientific conference, and you'll be too old to accompany me." I suspected she was only half teasing.

One afternoon I asked Jean Danysz to meet me in my office. He arrived breathless and sweaty, having run to make our meeting.

"How's your baby's fever?" I asked him. Jean reminded me of my brother, the same ebullience tempered by a conscientious streak.

"Better, Madame, but my wife needs to take him to the doctor."

I poured him a glass of water. "There's something I want to ask you."

He drank the water down, and I poured him another glass.

"Your work on magnetic deflection is superb. You have the makings of a fine scientist. I want to promote you to my laboratory assistant. I hope you'll say yes."

His eyes watered. "Madame. Honored doesn't begin to express . . ." He twitched around his mouth. He'd been under more strain than I knew.

"Do you have the money to pay the doctor?"

"I think so. I think I do."

"You'll have a salary now."

"I don't have the words to thank you."

"You've earned this, Jean. I've relied on you a good deal."

"If it's all right with you, I'll go home now. I want to tell my wife."

When he got to the door I said, "Oh, Jean—"

"Yes?" He turned back to look.

"Your kindnesses to me personally—they don't go unnoticed."

"Nie ma za co." Think nothing of it.

"Do widzenia, Jean."

"Do widzenia, Madame."

I went and stood by the window, a tear leaking down my face. With Jean, at least, I was doing something right.

On the last day of October, I boarded a train to Brussels for the Solvay Conference. I was immensely excited. André and I had done calculations that allowed us to estimate the number of atoms in a gram-molecule of helium, and from there, to derive a value for Avogadro's number. It was encouraging progress—something solid in hand. I couldn't help wondering whether quantum theory might someday shed light on radioactive decay. I'd be listening for any hint of it, even if that wasn't what we were at Solvay to discuss.

The chairman, Hendrik Lorentz, had sent out some of the reports in advance, and during part of the journey I found myself absorbed in his own contribution. The ideas weren't entirely new, but the clarity and elegance with which he laid out the problem struck me deeply. He showed, with an almost painful precision, how classical physics breaks down in the face of light's true behavior. The old theory of equipartition, when applied to blackbody radiation, led to a glaring absurdity—predicting infinite energy.

The wheels of the train clattered rhythmically over the rail joints, and the sky turned hazy, making it harder to read. My carriage was just behind the dining car; whenever the doors opened between, the smell of soup drifted in, rich and salty. My stomach growled. I set my papers aside and turned to the window. The fields rolled by, orange stubble glowing whenever the clouds parted.

Paul had left early for Amsterdam with Perrin and Poincaré; from there, they would travel on to Brussels. I told myself these travel arrangements weren't personal, that I understood why—

it would have been foolish for us to be seen together. Still, I felt shut out.

Seven months. I had endured the ache of him for seven months. We had kept our distance, obeyed the rules we had agreed upon. But I had marked this day in my mind, as if calibrated to it, and now just one more day felt unbearable.

In Brussels, we would decide what came next. I tried not to expect too much—our love had already cost us dearly. It was possible Paul wanted to end it. Yet I held fast to the hope that we might find a way forward together.

The train slid through pastureland. On a muddy riverbank, a gray heron stretched its neck out, a black stripe running from eye to crest. Then it was gone. A field of calves, all facing all one way. Gone.

I used to miss Poland the way I now missed Paul. A wreath of wildflowers, the scent of spring peas—these could bring back my homeland so fiercely my throat would tighten, my ribs ache. I still missed Poland. But now I knew—somewhere quiet, in a fold of my heart—that even if the Sorbonne and my laboratory were suddenly transported to Warsaw, and I lived on the cobbled streets near the house where my mother gave birth to me, by the muddy Vistula with its smell of fish and apples, even if I picked berries from the same fields of my childhood—still, I would not be appeased. I would still hear, on a cold wind, the howling from Siberia. I would look up at the gray herons above me and wonder what country they were flying toward and feel the ache of longing.

Perhaps it was like that with Paul. Perhaps nothing and no one could take this yearning away.

I carried my bag through the open sweep of Place de Brouckère. Trams rattled past. Women in high-buttoned shoes hurried by. In five minutes I arrived at the Grand Hotel Métropole: neo-Renaissance splendor, a massive front, three levels and nine bays. The lobby had statues and Corinthian columns, carved wood ceilings, mirrors and chandeliers. A polished man behind a marble counter handed my room key to a bellhop, his temperament as bright as his red uniform.

"My uncle Dagobert started as a bellhop—now he's a concierge. I'm Dagobert, too," he said, lifted my bag with gusto. I had to convince him not to unpack for me. My suite had a rich blue carpet with creamy flowers, golden drapes around the bed, and a balcony looking onto the square.

It would be ludicrous to sleep on such a bed alone.

Dagobert had barely left when I heard a knock at the door: tap, tap, tap-tap, tap-tap. Paul's knock. I opened the door to his square shoulders and broad brow, the compacted energy that made him burn, the oversized, ridiculous moustache. He was real. In some strange way, I had feared I had imagined him. But here he was, a fact.

"My God," he said, "look at you!" He barreled into me, he laughed.

"Let me look at you!"

He held my shoulders. "What do you see?"

"A drunken sweetheart."

"Right you are, and I've ordered champagne."

His moustache over my mouth made my body a swamp. "I haven't bathed," I said.

"All the better." He tasted the salt on my face, and he growled and drove me to the bed.

He made love to me hard and deep, and it hurt—the angle was wrong, the pressure struck something far back, so that I cramped and ached. But I didn't ask him to stop. I didn't want him to.

Paul was with me, and I was in his arms. We were alive, and we were still the two of us.

We bathed. We drank champagne and dined in my suite. Paul had pre-arranged a table with candles, starchy white linen and delphiniums. Fish stew, endive salad, goat cheese, apple tart. I kept reaching over and stroking his hand. He was really there.

He took the last bit of cheese and said, "Planck and Poincaré are going to challenge me." He was giving a paper too, on diamagnetism. "You know, not one of us has caught up to the ramifications of mass and energy equivalence."

"Do you think Einstein has?"

"Caught up with the ramifications?"

"Yes."

"That man cracks the earth open, destroys classical physics, and then tosses us the pieces. It's up to us to find the evidence. The great thing is, he has no need to prove anything. He's nothing but a pure knowing subject."

"The clear eye of the world."

"He wears a morning coat to dinner. He's immune to rank and prestige."

I pushed around a bit of apple tart on my plate. "That's just how you used to talk about Pierre."

"Ah, yes." He swallowed more champagne.

"You like someone to admire. To help you forget yourself."

He leaned back and looked at me. "Someone like you."

"I think I was that person for a while."

His eyes flickered. "I still admire you."

I took his hand to my lips. "I know."

I did know. And yet I felt that his excitement, and even his passion, was partly the energy of farewell. Perhaps he had already left me. Perhaps not. I didn't want to assume, and he might not know himself, but the feeling was there.

We made love again under the cavernous ceiling, in the glow of lamps. After, he lay with his head on my arm, drowsing. We didn't talk about our future. Clearly, he felt no pressure to make a plan.

"You're thinking," Paul said, in a sleepy voice.

"Just dreaming." These were the kinds of things that mattered in the end: Paul's soft words before sleep, the touching of our feet beneath covers.

"Of what?"

"All my dreams are of you."

He lay on top of me to kiss me, and with my hands I memorized his neck, his shoulders, the muscles tapering down his back. The smell that belonged only to him, and never to another.

We were discreet—we arrived separately at the first presentation of the conference.

The room felt tense—not surprising, really. Max Planck was cautious by nature, uneasy with Einstein's notion that light and energy are guided by chance, though it was Planck himself who first proposed that energy isn't continuous, but comes in tiny, discrete packets. Lorentz opened with modest and compelling authority, and before long, we were caught up in a debate about a factor in one of his equations. Paul and Planck responded by turning to ordinary differential equations instead of the newer expressions for fluctuations. Paul wasn't being conservative—he'd taught Einstein's boldest theories across Europe. But he wanted to test the new ideas against the old, to see what might still hold.

I sent letters to the girls, describing the hotel's splendor to Eve, and to Irène, the euphoria I felt, bearing down on problems with kindred minds. I shared that Einstein had invited us all to come hiking in Switzerland with him and his son, about Eve's age. I didn't say that he had invited Paul, too, or that Paul, at that moment, had touched my leg under the table, a thrilling touch that came, after all, with a vision of the future: my lover and my children and my life in science.

For nearly two whole days at the Solvay Conference, I felt I was back in my life.

Around six p.m. I was resting in bed before the evening reception when someone tapped at my door. Not Paul's knock. Nor would Paul come to my room at this hour.

An image of a checkered waistcoat and scarred face came to

my mind, and the memory of lavender, but I opened the door and found Dagobert, the bellhop, looking pleased with himself.

"A telegram for you, Madame. From Stockholm." He waited while I opened it.

My face must have shown my joy.

"Good news, Madame?"

He was so eager, I couldn't resist handing him the telegram to read.

> REUTERS 4 NOVEMBER 1911
>
> MADAME CURIE STOP NOBEL PRIZE IN CHEMISTRY AWARDED TO YOU STOP ONLY YOU HAVE WON TWICE STOP ANNOUNCEMENT NEXT WEEK STOP PLEASE WAIT TO DIVULGE STOP CONGRATULATIONS STOP SVANTE ARRHENIUS

"Again, Madame?" said Dagobert.

So he did know who I was.

"Yes sir, again. This time for chemistry, for the isolation of the elements polonium and radium."

"Wait till I tell my uncle!"

"Oh, Dagobert, I'm afraid I've been indiscreet. Can you wait to tell anyone, until it's announced in the paper? There's a rule about this."

"You can count on me, Madame. I've never betrayed a secret. My uncle says that's what makes a good bellhop and a good concierge."

"My money's on you for concierge, Dagobert, and before you're thirty-five."

"Thank you, Madame!"

I shut the door behind him and paced the room. The humiliation of the Academy vote? Gone. The chance of pushing through the Radium Institute? Much more likely, now. Two Nobel prizes. Never done before.

It was all I could do to stop myself from running down two flights of steps to the fourth floor and knocking on Paul's door. I wanted to see his joyful face. But someone might be in the room with him or see me in the hall. Instead I took the elevator to the lobby and sent a telegram of thanks to Arrhenius. The news wouldn't likely be published for a couple of days.

If only my father were alive to hear!

I smoothed my hair back into a new twist and framed my face with a few soft strands. Finally, at nine p.m., I found my way to the evening reception, the hall with its massive carved fireplace and more chandeliers. I said hello to Hendrik Lorentz, the organizer, who stood with Poincaré and Einstein. When I approached the group, Einstein wandered off as if he hadn't seen me. I was half amused—clearly, something was on his mind. I didn't see Paul.

Lorentz, by way of apology for Einstein, said, "He's in the midst of a divorce. Rumor has it he's in love with his cousin."

"Ah. Have you seen Monsieur Langevin?"

"He stood me up for an afternoon meeting."

Finally, Paul came into the hall, elegant but tense in his floppy tie, a flower on his lapel. I brought him a glass of champagne. My own few sips had already gone to my head.

"Paul, I have news."

"So do I."

"Yours first," I said. It was clear that his wasn't good.

He led me out of the hall—in front of everyone—and took me to a quiet room off of a corridor, an airless place with a faint stink of smoke.

He closed the door and faced me. His expression made the blood drain from my cheeks. "She's gone to the press," he said.

The events that followed seemed to unfold in a different kind of time and space. During the conference sessions, the speakers' words reached me at a ten-second lag. In a discussion on relativity—how time and space shift depending on the observer—I thought only, and oddly, that I was the one they meant: the observer, watching from a distant star. When Einstein spoke about energy fluctuations in solids and his fusion of wave and emission theories of light, Paul lit up, debating Brillouin, Nernst, and Poincaré. To me, he looked like a puppet—arms, legs, mouth moving.

Then one morning when I went down for coffee, a colleague from Paris looked at me with a raised lip corner and walked away. A table of scientists stopped talking when I came near. I froze in place.

"Madame Curie, sit with me," said Lorentz, taking my elbow. I didn't even sip my coffee, while he ate bread and ham and chatted at me, I believe about the mathematics of his theory of luminiferous aether.

"I'm afraid there's been some gossip," I finally said.

Paul had said that Jeannette had told the papers she was suing him, and that she had my letters.

Lorentz put down his fork and wiped his mouth with a napkin. "They say you've disappeared like the Mona Lisa from the Louvre."

"Disappeared?"

"Of course, we all know where you are."

That night, my Nobel prize was announced, presumably to raised glasses and hurrahs. I don't remember that.

In that side room at the Métropole Hotel, when Paul told me that Jeannette had gone to the press, my legs gave out. I lay on the floor for several minutes before I could stand up. Paul wasn't sure whether to call for medical help. Somehow, in the midst of it all, we agreed there was nothing to be gained by rushing back to Paris. We would stay, go to the sessions, act as if everything were normal.

When I told him about the Nobel, he said, "But this is marvelous," though he clearly couldn't take it in.

He came to my room the last morning. My bag was at the door, waiting for Dagobert. I didn't want Paul there—I was afraid of the photographers. Neither of us could offer the other comfort. We didn't know how to prepare for what might come next.

Our last hug was bloodless, devastating. I thought, Jeannette Langevin has stolen our love. I couldn't even cry.

In the hotel lobby: journalists and cameras, newspapers in my face.

I took the train from Brussels by myself. I sat by a window, and a thickset man, a Frenchman, sat next to me. He pulled a newspaper out of his briefcase. On the front page: a caricature of my face. The headline read, "A STORY OF LOVE: MADAME CURIE AND PROFESSOR LANGEVIN." I saw phrases: "suing her husband," "consorting with a concubine," "proof in the form of letters, held by Madame Langevin."

I turned my head to the window and stared out for the rest of the trip. There was pressure in my bladder, but I didn't trust my voice to ask the man to let me out. Time passed. Finally, the passenger put on his coat and disembarked.

He left the newspaper on his seat: on it, a gun drawn in scratchy ink, and above it, scrawled in black, "ADULTERESS."

Isle-de-France, July 1895

On our honeymoon, Pierre and I make our way on bicycles through villages of granite houses, where chickens peck in gravel. The roads swirl through the damp green landscape, tufted here and there with forests.

Pierre, I know, is asking himself the reasons why certain faces of a crystal have preferential development—do they have a different rate of growth, or is their solubility different? He is more fit than I am, and he speeds ahead of me, sometimes looking back and stopping, annoyed that I'm not just behind him. When I catch up, my shirtwaist drenched in sweat, he greets me with, "Can't you pedal faster?"

"Can't you pedal slower?"

"All right," he concedes, but as soon as we set off he forgets his promise, and off he goes again.

Each time he rounds a corner out of my sight, a little panic sets in. I imagine a dog running in front of his bike, and his body flying. If I reach him within a minute, he'll be all right, I say to myself, as if my eyes on him can keep him safe. If I see him before he crests the hill, no harm will come to him. It is highly unscientific. This problem is solved only by my assiduous pedaling and gaining strength.

XV

Paris, November–December 1911

ROMANCE IN A LABORATORY: THE AFFAIR OF MME CURIE AND M. LANGEVIN by F. Hauser

Le Petit Journal, 5 November 1911

. . . *le Petit Journal* interviewed Madame Langevin at her home in Fontenay-aux-Roses and found a woman in tears, terrified of the fuss that her conjugal misfortune was causing. "I would never have pursued my husband in court, but he has left the country with this woman, and I don't know where he is." Why, we asked, did she not shout out the betrayal of her husband and the one who has destroyed her home? "I have kept silent," she answered, "because it was my duty as a mother and wife, to hide the faults of the one whose name I bear." Now, however, she can no longer bear her martyrdom.

While this poor and unhappy woman whose heart is ravaged by undeserved misfortune was thus expressing herself, her smallest little girl, an adorable toddler, was pressing close against her and stammering, "Don't cry, maman, petit père will come back!"

Special Cable to *le Temps*

Brussels, 6 November 1911

. . . Madame Curie told *le Temps*, "I went to Brussels along with twenty French and foreign scientists, including Paul Langevin, to a scientific meeting of the greatest importance. They knew at my laboratory where I was. The story is pure folly."

SCIENCE AND VIRTUE

l'Action française, 8 November 1911

. . . This woman is not of our race, she is a Pole, a functionary of modest talent. She is backed by hypocritical Sorbonne professors, Israelites and Protestants who hide behind algebra, physics and chemistry treatises; she has willingly benefited from the prerogatives of men.

LETTERS TO THE EDITOR FROM MADAME CURIE AND JOURNALIST F. HAUSER

Le Temps, 8 November 1911

Nothing I have done obliges me to feel diminished. In spite of the wrong done to me, because of the formal retraction and apologies I have received—with permission, I have included one from F. Hauser with this letter—I will not currently waste my time with lawsuits, but I find the intrusion of the press into private life abominable, and particularly so when it involves people who have manifestly consecrated their lives to preoccupations of an elevated order. Henceforth, I will vigorously pursue all tendentious allegations, and I will demand damages and interest of considerable sums, which I will use in the interests of science.

M. Curie

Dear Madame Curie,

I am tortured by the thought of the harm that I have done to you. I am consoled only by the thought that the humble journalist I am will not be able to tarnish the glory and respect that surround you. Madame, I will never again write a word, signed or unsigned, about this sad affair. I bow to you in respect, and I authorize you to publish this letter.

Your afflicted,
F. Hauser

Sceaux, France
20 November 1911

Dear Monsieur Arrhenius,

. . . I remain grateful for your enthusiastic advocacy of my candidacy for the Nobel. I write you now to discuss the delicate matter of attacks on me by the family of M. Langevin. I would like very much to thank the Swedish Academy in person for the great honor, but I am afraid that the ceremony might be disagreeably troubled by rumors in the press. I would be grateful for your counsel as to whether you think I should come or whether it would be best for me to stay away.

M. Curie

Stockholm, Sweden
23 November 1911

Dear Madame Curie,

Here in Stockholm the chicanery and lies of the French press are very well known, but no one believes them. I assure you that the Swedish press will be free of any mention of the Langevin affair during your visit. You will be the guest of our nation.

S. Arrhenius

• • •

The girls were all right. Irène had heard rumors, but I reminded her of the craziness after the first Nobel, the stories and intrusions. Eve, almost seven, was attuned to my anxiety, but I thought it unlikely that she had been exposed to gossip.

Paul moved into a faculty apartment at the EPCI. He had lunch with the boys every day, and on weekends he took all four of his children for rambles in the countryside. Through Perrin, he sent me words of encouragement, urging me to ignore the gossip columns and the storm of public abuse.

I tried. But the exposure of my private life—and the speculation about my motives, thoughts, and feelings—brought about a kind of inner unravelling. A quiet panic took hold. It felt as if the threads that bound me to myself were loosening. The person I had become through decades of patient work and devotion—she was slipping away. I held onto my thoughts of the Solvay Conference, of the twenty-some scientists I stood among. That could not be taken from me—not by newspapers, nor tabloids, nor letters, nor lawyers, nor the rising tide of accusation.

I was like a spider casting a silk filament into the wind, hoping to be carried forward.

Each day I expected to find stories about my new Nobel in the papers, but there were only brief items, buried in the middle. Still, no one could take my achievement away, and the note from Arrhenius of the Swedish Academy fortified me. My letters to Paul were only a rumor—Jeannette still held the proof. The journalist Fernand Hauser's letter, which retracted his story in *Le Petit Journal*, was reprinted around the world along with mine, and gave me hope that the storm would pass.

In Brussels, after sex with Paul, the ache of it had stayed with me, as if I were bruised inside, which maybe I was. I had felt it when I was walking, or even breathing a little. But this had gone away. Home again, I developed a dull ache low in my pelvis. It burned when I peed. I drank water, and I rested, and I was relieved when I began to feel better.

One night, with the girls asleep and the moon shining, I sat on my bedroom floor, surrounded by papers and graphs. I picked up my copy of the official Solvay proceedings—Lorentz had carefully transcribed all our exchanges, every discussion. A cockerel roosting in my neighbor's tree let out a wild, misplaced crow. A fox in the garden? My nerves were so frayed I spilled my tea. Usually, the bird waited for morning.

I was deep in my reading when a spray of pebbles hit the house. I ducked without thinking. A clump of dirt thumped against the sill. Then a sharp ping on the glass—a web of cracks. Eve appeared in her nightdress, and before I could stop her, she looked out the window and saw three people standing under the lamp outside our gate. A woman pointed up at us.

"They're excited, right, Mé? About your prize?" Eve was trying to make it better.

"We'll ignore them, shall we?" I said lightly.

"Will you lie down with me?"

We went to her room, and I lay beside her. From across the hall, another ping. It had been two weeks since the stories broke in the papers—why now?

"Shall I sing you a lullaby? One your grandmother used to sing?"

Eve nodded, her little chin lifted, and I began, "*Na Wojtusia z popielnika / Iskiereczka mruga*," a lullaby about fairy stories, and how the tellers weave their tales as the fairy lights blink. My voice wavered at first, but I kept going, louder, filling the room with the sweet, haunting tune. I could almost hear my mother's tambourine, its rustle and jingle rising up to shield us from the noise outside.

The next morning Irène went as usual by train to the center city, and I walked Eve to school. I decided not to go to the police, but instead I did some errands and then went to talk to André. *Step left, step right, step, step, step.* I coached myself to keep moving forward.

Maurice stepped into the hallway when I came in. "Aunt, are you all right?"

André ushered me into his office and handed me a fresh copy of *l'Oeuvre*. "I'm sorry," he said.

"Please, André, that's one rag I can't—it's the worst of the worst." I tried to keep my attitude of protest. Gustave Téry, the publisher, fancied himself a "free thinker" and loved to attack "the German-Jewish Sorbonne" in his weekly paper.

From the next room came low tones from Maurice, Jean, and Agata.

André said, "Sit down. You need to know."

I couldn't remember when he had ever issued me a command.

On the cover of the weekly, I read, "My dear Paul, I think only of the moment when I will find again all the sweetness of your presence . . . I beg you, don't make me wait too long for the separation of your beds. . . ."

It was my letter from l'Arcouëst. I flipped the page. "You must decide to do all you can, methodically, to make her life with you unbearable . . . When I know that you are with her, my nights are atrocious, I can't sleep, I wake in a fever. . . ."

The room was freezing. My knees and elbows shook.

André stood behind me. "The bastards."

"There's just this letter?"

"It's ten pages of letters to Paul from you."

"Ten pages of letters," I echoed. They had been throwing stones at my house because of my letters to Paul. This weekly had reached the stands.

"Is Eve at home?" André asked.

"She will be soon. The nanny brings her at midday." This nanny, Lorraine, was temporary. She lived next door. The girls' cousin had gone back to Poland.

"You go to Eve," said André. "I'll pick up Irène from school."

As I approached the gate at my house in Sceaux, seven or eight people milled about with hardened faces. Some carried umbrellas though it wasn't raining. A man had set up a camera on a tripod. He smoked a cigarette.

I hadn't told André what had happened last night. I hadn't thought to tell him.

I cut around to the dirt lane that ran behind the houses on our street, along a deserted railroad track, and entered my house from the back garden.

"Mé!" said Eve.

I pulled her close.

"Dirty Jew!" came a shout through the window. "Husband stealer!"

Eve asked, "Are we Jewish?"

"No, little one."

"Do we like Jews?"

"Yes, of course. Where's Lorraine?"

"She has a stomachache."

"Where is she?"

"In the bathroom. She has a stomachache."

I went to the kitchen to make coffee, Eve clinging to my leg. She liked hot milk with sugar and a splash of coffee; it would be a treat. I would make some lunch. I set out three cups, for Eve, Lorraine, and me.

A stone knocked against the sill.

Irène had gymnastics until four p.m. Had André meant that he would pick her up right away?

The coffee pot gurgled on the stove. My hand trembled as I turned off the gas. The milk frothed to a boil.

Pebbles sprayed the kitchen window: another crack. I moved quickly to open the window, leaned out and caught the shutters. A red-faced woman screwed up her face and spit in my direction. I slammed the shutters.

Eve clamped her arms around my waist again. I had already picked up the coffee, and I set it down too fast: the pot tipped, spilling scalding coffee on Eve's arm. Her shriek ran through me like fire. I filled a bowl with water and held her arm in it. She screamed and tried to pull away. Did I need to get her to the hospital?

"Lorraine!" I called.

Eve writhed in my arms until, finally, she whimpered and went limp.

Lorraine came in, pale and splotchy, and I thrust Eve into her arms. "Keep her burn in water."

André would be bringing Irène. They would walk from the station, not knowing any better. I had no telephone to warn them.

Why hadn't I listened to André when he told me to install a telephone?

I latched all the shutters, upstairs and down, and double-checked the locks on the doors.

In the kitchen, Lorraine had set the water on the floor and helped Eve to lean over it. The burn was seven centimeters long and nearly as wide. It was swelling but not terribly.

With the shutters closed, the house was dark. When we sat in the parlor, Eve crawled into my arms. She was six years old and almost too big for me to hold. Her blouse and pinafore were stained, and she smelled of coffee. I held a compress to her arm and kept her arm above her heart.

Lorraine took up her knitting, but she kept having to undo her stitches.

I closed my eyes and rested my head, and I thought of Pierre's body in his coffin across the way. There had been times when I believed that he was with me, living in my chest beside my heart. He was not there now.

"Foreign bitch! Go home!"

Do not question yourself.

At Zola's funeral, the crowd had gotten ugly when Dreyfus arrived. Pierre and I had been fearful they'd throw fire. *L'Oeuvre* hated Dreyfus. The ones who hated Dreyfus also hated me.

Eve burrowed her head into my body.

Where was Paul? *The risk to you is high,* he'd said.

A motor approached from down the lane. Taxis didn't normally drive on the lane, and in Sceaux, not many owned automobiles.

Someone tapped at the back entrance. Lorraine dropped her knitting.

I went to the door.

"Marie!" came a low voice.

It was André, and Marguerite Borel in a cape. They stepped inside and André locked the door. Marguerite looked at the spilled coffee, the bowl of water on the floor.

"Where's Irène?" I asked.

Marguerite said, "We're taking you to my house."

André said, "I'll get Irène right after."

"I don't think I can go." All I could think was, I might never be able to come back.

"Of course you can. We'll help."

I heard André in the parlor asking Eve about her wound. When he came back, he said, "We'll get you out of here."

"They'll leave," I said. "We'll wait until they leave."

"I don't want to scare you, but there's talk of throwing you in the Seine."

"They only want to frighten me." The wooden floorboards widened and narrowed as André walked me to the parlor. Marguerite went upstairs to pack a bag.

André left first with Lorraine, to walk her home. He was back in ten minutes; they had managed without being noticed. All four of us then crossed the back lawn to the dirt lane, and headed toward the cab, which waited near the street. The ache in my pelvis had moved to my lower back, and I was walking strangely, and I could tell that André saw. He carried our suitcase. Marguerite held Eve's hand and mine.

We had nearly reached the automobile when a stone hit the windshield.

A man called, "She's here!" and the crowd moved in.

André shoved the three of us into the back seat and got in with the driver. A woman blocked our path. Red hair, square jaw, staring through the windshield.

An egg splattered on the window by my face. Eve began to cry.

The driver honked his horn and inched forward. The woman hung on to the hood but finally dropped off. She slapped an open palm over her fist in disgust. Our driver picked up speed.

We turned off the lane onto the open street; within seconds we had left all the people behind.

"Stop," I said. The driver stepped on the brakes.

"What is it?" said André.

"Irène. We forgot Irène."

"Carry on," he said to the driver, and to me, "I'll go straight to Irène. I'll bring her to you. She's at gymnastics, right?"

"But my briefcase."

"I'll come back and get it tomorrow. You go to Marguerite's, and she'll call a doctor for Eve."

Eve's dress was wet. I was wet, too. It had been drizzling on our walk to the cab. The people had been right to bring umbrellas.

The driver circled around past rue Sablons, past the house of Pierre's family, tucked behind an apple tree.

When we got to the Borels', I waited with Eve in their guest room, listening for Irène. Finally she came running up the stairs, ahead of Henriette Perrin. She barreled into me and clung to my waist. Henriette tried to coax her away. Later, I woke in the night, sweaty, with pain deep in my flank. Eve's hair was in my mouth, her bandaged arm on my ribs.

Mont-St.-Michel, Normandy, France, Summer 1905

We travel in a carriage pulled by tandem horses—Pierre, my sister Helena, Irène, her cousin, and me. As we draw closer, the tenth-century abbey rises from the sea on its granite perch. It looks like a floating castle.

"For three hundred years," Pierre says in his deepest voice, "this island was the center of Gallo-Roman culture. Then came the bar-ba-ri-ans."

We climb the battlements of Mont-St.-Michel, visit the prison, the abbey church. But these are not why we've come. It's the 30th of August. We've come to climb to the West Terrace by 12:45 p.m., and wait. Pierre hands out special lenses. There's a shadow across his forehead, and he limps like an old man, but he's jaunty, almost theatrical.

At 1:02, the moon catches the sun. The light dims. A long, narrow line of migrating birds flies toward us. Then, suddenly, they turn and veer south. Swallows drop from the sky. They shriek and whirl above our heads, a tightening storm. More and more of them fall down, roosting on the church spire, the galleries, the windows, in the reeds below. The sun thins to a crescent. The moon's shadow rushes across the sea.

"Mé," whispers Irène, throwing her arms around me.

The sun goes black.

The birds go silent.

XVI

Paris and Stockholm, November–December 1911

At the Borels', in the downstairs hallway, the telephone rang and rang. I could hear from our room upstairs. Marguerite said, "a sordid cabal," "of course we are," "yes, she's here," and "we don't feel that way." Émile's angry voice shouted into the receiver.

That first morning, Eve woke up cranky, her burn inflamed. I changed her bandage, helped her bathe, settled her with colored pencils. My back pain was worse, as if someone had slugged me under my ribs.

At least I was done hiding things. There was nothing more Jeannette could do to me.

Marguerite came in with a tray of ham and fruit. "Irène went to school. Henriette will bring her for a visit."

"Thank God for you and Henriette."

She seemed preoccupied as she set down the tray and laid out napkins.

I watched her. "Are my friends turning against me?"

"Of course not," she said, but she blushed.

"Who called Émile?"

"The minister of public instruction."

"What did he say?"

She busied herself with the tray.

"It's better that I know."

"He threatened Émile with a demotion."

"For harboring me?" These were college apartments.

"For sullying French academic honor."

I went to the closet and pulled my suitcase out.

"Stop, Marie. Émile won't hear of this."

"I can't put the two of you at risk."

"You'll embarrass Émile. It would look as if he were cowed. Would you do that to a red-blooded mathematician?"

I sank back into my chair. Marguerite was the daughter of Dean Appell. If his son-in-law could be demoted for giving me shelter, what would they do to me?

I spent an hour coaxing Eve to eat, and later that morning, André arrived. He found his way upstairs and handed me my briefcase, its yellow leather streaked and worn. I held it to my chest. The bag that Pierre had bought for me, after our Nobel prize.

André said, "Your house looked just as usual. No one about."

"You're a dear."

"Paul came to see me at the office this morning."

"What did he want?"

"To thank me, actually, for looking after you."

"Oh—" I was surprised Paul had come to André—this would have been uncomfortable for him.

"And to find out how you are."

"He's all right?"

"Of course."

I nodded, not wanting to press him about Paul or my research students. What were my students saying? Did they feel betrayed? "I'm sorry we have to delay our experiment," I said, "but I suppose I need to stay away for a while."

Eve said, "Do you want to see what I drew?" She held up a picture of our house and a family in front of it. The sun in the upper corner, the mommy and daddy holding hands.

My daughter was like me. She couldn't let go of what she wanted.

"Lovely," said André. "Now, draw me a picture of a lightning bug. Do you remember the one we looked at together, at l'Arcouëst?"

"It had a fire inside it. A chemical reaction."

"Yes, that's right."

She began another drawing. "Irène and Aline dug them out and made necklaces. I would never do that. That was cruel."

André said to me, "Your students are behind you, Marie."

I cleared my throat. "You'll oversee them?"

"Until you come back."

He took out his silver snuff box. André didn't have two weaknesses, he had three. His snuff, his twice-yearly tipple, and his loyalty to me. "Have you heard from Stockholm?" he asked.

I told him about Arrhenius's quick response to my letter. "He said in Sweden they pay no attention to the chicanery and lies of the French press."

"Chicanery." He held a pinch of snuff between his thumb and forefinger, with the precision of the chemist he was. "How's your back?"

"Worse." I'd found a bit of rusty red in my urine, but I didn't tell him that. I had no real fever, and there was no outward sign of infection. The stress of the last days had aggravated my condition. I thought it would improve after rest, as it had before.

"You probably shouldn't attend the ceremony," he said.

"Why? Do you think there will be trouble?"

"Marie, it's a train ride of forty-eight hours. Also, I've been thinking. What would you say to a house on the Île St. Louis? Move back into the city?"

Leave Sceaux for Île-Saint-Louis. The anonymity. The quiet.

"Shall I see what's available?"

"Oh yes, please. André, thank you for not—"

"You know that I don't judge you. Since Paul"—he glanced at Eve, still drawing in her notebook. "Since Paul, you've come alive. I don't want you to go away again."

I felt hot behind my eyes. I'd done little to deserve this friend.

"Hold your own, Marie."

When he said goodbye, I longed to follow him down the stairs, to walk with him down rue d'Ulm and rue Descartes, and back to my laboratory.

The next morning Mortier, a journalist who had defended me, fought a duel with Téry, who had printed my letters. Téry shot Mortier twice, in the biceps and the forearm. This idiotic event was all over the papers.

What had I to do with these people?

An insane energy ricocheted around me. I was being used, a woman either to rally around or pillory, an excuse for spectacle and frenzy. For men to fire pistols at each other. All my life I had known my purpose: to be honest and true and do good work; and yet I sensed, even in my shock, that this craziness wasn't entirely outside of me. My longings, my despair, and going after the man I wanted—a married man, yes, whom I was certain needed saving—in all of this, I had helped create the drama. I had not wanted it to happen, but I was a part of it.

I thought of the newspaper interview with Jeannette Langevin, the one that ended with little Hélà—"her adorable toddler," they called her—crying and consoling her mother. The story was horrible and manipulative, but also a piece of the truth.

Marguerite had to add leaves to her table and re-set it for lunch each day, as more visitors arrived. Most were members of Marguerite's salon—scientists, politicians, and writers. The attacks on me, they said, were part of the new nationalism, a turn to the right in France. Even Jan Paderewski showed up. Was it a year since I had taken Eve to his house, for him to hear her play? He took my hands and gazed into my eyes; his hawk-like nose, that unsparing, honest gaze. This man who had known my mother, who had heard her play.

One afternoon, when Eve and I were taking a nap, the telephone rang, and Marguerite came to get me. "It's Pierre's brother," she said.

Maurice's father, Jacques. Pierre's best friend in the world next to me.

Blood rushed to my forehead. I held tight to the banister going down the stairs. Marguerite disappeared into the kitchen.

"I'm sorry," I said, the cold phone to my ear.

"Are you all right?"

"Jacques, I—"

"Marie." Pierre once said that Jacques' voice sounded like a garden in the sun. "Don't let the bastards get to you, all right?"

"Don't be so kind, Jacques. Please don't."

"You were the happiness of my brother while he was alive. And my father, too." He paused a moment. "I love you, Marie. I love you like a sister."

"Oh, Jacques—"

"Take care of yourself, Marie. All of this will pass."

A letter arrived from Albert Einstein, words I printed on my heart:

> I'm incensed by the way the hoi polloi is attacking you, and I absolutely had to vent my anger. You must hold the rabble in contempt, whether they feign reverence or seek to satisfy their lust for excitement through you.
>
> I need to tell you how much I admire your spirit, your energy, and your honesty. I will always be grateful that we have among us people like you and Langevin, genuine human beings, in whose company one can rejoice.

I read it again. *People like you and Langevin, genuine human beings.*

Einstein was like Jacques, seeing the good in me. In Paul and me.

I went out into the Borels' back garden, unable any longer to stay inside, journalists be damned. This was where I'd arrived that evening in my white dress and eavesdropped on Marguerite's party, before joining in. No honeysuckle now, or blossoming roses.

I did not think I would be with Paul again, not in the old way. What I had now were the wrenching memories. Paul in his gray suit, on this very patio. In Brussels, in electric debate with Poincaré. Our joy exploding in that hotel room. The blow of bad news and the air sucked out of us. When we said goodbye, the dull embrace.

The constant pressure in my kidneys reminded me of the last time we made love, how Paul had plunged into me. I had sensed it then, and I knew it now, that the joy of our reunion was also the thrust of goodbye. He had left me with this pain that I couldn't wish away. It was what I had left of him.

One evening as I read to Eve, there was a commotion in the entryway. I looked out my window, and there on the street, in a buttoned frock coat, in a triangle of light, stood Paul.

Marguerite came out in her green cloche hat. I could feel her excitement in her sharp movements, her quick laugh. Paul ushered her to a carriage and climbed in after her.

The frock coat. A duel? Impossible. There was a mania in France for duels, but surely Paul was above such lunacy

Images scattered in my brain. Two shadowy men, Paul's seconds, pacing off the field. Paul fumbling as he loaded a pistol. I went back and forth between anger and fear.

In my nostrils, gunpowder, an eggy stench.

I hardly slept. In the morning, I waited until Émile went off to work, and then I looked for Marguerite. Her bedroom door was ajar, but the room was empty. She wasn't in the kitchen or the drawing room.

I gave breakfast to Eve, and a neighbor came to take her to

the park. I couldn't take her myself, according to Marguerite. "Wait a few days," she'd said.

I lit a fire and sat at the dining room table and made myself answer notes, though my handwriting looked shaky.

Marguerite did not return until half past four. I startled when I heard the door. Her hair fell over her face; mud covered her fine shoes. In her hands were two newspapers, the afternoon editions of *le Petit Journal* and *l'Intransigeant*. She shoved them across the table. "You're going to find out anyway," she said.

"Just tell me, please."

"Paul challenged Téry. It's done. No one's hurt. Christ, we drove all over Paris in a carriage, trying to find seconds. Finally, Painlevé agreed, and Paul's director at the École. Paul knew it was idiotic, but he felt he had to do it."

I took the newspapers over to the fire and watched the flames hiss up.

"I knew you'd be angry," said Marguerite.

"How could he have done this? And you, Marguerite. You're an intelligent woman. How could you condone it?"

"Téry insulted him in print and insulted you, too. You know how it is, Marie. The code of manliness, etcetera."

"Archaic nonsense."

"He's a man, Marie."

"He could have lost an arm or a leg. And he's made me look even more ridiculous." It was just as Einstein said, the lust for excitement. There was mud even in Marguerite's hair. "You're doing everything for me," I said. "I don't want to criticize you."

"I probably deserve it. I wouldn't say I egged him on, but I did sympathize."

I could well imagine her admiring eyes, and the courage Paul would have drawn from her. "I suppose he would have done it without you," I said.

She was disappointed that I wouldn't talk about it. She had hoped to tell me all the details that I later learned—about Paul's practice with a pistol at Gastinne-Rennette, where dueling Parisians went for firearms; the frightening fog at the Bois de Vincennes; Téry lowering his gun without a shot, in spite of the dishonor, because, he claimed, he didn't want to deprive French science of a precious brain. Henriette later told me the whole story, but that day, sickened by it all, silence was the only means I had to punish Paul and Marguerite.

I went upstairs and refrained from slamming my door. I sat for a long time, imagining Paul in his frock coat, a gun in his hand, and myself as I was, curled around my pain. Paul had challenged a man to a duel to preserve his reputation. He had risked his life. He couldn't leave his wife for fear of harming his children, but he would orphan them to preserve his dignity.

I had been reckless for the sake of our love. He had not been reckless for me.

On the 5th of December I received another letter from Arrhenius of the Swedish Academy. M. Langevin's ridiculous duel, he said, gave the impression that my letter, published in *l'Oeuvre*, was authentic. He urged me to decline the prize.

Anger burned in me. Scientists taking their orders from the press. Judging my private life while knowing none of the facts. Had they ever inquired into the sexual lives of a male candidate?

By the time he received my response, the Academy would have received a telegram from me, announcing that I would be in Stockholm for the ceremonies.

When Marguerite came into my room, with her wide eyes and cloche hat, she saw my face and said, "What happened?"

Eve was napping. I put my finger to my lips. I did not want to tell her about Arrhenius.

She took off her hat and sat next to me. "I have something to tell you," she said. "My father and I had a fight. He was dressing. He threw his shoe at the door." She pursed up her lips, imitating her father. "'Scandal makes a stain of oil.'"

"He's very angry?"

"I told him I'd never talk to him again if he—"

"If he—"

"If he asks you to leave the Sorbonne."

I pretended to look for a mint in my briefcase. "I'm sorry," I finally said.

"He should be the one who's sorry."

From the bed came a snore, and Eve flopped her arm around.

I sat down heavily. "I can't afford to lose my job."

"What will you do?"

I blew my nose. I thought of Dean Appell's mess of white hair, his joy in making academy visits for me. Choking up on the phone as he told me about the vote. The awful compassion in his eyes on the day of Pierre's death.

If he fired me, they would never re-hire me at Sèvres, to teach young women.

Once, at the Sorbonne, Dean Appell had defended a male research student who had been caught kissing another man. Surely he would come around for me.

I mustn't wait until he called me in to talk.

He stood up when I stepped into his office.

"Max Planck sends his regards," I said, before he had a chance to speak, reminding him that he and I were colleagues, on the same side, and I was a person of account.

"Ah." He looked confused. "He was in Brussels, of course." I could tell he wished to ask me about Solvay, but he only said, "Madame, I can't support you in this scandal."

"I thought you might want to know the facts."

"Are the letters yours?"

"I've done nothing to diminish myself."

He screwed up his eyes. "You had an affair with a married scientist."

"Am I the only scientist at the Sorbonne who's had an affair?"

"You know it's not the same."

"Oh?"

"Don't be naïve."

"I won't ask for favors. I want only to be treated as scientists before me have been."

"But Marie, the publicity."

"You read those rags?"

"At least three duels have been fought because of your actions, and one man wounded rather badly." The wounded man was my supporter Mortier, from the newspaper *Gil Blas*, who had been shot in the arm by Téry.

"You hold me responsible for men acting like children?"

He rubbed his forehead with his hand. "It's all quite a disaster."

I had been angry, but his tired forehead and frail hand moved me to sympathy.

He said, "The Sorbonne can't be associated with this disgrace."

"Can the Sorbonne be associated with this year's Nobel Prize winner in chemistry?"

"I'm responsible for order in the faculty."

"You've stood up to gossip in the past, admirably."

"I can't hold back the sea that's drowning you."

"I'm still the same person. You know me."

He raised his head. "We would like you to consider—"

I shrank, sensing something of what was coming.

"Perhaps a teaching post in Warsaw, at a girls' school. You would be more comfortable, wouldn't you? Among your people?"

Foreign bitch, go home.

Paul was married, but I wasn't. Paul had aimed a gun at another man, yet his dean at the *École* would never speak to him like this.

"I'm a French citizen."

He waved his hand. "All right."

I stood up. "Wait a little while, Dean Appell. See if this blows over. I need this job."

A colleague rapped at the door and poked his face in, saying, "There's a student here."

"Let him in," said Dean Appell, and to me, "I can't promise you."

"I'll take a leave. My health is poor."

"What will you do?" Just for a moment, he looked concerned.

"First of all," I said, "I'll take a train to Stockholm."

Bronia came from Poland through a snowstorm. She took a taxi from the station and came straight up to my bedroom at the Borel's. When she saw me, a frantic expression crossed her face, and I began to weep.

"Hush, darling."

I clutched at her. We sat in the loveseat for an hour; she didn't even take off her coat. I hadn't wept in Brussels, or on the train, or when I saw my words in a newspaper, but with my sister holding me, I couldn't beat it back.

"Hush. You don't have to go to Stockholm."

"I do. I will."

"There could be cat calls. Crowds. It could be ugly, *ma chère*."

"Apparently the Royal Princess of Sweden couldn't have me at her table, in case I corrupt her."

Bronia laughed, and I blew my nose and unbuttoned her coat, pushing each wooden button out of its tightly sewn hole. The coat smelled like Poland. Pinecones. Burning grass. My tears streamed down again.

"I want Irène to come with us," I said. "She needs to see her mother in a moment of triumph."

"Yes, that's right. We'll travel to Stockholm, the three of us. The King can fuss all he wants about his daughter. The Nobel Prize doesn't belong to him."

We changed trains in Cologne and headed north into Denmark through a mighty snowstorm. Irène had never seen such a thing; her visits to Poland had always been in summer. Bronia regaled her with stories about our childhood, riding on sleighs, building igloos, skating, cutting holes in the ice and fishing.

"I want to go ice fishing," she said. "Can we, Aunt Bronia?" The two of them sat behind me. I could hear but didn't have to talk. My back was worse. I had seen a doctor, who said to drink a tremendous amount of water. Not easy on the train.

Eve was staying with Henriette. She hadn't wanted us to go.

What I really wanted was to lie down in the fields of snow as we passed through. Lie down and go to sleep. I wondered if I would even have the strength to teach again. Yet I knew one thing, and I knew it like iron: I would get to Stockholm and survive any trouble it caused. I would stand before the royal family and the prize committee, my colleagues, the press, and the photographers, and I would give my speech. It would be like torture to push myself outward, but that was what I would do.

Pierre's "helpmeet." That's what Dr. Törnebladh had called me at the Nobel ceremony eight years before, in his presentation speech. "God said, 'It is not good that the man should be alone.'" This time, he would not call me a helpmeet.

"Is Mé going to be all right?" Irène was saying. "André said she shouldn't travel, because of her back."

Toward the front of the car, a wealthy Swedish woman seemed to be eyeing me. She wore a diamond brooch that could fund a laboratory.

"She's strong," Bronia said.

"I'm not sure we should be going."

"Don't you want to go?"

"Of course I do. But if Mé is sick—"

"Do you know, Irène, when your mother first came to Paris, she lived by herself in a sixth-floor garret, and it was so cold in that room that when she went to sleep at night, she piled not only her blankets but all her clothing on top of her, and then she even put her furniture on top of that! And did she complain? Your mother was happy."

"That was foolish. She should have got more coal."

"Your uncle kidnapped her and made her come to our house and eat a steak. We were living in Paris then."

"Why did you go back to Poland?"

My question exactly, although I knew the answer. Bronia had a life of her own.

The Swedish woman walked down the aisle toward me. I stared at my lap.

She passed me by, and in excellent French, she said to Bronia, "Madame Curie? My congratulations. Might I have your autograph? I'd recognize your face anywhere."

We saw the carriage even from the train, drawn up under the gas lamp, black and gold with four bay horses, snow coming down in puffs. The coachman's cloak had white stripes over the arms.

Dr. Dahlgren, a burly man from the Swedish Academy, greeted us amicably. He was secretary of the Nobel Committee which had bestowed and then tried to revoke my prize.

"Ho-ra, ho-ra!" a woman on the platform jeered. Bronia put her hands over Irène's furry hat, pretending to warm her ears. *Whore,* it had to mean.

In the Grand Hotel lobby, Arrhenius and I greeted each other civilly, though it took all I had to manage my contempt. That night I stayed up late, drinking all the water I could manage and revising my banquet speech.

On the evening of December 10th, Dr. Dahlgren ushered us, the Nobel laureates, into the Musical Academy. I shivered from cold and excitement. Fear. Arrhenius had said he didn't know what might happen.

But what could go wrong, really? I'd lived through stones and curses; I was a connoisseur of insults. All I had to do was survive the evening and make my banquet speech. Photographs would appear around the world and do their work. Science and my achievement would outlast gossip. I looked fine in my black lace, Bronia had made sure.

The hall was flowing with fabric, plants, and boughs of pine, thanks to the royal decorator. In the back hung an enormous laurel wreath wrapped with blue and gold ribbon, and next to it, a bust of Alfred Nobel. We laureates were seated near the front of the stage, with hundreds of eyes on us. Behind us was a semi-circle of distinguished men, Swedish military officers and intellectuals; before us, a sea of people in tiered balconies and private boxes, wearing evening dress. In the front row were Bronia and Irène. Irène wore a new gown—Bronia had insisted, dressing my daughter as she dressed me, my fourteen-year-old girl with her lovely, sloping neck. Irène had refused to be impressed by the ceiling paintings at the Grand Hotel, and the gold chandeliers, but even she looked star struck now. Bronia whispered something in her ear, and she closed her mouth.

When the royal family filed in—the King, famously tall and slim, and the Queen-consort, and their eldest son—the orchestra broke into a grandiose overture. I didn't dare look at Bronia. We would have smiled inappropriately.

In this great hall, where form and ritual were uppermost, who would cause trouble for me? I tried to summon Pierre, as if the thought of him could buffer me. What was I afraid of? A snub from the Royal Highnesses? The King?

In the event, when Dr. Dahlgren presented me in his sonorous voice, the atmosphere was hushed, and the expected insult was only a bit of self-defense ("the Royal Academy of Sciences considers itself well justified in awarding the Nobel Prize for Chemistry to the sole survivor of the two scientists to whom we owe this discovery"). And Dr. Dahlgren, after acknowledging that I had been awarded this prize before—the first time the Academy had awarded it to someone twice—redeemed it all. He turned his round face to me, and with the look of an apology, he said, "I beg you, Madam, to see in this distinction a proof of the importance which our Academy attaches to your most recent discoveries."

My "most recent discoveries." My discoveries post-Pierre. My work was truly being acknowledged. I had an upwelling of joy, a warm, fluttery feeling in my chest.

He gave me the cue to walk over to King Gustaf to receive my prize, and applause lifted me across the stage. The King appeared even taller at close range, with sculpted cheeks and an ironic expression—the look comedians wear, watching people from another plane.

He handed me the paper and the medal, as protocol demanded, and then he bent and whispered in my ear, "I assure you, Madame, I too am more than just a pretty face."

I sat next to King Gustav at the banquet, and he made me laugh. We ate quail, turbot, chicken, and artichokes. Irène ate both her own dessert and mine—Charlotte à la Râchel. I studied the wine labels: Chateau Montrose 1896; Liebfraumilch 1904; Charles Heidsieck, Sec, 1900; Porto Sandeman. I studied them as if I still had someone to tell.

In my banquet speech, I acknowledged the work of other scientists, and, of course, I honored Pierre's memory and our mutual work. But whereas, in my initial draft, I had frequently written "we"—after all, one has assistants—the night before I had crossed out that word and put "I."

To the audience before me, and to the world, I asserted that the history of the discovery and the isolation of radium furnished proof of my hypothesis—my hypothesis—that radioactivity is an atomic property of matter. I affirmed that the chemical work of isolating radium in its metallic state, and characterizing it as a new element, though intimately connected to my work with Pierre, was carried out by me alone. I pointed out that Rutherford and Soddy's bold interpretation of the relationship between radium and the gas helium rested upon the work for which I won this prize: the proof that radium is a chemical element.

I said everything I needed to say.

Whatever else might happen, this will be there, in the record, for centuries to come.

While I was in Stockholm, André made good on his word and secured an apartment for my daughters and me on the Île Saint Louis, on the quai de Béthune, in a large building a few steps from the pont Sully. When I saw the four flights of stairs, huge stone stairs that circled through the center of the building, I didn't know if I could climb them. When I succeeded, I couldn't imagine how I would get back down. In Stockholm I had used up my reserves and my defiance. The pain in my back and sides grew worse.

Even when we were all moved in, Eve wandered through the rooms saying, "When will the furniture come?" She would have liked sturdy sofas, velvet drapes, paintings on the walls—something more like Hertha's Norfolk Square. Though she couldn't remember her father, I believed she sensed his ghost in the airy corners and the space below the ceiling, and suffered from all the other losses that haunted us.

Though I had known in theory—my attorney had informed me—it began to sink in that according to French law, if Jeannette Langevin named me as Paul's mistress in the trial, he and I would never be able to marry.

It didn't matter. Our relationship was over. I felt this more than knew it. Our cruel exposure, my letters in the press, had wrung the last goodness out of our love. When my legs gave out in that side room at the Métropole Hotel, where had Paul been, really? And when I was prisoner in my house in Sceaux? Of course, he was shocked in his own right.

He had, at least, written to Arrhenius when he discovered that they'd tried to take the Nobel Prize from me. He called me an irreproachable woman being crucified for trying to save him, at his own request, for the sake of his scientific future. He said I had written the published letter at a time of great anxiety, having been threatened with murder by his violent wife. My mood had lifted for a while when Henriette told me about this, and then I felt pitiful, that I was glad even for crumbs.

I pieced something else together. When Paul had taken his sons to Leipzig without telling Jeannette, she had sued for divorce. Had he told her in advance when, after this, he had traveled to Brussels for the Solvay Conference? Of course, by that time Paul's travel wasn't her business, as long as it didn't involve the children, but everyone in our circle knew that I would be there, too, and this was also in the newspapers. Had he taken any precautions to ease her jealousy, or had he stubbornly gone his own way? Had he thought of me? He had been more concerned about the insults of a third-rate newspaper man.

Would she have published my letters if he had taken more care?

In our drafty apartment, in my drafty room, I lay on my bed, my arms weakly at my sides. I wanted only to escape. My mother had been forty-two when tuberculosis took her. I was now forty-four; I should have died two years ago. I had been ten when my mother died, and Eve was now six—I might live for four more years. This was my feverish math.

Pain gnawed at my back. I suspected a full-blown bladder infection, or my kidneys, even. I thought of Paul, thrusting inside of me at the Hotel Metropole. His passion had left me bruised. Now my bladder burned all the way up to my heart.

I wasn't getting better, and I needed to return to the doctor. The first time, he had asked about sex. He hadn't said it outright, but he knew—of course he knew—about Paul. I felt the tug of his curiosity, the effort it took to keep his tone clinical, but I would not let him make me feel cheap and dirty. I told myself that what was said in that room would stay there.

In theory, my isolation would starve the gossip columns, and at least I was spared the glares of colleagues and strangers.

Too ill to teach, I could only wait while Dean Appell decided whether to keep me on, hoping the delay might work in my favor.

Once classes resumed in the new year, Irène was set to attend the same lycée as before our move, and Eve was to go to a neighborhood school. I hired a new nanny, who would be able to take Eve to her piano lessons. Her piano teacher had shunned me since the scandal, but she was good at what she did, and Eve loved her.

"Mé, Mé," both girls chirped, trying to draw me to them.

We managed a feeble Christmas with the Perrins. Throughout the meal, I thought I heard a distant wail, like a foghorn on a looming ship.

One evening the following week, when the girls and I were at the table having supper, I stood up to go the toilet. I had to go all the time.

Irène stared at me.

A crash of pain.

The next thing I knew, there were sirens and a man's voice saying, "Madame." I opened my eyes to strangers. I was lying on a stretcher.

From above me in the echoing stairwell I heard Eve crying, and Irène saying, "Shut up, you idiot. She's going to be all right."

PART THREE

XVII

Highcliffe-on-Sea, July 1912

THE AIR SMELLED OF SALT. Where was I? When I opened my eyes I found a green wardrobe in the corner, a rocking chair, coco matting on the floor.

I went to the window. A white mist hovered above the earth, as if guarding it in sleep a while longer. Beneath it was a meadow, intensely green, a country lane, and a pebbled stream. Two small cottages drowsed beneath their thatching. I heard the rhythm of waves, though I couldn't see the ocean.

Hertha must have fetched me from the ferry. The buzz and rumble of the engine; the stop-and-lurch into harbor; a woman in a hat with enormous ostrich feathers. Images floated like fragments of a dream.

"You must take refuge with me in England." Hertha had written me a letter. She first reached out to my sister in Poland, who told her about the Alpine village where I was seeing a doctor and taking thermal baths. She wrote that she had taken a house by the sea in Dorset—the Mill House, it was called—so I needn't come to London. "You shall have two months of sunbathing." I should travel under a different name, she said, but that was nothing new. I had been hiding for months.

I made it back to the bed before exhaustion overcame me.

A dog barked. This time, when I opened my eyes, the world had brightened. Out the window I saw a stone bird bath, vines climbing over a trellis, purple foxgloves along the lane. An old woman emerged from one of the cottages in a sun hat and flowery shift. A dog poked around in the weeds.

My suitcase lay open on a bureau. I washed at the basin and changed into my dress. Sunken eyes in the mirror. I brushed my hair into a bun—mostly gray now, hardly blonde at all. I covered the mirror with a scarf.

In the hallway a newspaper lay on the table, and my skin chilled. At a low moment, I had written another letter to Paul. I'd taken every precaution, but could it have been intercepted? Used again for blackmail, or appearing with a photograph and in a hundred languages? When I was in the hospital after my collapse, nearly dying from kidney disease, a rumor spread that I was giving birth to Paul's child. I had wished that it were true.

"Greece joins Balkan League: Allied against Ottoman Empire." "Woodrow Wilson is Democratic nominee for American presidency." "Harriet Quimby, celebrated for flying across the English Channel, dies in plane crash: Monoplane falls 1000 feet into Dorchester Bay." This newspaper was two weeks old.

Henriette had promised to keep me informed about Paul. Why hadn't she?

Calm down. You're in England now.

Hertha would know how to keep me safe. This spring in London, in her house in Norfolk Square, she had harbored forty census-resisters who were hiding from the government. "If women don't count, neither shall they be counted," was their motto.

I found my way downstairs where, from the kitchen, came the clanging of pots and pans and the smell of lunch, rich and savory. Roast chicken? I was hungry, that was new. Someone chattered in English. A cook, perhaps. Hertha had said that she would bring in help.

You have my sympathy, she'd written, *in all your great and unmerited troubles, as well as your well-merited triumphs. Dear Marie, do not lose heart!*

The drawing room of the Mill House was large and airy with

its bare plank floor, furnished with a sofa, a few chairs, and an upright piano. The room was crowded nonetheless: behind the sofa were two long tables, and on them, Hertha's familiar glass tanks, mounted on rollers and imported from Norfolk Square, filled with water and layered with sand. On the bookshelf behind were various supplies: permanganate of potash; India rubber; gloves.

From behind me: "My dear Marie."

Her voice. I'd forgotten what a spell it cast, deep and musical. And her full-hearted gaze, as if there were nothing else in the world but what she was looking at. I took her in, her expressive, gray-green eyes, eyebrows rising in the middle, her fuzzy black curls, her strong figure—but none of this describes her. There was compassion and lightness in her being, which simply startled me.

Had we talked the night before? It made me uneasy, not to remember.

"Have they found me?" I was no longer the favorite scandal, but if word got out that I had left the country, the embers of gossip could easily flare again. In these last months, I had learned how a passing glance might become recognition—and recognition, another sordid tale.

"No one knows where you are, nor shall they."

"Do you think I'm insane?"

She smiled. "I haven't seen any evidence. Yet."

"I hope not to give you any!"

"I'm so glad you've come to me."

I rubbed the cracked tips of my fingers together.

"Let's have tea in the garden," she said. "I've made up a tray."

"I can barely remember arriving last night."

"You collapsed at my feet when you disembarked. It took all my strength, and the driver's, to get you into the cab."

"What trouble I am," I murmured.

"It was dramatic, but now you're here, and you shall sunbathe and restore yourself. Let's go to the terrace." She refrained from touching on the matter I couldn't bear to mention. Her kindness steadied me, and her lack of fuss.

The garden smelled of honeysuckle, warmed by the afternoon sun. The lawn sloped to a leafy hedge of spirea with misty blue blossoms. We sat under an awning and had buns with dried fruit and strong tea. We were in Highcliffe-on-Sea, near Bournemouth. We could barely hear the surf this time of day, though the English Channel was just over the cliffs. A stream wound through the property; in the previous century, Hertha said, the house had been a water-driven corn mill. Behind us was a deep woodland.

An enormous cat with golden fur rubbed against my legs. Nelly. I'd met her when I visited Hertha in Norfolk Square.

"Sometimes I think her mother mated with a mountain lion," said Hertha.

I didn't understand why cats liked me. "Doesn't she hate to leave home?"

"She hates it worse to be left behind." When Hertha saw my expression, she said, "Ah, Marie. I'm so sorry. So angry and so sorry."

I added sugar and milk to my tea, though normally I took neither—it was a way to keep busy and not tear up again. The dog I'd seen from my window came trotting toward Hertha. Maybe he wanted sweetness and comfort, too. Hertha's real name was Phoebe, I remembered. Her friends had called her Hertha, after the goddess of fertility and healing.

"Shall we send for your daughters from l'Arcouëst? I'm longing to know them better."

When I hesitated, she said, "Aren't you eager to see them?"

In the past seven months, since my collapse just after Christmas, I hadn't seen my girls very often. I was three months in the hospital, before and after surgery on my kidney, for pyelonephritis—three months of hazy consciousness, nuns padding about in gray-blue habits. No one knew if I would make it, so I had made plans for my daughters and my supply of radium, in case I died. When, finally, the doctors announced that I could leave, my nightmarish memories came faster and harder. Crazed women under eerie streetlight. Tomatoes streaking the windshield of our cab. The smell of coffee, my daughter's burning flesh. The cold bank counter where I had handed over my savings.

I couldn't go back to Paris and keep my mind, so at first I rented a house in a village north of the city. The girls were living with their nanny. André often went to see them, and he or the nanny brought them to visit me.

I didn't always know the difference between nightmares and reality. Sometimes I woke in the morning with my scalp aflame; I was surprised, when I touched it, to discover that my hair had grown back. If I caught a glimpse of a man in a checkered waistcoat, or imagined a hostile glare, I packed my bags and moved to a new town. I rented houses under false names until finally, in May, I fled to Thonons-les-bains. To the shopkeepers there, I was Madame Sklodowska, as my mother had been before me, when she took her cure in the Alps.

"I miss the girls," I said to Hertha. "but I'm afraid to see them." These were other images: the top of that cold stairwell. Myself on a stretcher, winding down the concrete stairs. Eve crying. Irène's voice. *Shut up, you idiot.*

"I wonder why," said Hertha.

"I don't know. I feel . . ."

"You feel . . ."

"An anxious dread." I rubbed the tips of my fingers together.

"There must be a reason."

I sipped my tea, hoping to deflect. Hertha seemed to listen with her skin, as if her own sorrows had passed from her memory into her body and become an organ of perception.

"I'm ashamed, Hertha."

"My darling."

"I can't face my girls." I had said it now, and it was true. I couldn't even bear to use the name Curie; it was as if I'd defiled it for my daughters, and for Pierre and his parents. My face had been plastered across newspapers around the world, the villain in a cheap romance. When Dr. Curie and his wife had welcomed me into their family, could they have imagined the muck now dripping from their name? My siblings in Poland were supportive, but what did they think, really, of the sister who had once made them proud?

Hertha took my hand. "You feel this way now. It will change."

I looked at her. She seemed so sure.

She poured more tea, leaf-flecks swirling in our cups. "For two months, you've nothing to do but rest. I've hired a cook, and a Miss Fanning to supervise the girls and give them English lessons. Wait till I show you the beach."

A bicyclist went by, a big girl pumping away with a little one behind her in a basket. When they swerved on a rise, the rider stepped off and pushed the bike uphill.

Could I do it? Relax into Hertha's care? I didn't want her hovering around me, concerned each day, and I wasn't sure I could stay put. For seven months I had been wandering, weary of life and weary of myself. At times the pain in my kidneys was the only way I knew I had survived. My misery was both physical and emotional; the two blended together. The worst of it had subsided. I dreaded its return.

I had one bag. Easy to pack and leave in the night.

I said, "You need a rest yourself. You've spent so much time nursing other people."

"Ha! Three people dead in three years! My husband, my nephew, and Barbara. You know about my guardian angel, Barbara Bodichon—"

"Of course—"

"She put me through Bedford College and left me some money. Am I scaring you?"

"They'd have died sooner without you."

"And the hunger-striking suffragettes, who at least had the

decency to recover. Thank God I have my daughters. My Barbie's married, did you know?" She squinted. "You're awfully thin."

I obliged her by biting into a tea bun and managing to chew. "Mm, orange rind. We have buns like these in Poland, but with cheese curd."

Hertha buttered one for herself. "When I was taking care of my husband and Barbara," she said, "I amused myself by planning my own funeral. A chorus of castrati singing Mozart. Fresh-killed lamb roasting on spits."

Her fantasies made me less embarrassed of my own. "I sometimes pretend I'm already dead," I said.

She put down her plate. "Did you ever—"

I was annoyed, but her unspoken question wasn't unreasonable—here I was, collapsing at her door. "I'm going to tell you something, and then I've nothing more to say about it."

"All right."

"In Thonons-les-bains, I mixed half a vial of oxalic acid with water." I leaned back in my chair. "There you are, I've come clean."

"Why didn't you drink it?"

"I'm not sure."

Hertha looked at me with the same clear eyes as before. Could it be, she wasn't judging me?

I said, "I think I would have drunk it, but I found your letter. I telegraphed you instead."

I had opened a book with no conscious intention, and there it was. *My darling Marie, you have shown women a way to avoid the shipwreck of their minds and lives. I could not bear it if now your fine powers were added to that saddest of human sacrifices.*

Hertha said, "There's something in you that really wants to live."

I thought of homeless people I'd seen in Poland, who had lost their feet to frostbite, hobbling along the sidewalk. I thought of my own mother, ill beyond what a person should have to bear, yet breathing, coughing, breathing.

"And now? Would you ever do it?" she asked.

The other half-vial was still in my suitcase, the size of my little finger. I couldn't answer her.

She said, "It's not fair to make me worry."

"I wouldn't do it here!" I wanted her questions to stop. A stag beetle dropped out of nowhere and clattered onto the table. It had huge red mandibles. I swiped it away.

"Poor beetle. He makes such a racket," said Hertha.

"Stag beetles have two weeks to find a mate. Pierre used to teach me insect facts."

Hertha was quiet. Heat climbed up my chest into my face.

"Look," I said. "I'll try to be a good patient, on condition you won't blame yourself if I don't improve. I'm not optimistic."

"We'll take it as it comes."

This made me feel lighter. No need to think or look ahead.

In truth, I was a bit afraid of Hertha. I didn't want her looking into my heart. The pathways of my misery were narrow and dark, and I'd been traveling them alone. Even when I turned to the business of my days, dread fed like a worm on my mind.

Hertha lay her head back on her chair and rested her eyes. A thrush sang in the woods behind us, and a butterfly—black with golden spots—fluttered over her nose. The corners of her lips turned up, as if she sensed the butterfly's nearness.

I would try to get better. I would do the exercises my doctor in Thonons-les-bains had prescribed and measure my urine output, three times a day, to monitor my progress. I would swim in the sea and read books for pleasure, and I'd eat what the cook prepared. I would put myself in Hertha's hands.

And supposing my daughters came for a visit and it went well, and my spirits improved—what next? I stirred uncomfortably. Hertha was prodding at me, wanting me to come toward the sun, out into the open.

In the back of my mind was a ticking clock. Come mid-September, Hertha would return to Norfolk Square, to her science and her suffragettes, and my girls would go back to school. I had a job, at least. My decision to go to Stockholm had been right. I had stood behind myself, and afterwards, Dean Appell had decided to stand behind me after all. I had told him I would teach in the fall, but I didn't see how. Could I recover my mind and my health, and bear whatever insults came my way? If not, then what? Seven more months of traveling incognito, fleeing from one village to the next?

The following morning, Hertha rented a carriage, and we set out on a tour along the coastal road, past cliffs of sandstone and clay, the sea crashing below.

Hertha in her billowy skirt held the reins. "Shall we go into town?"

"I'd like to get a newspaper." I needed to rule out that something bad had found its way into the gossip columns, something to do with Paul, or me.

I was quiet for a while, and Hertha said, "Are you worried about Paul?"

"A little." So many bad things had come from our relationship, and I couldn't bear for there to be more. If Paul lost the right to see Jules, André-Phillippe, and his girls, for instance. Or if his divorce were financially ruinous, and he had to leave his research. An image came to me of Paul in an attic, thick dust and a small high window, a wooden beam, a rope in his hand. I shook it off.

"You must remember," Hertha said, "men don't suffer as women do."

I flushed. "That's ridiculous. You don't know him."

"The son of a workman fighting in a duel, obeying the *point d'honneur*! And you say he worships reason. Really, Marie. I don't know why you didn't knock him over the head with a pan. Why didn't you, really?"

I had the same question, but I didn't like it coming from her. "His wife took care of that for me," I said dryly, and she laughed. "I wish you'd have a little sympathy," I added. "Téry wrote a diatribe."

"In which he said that Monsieur Langevin was a coward, hiding in your skirts. A duel! How awful for you. And the way you've been treated! It would never have happened to a man."

"I've seen men of genius dragged through the mud. Paul devotes himself to elevated causes, and—"

"Men of genius! You and your great men."

"Well, he is a great man, I'm not ashamed to say it."

Hertha rolled her eyes, though with a smile.

I said, "I can see you'll spare me nothing today."

Hertha laughed. "You're splendid, Marie. Of all the women in the world, I have the highest regard for you." She squinted. "But I'm worried that you haven't given him up."

"What?"

The carriage lurched down a dip in the road. "Have you?"

The air shifted oddly, a blurry glare. "For pity's sake, Hertha, I'm not devoid of self-respect."

"Well, good, then." She clucked at the horse, and we turned toward town, through a stand of oak, shielding us from the sun.

I was annoyed with Hertha. Had I asked her to straighten out my life? She spoke too loudly, and her questions—she went too far.

Of course I had given Paul up. Our relationship had become impossible from the first newspaper story. And yet, as Hertha and I bumped along on the road, a memory rose unbidden, of waking up with Paul, at our place, at the first light of day. The air was cool. Paul's head was on the pillow next to mine, his breath against my cheek. Through the open window were the squawks of chickens being hauled to market, the patter of rain, the smell of wet cobblestones, and from the bakery across the way, new bread.

There was a line outside the fishmonger in town, holiday-makers and villagers placidly waiting their turn. We headed to the tobacconist to buy a newspaper, further down the High Street.

I was worried about the letter I had written to Paul, on the day that I mixed oxalic acid into a glass of water. In seven months, I hadn't before been tempted to write—my words in the newspaper had nearly stopped me from putting pen to paper altogether. But that day, I was compelled.

I had hinted at taking my life.

If one more foolish word of mine saw the light of day, I wouldn't be able to bear it. I still had half a vial of oxalic acid left. I would want to use it.

Hertha scanned the paper for me. "Nothing. I'll check again on Monday."

We walked back past the fishmonger; the line was longer now. There was a dragging sensation in my back.

A man stepped out of a photography shop with a tripod and a Kodak. It was one of those shops that sprang up in seaside villages, making holiday portraits for vacationers. My heart sped up. I felt certain I knew what sort of man he was—slippery, cold-blooded—and what he would do if he recognized me, where he would sell his photograph, for how much and to whom. A colony of gulls, black-headed with broad gray wings, came cawing and screeching and swooped down over the street, just above the head of this man. The photographer ducked. The gulls scattered.

When he picked up his equipment and came toward us, I gagged.

"She's ill," he said to Hertha. He held out a handkerchief.

"Get him away," I whispered.

He said, "Can I do anything?"

"Reptile! Get away."

He looked confusedly at Hertha. "Mrs. Ayrton?"

"Never mind," she said.

She took my arm and walked me to the carriage. I was ready to pounce if she chastised me. Just one word of "he meant no harm," and I'd have had her neck. But Hertha didn't speak. Perhaps she thought I was truly mad—and for the moment, I was—but I was unrepentant. I was finished being a martyr. I would rather lash out and be in the wrong than tolerate one more moment of hatred and bigotry. The reptiles had driven me from France; they'd sickened me; they'd taken my life away. I would give them nothing more.

That night I awoke to the sound of a woman crying. The sobs were eerie, deep and guttural, past embarrassment. Who was this? What was happening? My bedroom door opened, and before I understood what was happening, Hertha had gathered me in her arms.

"Poor darling," she whispered.

The cries were coming from me.

She stroked the hair from my forehead. She had been to the beach and smelled of sulfur, seaweed. Her fingers were dry, her breath smooth and even. Gradually, my body stopped shaking. I fell asleep thinking of the ocean, billow upon billow, dark waters I could rest on, holding everything I could feel.

When I came downstairs the next morning there were two other women in the kitchen with Hertha, sitting at a table with blue and white crockery. One had a thick Scottish accent, and her voice was like a corncrake, the raspy bird that used to wake me up at night when I visited my cousins in the country. The other had a soft, angelic face—Miss Sharp!

"You want me to stay comfortable, with all the other silken petticoats," Hertha was saying. "We'll never win the vote that way."

Miss Sharp puffed her cheeks in protest, but she only said, "Oh Hertha, you're such a radical!" prompting laughter all around.

I stepped back out of the kitchen, but too late.

"Marie!" Hertha put her arm around me and brought me to the table. "I meant to tell you, but Miss Sharp and Miss Beattie arrived ahead of schedule. We have so many bedrooms."

The raspy one wore trousers. She pumped my hand. "I hear we're to meet your daughters. I'm Ada Beattie. We're telling Hertha she shouldn't march in the next deputation. She's still bruised from when the bobby stepped on her chest, the poor wee thing."

"Madame," said Miss Sharp. "I'm so glad to see you again. We're not here on business, but I do hope you'll sign our petition."

I said, "I'm rather staying out of the public eye."

"Your name is a household word," said Miss Sharp. "It commands respect from the whole civilized world."

Was she mocking me?

"Evelyn's a journalist," said Miss Beattie.

"I know. I'm wary of journalists, but pardon me."

"You have cause," Miss Sharp said kindly.

Hertha said, "We're working to get our leaders out of prison. They're persons of the utmost integrity. We could use your help."

Hertha was speaking too loudly again. My patience was used up. "May I sign as Madame Sklodowska?"

They all stared at me a moment, and then they laughed. "We're terrible, we're absolutely awful," said Hertha. "Go away," she said to the others. "Madame Sklodowska hasn't had her tea, and neither have I."

"Far be it from me," said Miss Beattie, clearing her plate from the table, "to interfere with a lady's breakfast. We'll go for a wee ramble."

"There's campion and dog rose still blooming," said Miss Sharp, and the two of them hurried off.

Hertha covered the table with plates of food, moving in her bustling way. I ate toast and a boiled egg, more than I'd eaten all at once in months, while she had two pieces of toast, two eggs, bacon, and two big cups of tea. The kitchen was blessedly quiet.

"I'm embarrassed about my appetite," said Hertha, "but I do so love my food."

"You don't look embarrassed. You look as if you're enjoying every bite."

"I am indeed."

"Are you really going to march? Will there be more violence?"

"You still disapprove."

"Yes, I do." Newspaper images came to my mind, of postboxes in flames. It occurred to me now that Hertha might have tossed a match. "I still say violence never helps."

"It's terrible. We do our best to contain it. But what do you suggest?"

"Don't burn postboxes; set fire to people's minds. Subversion through education. Nudge evolution along." This might have sounded lofty to Hertha, but in my mind I heard my father. I saw Monsieur Slosarski in front of our class after Jakub Kunicki was hanged, his brown curls falling back, his hand extended to me. *We don't carry rifles.*

Hertha narrowed her eyes. "The English also love their logic, but it hasn't helped women very much."

"Women need to discover that logic is their friend," I said, and blood rose to my ears. I felt like a hypocrite.

She brushed crumbs off the table. "It's absurd to set a few windows against the damage being done to women. We break what's breakable. They try to break *us*."

She flushed with a look of love and annoyance, and I suddenly realized: I didn't want to share her. I wished the other women hadn't come. Why was Hertha making me socialize? I liked Miss Sharp, but now I cowered even in front of her. And Hertha was about to make me face my daughters, too.

I refrained from saying all this—my feelings weren't worthy. Hertha's attention had rekindled my old longings. I could feel like a child, wanting her to take over my care, but I mustn't be too needy or let her matter too much. Though like an angel she had beckoned me to Highcliffe, she had her own needs and her own life.

Miss Beattie and Miss Sharp had left the petition on the table. I said, "I'll sign it," and I wrote my name on the line.

Hertha took the petition with satisfaction. "I'll be working this morning, you'll be pleased to know, in my laboratory. I've a new idea."

"Another one!" I teased. Hertha, when inventing, jumped ahead as soon as she had a smattering of knowledge, applying it as best she could, and then she went back to catch up on her understanding.

"I know I'm terribly rash," she said, "but it's immensely more interesting to plunge straight into a thing, and not begin with the alphabet of it."

I would never have allowed this approach in my own laboratory—it was counter to everything I knew and taught: never to shirk the task of mastering essentials, and never to rely on native talent. But then, this wasn't my laboratory.

We piled the dishes onto the counter. "I envy you," I said. "I don't know when I'll get back to rue Cuvier." It had been eight months since the Solvay Conference. Quantum theory and the science of radioactivity were developing at breakneck speed. I read the journals, I knew the research, but I hadn't been part of it.

"Don't worry," said Hertha. "Science is always there, grand and calm. That's what I feel when I settle into my laboratory, and that's what you must remember."

I warmed my hands in sudsy dish water.

"The question is," said Hertha, "what do you want now?"

I washed the yolk out of an egg cup, a little rooster with the tail broken off. "Truthfully?"

"Of course."

"I'd like to drown Jeannette Langevin in one of your tanks."

I'd hoped to make her laugh, but the air around us went still. Hertha had heard the feeling beneath.

I ran the hot faucet until it scalded my hands. My hatred was real. It didn't help that I knew better.

"And short of drowning Madame Langevin?"

I looked at her. Her hair seemed to send out light. "I want my dignity back."

"Oh, Marie. Your dignity, and so much more."

She kissed me and left the kitchen.

Hertha arranged for my daughters to take the ferry across the Channel and insisted on meeting them at Dover herself, leaving me at the Mill House to rest. After lunch, I sat in the garden with a monograph. Miss Beattie and Miss Sharp, too, were headed to the coast for a WSPU meeting—Women's Social and Political Union. They seemed to be planning another action.

All this activity stirred memories of my days at the Flying University in Warsaw. How thrilling it had been—the principles, the risk, the camaraderie of women bound together by purpose. We switched locations constantly to avoid the Tsar's police. Under those very noses, I carried forbidden books into a garment factory to read aloud to women workers. At the Zorawskis', as governess, I taught illiterate peasant children to read Polish in my bedroom on Sunday afternoons. Kazimierz's parents knew of it—and allowed it, even permitted their elder daughter to join us—though we all risked arrest.

In the drama with Kazimierz, I had forgotten what I once admired in his family.

How daring I had been then—imaginative, energetic, always pushing forward! All this before Pierre. I had been an accomplished and confident young woman when I met him at twenty-six, before he was there to embolden and enliven me. What had become of that person? Would my daughters ever get a glimpse of her? While they were with me at Highcliffe, could I banish my fears, keep my spirits from sinking, stop worrying about Paul?

I had the oddest sensation that his and my story was not finished. Everything that had happened between us seemed unreal, too dramatic to be final. It felt like a decade since Brussels, yet I still half-expected to turn a corner and see him there—"Marie!"—take my hands as if nothing had ever gone amiss.

The garden at the Mill House was beautiful and fresh. I had just begun to drowse when Irène rounded the corner and flung herself into my arms. The monograph went flying.

"Darling Mé!" she said.

"Darling girl!"

She was taller now, sturdier—as she should be at nearly fifteen—still with her lovely, sloping neck. In her letters she had boasted about long bicycle rides.

She took my hand, examining each fingertip in turn. "They're a little better," she said. "I know you don't like time away from your laboratory, but I think it's good for you."

"Just a bit of radiodermatitis."

Eve, still only seven, seemed younger than when I'd last seen her. She stood apart with her doll, its bow tied neatly to match her own.

"You brought Fleur," I said. "May I see her?"

"Her head keeps falling off," Eve replied. "Nanny says it's a factory defect."

She handed me the doll, and there, on her small forearm, I saw again the wrinkled pink skin, the shiny scar. At once I smelled the coffee, heard the rattle of dirt and pebbles against windows, the shouted slur—*Polish whore, go home*—and Eve's shriek.

My memories erupted like this, in shards and flashes.

I pulled Eve onto my lap. It helped—the weight of her.

Hertha said, "The transfer went smoothly. They had a good trip."

"I don't agree," said Irène. "I wasn't happy about calling myself Irène Sklodowska. My name is Curie, and it's a good name, too."

"Isn't Sklodowska a fine name?" I said gently. "It's the name of my childhood, and of your grandparents."

"I like it—for your sake."

In the past seven months, Eve, as if she too were a fugitive, had taken to signing her letters with her middle name, Denise. And not in her usual neat hand, but in thick black quavering strokes.

"You'll soon have your name back," said Hertha to Irène. "But here, in Dorset, you're going to practice not being famous for a while."

"That will have its advantages," my daughter conceded. "But when we go back to Paris, we're all Curies again."

Irène was strong. She would be all right.

The next day I disguised myself with a sunhat and a shawl and headed down to Highcliffe beach, a sandy flat of peach and tan and green, with Hertha, the girls, and Miss Fanning, the nanny Hertha had brought with her from London. Miss Fanning looked like a peach. Her fine blonde hair had fire in it, and she had a ripe look of expectancy, as if any moment something terribly exciting might happen. She made me nervous—who might she talk to?—but Hertha said that she worked odd jobs for her at Norfolk Square and had proven her discretion.

"The tide's out," said Irène. "It's gorgeous!" Her English was excellent. She had brought a children's version of Shakespeare's history plays with her, and had read *David Copperfield* that spring.

"Let's go in!" said Miss Fanning. She and Irène set off running across the flat.

Like Miss Fanning, I had been ready for anything once. I had run like that.

Eve and I collected sea glass and assembled the shards into crabs and seahorses, pink and green and blue. "Did you see the piano at the Mill House?" I asked her. "Hertha said she'll play duets with you."

Eve didn't answer. I thought to chide her—at seven, a girl should answer—but I let her be. She attracted admirers with her broad forehead and big eyes. When they stopped to chat, she gave them a tremble of a smile.

Hertha came to join us, balancing on one haunch and adding stones to our creations.

"It worries me that she's so pretty," I said, when Eve was out of earshot.

"Whatever for?" said Hertha. "Both of my daughters are beautiful. It gives me enormous pleasure."

"I've rarely seen beauty in a woman come to any good."

She tugged at the leg of her swimming costume and settled into a more comfortable position. "Are you thinking your life would have been easier, if you hadn't been so lovely?"

I smiled. "I don't know how to answer that question, but I can't deny that it makes me feel a little better. Only I think you're lying. I'm not so lovely now."

"You're like a peasant, afraid of the evil eye. You shouldn't let anyone spoil what you have."

I stirred the sand with a stick and tried to imagine recovering what I'd had in Paris. It looked as if funding was coming through for the Radium Institute. It might all have fallen through with the scandal, but, thank God, this hadn't happened. I'd been smart to be proactive once Jeannette found my letters, meeting with allies, and getting things started. Those efforts were paying off.

Yesterday's post had brought a packet from André with forwarded business, including a rogue hateful letter—normally, André managed to weed these out—and a request from the Sorbonne for my course requirements. Could I face Dean Appell? Could I stand before a classroom, knowing half the students had read my most intimate letters? Some of them knew Paul. They listened to his lectures, drank coffee with him at cafés. If they gathered around his workbench, they knew his very smell.

"There's something that haunts me," I said. And I told Hertha about the image that pressed at the edge of my mind whenever I thought of Paul: the small high window, thick dust, a rope slung across a wooden beam. He was living alone now in a flat in Paris—he'd be lonely, he wasn't meant for solitude. My grandmother had visions that sometimes were true. Paul was volatile, and the scandal had shamed him, too. I didn't know what he might be capable of.

Hertha listened, her eyes intent.

"Do you think it means anything ominous?" I asked.

"Well, of course you want to hang him," she said loudly.

I gaped at her. "Really, Hertha, you say the most ridiculous things."

She laughed. "And you lecture me about violence."

When bad news did arrive in the post, it was for Hertha and not me. Another of her articles, rejected. She paced the drawing room, perspiration dripping from her brow. The air was humid. Her hair had grown to twice its normal volume.

"They won't even disclose the name of the referee." she said. "Whoever it was never even saw the experiment. He didn't attend when I read my paper!"

"Oh Hertha, I'm so sorry."

"They're punishing me. It's because of women's suffrage, I know it."

That night she went early to bed with a migraine. The next day, too, she stayed in her bedroom with the shades drawn. Irène, who missed her math companion—they'd been doing trigonometry together—asked, "Is she very ill?" I was unnerved. I needed Hertha to go on as she was, scornful of the men who put her down, contented with her own self, her light-filled hair, her wit, her appetites. I saw more clearly the price she paid for being brave. Like me, she had episodes of nervous exhaustion. She too lost her confidence.

I tried to rest before dinner that evening—my kidney was tender—but my mind had reverted to the last actual sighting I'd had of Paul, in a frock coat, standing in a triangle of light on the sidewalk at Marguerite's. What a farce that duel had been, a caricature of everything it meant to be French and male. How could a person of Paul's intellect—a serious man, a scientist, who aligned himself with the downtrodden, and marched with factory workers—how could he place "chivalry" over his genuine values? Succumb to romantic drama over science? It was the kind of behavior Jeannette would find appealing. The two of them deserved each other.

Why *hadn't* I hit Paul over the head with a frying pan, as Hertha put it? Jeannette had broken a bottle over his head!

I could ask myself this question now, but when his dear face had been in front of me—those dark eyes deepened by pain—all I had wanted was to comfort him. I sensed the striving boy still alive in Paul, the one who had come to Pierre with scuffed shoes, long hair, and a love of music hall theater, soon to fall in love with experimental physics, Debussy, and Chateau de la tour. His home life with Jeannette had confounded him. Mostly, he blamed himself, but he hadn't meant to make a mess of it—no more than my father had meant to get fired from the Nowolipki gymnasium, or to lose the money he had saved for our education in a foolish scheme.

Even when we were grown, my father had mourned his own stupidity. I told him that he had done everything a father possibly could. I begged him to believe that we had turned out all right, even without his money, but he refused to be consoled. I was seven when he got fired. We children came home from school to find our mother packing. Our father stood beside her, clasping his hands, shoulders sagging, his mouth slack.

Paul, at least, could perhaps still see a way forward. He had separated from Jeannette.

When I went downstairs I found Eve and her doll lounged on the love seat with Miss Sharp, who clicked her knitting needles. The Scottish one in pants, Miss Beattie, sprawled on the floor. She said, "You're looking awfully peely wally."

Her voice scraped in my ears. *Peely wally*, what was that?

"I'm fine. I had a nice rest." Perhaps, I thought, I should remove my scarf from the mirror and look at my peely wally face more often.

Irène, at the desk, had the eraser of a pencil in her nose, and she was tugging at her nostril while staring at Miss Beattie—I could see that Miss Fanning was itching to teach her better manners, and she was right, though in truth I was pleased that my daughter didn't care about appearances. Irène said to Miss Beattie, "Are you married?"

"Never, by God. Marriage is a male invention designed purposely to ensnare women. I shall never be ensnared. Now this one"—she pointed to Miss Sharp—"that's a different story."

Miss Sharp looked up from her knitting and smiled sweetly. "I'm not ensnared."

"Are you married?" asked Irène.

"No dear, I'm a spinster. But I have a lover."

She talked this way to Irène? Though I was startled, it occurred to me: what if I could say such a thing to my daughter? *I have a lover, darling.*

"Aye, her lover, he's great with his words," said Miss Beattie, "but I wouldn't trust him. He's a sleekit bastard. I shall never be ensnared."

"Sleekit?" said Irène.

Eve put a trusting hand on Miss Sharp's face, and said, in French, "Do you have a little girl?"

"No, my darling," she responded in French, "and it breaks my heart."

Irène said, "Is your lover married to someone else?"

I said, "Irène."

Miss Sharp only looked at her intently. "Yes, he is."

Miss Beattie said, "She's not one to make a fuss, which is too bad under the circumstances. I would be fussed."

"You forget the fusses I've made when there's a point to it," Miss Sharp said.

Her friend turned to her with frank admiration and shining eyes. "Aye, that's so."

Irène dug into her notebook with her pencil. She was working on derivatives, which she declared "adorable."

I dusted the piano keys. What did Irène think about all that had happened to me? In the months since the scandal broke, this question had been part of the static of my mind. She had stayed with the Perrins in the first torrential weeks. André had told her to pay no attention to the gossip, but I wasn't sure what she knew. Soon, we had all moved out of our house in Sceaux and into the apartment in the Île Saint Louis. It hadn't been two months before my bladder infection traveled to my kidneys, and I collapsed. Ever since, the girls had been cared for by their nanny. Seven months.

Irène's tense hand moved across the page, now covered in equations. I pulled a chair up beside her. She'd grasped the concept of derivatives, but she wasn't getting accurate results. In the margins were Hertha's markings, hard to decipher.

"Do you make the calculations in your head?" I asked.

"Like you taught me."

I took her pencil and circled the errors. "The mind of a scientist develops with patience. Attention to details. You learn to make no mistakes."

"No mistakes. That's rich."

I was taken aback. Did she know what she was saying?

"Do you mind?" she added. "You're blocking my light."

"Don't block the princess's light," said Miss Beattie.

My irritation with Miss Beattie vanished.

That night Hertha came down for dinner. "By tomorrow," she said, "I shall be in working trim." We drank wine and ate lamb chops. Miss Sharp told a story of a lecture tour in Denmark, where men didn't stare or hurl insults or innuendos, nor did they fuss or act gallant. At one museum, a gentleman had wondered if they might like to see a special collection and had unlocked the rooms for them. It was completely unremarkable, she said, except that they had never before been treated so matter-of-factly by a man. Then, in London, she met the painter Whistler, famously a rebel and a pioneer, and he learned that she earned her living as a writer, and he said to her, "Not understood at home? No scope for the development of your personality?" These experiences made her want more than ever to fight for women's rights.

"I certainly know the feeling," I said. "But for the most part I've been lucky. In science, a mind really has no sex."

Hertha stopped with a forkful of peas halfway to her mouth. Miss Sharp and Miss Beattie gazed at their wine.

Hertha said, "You still think you're above the fray, after what you've been through? Really?"

I flushed. I had, for the moment, been peacefully living in the self I was before the scandal and the debacle with the Academy of Science, the self who believed, in spite of everything, that she belonged to a community of scientific minds, sharing serious goals, impervious to prejudice and crass, personal strivings.

"I'm sorry." I was embarrassed, shaken.

"You and I agree that the mind has no sex," said Hertha, "but come now. You know too well the world we live in."

"I know the world I want to live in," I said hotly. With my daughters present, I felt I had to defend myself.

"And yet you judge us."

"Hertha," I pleaded. "You must know I'm on your side."

"My paper has just been rejected by a set of minds which you say have no sex."

"It's terrible. It's wrong, but it's all the more reason to prize objectivity, isn't it? And surely, not all men are the same."

Miss Beattie said, "Nor all orangutans neither, but they have certain features in common."

"I believe I have more in common with men who are objective than women who aren't. Men with ideals, who devote themselves to elevated causes." I looked around the table. "Like all of us."

Hertha said, "The great and good Madame Curie."

"I didn't mean—"

Irène tipped her glass and dripped red wine on the tablecloth. Intentionally? or in a trance?

Hertha casually took the wine from her.

Irène said, "I'm going to be a chemist or a physicist. I plan to study radium."

My girl, standing up for her mother. Of course she would be a scientist, but what kind of life would she have? I ached for her. It was true, what Hertha was saying. My daughter's path as a scientist would be hard.

Hertha knelt beside Eve, who combed her doll's hair with an intense expression. "Do you know how to sew?" she asked. "We could make Fleur a bonnet to match her dress."

"I want to go home," said Eve. "I want to go home with my mother."

That night, at last alone, I sat in the dark in my bedroom's rocking chair, gathering my composure. Hertha had gotten under my skin, and in front of my daughters. And clearly, I had gotten under hers.

What had we been fighting about, really?

At the table, I'd fallen back into my habit of believing that I was an exception among women, that my hard work and my mind were a bulwark that could keep me safe. Of course this irritated Hertha. In my life I had fought off many challenges related to my sex, but whenever possible, I had blocked out my awareness of the very threats that drove Hertha and her friends into action.

And why wouldn't I? My body grew hot as I thought of my days as a Polish girl in Russian schools: the sticky, oppressive air; the constant suspicion; the fear that a single careless word might send a parent to Siberia.

You know the world we live in. The world in which divorce is a scandal, while affairs and abortions are perfectly fine, as long as no one knows. In which keeping a family intact trumps honesty and love and the wellbeing of the children. In which respectability covers over blackmail and threats of murder. Yes, I knew this world.

The coco matting scratched softly as I rocked, and a dim awareness stirred in me of a charge I had to bring against myself. It wasn't only Paul who had failed to live up to his intellect, and his calling as a scientist. I, too, had betrayed my values.

A true scientist starts with a plan but stays flexible, open to new information. She pauses, corrects herself. This is the scientific frame of mind: adapting to reality, or else becoming ineffective. It's not only a method for the laboratory, but a total way of living.

I hadn't been true to this ideal. I had refused to see where my relationship with Paul was headed; I closed myself to unwelcome evidence. I'd been afraid to discover what I didn't want to know, afraid because I wasn't willing to act on that knowledge or change my course. I wanted too much—for Paul to be the man I needed, for things to go my way. I had tried to bend the world to my will.

Paul and I had related in other ways that I preferred not to remember. When I was jealous of his wife, he would subtly take the high ground, as if the drama were playing out between two women and he was above it. If ever I criticized Jeannette—something I long avoided—he would make excuses: the tolerant gentleman, the good Christian man, only without the religion.

After Jeannette's threats and the assault, yes, he was remorseful, ashamed, but what good had that done me? He took no action on my behalf. His passivity with Jeannette left me stranded, so I had stepped into the vacuum he created. I had tried to think for Paul, as if he couldn't think for himself. I wrote that letter from l'Arcouëst, telling him what to do.

The thought of that letter blurred my vision. I had been in

a bad state—just after Jeannette and her sister. Why hadn't Paul destroyed it and acted to ease my jealousy? Wasn't it natural that I burned with humiliation, knowing he was sleeping with the woman who had attacked me in the street? Night after night, images of their naked bodies roiled through my mind. He knew this. But was he concerned? He answered with cool detachment, while I carried the weight of his weakness.

He told me that his home life was desperate, that I was his sanctuary. But perhaps he thrived on drama after all.

I had dreamed of Paul inhabiting his full mind and heart. I believed I could help him become the man I thought he was.

You and your great men, Hertha said.

Whatever she thought, I wasn't wrong in loving the swift movement of Paul's mind, the wordless space he inhabited. The way he grasped essentials in an instant. The passion of his causes, his inventiveness. I would not let anyone take that from him—or from me. His achievements spoke for themselves, and if he could believe in himself, there would be more. I was not ashamed of loving the genius in Paul.

From the next room came the rustle of Hertha settling in. It was time to stop thinking and go to bed.

I lit my lamp. As I undressed, someone tapped at my door. Hertha, come to make up? I hesitated, then said, "Come in."

It was Irène, barefoot in her nightdress, her scraped ankles poking out, her hair loose and unkempt.

"I thought you were asleep," I said.

She closed the door and stood there. "Didn't you love Papa?"

My insides tightened. My still fourteen-year-old daughter, speaking to me this way. "Of course I loved Papa."

"Then why did you go with Monsieur Langevin?"

"What do you know about that?" I picked up a hairbrush, but I didn't know what to do with it.

"I read it in the paper. At the gymnasium. The day André came to get me." Her lip trembled. She fixed me with her gaze. "You wrote him letters. He has a family."

I hung my dress up and put on my nightgown as she stood watching. I would rather have been naked in front of an army.

"I have a right," she said.

I sat on the bed. I also had a right.

"I loved your father more than my own life. I've never loved anyone as much as him. I never will."

Her eyes had a pale, inward look.

"Do you miss your father?" I asked.

"Was Papa against violence?"

"Yes."

"Why? Why are you against violence?"

I was about to tell her about her ancestors in Poland—how they had learned through bitter experience what comes of violence—but my daughter stood before me, lanky in her nightgown, and I could only marvel at her. I had watched over her cradle, nursed her fevers, changed her nappies a thousand times. There had been math lessons, midnight conversations, and the poignant letters we exchanged whenever we were apart. All the love of my life I poured into this girl.

"So much goes into a human life," I said. "To harm a person who's been loved so much—there's nothing more grotesque."

"Grandpére wasn't against violence. He supported the Communards."

"Yes, but they didn't get what they wanted, did they."

"Maybe the suffragettes will help the women get the vote."

"I hope so. Maybe they will."

"They're not killing people with arson, are they?"

"I don't think so, darling. That's not what they want."

I would have held out my arms to her, but she was separate and defiant, her chin pitched forward, her forehead in a pout. I saw that she was wholly herself. A soft kind of deference came over me. Irène was strange, sometimes slow, even downright offensive, but she had her dignity.

"I agree with you about violence," she said. Then she left without kissing me goodnight.

I sat in the space she left behind. The window was open. Waves washed the shore.

All this time, Irène had known about Paul—she had read my letter in the paper. She had carried this knowledge until she could ask me, without letting it knock her off course. What a brave and wonderful girl. She was protective of her father. Of course she was. There would be more questions. We would talk.

I had always felt that my daughter would die for me, just as I would have died for my mother. Yet it was also true—I saw this now—that Irène had been keeping an invisible scale, collecting facts like pebbles, weighing them in my favor or against. She had made me her measure of goodness. And if I wasn't good, whom could she trust? Though I was disgraced in the world, and I had been ashamed, it was she who made me feel true guilt. I could fend off the vile Téry, I could hate Jeannette Langevin, I could blame Paul—but I would have to listen to my daughter. And what would her judgment be?

When I told Hertha that I stayed alive for my daughters, I had spoken the truth. Even when all I wanted was relief from consciousness, I had loved them like a hawk, watching the ground to keep my hatchlings safe, plotting their survival. Even, I realized now, even my love for Paul had been partly for my girls, because after Pierre, loving him was the only path I could find to come alive, and only by coming alive could I give them back their mother.

A little later, restless, I put on a robe and descended the creaking staircase. In the kitchen I found a torch and went outside.

Insects swarmed the light. I switched it off and felt my way among the rocks toward the cliff over the beach. A cloud covered the moon, so it was hard to see, but on a ledge above the water I made out an odd shape: Miss Sharp, sitting on a rug in the grass. She looked no bigger than Irène, with delicate shoulders and a wispy neck. Miss Beattie had told me that when Miss Sharp spoke at a protest, people were startled that such a big voice came from such a small chest. Once, after she had rallied the crowd at a meeting house, a man picked her up and threw her down the stairs.

"Hello?" I said.

She didn't hear me over the din of the sea. Her head was bowed. She was crying.

When she noticed me, she made room on the rug. A wave crashed, spraying us with salt.

"Are you all right?" I asked, lowering myself beside her.

"I'll be all right. It's just a private sorrow."

A private sorrow. I was glad for her, that it wasn't torn open to the world.

I wanted to say so, and to confess my own loneliness and shame, but just then the moon broke from behind the cloud. We both looked up. For half an hour we sat like that, watching the moon appear and disappear.

Skalbmierz, Poland, 1882

"**W**hat's wrong?" Papa asks. I don't know what's wrong—only I can't stop crying, and I can't eat.

"Aren't you happy with your gold medal? First in your class?"

I am Papa's third child to walk away with the gold from a Russian gymnasium, after Józef and Bronia. Almost, I didn't have the chance to go. The headmistress at my primary school told Papa I needed a gentler education, because I drove myself too hard. Papa disagreed, but now, I think, he wonders.

He decrees that for a year I shall abandon intellectual pursuits. He sends me to my cousins in Skalbmierz, in the south of Poland, where the households are gay. There a person may speak Polish and sing patriotic songs.

And oh, what larks! My cousins and I swing ourselves hard and high, we swim in the river, we go torch-fishing for shrimp. We don crowns of vegetables for pageants, and with my aunt we weave wreaths of poppies, wild pinks, and cornflowers.

When winter comes, the kuligs begin. We travel from manor to manor in our sleighs at night, with blazing torches and jangling bells, our horses tossing their harnesses. You can't imagine how delightful it is to dance the mazurka with boys in Krakow dress—red and white striped pants—while I wear a bright full skirt and beaded vest. I do an exquisite oberek: high kicks, flying steps, until I wear out my shoes. During the waltzes, partners crowd the doorway, waiting their turn with me. I've turned stupid and sublimely happy.

When it snows on the sleigh ride home, we can hardly see the road.

I call to the driver, "Look out for the ditch! You're headed straight into it!"

"Never fear!" he shouts—and over we tip.

These tumbles only add to our merriment.

XVIII

Highcliffe-on-Sea, August 1912

I WAS RESTING UPSTAIRS after lunch one afternoon when, out on the pavement, a motor car door slammed. I looked out the window. In a fresh white blouse, Miss Sharp was kissing a man in a straw boater hat, next to an apple-green Rover. Henry Nevinson. He hooked his ankle around her calf, right there in the street.

A pebble dropped in my stomach. Paul and I had kissed like that. Joyful. Ravenous.

I succumbed to curiosity and went downstairs. Everyone was gathered under the garden awning. Miss Beattie stood close to Miss Sharp, her legs planted wide, protective, as if, given the chance, she might kick her friend's lover to the curb. Eve giggled and hid behind Mr. Nevinson, slipping sugar cubes into his jacket pocket. He pretended not to notice. His tweed suit looked as if it had traveled to Timbuktu and back.

"What do they throw at you?" Irène was asking Miss Sharp. She'd been swimming; her hair hung damp and tangled.

"Sometimes live mice," said Miss Sharp. "Tomatoes. Herrings. Chestnuts!" She knitted with quick hands, a yellow sweater for her nephew. I was a little in awe of her—her simplicity and composure despite such a tangle of love and loyalty. It wasn't really a love triangle—there was no word for this geometrical shape. It occurred to me that while I sometimes cast myself as the villain in the saga with Paul, I could not see Miss Sharp that way.

Mr. Nevinson said, "She caught an egg once without breaking it, and hurled it straight back at the hooligan. Splendid, I must say."

"Accidental prowess," Miss Sharp said. "But I'm famous for it."

"Aren't you scared?" asked Irène.

"At least when people throw things at you, you know what they feel. Drawing rooms frighten me more—all that frozen hostility."

For a moment I froze too, my memory flashing to Jeannette, her ugly laugh, that day when she invited me for coffee, to complain about Paul. *I'm not like fancy people who hide everything.*

Hertha said, "Here's Madame Sklodowska."

Though Mr. Nevinson knew who I was, I was glad for Hertha's care.

"Madame Inquisitor." He tipped his hat.

"I've been hearing all about you," I said.

"I don't like the sound of that."

"Not everyone loves you, Mr. Nevinson," said Hertha, "but Eve here is a fan."

"Swing me around," said Eve.

"Again?" He turned to me. "Your daughter is hard to resist."

"Don't break your back," I warned.

They went to the far end of the garden where he spun her until they reeled and collapsed in a heap. Miss Sharp looked on with what seemed both pride and sadness.

Hertha put a teacup into my hand and murmured, "If looks could slay—again." I smiled despite myself. It had been little more than a year since she'd caught me glaring at Nevinson in London. I couldn't deny the anger I felt toward him, though I had no real reason. Nor the edge of attraction, which perturbed me.

"Why do you do it?" Irène pressed Miss Sharp. "What about

passive resistance? Why not that?" She could never leave the subject alone.

Miss Beattie leaned back into a chair, hands clasped on her stomach. "There's plenty of violence in passive resistance, lassie, only it's all used against us."

Miss Fanning said, "Men kill other men for freedom, and we give them badges of honor, isn't that right, Mrs. Ayrton?"

"That's right," Hertha said.

At the far end of the garden, Eve chattered at Mr. Nevinson. He listened as if no one in the world mattered more. I could almost smell his manly privilege, the world opening before him, he in the fortunate position to flout convention and champion women's rights. He really had ridden on his war horse at the front of suffrage marches, Miss Beattie told me.

I went to sit on the grass with them. Eve was showing him her front tooth.

"It wiggles," she said. "It's almost ready. I've lost both bottom teeth, too, but not my cuspids. Cuspids come later. My sister lost hers when she was eleven."

"I have a favor to ask, Eve," he said. "Will you pick me a bouquet of flowers?"

"Mrs. Ayrton said I mustn't."

"Never mind, it will be my fault."

When she hesitated, he added, "I'm partial to yellow ones," and off she went.

It will be my fault. Undermining Hertha, telling Eve she needed his protection.

He lit a cigar and blew the smoke away from me. "A capital girl, your daughter." He turned to me—sensitive brow, rakish mustache, those full-on eyes that made a person feel chosen.

I rolled a blade of grass between my fingers. It had a sharp-sweet smell.

"Don't scowl," he said. "I've done something you'll approve of."

"Tell me," I said. "Tell Mother."

He laughed. "I've broken it off with Nannie, my other mistress."

Surprise—and a flicker of pleasure—quickly hardened. What of Nannie's feelings? What of Miss Sharp's? My wish to snap at him and my wish to stay superior balanced into silence.

"You've no sympathy for me," he said, "but it was damn difficult. Evelyn knows, of course."

"There's still your wife, Mr. Nevinson. What about her?"

"Yes, well, you have high standards, Miss Sklodowska. It's not the new world yet. I could manage a divorce, but it wouldn't be good for her. I'll have to live with this."

"As will Miss Sharp. Have you ever thought what it's like for her when you go home to your marriage bed?"

"It's my business, isn't it?"

"Your business has a way of pulling in other people."

"That Paul of yours, was he a rascal?"

I was shocked, but in a funny way, relieved. "Why do you ask?"

He shrugged. "You seem to think I am."

"He's not a rascal. Just weak. Men in general are weak." The words surprised me, but once spoken, they felt true—or true enough. I would rather rely on a woman.

Mr. Nevinson gazed across the grass. "I do like to live."

I had to grant him this: he had put himself in the path of bullets for the sake of truth.

From under the awning came laughter. Miss Sharp, hands flying, argued some point with Irène.

I said, "Hertha says that there's to be a new action. They might cut telegraph wires. Are you worried for Miss Sharp?"

"Miss Sharp has her own mind, and a galloping mind it is. You should hear her speak in public. It gives her a cold feeling in the pit of her stomach, but she's often the best speaker among the suffragettes. She makes people laugh. And once they laugh, they're yours."

We stood and brushed off the grass just as Eve arrived

clutching her flowers, her belly protruding in its adorable little-girl way.

"You're back, darling," I said.

Mr. Nevinson bent to her bouquet. "Zinnias and marigolds. And dandelions!" He spoke to her in French.

"I like dandelions," she said shyly.

"Some people call them weeds," he replied, "but I think they're beautiful."

She lifted her dark lashes to him, all openness and love—unsuspecting, unguarded.

Such civilized courtesy, so flattering. Why wouldn't she fall for it?

I pictured her twenty years older, still with those lashes and that curly hair, in a glamourous dress with a low back—and on her face a look of confusion, of pain.

A vision came to me then: a dozen suffragettes climbing telegraph poles, straps cinched at their waists, canvas cradles heavy with tools: wire-cutters, hacksaws, axes. I was among them, with Miss Sharp, Miss Beattie, and Hertha, all of us shinnying up to the crossarm bristling with insulators and wires, ready to cut them down, to make a new world.

Before Mr. Nevinson left that evening, he took me aside and said, "I've been thinking about your health." Nearby, Eve clambered in his apple-green Rover.

"Mine? I'm not the one risking prison a second time."

"Evelyn? She'll be all right. She's a fire brand." Tenderness softened the muscles of his face. "But your ailments . . . the back pain. I see it in your walk. Could it be from playing about with radium? I'm a journalist, you know, I've looked into it. Rather dicey—people losing their hair."

Why did no one else talk to me this way? There was a freedom in it. It scared me a little.

"I've sometimes wondered," I said. I had never confessed this to anyone—nor had I ever admitted that sometimes I blamed it on sex with Paul. Really, there were many reasons why a bladder infection might climb to the kidneys. Yet radium could have been part of it. Perhaps it had been part of Pierre's bone pain, too. We couldn't know. The research was still thin.

"There's a Hindu myth," Mr. Nevinson said, leaning in toward me, "about the elixir of life—a pot of nectar at the bottom of an ocean of milk. The gods, desperate to live forever, stir the ocean up and set it churning. The ocean boils, it foams, until at last the nectar shoots up into the sky." He lifted his hand, showing the rise. "But"—he dropped it—"with it comes a deadly poison. It hangs above the nectar like beads of rain, caught in the sun, ready to fall and ruin everything. Then Lord Shiva steps forward and swallows the poison. What agonies! But he's the only one strong enough to bear it."

I knew about Shiva, creator and destroyer.

"It burned his throat," Nevinson went on softly. "Turned it blue."

I shivered and said, "You speak in parables, Mr. Nevinson." But I understood. Every act of creation released its poison. We stirred the ocean for its nectar, and the poison rose with it. It had been that way with radium. And with Paul.

I was the one who swallowed it. The poison had turned me blue.

Yes, I had caused harm—in my ambition, in my love—but harm was woven into creation. It was this way for everyone.

What Mr. Nevinson had helped me see was too raw, too immense, to speak out loud.

"You've had your throat burned," he said.

I had indeed.

"In science, one never knows how things will turn out," I said. "That's half the adventure—discovering what comes next."

"That's right—that's the spirit."

I gave him a smile, and he smiled back. Then, with a gallant flourish, he opened the door for Eve to step out of the Rover.

After Mr. Nevinson's visit, I didn't worry so much about Paul. My urine chart didn't show any change, which the doctors wouldn't like, but my kidneys weren't bothering me. Twice a day, the postman came and went, sometimes without my noticing.

It seemed to me now that if I had miscalculated, indeed overreached, with Paul and in my life—given the constraints, and that I was a woman—well, I was in good company, stirring up the ocean to get to the nectar of life. It was my nature, it was human, to hunger for things that are beautiful and good. I would never give up wishing as long as I was alive.

In many ways, I was returning to myself. When Miss Fanning asked me to teach her the structure of the atom, I step-by-step described Rutherford's gold foil experiment, drawing pictures for her. Later I found her with Eve's pencils, drawing an atom with a fiery red core and deep blue electrons in their orbits. I dreamed that night about my laboratory on rue Cuvier and woke up smelling our wood benches—the linseed oil we used on them. For the first time in nearly a year, I itched to return to Paris.

Toward the middle of August, I received an invitation to speak at the Physics Society in Paris. I showed it to Hertha at breakfast while she tucked into her eggs. My colleagues in France were sending me a vote of confidence.

"You could write a paper," said Hertha, dabbing her mouth. "You wouldn't have to deliver it if you're not well. Just prepare it, then see."

I decided to write about challenges to the theory of the emission of continuous electromagnetic waves. New research suggested there might be discontinuities in their structure. I felt the old, familiar thrill of an unsolved question: could these two conceptions—continuity and discontinuity—be reconciled?

Something deeper stirred. Continuity. Discontinuity.

When Hertha left the table, I sat on, dreaming of the Vistula swirling around its sandbanks, the smells of fish, apples, and garbage heated by the sun. In my own life—from childhood in Poland, to Paris and Pierre, through scandal to this moment—was I really continuous, a single describable thing? The motherless girl ready to sacrifice her future for a forbidden boy, until he abandoned her, or the studious one, the ardent positivist? The atheist since age ten, yet stunned into reverence by oceans and chemistry experiments?

Hertha said that I didn't know my own goodness, or my strength, yet she also complained that I was stubborn and self-righteous. The papers called me a calculating, chilly-hearted adulteress. Marguerite Borel said I was a woman who walked through fire for those she loved.

I was not quite like an electromagnetic wave—continuous and discontinuous at once. The comparison failed. Yet surely my selves were many.

When I was little, my Auntie Lucia told me I was named for the Virgin Mary, but when I asked my father, he said no, I was named for the Black Madonna, the one who drove off four thousand Swedish invaders, appearing on the wall of Częstochowa in a glowing robe, priming the cannon and throwing the enemy's shells right back at them.

I smiled and got up from the table. I would have to tell Hertha. No wonder if sometimes I was a tad too grand.

The next morning I dreamed of my mother. She wore a red cloak, like Hertha's. She looked fresh and happy. I leaned in to kiss her—her skin was cool as milk, and sweet.

When I woke, I lay still, cherishing the vision. In life, my mother had never allowed me to kiss her, and she never kissed me. As a girl I believed there must be a reason she held me at arm's length—something lacking in me, some way I had fallen short.

But perhaps, after all, she had only wanted to protect me. The doctors had told her tuberculosis wasn't contagious. Yet she knew she had fallen ill after nursing her brother, and she may have suspected, even then, that her sickness could be spread from one person to another. Perhaps this was why she never kissed me.

One afternoon when I was working on my lecture a door slammed hard. Miss Beattie called urgently, "Madame Sklodowska." She came tearing up the steps. "We're packing our kits," she said. "We're going to London."

"What's happened?"

"A telegram. I can't say more."

Everything happened quickly after that. A carriage was arranged, and the cook packed up a meal. Hertha changed into her traveling clothes—at first, she planned to go as well. "You'll be fine without me, and I'll be back in a week," she said to me, but Miss Sharp argued against it. "You'll do more good for the movement if you stay here," she insisted. "We'll need you later on."

When Miss Sharp came downstairs carrying her suitcase, she saw me standing amidst Hertha's tanks and rollers, unsure of how to help. She put down her bag and took my hands. Her own were dry and soft.

"You are exquisite," she said.

"Oh, but—"

"You make me want to write again. One day, maybe I will."

I pictured her being pushed inside a cell, and I heard the click of the lock. "Are you frightened?"

"Yes," she whispered.

If she were imprisoned, she intended to go on a hunger strike. They would keep her until she was close to death, and then release her to Norfolk Square.

I said, "Couldn't you leave the protesting to others for a bit?"

"Not at all. 'God gave thy soul brave wings. / Put not those feathers / Into a bed to sleep out all ill weathers.'"

"I suspect the author of that poem wouldn't approve of you."

"George Herbert, probably not," she laughed.

Eve clutched at me as we waited for the carriage outside. "I'm not the one leaving," I told her. Hertha stood apart in her broad hat, her duster, white blouse and black tie. Travel clothes she wouldn't need after all. She seemed distant from me—I thought she must be worried about her daughter, who also planned a hunger strike. But the hardest part of prison, Hertha had told me, was the isolation, and being watched through a thumb-sized hole in the door. And when, in another cell, someone loses control, someone who might never get out, and screams through the night as if she is being tortured.

I was reminded of Uncle Henryk. All the men across Siberia, roaring.

One of the horses reared up before the carriage set off and had to be settled before they could leave. I put my arm around Hertha's shoulders.

"I don't know what they're going to do," she said, "but I'm sure you'd disagree with it."

"Oh Hertha, you *know* I'm on your side," I said, but she was angry, she was scared. I went upstairs to my bedroom and looked in my bag for my red and white cockade, like the ones used by Polish insurgents. I carried it for courage, and in solidarity. I had kept my Uncle Henryk's for years, and when it got ratty and fell apart, Irène had bought some ribbons and made me a new one.

I found the cockade and went down to Hertha and pinned it to her shirtwaist. "In Poland, when someone in the family is in prison, we consider it a badge of honor."

Her lip trembled. I opened my arms, and she clung to me—her back shaking, her hair scratchy against my cheek. Her tears and snot ran down my neck. I started to tell her how brave she was, but what I wanted to express went beyond praise. It was a connection so close it was almost carnal. I had fallen asleep in her arms, my body moaning, beyond my control, and she had soothed me, her chest rising and falling like the sea.

Now her salt was on my lips, my collar damp with her tears. I felt the ache inside her chest as it rested against mine, her pain and my love passing between us, through her body and back again through mine. It seemed to work that way: love begetting love, healing flowing both ways, the giving and the receiving nearly the same thing. Which Hertha had known all along.

And to think that all my life I had worried that love itself would vanish, once the people who loved me were gone.

That evening I heard a shattering in the kitchen and found Miss Fanning standing over broken plates, her red hands shaking. "They chain the ladies to the prison bars," she said. "They chain their arms above their heads."

"Don't go scaring Irène and Eve, will you, Miss Fanning?"

"Oh no, ma'am. I won't scare them, you can count on me."

The next morning as I combed Eve's hair, she said, "Are they going to hang Miss Sharp? Miss Fanning said they hang criminals. Are you going to jail, Mé?"

"Idiot," said Irène. "Mé hasn't done anything wrong."

Eve said, "Are they going to hang you, Mé?"

"Oh my God," said Irène, and I said, "No one is going to be hanged."

After Miss Fanning broke several more plates, Hertha decided she needed a break and sent her back to London for a week with her mother. "I'll come back right as rain," Miss Fanning said.

"Meanwhile," said Hertha, "we'll all pick blueberries."

We did pick berries, blue bulbs with a powdery white bloom, which we made into jam. The girls scraped the syrup from the pot with spoons. Hertha and I also worked on the design for my courtyard at the Radium Institute. We drew rows of linden trees and an arrangement of rose bushes, and we discussed which plantings would draw bees and butterflies.

As I made last touches, sitting at the dining room table, Hertha, in the drawing room, focused on a difference-of-pressure gauge which was to exonerate the experiment that the Royal

Society had rejected. She hummed as she worked, over the top of her anxiety. From around the corner, I could see odd bits of tubing and a mess of drawings. Privately, I shook my head—her lack of a disciplined approach still bothered me.

A crash came from the drawing room—breaking glass—and from Hertha: "Oh shit!"

I had to laugh. Hertha was right, it was no good being righteous. I called, "Can I help?"

"Never mind, it's just a beaker." She popped her head around the corner. "Once I knocked a whole shelf of beakers off the wall. It's how I met my husband. He heard the crash and came to see." She continued to hum as she swept up the glass.

I had always thought that determination was the way through any problem, force of character and force of will. But life didn't just happen through a person, it happened to a person as well. Both things were true. Maybe accepting this was what helped Hertha, even in the midst of chaos, to open her spirit and carry on. Even worried about her daughter and her friends, she kindled the spark of what she wanted.

Later that afternoon, in a journal, I came across a review of my *Treatise*, in which the author described me as the widow of a great scientist. An image of Miss Sharp climbing into the carriage flashed through my mind, and the thought came to me: *I could get sick, or I could get angry.* A wave of anger coursed through me—*that reviewer can go to the devil*—and then it passed by. My skin tingled. I wasn't tired at all. In the midst of what I couldn't control, I was discovering an area of choice.

A few days later, for exercise and to think through a rough spot in my lecture, I took a walk through a wooded river valley where the trees formed a canopy of shade. Japanese anemone sprawled beneath the branches, with their airy stems and soft purple petals, their clusters of bright yellow stamens. Each step released the tangy scent of herbs beneath my feet. Hertha and I had passed through this valley on our ride into Highcliffe on my second day at the Mill House, six weeks earlier, when I had little in my heart besides fear. It was good to be freer in my mind. Good to be writing a lecture.

Except for the hospital, my time in Highcliffe was the longest I had been in one place for a year—I hadn't bolted after all. My thoughts went again to opening a book when I was at my lowest point, in Thonons-les-bains, and finding Hertha's words, *You must take refuge with me.* What a lucky thing that was. Perhaps, in some part of my mind, I had remembered putting her letter there. However it happened, the energy of Hertha's love had traveled to me. Then, at the Mill House, she'd shielded me from the wind and shared her light so I could see my way again.

If Pierre were alive, we would have wondered together about these mysteries. All matter in the universe vibrates, he might have said. Even feelings and thoughts create electrical activity.

I would have loved to talk with Pierre about the lecture I was writing, about luminous waves and how they moved through space. So recently, we scientists thought that light was carried through space by luminiferous ether. Now this theory seemed quaint, but it wasn't surprising that it had held sway so many years—after all, all other bodies, all other kinds of matter, needed a medium through which to travel.

Thinking about Pierre brought a warm feeling in my chest. I had been shutting out his memory, too guilty to allow him close. How strange it was, this process of letting go. A space inside of me opening up.

A river ran through this part of the woods. The forest floor was wet and lush with sedge. Twice, I slipped and nearly fell. I sat by the river to rest, watching the water as it pleasantly sloshed over stones. If Pierre had been with me, he would have been wading through the mud, looking for species of frogs.

I was beginning to feel that I was ready to return to Paris, to teach and oversee my lab, build up the Radium Institute, and fight for my reputation. My urine output still hadn't really changed, and my kidneys often ached, but my spirit at least was lighter. I could remember, now, all the good things I had, especially the friends who had fought by my side. I had made mistakes, but I had kept my dignity. I had fetched my prize from the Swedish Academy. Most of all, I still had a life in science, and I could still do useful work. The foundations of the Radium Institute might be laid by spring. France, which had always been my daughters' home, had become my home as well.

How long before the poison letters stopped coming, the threats on my life, and the nasty gossip columns? Certain phrases were seared onto my mind. "A masculine face full of lines." "Dowdy." "Unlimited selfishness." Even "cunt" and "whore."

I would not be invited into the homes of the bourgeois, but I had never cared about that—only Irène and Eve might suffer if I were excluded.

Paul and I would still be colleagues. When our friends gathered, I supposed that one of us would have to stay at home.

Did Henriette, when I wrote to her, give news of me to Paul? What did he think about my being in England? Henriette hadn't written to me for weeks.

As I walked back to the Mill House, the path I followed led me through a grove of hawthorns with gnarled trunks, covered with gray-green lichen. The silence deepened. A weird sort of fleshy, red fungus grew on the dead wood.

My mind was still on Paul. Yes, he was contradictory, with his devotion to logic and the chaos that followed on his heels, and he was weak in certain ways. But we had loved each other. He was who he was. If I had hoped, against all evidence, that he would turn out to be someone else, whose responsibility was that?

He came back to me now in his sweetness—the way he turned his head to the side when he laughed, as if embarrassed, and looked down thoughtfully. His troubled forehead, the mind that needed to be harnessed. The gap of sadness between his innermost self and the charm he turned on the world. When I wasn't angry, I could still remember his love and draw on it. He had valued me. After Pierre's death, when I'd felt like the shell of a human being, he had discerned what was true in me. If I hadn't fully given him up—if Hertha's intuition had been right, that time together in the carriage, riding into Highcliffe—if I felt him to be my friend, and one day maybe even more than a friend (no one could see this far into the future)—what was wrong with that?

It wasn't his fault that society blamed me. He too was being punished. Thirteen years in a violent, suffocating marriage, and now he was separated from his children. He missed them; the loss tore him apart. And Jeannette—nearly shredded by fear—her madness rooted in the terror of being a woman left alone with her children, with no path forward. I didn't need Hertha to explain it.

I remembered Jeanette on the train to Châtillon-Coligny, her brilliant blue feathers, her handsome and hilarious airs—*I'd come to see the hats alone.* Her tenderness in that stone-cold chapel, pressing a handkerchief into my hand. She had a spirit; I had to grant her that. Who might she have become, in another world?

In that same chapel, Paul seemed to blend in, and yet he didn't. His fragile confidence, his passionate gloom—Pierre's thunder boy. Elegance notwithstanding, he had never stopped being the working-class boy among scientists parading their Royal Medals, men who expected nothing from him. He struggled to believe in his own achievements. Maguerite was right—what Paul did believe was the man's code: that his family's unhappiness must be his failure. It was unjust, a burden no man should have to carry.

Though women had it harder, I still believed that men also suffered from the world as it was. But that did not make it a world I could accept.

One morning when I was answering letters, Irène came in from outside. She carried a newspaper. I stood up, in spite of myself.

"May I see it?" For weeks, I had stayed away from the papers.

"I'm reading it." She spoke in English, though we'd been speaking French to each other. "There's trouble in the Ottoman Empire." This, of course, I knew.

Hertha stepped into the dining room. "Irène, perhaps you can read it this afternoon. Your mother is rather eager."

"I know," said Irène.

Her behavior made me certain there was news of Paul in the paper. It took all of my restraint not to rip the paper from her hand.

"Irène," said Hertha. "Give your mother the newspaper."

"Is there news?" I asked Irène.

"Miss Fanning wrote to me. She's staying in London. She isn't coming back."

Hertha glanced at me—she seemed already to know.

"Oh?" I asked. "Is somebody ill?"

"It's because of you," said Irène.

Hertha said quickly, "She didn't want . . . They're a poor family. A girl like her who wants an education . . ."

"Oh! I understand." Miss Fanning had told her mother I was here. Her mother could tolerate a suffragette, but not a woman like me.

Irène tossed the newspaper on the table and went upstairs.

I fumbled for the magnifying glass.

"Shall I?" asked Hertha. She took the glass and flipped through the first few pages, turning to the gossip column. "You probably don't want to see it," she said, but she gave me the paper, pointing to a brief little item.

> A good week for families, a bad week for foreign women. An anonymous source at the Sorbonne confirms that Madame Curie has fled the country in shame. In her absence, Madame Langevin has dropped the legal case

> against her husband. Monsieur Langevin has moved back in with his wife and children. A French family is restored.

That night I went to bed early. Pain in my kidney twisted through my back. As if my body recognized no difference between pyelonephritis and unhappiness. I had known for months that my relationship with Paul was over. His move back with his wife exposed a hidden corner of my heart that had refused to understand.

If I relapsed, it would be like a cry for pity. I didn't want that.

Downstairs, Hertha played "The Maple Leaf Rag" on the piano. She'd been teaching the girls how to dance the Turkey Trot. I'd watched them earlier, Irène flailing about with her arms, too much like a real turkey, while Eve caught on easily.

Paul liked to dance, but he had gone back to his wife and would never dance with my children. He would never again grasp my head between his hands and press his forehead against mine, or smother my face with his moustache, leaving me smelling of him.

I would sleep with the ghosts of two men beside me.

The story Paul and I had told each other about our love was shredded. If I had survived the misery of the past year with my dignity somewhat intact, this was in part because I had a seed of faith that Paul and I, beneath it all, had a shared understanding of who we had been to each other. As long as he stayed away from his wife, my position, over time, might have been tenable. Now he had chosen her over me. I had become the woman who nearly broke up his family.

Perhaps he had never wanted to leave Jeannette. I had been deluded, and everyone knew it except me.

A masculine face full of lines. Unlimited selfishness.

No wonder Henriette hadn't written. She would have told me if Paul had died, but she didn't want to be the one to tell me this.

My limbs were cold. I felt as if I were naked in an icy wind, on a tundra of frozen black soil.

Early in the morning I heard Hertha up and about, and I went downstairs to find her while she was alone. I tried to disguise the hitch in my gait—my kidneys, my distress, who knew. Rain spattered against the window over the sink.

Hertha handed me a cup of tea, and I cupped my hands around it. The first cup of tea in the morning, still a pleasure.

"I can't go back to Paris," I said.

She bristled. "Of course you're going back."

"Yes, I will, but not yet. I can't do it, Hertha."

An old man carrying a plucked chicken arrived at the door. "Here it is, Mrs. Ayrton. You said you wanted one."

Hertha paid for the chicken and placed it on the cold slab, keeping her back to me. In a while she wiped her hands on a towel. "Come with me to Norfolk Square. I could use your help with the nursing. But I don't plan to be around the day you tell the girls."

The weather in Highcliffe continued wet and thundery, with a sharp edge of cold, and we wore all the woolens we had brought with us. The girls took turns getting scuttles of coal from the outdoor bunker, and we kept a fire going, but the coal got damp, and starting the fire was a challenge. I found an old asbestos sheet and set it in front of the fireplace to keep out the draft until the flame was good. One day the sheet itself got wet and, not knowing any better, Irène still set it in front of the fireplace. The moisture in it vaporized, and the sheet exploded: pieces of asbestos flew across the drawing room. It took us all morning to clean it up.

I chose an evening when the girls and I were doing a puzzle in the dining room at the Mill House, to tell them the news they didn't want to hear. Irène, Eve, and I sat at the table near the fire, finishing a jigsaw puzzle that Eve had started with Miss Sharp, made of hand-carved wood and featuring two characters from one of Miss Sharp's fairy stories. Eve surprised me with her level of concentration. "Mr. Nevinson gave this to Miss Sharp for her birthday," she said. "I think it's beautiful."

"Everything to do with Mr. Nevinson is beautiful," I teased.

"She's in love," said Irène. "She thinks Mr. Nevinson will marry her."

I felt the stab, though Irène didn't seem conscious of it. Eve pursed her lips as if she were saying, I'll show you all.

I said, "I can return the puzzle to Miss Sharp myself. I've decided to go to London for a visit, with Hertha, and to help her with the suffragettes. Just for a few weeks."

"I guessed that already," Irène said, and she went haughty and silent. Eve, as if she hadn't heard me, marched her doll across the table, saying, "Fleur, you're very naughty, and you're going to bed without supper."

I was glad for Irène's punishment of me; it made it easier to manage the guilt. The girls would have to bear up a while longer. I had tried to shield them from my fame, my illness, and the scandal. I had tried to give them a structured life and courage when their father died. I wished I were ready to go back home with them, but it was no good pretending I could handle what I could not. Since I'd heard the news about Paul, memories and nightmares had risen up again. In one, a crowd of protesters broke down my door and carried me toward the Seine. Now was not the time to expose myself to insinuations and hatred. The buffer between me and the world was still too thin. I thought of that day in Thonos-les-bains, when I had mixed oxalic acid with water. I had gotten rid of the remaining poison, but I must never allow myself to feel that way again.

The girls would go back to our place in the Île St. Louis, which they had come to like. They had written to their nanny; she had responded kindly. Their school plans were in place.

At the end of August, in a rare clearing after a rain, I set out after dinner to watch the sun go down. The mud was slippery, and the air fresh. I was glad to escape the coal smoke and Irène's silence, but as I climbed up the cliff, world news was most on my mind. That morning we had heard about a marketplace massacre in Turkey and uncertainty about the Balkan treaty. Military alliances were being actively strengthened. "Will there will be a general war after all?" I had wondered out loud at breakfast. Hertha said it was too horrible to contemplate.

I tested my shoes' grip across each of the muddy stones.

The sky had cleared enough for the steep chalk cliffs on the Isle of Wight to be visible, and the astonishing white Needles, three in a row. Once a fourth Needle had stood in the gap, but it had fallen a hundred years ago. People called it "Lot's wife." I suppose it made the mistake of looking back, and let that be a lesson to me. I settled myself on a bench and looked out at the western horizon, streaked with orange and red. A young family down on the beach was gathering toys into a basket. We still had four days at Highcliffe-on-Sea, but I was missing the girls in anticipation, the simple tasks I'd be absent for. Brushing their hair. Helping them gather their clothes and books.

Footsteps came up behind me, and the swish of a woman's skirts. Hertha. She sat on the bench next to me, and we looked out at the sea together.

"When the world's so beautiful," she said, "it's hard to believe there are men ready to destroy it. But their backs are against the wall. Or so they believe."

"So beautiful," I echoed. The sky was lit from below, and the golden clouds, reflecting back, made the blue water glow. All along the beach people stopped what they were doing and turned in the same direction.

"Have you heard any more about Paul?" Hertha asked.

"He's back in the laboratory. He's all right. Jeannette has calmed down, now he's home." Henriette had finally written. Mostly I wished Jeannette no ill, but I was not above fantasies that she would trip in her hobble skirt and fall in front of a train.

"Restored to honor," said Hertha. "What's wrong with the French feminists? It would be nice if they put in a word for you."

"I don't think like that. As you know, I like to keep my head down, out of the fray."

"Not quite out of the fray," she laughed.

I said, "I'm a distance from joking about it."

"You'll get there. Deep suffering, deep laughter." She sat up straight. "Oh look—the puffins are back."

A raft of them came beating by, white-jowled, black-capped, orange-beaked, well above the water. One swooped down and dive-bombed for fish, and others followed. Puffins had been hunted nearly to extinction, but these ones didn't seem to know it.

Hertha rested her gaze on me. "In the end," she said, "we make our own lives as best we can."

"I sometimes think there's something missing in me."

"I know you think that."

"As if I can't be happy on my own."

She took off her shawl and wrapped it around me. "I wish you could see yourself as I do," she said. "See who you are."

I heard in her words an echo of something I had said to Paul. I took her hand. "You don't see a woman who's made a big mess?"

"You've made a big mess, yes. But it's arrogant to expect to get everything right."

I laughed. "When you sat down next to me, I expected a different kind of comfort." I wrapped her shawl tighter around me. "It's just like you, to take the wind out of my suffering."

"Your suffering sails."

"I know you're right, but honestly, Hertha, do you always have to be so wise?"

"It's a failing of mine, darling. I hope you can live with it."

Although the news about Paul had thrown me back on earlier doubts, underneath I felt freer, and clearer. I was still avoiding Paris, but going to London wasn't merely an escape. I wanted to stay with Hertha a while longer, to soak her up, her anger and her love, her matter-of-fact acceptance of my faults and hers. I wanted to see her in action, answering the assaults she faced, the minor and the grave.

"I'm all right," I said, "but I'll never be the same."

"No," she said softly. "I don't expect you will."

"I hope you won't throw me out of Norfolk Square. I've gotten my mind around window smashing and destroying mail, but arson? Throwing a burning chair? Someone could be badly hurt." Along with the world news, we'd read that morning about two women from the WSPU setting fires at a play in London attended by the Prime Minister. The whole building might have burned down. "I won't hide what I think, if anybody asks."

"Oh well," said Hertha, "let's take it as it comes," and she kissed my cheek.

The tide had receded. The beach stretched broad and empty, and the last of the light faded on the water. In the time we had been sitting there, the beacon at the Needles' lighthouse had changed from red to white, flashing over the broken chalk of the Wight.

The next morning we were sitting in the garden when Hertha received a telegram. She opened it with eyebrows lifted, as if preparing herself not to let bad news get the best of her.

Her face went white. "Barbie's been arrested. And Miss Sharp." They were being held at Halloway. We didn't know the charges.

Hertha got up and went behind a bush and retched.

A stone of fear sank into its spot, deep in my solar plexus. Miss Sharp had only recently been released from prison. Even if her charges were minor, her sentence could be harsh.

By afternoon, Hertha had a man packing up her laboratory and loading it into his truck. She wanted to visit Barbie in jail, and to be at the police court in Canon Row if she and Miss Sharp went before the Magistrate. She was all business, but the news, though it hadn't surprised her, had knocked the stuffing out of her. I brought her cups of tea and kept the girls out of her way. By evening, Miss Beattie had arrived from London in her Model T.

We were to leave for Dover at noon the following day, but when the hour came, Irène was nowhere to be found. Could she have gone for a swim? I checked her suitcase: swimming costume neatly folded.

"I'm not concerned," I told Miss Beattie, but she combed the woods near the house. Hertha went to check at Mr. Everett's farm, where the children had been feeding the goats. Meanwhile Eve and I visited the nooks and crannies of the Mill House to say goodbye—one would think that she was leaving her childhood behind. "We'll come back, Mé, right?" She had lost her front tooth that morning, and her tongue was in the gap, giving her a lisp.

We needed to leave soon, or we'd be driving in the dark. My skin pricked. Was Irène still punishing me? Was she hiding? Tourists came and went through Highcliffe, but I hadn't heard stories of anyone suspicious. I had a hollow feeling in my throat.

I was in the girls' bedroom when Miss Beattie hollered outside. I opened the window and saw my daughter pedaling up the road on a bicycle I'd never seen, her legs pumping, her thighs so long that her skirt skimmed the handlebars, gorgeous, free, riding up the hill. She stopped in the front garden, panting, and wiped her forehead with a handkerchief.

"I've been all along the coast," she said to Miss Beattie. "You've no idea how many miles."

"If I might voice an opinion," said Miss Beattie, arms akimbo, "you might've told us where you were and spared your mum a bit of worry."

Oh, so sweet to have an ally.

"I'm very independent," said Irène.

"Aye," said Miss Beattie. "Your mum knows how to raise a girl."

Miss Beattie wore goggles and a cap and hunched over the steering wheel as if she were a pilot fighting the Turks in Tripoli. Irène sat next to her, spare cans of gasoline between them, and we set off for Dover where we would spend the night at a hotel and, the next morning, meet André at the ferry. He would accompany the girls back home. Hertha and I would carry on with Miss Beattie to London and settle into Norfolk Square.

An hour into the journey, Eve began to cry.

"What's all this?" I asked.

It was Mr. Nevinson. She was afraid she would never see him again. She wanted to show him her front tooth. Could she go to London, too? Would he ever come to Paris?

"Oh, sweetheart," I said, "when you get back to Paris, you'll forget about Mr. Nevinson." We turned a corner to find a dozen horses running across a pasture, a golden brown, muscular river. "Look, the horses!"

"I *won't* forget him." Her chest curled in; she struggled to breathe between sobs.

I put my arm around her shoulders and nuzzled her. She smelled of leather, like the seats, like Mr. Nevinson. "Oh, my girl. I know, I know."

There were mud grooves on the road from last night's rain, and Miss Beattie had to slow down. Fumes of gasoline rose from the engine and whiffs of manure from the fields.

Who was Eve crying for, really? Her sobs swooped around, and it seemed to me as if they gathered up long ago losses, not her own but making a home in her. In my mind I saw a droshky carrying my mother and my sister Zosia away, off to take a cure. Horse hooves splashing through puddles, across the bridge over the Vistula and into distant fields. Plumes from factory chimneys darkening the sky.

Must everything circle back? What was it about this world, where nothing gets lost, nothing truly goes away?

I do take some comfort in the laws of thermodynamics. It was Paul who said this to me. I thought he had been talking about energy, life. The life that had shown itself in the baby whom I knew, for a moment, at the edge of the sea in Arromanches.

We stir up the nectar, the elixir of life, and when it shoots up, the poison shoots up, too.

Eve still whimpered. I tried to comfort her. "Hush, hush my darling."

Hertha breathed into my ear, "Why not let her write a letter to him?"

"Eve," I said, "would you like to write to Mr. Nevinson? We'll wrap your tooth in a scrap of handkerchief. Won't he be surprised?"

"You'll give it to him? You will?"

I held her close. I kissed her scalp. "Yes, my love. I promise."

Everything unfolded. It would be all right.

People said that Irène was like me, but so was this little girl. My desires hadn't left me when I became a scientist. I had always needed someone to be close to, someone to love. I knew the euphoria of the world's secrets opening up to me, but even this had not been enough. I wanted all of it, even more, a beloved one beside me—no matter how wounded, no matter how imperfect—to share the mysteries.

The engine vibrated through our backs, and Eve fell asleep with her head tucked under my arm. A few minutes later, a gentle weight landed on my other shoulder. Hertha, also asleep. I lay my cheek on her fuzzy head. My worried friend.

I have taken a house by the sea.

The road to Dover stretched ahead, gleaming white. When we drove through a stand of cedar, a softer light fell over us. Cedar, with its prickly, camphorous scent. Like an old chest when you open it.

Irène in her traveling hat turned around. She saw Hertha asleep and her sister snoring, and looked at me and smiled. Pierre was in the angle of her cheek. "We'll see André tomorrow?" she asked.

"We'll meet him at the ferry. I have blueberry jam for him."

"And for the Perrins?"

"A jar for the Perrins, too."

The Model T jostled. Miss Beattie was intent, her shoulders tight. She would need a hot bath tonight.

I closed my eyes and drifted, and a golden cornfield opened in my mind. Bronia digging up onions. Pierre taking her hands. *Thank you for being a good sister to my wife.*

Jean Perrin opening his door. Henriette's good wrinkles around her eyes.

A softness over my husband's face. *Was it very painful?*

You are exquisite.

I seemed then to enter my childhood house on Nowolipki Street. In the parlor, my mother punched holes in leather at her cobbler's bench, and down the hall, my father, with schoolboys gathered round, spoke of the properties of matter. I walked into the garden and up a small green hill, looking for our linden tree. And there it was: broad and glorious, three hundred years old, thick gray bark and floppy leaves, smelling of lime and honey. Zosia was padding a branch with cabbage leaves, to make it softer for me; she put her hands under my arms and scooched me up. When she climbed up after, her goofy feet disappeared into upper branches. She, Józef, Bronia, and Helena roosted above my head. We were five Sklodowski children in a linden tree, our roots in Polish earth. We had been there forever, since before the Russian invasions, before, even, the Swedish marauders stormed Częstochowa, and my namesake, Maria, the Black Madonna, turned their own shells back at them and drove them out.

I must have slept in that Model T. When I opened my eyes, we were nearing Dover. Bands of thick clouds had gathered. The road turned in toward the coast, and the bay came into view, ferries passing each other in the straits. A naval ship moved into Dover Harbour. We passed a pub on our right, and a cemetery, with ancient, tipping-over stones and unmown grass. A dog with a bandage on its paw limped at the side of the road.

The clouds created deep shadows and a quiet light. The air was chill, and I was glad for Hertha and Eve, jostling beside me, their bodies giving off warmth. Miss Beattie's scarf fluttered in the wind. We slowed down for a horse-drawn cab and pedestrians along the grassy cliffs. A man with a beard, gnarly and stooped, lumbered up the hill toward us. A woman took a girl by the arm and pulled her along, looking tired and impatient. I wondered where they were going and what they would have for dinner. I didn't know these people, and yet it seemed to me that I did know them, that they were like me and I was like them. I sensed in their spirits something of what I knew—sadness, disillusionment. Yet I also sensed that in their inner bleakness, there was something else, a source of vibrancy and life. Of course, they couldn't know this, or that, even now, they were giving off light. Nor could I have known, when I thought that I had withered on my stem, that in the darkness strange new blossoms were growing.

Epilogue

FRANCE, MAY 1915

THE PHONE RINGS in our apartment at three in the morning: heavy shelling at the front in Verdun. The radiological car damaged, dozens of injured men. Another car is needed.

Verdun is two hundred fifty kilometers to the east; we can average twenty-five kilometers an hour at best. How many men will die before we arrive? How many needless amputations, and surgeries searching for shells?

My ears buzz, making me queasy, but I feel better after toast and tea. I leave a note for the nanny and Eve, and I find my coat, my yellow leather bag, and the soft, shapeless hat that comforts me. It's a twenty-minute walk across the bridge to rue Pierre-Curie and the Radium Institute. My driver and I load up a van with the X-ray apparatus, cables, cases of equipment, and extra gas. Within minutes we're on the road.

Irène is in Hoogstade doing this same work. At seventeen, she's young to be working near the front, but who is more competent? She tells me I should get my license so that I don't need to rely on a driver. Like me, she trains the X-ray technicians, and she complains that the army selects these men for their social class, and they really can't learn because their pride gets in the way. She's right about all this. Also, we need hundreds more technicians.

Daylight comes softly as we drive along, mist rising from the fields. When a tire bursts, and we have to pull over, the meadow pipits chirrup lustily; we have entered their kingdom uninvited.

How charged and beautiful the world is, in spite of everything.

Last week, I sat at a wounded soldier's bedside, and all he wanted to talk about was birds; anything else and he would cry. In the flattened villages he had seen wrens and the odd dunnock, also mistle thrushes. From the trenches he'd watched flocks of swallows and sand martins crossing over.

Jean Danysz's father sent me a letter. I knew, as soon as I saw it, what was inside. I read it in hasty suspense. Jean was dead. I walked to my dining room, unsure if my legs would carry me. I sat for an hour staring at a cup of tea. All I could think of was that time in the laboratory, when Jean noticed my tremor and brought me tea brewed with blackberry preserves. I felt like a porcelain cup myself, cracks spidering all over it.

I must write to someone, must try to get Maurice out of the trenches and reassigned to the rear.

I don't worry for myself when I travel to the front, though I feel guilty to be free when thousands are dying every day. Each time I approach the battlefields, sentries stop me and ask me questions: where am I going, what am I doing, and where are my papers? They ask about my Polish accent, and they want to know who authorized me to travel to the front. One thing, however, they never ask: Who have I slept with, and what French family have I wrecked? The world is grotesque with violence, men blown apart and fascists at our borders. People no longer amuse themselves with gossip about the private lives of professors at the Sorbonne.

By the time we arrive in Verdun, night has fallen over the hills. No rain or snow, only two burst tires, cooperative sentries. A good day.

Amidst the moans of the injured and the rumbling of the cannon, I improvise a darkroom, assemble the instruments and set up the folding table, while the driver rolls out and hooks up the cable which connects the X-ray apparatus to the generator. We test the current—it's all right. Within half an hour the apparatus is powered, a halo glowing over it. The surgeon arrives, and the procession of stretchers begins. I forget about time as we pass the X-rays over men's bodies, the rays passing through tissue to outline the skeleton, an eerie intimacy. We write down our observations and make calculations to locate the problem precisely.

One man has four projectiles in his hand, including a piece of metal in the midshaft of the ring finger metacarpal. We take films from different angles, bringing into view the carpals, metacarpals and phalanges. It takes us hours, but we remove all four of the foreign bodies.

Who could have known that roentgen waves, when they were first discovered, would save this soldier's hand?

Next up is a man with his femur protruding through the skin. The army technician setting the voltage has bloodshot eyes and is drifting off at his task. I fear he'll overexpose the X-ray plate or burn out the Crookes tube. The nurse, an Irish girl who spent a decade as a maid, is taking over some of his duties, positioning the plate behind the wound and reviewing the exposure calculations. My memory flashes to Miss Fanning, drawing the structure of an atom.

"Are you tired?" I ask the nurse.

"I'm too excited. I'll not be needing a nap till dawn."

"Would you be able to take his place"—I gesture to the technician—"for an hour?"

"I would," she says simply. "I'm happy to, Ma'am."

I send the technician for a break and show the girl what's needed. Watching her competent movements, it occurs to me: I'll train women to be technicians! I'll devise a course in radiology for nurses, including lessons on electricity, X-rays, and anatomy. Irène can help me teach, and we'll train women of all classes, from chambermaids to socialites. It won't matter their accent or their background, as long as they're capable of acquiring the physics they need to operate and maintain the equipment. They'll be proud of their work, conscientious. I'll make plans immediately. We'll start in the autumn.

A bit of worry nudges me. I'll warn the nurses of the dangers, and I'll make them wear smocks, but inevitably, they too will absorb X-rays. Each time, a few hours after surgery, my skin gets hot and prickly. There's a constant humming in my ears.

The surgeon determines there's no hope of saving this soldier's leg: two bullets have destroyed too much bone. The nurse administers chloroform. The amputation takes an hour.

What will this man feel when he wakes up? What agonies, in his body and his mind?

The next fellow comes in on a stretcher with a piece of shrapnel in his skull. With the nurse's help, I am able to locate it.

Will these men be able to salvage something of their lives?

Perhaps they will. If all goes well, the amputated man will be fitted with an artificial limb. His life going forward might not be what he had wanted, but he will have a life nonetheless.

It's four in the morning when I take a break. I walk out into the starry fields, to the hiss and spit of cannons. The night is cold and clear.

Irène is sleeping in a tent in Hoogstade, under this same sky. I'll write to her about my plan for training women. Already I can feel her excitement. I like to wonder about her future. Clearly she will follow her parents into science, but what will be her specialization? She still says she'll study radium.

I walk along the border of the field and among the tents, breathing the cool night air. I fill my lungs and tilt my head up. Is it because my eyes adjust? Or has the sky suddenly lit up? There are stars, millions of them, shimmering across the dark. I have never seen a more brilliant sky, not even on a clear night in Poland.

All around me are sleepers in their tents. I hear one turn; another mumbles and belches. I gaze at the stars—the constellations, the planets, unknown worlds in streaks of light—and my thoughts subside, as if they have dispersed into the night and left a vibrant open space in my mind. I know this feeling.

It's the best part of science, how my breath arises from somewhere strange and quiet, a place of yearning and a place of calm, where I am utterly myself. The self I was as a girl. The self I am.

In the morning, when my job is done, I'll get into my Renault and head back home. I'll go back to work on my emanation service, capturing gas from my gram of radium, and sealing it in tubes to send to the army hospitals, to help cure lesions in the skin.

I'll be in Paris, but the men in the trenches will still be here in their pits of hell.

I fill my lungs from the bottom to the top, taking in the blessed, free air. I need sleep before the next round of patients—I should go to my tent—but the stars are just so astonishing, a golden dust, stars behind stars, showering across the arc of the sky.

There is so much more to see.

Afterword

AFTER THE WAR, Marie and Irène worked side by side at the Radium Institute, an international center for research and medical applications of radium. Due to Marie's prowess as a fundraiser, the Institute contained the largest sources of radioactive elements in the world. She considered it her calling to nurture young researchers, many of them women. In 1932, Irène (the "crown princess," some called her) took over as Director.

At first Marie wasn't pleased when Frédéric Joliot—recommended to her laboratory by Paul Langevin—proposed to her daughter, but after a couple of years she stopped introducing him as "the man who married Irène." In 1935, the couple were awarded the Nobel Prize in Chemistry for their discovery of artificial radioactivity, making Irène the second woman to win the Prize in science.

Marie didn't live to see it. She died of aplastic pernicious anemia, probably as much from X-ray exposure as from radium, on July 3rd, 1934, in the French Alps, where Eve had taken her to try to restore her health. She seems never to have taken full stock of the dangers of working with radium, at least not publicly. She even tried to hide her near-blindness. Perhaps among many possible reasons for hiding both the risks of radium and her debilities was her fear of public backlash. She had no reason to expect civility from the press.

Eve quickly wrote *Madame Curie*, a wonderful if idealizing biography of her mother, and an international bestseller. She didn't mention Marie's scandalous affair. Though a concert pianist, Eve, who was known as one of the most beautiful women in Paris, said she struggled to find direction, and acknowledged that her young years "were not happy ones." During WWII, she traveled to battlefronts around the world as a war correspondent, working for the French resistance. After her husband, Henry Labouise, accepted the Nobel Prize for UNICEF in 1965, Eve liked to say she was the only one in her family who hadn't won a Nobel Prize.

By the end of WWI, over 100,000 of Hertha's "Ayrton fans" were used in the trenches on the Western Front to dispel poisonous gases. Hertha fought for their acceptance and oversaw production, but not without three years of discouragement and obstruction from the War Office. According to Miss Sharp, who wrote a biography of Hertha, what mattered to Hertha "all that terrible time, was that men and boys were coughing their lives out in the trenches when she believed confidently that they might have been saved by her fans. . . . The pain that this brought to her was never forgotten or lived down. . . . She was never physically strong again, and never really lighthearted." In 1923, at the age of sixty-nine, Hertha died of blood poisoning after an insect bite. She and Marie remained friends to the end.

Miss Sharp had her own war challenges. Though the WSPU called a moratorium on campaigning for the duration, she ignored this decision and continued to fight for women's rights, believing that if women were to be enfranchised after the war, the cause must be kept alive. For this she was painfully shunned by the suffragettes. In 1933, she married Henry Nevinson, after the death of his wife.

Marie and Paul remained friends. When Paul asked Marie to give one of his lovers a job at the Institute, she didn't refuse (Paul later had a son with this woman). When he died in 1946, he left a sum of money to Irène and Eve. (My fantasy is that he was finally repaying Marie for the money she gave to Henri Bourgeois, their blackmailer.) Paul continued to be active in science and in social and political causes. During World War I, collaborating with Jean Perrin, he drew on Jacques and Pierre Curie's research into piezoelectricity to develop ultrasonics. In 1940, he was arrested and imprisoned by the Nazis for antifascist activity. His daughter Hélène Solomon-Langevin was deported to Auschwitz for her resistance to fascism (she survived), and he escaped to Switzerland, with the help of Irène's husband.

Though Marie and Paul never had a child, they share a great grandson: Yves Langevin, an astrophysicist. Yves' parents were Hélène Joliot (Irène's daughter) and Michel Langevin (the son of André Langevin, called André-Philippe in this novel), both of them also physicists.

Marie's discovery with Pierre of radioactivity, and her assertion that this energy was not due to molecular interactions, but was an atomic property of certain elements, set in motion a series of epochal discoveries and brought into being the field of atomic science. All medical treatment that involves irradiation can be traced to Marie Curie. She trained dozens of women scientists and teachers, who went on to train other women. It would be hard to overestimate Marie Curie's example in encouraging women to live and work at the forefront of science.

Acknowledgments

READERS WHO WANT to know more about Marie Curie, her friends and her family have a wealth of options. The biographies I consulted include: Denis Brian, *The Curies: A Biography of the Most Controversial Family in Science*; Eve Curie, *Madame Curie*; Marie Curie, *Pierre Curie*; Barbara Goldsmith, *Obsessive Genius*; André Langevin, *Paul Langevin, My Father*; Rosalynd Pflaum, *Marie Curie and Her Daughter Irène*; Susan Quinn, *Marie Curie: A Life*; Lauren Redniss, *Radioactive: Marie & Pierre Curie*; Evelyn Sharp, *Hertha Ayrton, 1854–1923, A Memoir*; and Dava Sobel, *The Elements of Marie Curie*. Letters between Marie and her daughters can be found in the original French in *Marie Curie et ses Filles: Lettres Tendres*.

Polish novels familiar to Marie proved useful to me, especially Bołeslaw Prus's *The Doll* and Eliza Orzeszkowa's *Marta* (translated by Anna Gaşienica-Byrcyn and Stephanie Kraft), as did Evelyn Sharp's *Unfinished Adventure: Selected Reminiscences from an Englishwoman's Life*.

I have also made use of the archives at the National Library of France, in Paris and online. My gratitude goes to the staff of the Musée Curie in Paris.

I am indebted to Ursula Klein, senior research scholar at the Max Planck Institute for the History of Science in Berlin, for her help on matters of science, as well as Stephen Sontum, Richard Wolfson, and Pete Schumer, professors emeriti of chemistry, physics, and mathematics and natural philosophy, respectively, at Middlebury College. Any mistakes are certainly my own.

When I look back at my earliest drafts, I wonder how I kept going—that I did so is largely thanks to support from my husband, Jay Parini, who also read, listened, and made me laugh. Michael Lowenthal's smart and generous feedback was indispensable. At crucial junctures, Margo LaPierre, Harriet Chessman, and Pamela Erens offered essential help. I appreciate those who inspired and supported me along the way—you know who you are—especially my readers: Claudia Cooper, Robert Cohen, Elizabeth Keathley, MaryEllen Bertolini, Katherine Branch, Emily Wheeler, Pauls Toutonghi, Lola Van Wagenen, Amy VanEchaute, Jennifer Green-Lewis, Phoebe Lewis, Ximena Mejia, Samantha Silva, and Claire Harman.

Thanks go to my agent Heather Schroder of Compass Literary for her enthusiasm and confidence; also to Geri Thoma, formerly of The Writers' House, who had faith in this novel well before it took its current shape.

I'm so pleased that *Luminous Bodies* found a home at Paul Dry Books. Deep thanks to the whole team, especially Paul Dry, Julia Sippel, and Mara Brandsdorfer.

photograph by Oliver Parini

Devon Jersild is a writer and psychotherapist in Weybridge, Vermont. She won an O. Henry Award for a story that appeared in the *Kenyon Review,* and she has written for many other publications including *New England Review, Times Literary Supplement, New York Times, USA Today,* and *Redbook.* She has also been Associate Editor at *New England Review* and Associate Director of the Bread Loaf Writers' Conference. Her book of nonfiction, *Happy Hours: Alcohol in a Woman's Life,* was widely acclaimed. *Luminous Bodies* is her first novel.